THE ULTIMATE
ALIEN

THE ULTIMATE
ALIEN

BYRON PREISS
JOHN BETANCOURT
& KEITH R.A. DECANDIDO
EDITORS
▼▼▼

ILLUSTRATED BY
CHRISTOPHER H. BING

A BYRON PREISS BOOK
A DELL TRADE PAPERBACK

Special thanks to Jeanne Cavelos, Eric Wybenga, and Leslie Schnur

Book design by Fearn Cutler

Copyright © 1995 by Byron Preiss Visual Publications, Inc.

Illustrations © 1995 by Christopher H. Bing
"Introduction" © 1995 by Agberg Ltd.
"This is the Universe" © 1995 by E.A. Holliday
"Alien Radio" © 1995 by Mike Resnick and Nicholas A. DiChario
"Before Eden" © 1961, 1995 by Arthur C. Clarke; reprinted by permission of the author and the author's agent, Russell Galen
"The Mallword Falcon" © 1995 by Somtow Sucharitkul
"Bride 91" © 1967, 1995 by Agberg Ltd.; reprinted by permission of the author and Agberg Ltd.
"The Ghost in the Machine" © 1995 by by Mel Gilden
"Duty Calls" © 1988 by Anne McCaffrey; first appeared in *The Fleet*; reprinted by permission of the author and the author's agent, Virginia Kidd
"The Pick-Up" © 1995 by Lawrence Watt-Evans
"The Brasher Girl" © 1995 by Ed Gorman
"The Phantom of the Space Opera" © 1995 by Don D'Ammassa
"The Invasion" © 1995 by Peter Crowther
"First Contact, Sort Of" © 1995 by Karen Haber and Carol Carr
"Empathos" © 1995 by Lynn D. Crosson
"Interstellar Love" © 1995 by Ron Dee
"Fast Seeds" © 1995 by Nina Kiriki Hoffman

ISBN: 0-440-50631-X

Printed in the United States of America

Published simultaneously in Canada

October 1995

10 9 8 7 6 5 4 3 2 1

CONTENTS

THE ULTIMATE ALIEN:
INTRODUCTION
▼▼▼

BY ROBERT SILVERBERG

FEAR of the Other, inextricably mixed with eager curiosity about him, goes a long way back. Aliens haunted the dreams of our earliest ancestors, perhaps: the boogeymen, the strangers, the ineffably mysterious creatures who lurk at the fringes of our lives, those who are Not Like Us. It may be that the hominids of two million years ago told tales around the campfire of the different-looking beings on the far side of the mountains, the strange ones who were following some different evolutionary track that was destined not to lead to *Homo sapiens.* And *Homo sapiens* himself, sitting snug within the Aurignacian or Solutrean caves while the icy winds of the Pleistocene whirled across the tundra, may have chanted throaty epics of the great war against the shaggy Other Ones whom they had overcome, the ones we call the Neander-thals today.

I think it must be true that we have always looked with min-gled fascination and horror at beings who do not belong to our own tribe, whether we consider our tribe to be the twelve mem-bers of the clan of Unghk the Barbarian or the teeming billions who make up the total population of Earth. In our struggle to understand who we are, we establish boundaries defining Us and Not-Us; and then we strive to comprehend what those who are Not-Us are like, what defining characteristics they have that make them Not-Us, for then we have a better idea of Us. And it has been this way, I suspect, since the time of the australopithecines and *Homo habilis*.

Traces of the encounters-with-aliens theme turn up at least as early as *The Odyssey*: Odysseus, making his long journey homeward from the Trojan War, runs into one bizarre monstrous creature after another (the one-eyed giant Polyphemus, the six-headed predator Scylla, the insatiable all-devouring creature Charybdis, et cetera.) A later Greek, Iambolos, wrote an account in the third century B.C. of an archipelago in the Indian Ocean populated by people with flexible bones and forked tongues, which enabled them to carry on two conversations at once. Five centuries after that, Lucian of Samosata sent the voyagers of the *True History* to the Moon, where they found, among many other marvels, a warrior race that flew on the backs of giant three-headed vultures, a tribe of archers whose steeds were fleas the size of elephants, and dog-headed men native to the star Sirius.

The eighteenth century was a particularly fertile time for the creation of fictional aliens—the primary purpose of which was, as usual, to provide a clearer perspective on our own nature. Swift's Gulliver, of course, met with a race of tiny people and one of giants, and, finally, a species of intelligent horses. A few years later (1751), Robert Paltock's *Peter Wilkins* told a tale of mariners who enter the interior of the Earth through a hole in the Antarctic Ocean and find a cavern populated by bat-winged folk. The great Danish fantasy *Niels Klim*, published about the same time, offers a planet of intelligent humanoid trees, with branches for arms and twigs for fingers. And Voltaire's satire *Micromegas* (1752) told of the visit to Earth of two gigantic beings, a native of Sirius eight miles tall and a somewhat smaller, but still immense traveler from Saturn: they had no need of spaceships, but moved from world to world in immense leaps, or occasionally hitched rides on passing comets.

And then, as we come closer to our own time, the fictional aliens become more numerous, more vivid, and, usually, more menacing. The most famous ones of all arrived from Mars in 1897, in H.G. Wells' *The War of the Worlds*:

> They were, I now saw, the most unearthly creatures it is possible to conceive. They were huge round bodies—or, rather, heads—about four feet in diameter, each body having in front of it a face. This face had no nostrils—indeed, the Martians do not seem to have had any sense of smell, but it had a pair of very large dark-colored eyes, and just beneath this a kind of fleshy beak. In the back of this head or body—I scarcely know how to speak of it—was the single tight tympanic surface, since known to be anatomically an ear, though it must have been almost useless in our dense air. In a group round the mouth were sixteen slender, almost whiplike tentacles, arranged in two bunches of eight each. These bunches have since been named rather aptly, by that distinguished anatomist, Professor Howes, the *hands*. . . .
>
> The internal anatomy, I may remark here, as dissection has since shown, was almost equally simple. The greater part of the structure was the brain, sending enormous nerves to the eyes, ear, and tactile tentacles. Besides this were the bulky lungs, into which the mouth opened, and the heart and its vessels. The pulmonary distress caused by the denser atmosphere and greater gravitational attraction was only too evident in the convulsive movements of the outer skin.
>
> And this was the sum of the Martian organs. Strange as it may seem to a human being, all the complex apparatus of digestion, which makes up the bulk of our bodies, did not exist in the Martians. They were heads—merely heads. Entrails

they had none. They did not eat, much less digest. Instead, they took the fresh, living blood of other creatures, and *injected* it into their own veins. I have myself seen this being done, as I shall mention in its place. But, squeamish as I may seem, I cannot bring myself to describe what I could not endure even to continue watching. . . .

Wells's all-conquering Martians gave nightmares to two generations of readers, and then, in 1938, caused something close to national panic in the United States when Orson Welles's radio dramatization of the Wells novel led careless listeners to believe that the Martians *had* actually landed (in New Jersey, not in Wells's London suburb.) The Welles broadcast made the Martians even more ghastly, more terrifying, than they had been in the original:

Good heavens, now something's wriggling out of the shadow like a gray snake. Now it's another one, and another. They look like tentacles to me. There, I can see the thing's body. It's large as a bear and glistens like wet leather. But that face. It's—it's indescribable. I can hardly force myself to keep looking at it. The eyes are black and gleam like a serpent. The mouth is V-shaped with saliva dripping from its rimless lips that seem to quiver and pulsate. . . .

The world had not yet been science-fictionized by endless movies and television shows, and people who tuned in in the middle of the broadcast were scared silly by it. Experienced science fiction readers took a different view, as one tells us in Hadley Cantril's classic study of the event, *The Invasion from Mars: A Study in the Psychology of Panic* (Princeton University Press, 1940):

At first I was very interested in the fall of the meteor. It isn't often that they find a big one just when it falls. But when it started to unscrew and monsters came out, I said to myself, "They've taken one of those *Amazing Stories* and are acting it out." It just couldn't be real. It was just like some of the stories I read in *Amazing Stories* but it was even more exciting.

Regular sf readers, by then, had experienced the alien menace again and again—and had met a few benevolent aliens, too, notably Stanley G. Weinbaum's comic, lovable Martian Tweel (*A Martian Odyssey*, 1934), and the philosophical Martian of Raymond Z. Gallun's "Old Faithful," published in the same year. Since then, although plenty of horrific aliens have been offered to the science fiction readership—as in John W. Campbell's "Who Goes There?" (1938), which became the movie *The Thing*, A.E. van Vogt's memorable "Black Destroyer" (1939), and Fredric Brown's "Arena" (1944)—many noteworthy attempts have been made at depicting aliens sympathetically and rendering their alien minds as comprehensible to us as possible. Significant among these stories are Eric Frank Russell's "Metamorphosite" (1946) and "Dear Devil" (1950), Edgar Pangborn's *A Mirror for Observers* (1954), and Orson Scott Card's *Speaker for the Dead* (1986), among many others. Science fiction has examined the possibilities of sexual relationships between humans and aliens (Philip Jose Farmer's *The Lovers*, 1952); it has looked at the theological aspects of the existence of intelligent non-human creatures (*A Case of Conscience* by James Blish, 1953, and "For I Am A Jealous People," Lester del Rey, 1954); it has explored the problems of communicating with aliens ("The Gift of Gab," Jack Vance, 1955), has posited the existence of aliens as a way of satirizing human foibles (*The Dark Light Years*, Brian W. Aldiss, 1964)—has, in fact, approached the concept of Us/Not-Us in a multitude of ways.

But the subject is as inexhaustible as human nature itself, and in the long run what the creation of fictional aliens is all about is self-understanding; for when we write about aliens, we are in fact writing about ourselves as seen through a distorting lens. Behind the fantastic trappings of the science fiction story lies a mundane core. What the science fiction writer writes about comes from within, from the mind of someone who has never visited another world or laid eyes upon an alien extraterrestrial being. Translating his own experiences and speculations into the soaring wonders of science fiction, the writer hides real experience under a cloak of fantasy. And so we look at the alien, however strange it may be, and we see ourselves; for what else, really, can the Earthbound writer write about, except the perception of the experiental world, transformed in this or that metaphorical way but always starting from a base in reality?

Here, then, is a book containing the latest bulletins from the human/alien frontier. Lynn Crosson, Mike Resnick, Karen Haber, Anne McCaffrey, and the rest of the contributors to this anthology want you to believe that you are reading stories about strange creatures from far-off places; and so, in truth, you are. But take a closer look. Behind the tentacles and leathery scales and dripping rimless lips, the sinuous limbs and the masklike faces, you are likely to find something very familiar indeed, transformed in unexpected ways, but uncomfortably recognizable all the same.

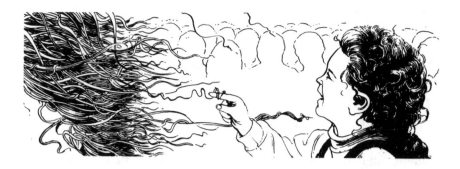

THIS IS THE UNIVERSE
▼▼▼

LIZ HOLLIDAY

THE aliens were dancing in the Carnival.

Celia Evans leaned over the railing of her balcony. Her daughter, Melanie, peered through the wrought iron railings next to her. Music from a hundred soundstages pounded the air of Notting Hill, reggae and blues, steel-drum and rap syncopated together, pierced by a thousand shrilling whistles, a hundred thousand voices singing and shouting and laughing in the pale London sunlight.

Celia hated it. She always had.

Her friends envied her flat. They thought she was lucky to live there, in the middle of the Carnival. A little bit of Jamaica come to London, the papers called it. But every year Celia promised herself she would find the money to go away over the Bank Holiday. Every year she failed.

And now there were bone-thin aliens whirling and curveting ahead of the parade, with their skin—or maybe clothing—arching and falling in rainbow tatters over their heads, and patterns like iridescent oil on water chasing over their faces, changing as the music changed. Even the police who surrounded them—

kept the humans out, the aliens in—seemed to be having a good time, with their shirt sleeves rolled up and streamers round their necks.

It wasn't right. Wasn't right.

"Want an ice cream," Melanie said. Celia could hardly hear her through the music that pummeled the air like a fist.

"We can't go down there," Celia shouted. "It's too crowded." She shook her head to reinforce her words. Melanie's mouth trembled. At four, she had already developed a passable imitation of her father's pout. Celia looked away.

In the street below, an old man detached himself from the crowd. He was wearing a shiny brown suit a few sizes too small. He used his cider bottle for a partner as he danced into the crowd, closer and closer to the aliens. Celia recognized him. He was one of the winos who hung around the park opposite the church. *Bad Celia,* Celia thought. *They're homeless people; a good little primary school teacher like you should know that.* But political correctness be damned; she had always taken great care to keep Melanie away from them. And this one was clearly crazy. He sent shivers down her back.

Closer and closer he went to the aliens, dancing with his cider bottle. Celia saw now that some of the other homeless people were sitting on the steps and pavement. She had always thought they went away for Carnival, to Kensington or Hammersmith, like birds migrating for the winter. But they were there, just sitting.

Distinctly, over the noise of the music, she heard one of them shout at the old man. He looked round, danced closer. A policeman tried to bar his way but one of the aliens stopped dancing for a moment, so that all the tatters of flesh or cloth fell out of the air and settled around it. It held out a hand or tendril. The old man reached out and took what the alien offered. He stepped into its charmed circle, and they went dancing down the street.

Celia found that her heart was pounding, her mouth dry. It had taken a minute, maybe less; and she was filled with a fear she could not articulate, for a man who had always scared her.

"I want to go an' talk to ET," Melanie said, dragging her back. Celia scowled, despite her best efforts not to. "Can I, Mum?"

"Don't be silly," Celia said. "I told you, it's far too crowded down there. Besides," she said, playing a trump card, "it's not *for* children."

"Daddy would let me," Melanie said. "He'd let me talk to ET." She put her head on one side, thoughtfully. "He'd buy me a ice cream, too, I 'spect."

"Yes, well he's not here now, is he?" Celia said, surprising herself with the venom in her voice. *Of course he's not here now. Why should he be? He only promised faithfully he'd be here ... after all the fuss he made about having access.* "Time to go inside for a while, anyway," she said. "Tell you what, I'll see if there are any lollies in the freezer."

"Don't want to. Want to see ET."

"It's a tough life, kiddo," Celia said. She smiled, though, to show she'd stopped being angry. Then she turned and went in.

Melanie followed, all frizzy orange pigtails and pink-cheeked indignation.

▼▼▼

In the living room, Melanie threw herself down in front of the television. Celia fed Orlando, their marmalade cat, then started to make a cup of tea. Her hands shook as she filled the kettle. *Damned things don't even have any eyes. And the tentacles ...* She thought she'd got used to the idea of the aliens. Then again, she'd only ever seen them on TV before.

The switch on the kettle wouldn't stay down. Something else that needed replacing. She slapped at it in frustration.

She looked in the freezer for an ice lolly for Melanie. There weren't any. "Damn," she muttered, anticipating trouble. *Damn damn damn.* She slammed the freezer door and went to tell Melanie.

"I'm watching Batman," Melanie said, unconcerned. Orlando stalked in and stretched out in a patch of sun.

"Oh. Well, would you mind if I turned over for the news?" She liked to pretend things were normal over the Carnival week-end, even though she could hear the evidence to the contrary all around her.

"Mu-um," Melanie said. "You always do that. *Daddy* doesn't do that."

"Just for a minute," Celia said. She turned her attention to the screen. Nothing about the aliens, thank goodness. When they had first arrived, they had been the lead story in every bulletin. Even the Wimbledon tennis coverage had been interrupted; even the *football.* Celia hated sports, but she was glad those days were over. Out of the corner of her eye, she noticed Melanie start to draw a picture. She smiled encouragingly, while straining to hear what the announcer was saying about the balance of payments.

"Look, Mum," Melanie said, "I drawed ET." She held up a piece of paper with a scrawled brown circle in the middle of it.

"Drew," Celia said automatically, but she thought, *Stop it. I don't want you even thinking about that . . . thing.* She was far too good a teacher to say it though. *If I ignore it, it'll go away.* "Why don't you draw a picture of you and Daddy? That day he took you to the zoo. Remember that tiger you saw? That would be a good picture."

"An' a camel. An' a rabbit. An' Suzie came with us," Melanie said. She paused. Then she looked straight at Celia. "She bought me a ice cream."

"I'm sure she did," Celia said, keeping the tightness out of her voice with an effort. *Bloody woman,* she thought. The phone rang.

It was Bill, ringing to say he couldn't make it.

"Actually, I was going to grab a swim this afternoon," Celia shouted over the hammer-blow beat of the carnival bass. "You know; anything to get away until the noise stops." She waited for him to point out that she never left the flat during the Carnival. He didn't, which annoyed her even more than if he had. She swiveled round to see if Melanie was listening, but the child was drawing another picture. Her pigtails bobbed up and down as she scribbled furiously on the paper. "No, I don't want to take her with me," Celia said, knowing Melanie wouldn't be able to hear for the din. She stared at Melanie while Bill made soothing noises on the phone.

Orlando stood up and stretched, then padded over to investigate the moving end of Melanie's pencil.

"Yes, I'll give her your love." Blat! went Orlando's paw against the pencil. "Yes, and Suzie's too." She slammed the phone down. *Nothing changes*, she thought. *Nothing around here ever goddamn changes.*

"Stop it, Landy," Melanie said. "You're spoiling my picture." She pushed the cat away roughly—

"Don't—" Celia said sharply, over the cat's startled yowl and Melanie's yelp.

Melanie held up her hand. Three parallel welts ran across the back of it and up her wrist. Celia crossed the room in three quick strides and scooped her up. "Hush," she said to her crying daughter. "Mummy make it better. I'll put some cream on it and you'll be fine, you'll see."

"Don't want it," Melanie said. "It hurts, it hurts—" She broke off into a long sobbing wail.

"Sh. Sh. It's all right," Celia said.

But Melanie twisted round, flailing her hands about. Her shoulders heaved up and down. "I want Daddy," she howled in between long gulping sobs. "I want my daddy."

Celia grappled her, trying to force calmness on her. It didn't work. The child's keening cut through the pounding music, until

Celia wanted to join in with it. Anything to prove that she still existed. That she could affect the world too.

"Stop it," she shouted. "Stop it stop it stop it!" She meant the noise. All the noise, everywhere. All the people who wouldn't leave her alone. But she found she was shaking Melanie. The girl's head jerked back and forth. She was quiet now. Her crying had stopped, the breath jolted out of her. She stared at Celia out of frightened blue eyes. Her cheeks were flushed.

Christ, Celia thought. *I could have broken her neck.* She let Melanie go. The girl flopped back onto the sofa. The marks of Celia's fingers were livid against her white skin.

A whistle shrieked through the heavy reggae beat.

"I'm sorry, Mummy." Melanie's lower lip trembled.

"No, I am," Celia said. She couldn't think. Not with the music: it seemed to have turned the air solid, so that she could not breathe. It would squeeze the life out of her, squeeze the humanity out of her. *I could have killed her,* she thought. *We have to get out of here.*

"Listen," she said, "we're going to get our things, and we're going to go outside. We're going to walk and walk until we get to Holland Park, and we'll have a lovely afternoon feeding the ducks, and when we come back, all the people will have gone." It was like a litany. It made her feel better.

Melanie nodded. She slid off the sofa and got the white plastic shoulder bag Bill had given her for her birthday.

▼▼▼

The front door slammed behind Celia like the crack of doom. *Abandon hope, all ye who exit here,* she thought, and was careful not to let herself start laughing. She held tight to Melanie's hand as she pushed her way between the people who squatted on the steps. Her foot slid on a kebab wrapper, and she skidded into one of the men. She felt her heart pounding as if it were trying to escape the cage of her ribs, but the man—man? he might have been eighteen, she realized—turned and smiled. He waved. Celia clutched Melanie's hand even tighter. Her lips pulled back from her mouth in something that felt entirely unlike a smile.

The music was everywhere. The air filled her throat as if it were as thick as treacle.

The aliens had left the parade. They were dancing in the street, round and round and up and down they went. The wino in the brown suit was still with them, but now he had been joined by some of his friends. The police encircled them, but they clapped in time to the rhythm, the sound lost in the greater sound of the music.

Aliens, dancing in the carnival. *No one thinks it's strange,* thought Celia. *Only me. Only me.* She felt as if she had slid sideways, into another universe where monsters danced together in the sun, and she almost killed her only child, and the police stood by, applauding.

And this was the universe, *this* where Melanie was going to have to live. There was no way back.

Melanie turned round. Her mouth opened wide. She was saying something. *ET.* Surely she was saying that. She twisted away from Celia and down the steps. Lithely, she eeled her way through the crowd. Celia followed, pushing and shoving.

"Take it easy," someone said. She wanted to kill him, to scream that her daughter would be lost. But he moved aside, and so did the others, once they realized why she was hurrying.

Celia arrived just in time to see Melanie dive between two of the police officers. She yelled something incoherent and threw herself at the policewoman nearest her. The woman yelled something. Celia ducked beneath her outflung arms.

She was too late. Melanie ran up to one of the aliens.

"Don't," Celia screamed. Surely they must hear, even over the sound of the music? But Melanie stared up at the alien, rapt . . .

This is the universe she has to live in. There is no going back.

. . . and the alien folded down towards her on its stick-insect legs. Its tendrils feathered across the air close to Melanie's face, as if it were taking her scent.

"She be fine," a voice at Celia's shoulder said. She turned. It was the wino in the brown suit. For a moment Celia wondered if he meant her daughter or the alien. He was swaying in time to the music, and his eyes seemed to be staring at something very far away. He waved his cider bottle around, then put it to his lips. Celia saw that it was empty. He put it on the ground, taking care to make sure it stood up.

"Lady," he said gravely, "woulds you dance with me?" *I can't,* Celia thought. *I can't. He's a wino; a homeless person. What's in a name?* She stared round desperately, hoping one of the police would see her predicament. They were looking in her direction, but they were smiling and clapping.

She caught sight of Melanie. The child was staring at the alien, at its tendrils. Her hand moved out, ever so slowly, as if she finally realized the enormity of what she was doing.

She's scared, Celia thought. *She probably ought to be.* And then she stared all around her, and she thought for the second time, *This is the universe she has to live in. There is no going back.*

Melanie looked at her. She smiled, a small trembly smile.

I never wanted you to be afraid of things, Celia thought. But it seemed to her that fear was all she had taught her daughter; fear and anger. *Go on. Touch it.* But Melanie only stared. *You have to touch it,* Celia thought. *How else will you ever learn to deal with it? Or will you grow up afraid of everything that makes your world special?*

She wants me to go and touch it first, Celia thought. *But I can't. My universe never had such things in it.*

She turned away, feeling confused and hypocritical. She felt something touch her hand. She turned, sharply.

"Won'ts you dance with me?" The wino held her hand in his. His grip was firm and warm.

She stared at him, ready to tell him to piss off. His eyes were full of distant pain. She wondered what had put it there, what had put him on the streets.

This is my universe, she thought. *This is normal. I can deal with this.*

The retort died on her lips. She let the man—the *man*—lead her into the dance. Over his shoulder, she saw Melanie reach out at last, and take the alien's tendril in her small hand.

And they danced. And they danced.

ALIEN RADIO
▼▼▼

MIKE RESNICK AND
NICHOLAS A. DiCHARIO

MUST I use this headphone unit? It appears my skull is ill-shaped for such a device. I can just speak into this? Very good. What does that mean? That red light? Oh, are we on? I can go ahead and speak, then? Excellent.

Hello, people of Earth, and good evening. As many of you already know, I have come to your world for the express purpose of studying your race, so that I may offer you the five basic truths of your existence.

But before I begin, I have been asked to deliver this commercial message for a new product called Heaven Scent. Heaven Scent is a liquid chemical bleach used in conjunction with your laundry soaps to whiten whites and brighten colors, and it can be purchased at your local supermarkets, where you will find an introductory rebate offer. The manufacturer claims that the bleach will cause cleaner, fresher-smelling fabrics, and will not be injurious to your garments. They will come out thirty-seven times brighter than the sun, and of course I couldn't say this on the public airwaves if it were not the literal truth. Heaven Scent is the answer to the housewives' and househusbands' prayers. Whoopie.

End of commercial message, the funds of which have been donated to the Home for Terminally Morose *Phlezms* of Indeterminate Gender.

Now, let me begin by saying that you live in terror of your mortality, and while this is a realistic fear, it is also a universally repressed one for all members of your species. You carry on as if your deaths are avoidable, in some way, via your professional or family or religious associations, and therefore, although you can look at your deaths rationally, you cannot *feel* them. Your ultimate fear is repressed.

Although your race has for some reason deemed it necessary to deny yourselves this self-knowledge to proceed with your daily lives, I submit to you the first basic truth of your species: Lurking beneath all your abundant insecurities and depressive states and schizophrenias, is this fear of death that you cannot reconcile. The denial of the death-state is directly responsible for your vast numbers of oppressors and victims, and your wars and injustices against the sanctity of life.

I therefore offer you this solution to the first truth: If you can open your minds and peer into the darkest corners of your hidden neuroses—which every one of you have, without exception—and admit your helplessness in the face of real death, then you will not be such self-destructive animals, creating obscure reasons for your acts of cruelty against self and society, and you will not live in such utter terror of the world that your fear of death makes you unable to live your lives.

Ah, my engineer has indicated that we have our first caller. Hello.

Hello?

Hello. You are on the air.

Uh . . . yeah, I have a question for you.

Proceed.

*Do you think you could do something about controlling your
kids? I mean, we're really glad to have you here visiting our planet
and everything, you know, but—*

My children? What have they done?

*Well, they've kind of built their own little community center
down here in our neighborhood—which is OK, you know, they
need a comfortable place to hang out and all, but the thing is,
they're printing their own money, and that's kind of got the local
businesses upset, if you know what I mean.*

I have told my children not to meddle in native affairs. If
they are in some way harming your economy or threatening
your sense of financial stability I shall banish them from the
planet's surface.

*Well, I don't want you to think we're prejudiced. I mean, that
would be a really bad rap to spread across the galaxy.*

Fear not, I shall handle it. My engineer has indicated I have
another caller. Farewell, kind person. Hello, you are on the air.

Yeah, I'm on, really? No!

Yes.

*Cool! I just wanted to say that this used to be a great hemi-
sphere until the Man started bringing it down.*

The man? What man?

*The Man. You know—like the uniforms, the military, the suits
and ties, you know. The government. The Maaaaaaaan.*

Hmm, no, I am afraid I do not know to what man you are
referring, and I fail to see the relevancy of your comment in
light of the basic truths of your species. So, farewell, kind person,
and thank you for calling. Next caller, please.

*Hello, Pop? We've been listening to your show down here at
the ACC—*

The ACC?

*The Alien Community Center. We just built it, and we thought
one of us should give you a call and explain about the currency.*

Yes, perhaps you should.

Well, we're operating in complete conformity with the local government's laws and barter articles, which do not prohibit the establishment of a community currency. Our dollars are of different sizes and designs from the existing tender, and we use our own special ink and a different texture of paper. We've established our own serial-number code and value structure that's a little too complicated for the natives, but our actions are in no way conspiratorial, and developing a currency is something that any local community is free to do within their existing legal system.

Nevertheless, you are upsetting the natives, and I want it stopped immediately.

But, Pop—

No buts! Just do as I say. You are interfering with the message I am trying to deliver to these life forms. Now, I should like to continue with the second basic truth. Mr. Engineer, please disconnect that problem child so I may proceed. Thank you.

Ahem. The second truth deals with sexual relationships, a matter of utmost importance to your race. Other than the obvious physical differences between the male and female of your species, there is a basic psychological truth that both the male and female must accept in order to secure a happy and peaceful co-existence with his or her mate.

The female of your species demands to be loved for the person that she is. A good mate should want "her" and not just "her body." She lives in utter terror that the sexual act will destroy her mate's perception of her inner personality.

The truth your female species must accept is that the male does in fact want only her body, that he is attached to his animal role, a role that thousands of years of evolution cannot and will not and should not obliterate, for it is an essential ingredient in the procreative drive of your race. This is not to say the male is incapable of appreciating a female for who and what she is. I merely wish to point out that the sexual act carries a different meaning for him.

Likewise, the male must accept this truth about himself. Although the "sensitive, caring male" is much in demand in your current culture, and many males, contrary to their natures, are striving to attain this posture to answer the needs of the females and arouse their receptivity, the male should not be anchored in guilt or shame concerning his purely sexual tendencies, for it is the guilt that shrinks his male personality (and we all know what *that* leads to) and threatens to destroy the animal that he is, and indeed must be.

To reconcile the second truth, your species must practice what I call "regression intercourse." You must allow each other to be reduced to nothing more than physical objects during the sex act, to absolve yourselves of the mind and grasp your primal instincts, for the female is a sexual being as well, although much repressed. You must allow the love and attachment you have for each other to grow out of your natural animal aggressions. Your sex will be happier and healthier and less rooted in the machinations of the mind, and your roles outside the sexual arena should be enhanced as well, since you will not have the insecurities of sexual misinterpretations spilling over into the obligations of your social and professional lives.

Ah, I have been informed I have a caller on line one. Hello. You are on the air.

I would love you to use my body like an animal. When can we get together?

I believe you have misconstrued the second truth.

Oh, yes, I want to misconstrue you desperately.

Please, I fear that—

Don't be afraid. I know exactly what I'm doing.

I am quite certain that you do, and I suggest you do so immediately, but with a member of your species. Next caller.

Eh, yeah, hi. First off, I'd like to say welcome to our planet.

Thank you, kind person.

How do you like the weather here?

As a matter of fact, I can adapt to any kind of weather.

Wow, that's really neat.

Did you have a question concerning the first or second truths of your species?

Well, actually, I was calling to complain about your kids.

My children?

Yeah. They're selling cosmetics. Not that selling cosmetics is a bad thing in and of itself—don't get me wrong, I mean I don't want to offend you or anything—it's just they've created their own company, and to be honest they can make a better product than we can—you might have guessed I'm in the cosmetics business myself, heh, heh, heh. Anyway, it's not exactly fair competition since you aliens are a lot more intelligent than us, and you've been all over the galaxy—and that kind of free spirit, that daring to explore the universe attitude, well, it really sells in cosmetics because we're youth-oriented, you know. Like, you can make your-self into the kind of person you want to be, or thought you once were, because who you are just won't cut it. Anyway, your kids are taking over a good portion of the market.

I wanted them not to interfere. Why won't they listen?

Kids, you know, that's just the way they are. I couldn't imagine having, what?, eighty or ninety of them like you. I can barely handle two. No matter what I tell them they have to challenge me. My son, he's into sports this, sports that. Do you think I could get him to read a book? My daughter is just as bad with her wild music. Dance, dance, dance, that's all she cares about. I keep telling her, what would happen if you were in an accident and lost your legs, God forbid? What would you do with your life? But does she ever think about it? No, she just keeps dancing and saying acid rock is too tame and she's waiting for them to invent base rock.

Fear not, I shall handle my children immediately.

Thanks, I'd appreciate it.

A call awaits me on line two. Farewell, good caller. Hello.

Yeah, I'd like to order a large pizza with pepperoni and mush-rooms, two tossed salads with feta cheese and no dressing, and a small order of chicken wings.

I'm sorry, but I do believe you have dialed an inappropriate telephone number.

Last time you guys put dressing on the salads, so make sure this time you get it right, OK?

I am sorry to inform you—

OK, then, buffalo wings. Boy, you guys are sticklers for termi-nology. And hold the horns, yuk, yuk.

No, no, please hang up your telephone device and dial again, thank you. Next caller, please.

Hello, Pop? We've been listening to your show down here at the ACC—

I am aware of that. Do you have an explanation for the cosmetics?

Well, we were a little bored, and we saw an opportunity to break into the cosmetics industry because, frankly, there's plenty of room for everybody. I'm telling you, there's no top to this market. These people are hungry for new products. We've developed our own line of body spray, perfume creme and lotion, talcum powder, cologne, shampoo and conditioner. We've got foundations, finish-ers, skin enhancers, eyeliners, glimmersticks, not to mention lip glosses and nail polishes in colors these people have never even seen, like yordishale 2.2. Our customers love it! Our signature fragrance is selling out all over the planet. We call it Star Byte, and we're gearing it toward professional females who dream of transcendence (as if there are any who don't). We were thinking of branching out into accessories. Jewelry, for instance, and clothing.

Enough! Put an end to this nonsense immediately!

But, Pop—

You are trying my patience. One more incident and you shall all be confined to the ship for the duration of my stay. Do I make myself clear?

Aw, jeez, Pop . . .

Mr. Engineer, disconnect that problem child so that I may continue. Thank you.

It is now time for me to reveal the third great truth to your people. I call this the truth of self-imprisonment, and—Excuse me? What about it? Oh, I see.

Dear listeners, I have been asked to endorse yet another product. For those of you who appreciate the rich flavor of a strong beer, and the refreshing flavor of a light beer, Bestend Brewing Company would like to inform you of a new product called On-Tap. On-Tap Beer Tablets can offer you the best of both brews. You may purchase a blister pack of one hundred of these tablets, fill a glass with tap water, drop in the tablets, and convert your water to beer, thus making the mixture as dark or as light as you wish. The manufacturers suggest you use no less than two tablets and no more than twelve tablets per average serving.

Now, if I may continue—Pardon? Oh, yes, I must thank them for sponsoring my telecast.

Back to vitally important business. The third basic truth of your species is the truth of self-imprisonment. You are all slaves to your particular cultures. The societal boundaries that you have established are fashioned to encourage *failure*, of all things. To become an accepted member of the fold, you must limit your thoughts and deeds to the status quo. As a result of this, you take your freedom of personality, your freedom of spirit, and stifle it. You crush your individuality. To further complicate this paradox, your enslavement into the group consciousness, your belittling social intercourses and daily routines, works as a shelter. You are safe as a social conformist, and this safety prevents you from reaching the core of your uniqueness.

In order to avoid this breakdown of individual personalities, you must develop a faith in the true self. You must be able to step outside of your boundaries with impunity, so that the despair of self-limitation does not obliterate the natural curiosity and creativity of your species.

Ah, I have a caller.

What are your political associations?

I have none.

Religious beliefs or preferences?

None.

Special interest groups?

No affiliations of any kind.

Have you ever used illegal drugs?

Absolutely not.

Have you ever been arrested for a misdemeanor or a felony?

Don't be ridiculous. What is the purpose behind this line of questioning?

Have you ever cheated on an exam, or your income taxes, or lied to your spouse or significant other?

Definitely not.

Congratulations, you fall into the target market for our new underarm deodorant, called Squeaky Clean, and we would like you to sample our product free of charge for one month, at the end of which we will contact you for your comments and opinions. Would you like to participate?

I don't have any underarms!

Hmm . . . That might pose a problem.

Next caller!

Yeah, this is the military head of NATO calling, and we have a big problem with your kids. We just discovered they've been building and selling hi-tech long-range weaponry and advanced radar equipment to our enemies.

My children? I can't believe they would do such a thing!

Listen, fella, we've got high-speed missiles headed this way that are superior to our defense mechanisms! What are you going to do about it?

My engineer tells me one of my children is on line three. I'll straighten this out posthaste.

Hi, Pop, you sound really good on radio. I think the show is coming along nicely.

Do you really think so?

Absolutely. You're a natural.

No, you're just saying that.

Honest! We all think so.

I find radio a comfortable medium, although a bit detached. I would have gone with television, but I was afraid my looks might frighten some of the populace. Now, what about these missles?

Just a crazy misunderstanding, Pop. You've got to believe me. Here's the thing. Although there are international rules and regulations limiting arms sales on this planet, we discovered plenty of precedent for covert transactions. Naturally we assumed this was common practice. All the world leaders have taken part in below-board arms deals. So when we saw how archaic their weapons systems were down here—they haven't even discovered simple quantum-wave explosives yet—we just thought we'd jump into the market. We didn't mean any harm.

Well, maybe you didn't intend to cause any harm, but you've certainly done so. I want your Alien Community Center shut down, and I want all of you to return to the ship.

But, Pop—

No buts! Just do as I say. Is there any way to stop the missles?

Uh, no, 'fraid not.

What kind of damage are we looking at?

Well, pretty bad.

Please define "pretty bad."

Catastrophic. Cataclysmic. One of those big words that begins with a "C." Unfortunately, we sold counterstrike weapons to the West, and from the looks of it, everybody is going to be wiped out.

What about defense systems?

Nobody was interested in those. We had some really good stuff, too.

Curses! I've failed again.

Don't take it personally, Pop, you gave it your best shot, that's the important thing. I'm sure you'll do better next time around. Anyway, we're kind of curious about the fourth truth. What is it?

Thank you for asking. The fourth truth is the truth of "collective destructive realization." Because the beings in question are the only life forms on this planet who are free of instinct, who are capable of conceptualizing their deaths, repressing reality, hiding within social structures and self-limitation, because they fashion their existences around the power of denial, they are subconsciously rooted in self-destruction, and are destined to annihilate themselves unless they can radically restructure their psyches.

Too late for that, I guess.

So it would seem.

Well, to be perfectly honest, we're all kind of bored down here. We're anxious to move on. Where are we going next?

I've had such rotten luck in this galaxy. I thought maybe we'd try M33 in Andromeda next. I just have to give the fifth and final truth, and then we'll leave.

No time, Pop.

But it will tell them how to overcome the fourth truth, live forever, achieve Utopia, rid themselves forever of body odor and halitosis, and become one with the Star Maker.

Pop, you've only got about a minute to get out of there. Can you state it in forty-five seconds?

The fifth truth in forty-five seconds? Well, if I say it very fast . . .

You're down to forty.

Oh, well, maybe the Adromedans will appreciate it. Ladies

and gentlemen, we now return you to your regularly-scheduled programming. . . .

▼▼▼

"Jose Canseco steps up to the plate, with two men out and a runner on third. He takes his position, hitches up his pants, and shades his eyes . . ."

"Sure is a bright afternoon, isn't it, Al?"

"Sure is, Ed. Can't remember the last time I saw such a bright sun . . ."

(Long pause.)

"Or so many of them?"

BEFORE EDEN
▼▼▼

ARTHUR C. CLARKE

"I GUESS," said Jerry Garfield, cutting the engines, "that this is the end of the line." With a gentle sigh, the underjets faded out; deprived of its air cushion, the scout car *Rambling Wreck* settled down upon the twisted rocks of the Hesperian Plateau.

There was no way forward; neither on its jets nor its tractors could S.5—to give the *Wreck* its official name—scale the escarpment that lay ahead. The South Pole of Venus was only thirty miles away, but it might have been on another planet. They would have to turn back, and retrace their four-hundred-mile journey through this nightmare landscape.

The weather was fantastically clear, with visibility of almost a thousand yards. There was no need of radar to show the cliffs ahead; for once, the naked eye was good enough. The green auroral light, filtering down through clouds that had rolled unbroken for a million years, gave the scene an underwater appearance, and the way in which all distant objects blurred into the haze added to the impression. Sometimes it was easy to believe that they were driving across a shallow sea bed, and more than once Jerry had imagined that he had seen fish floating overhead.

"Shall I call the ship, and say we're turning back?" he asked.

"Not yet," said Dr. Hutchins. "I want to think."

Jerry shot an appealing glance at the third member of the crew, but found no moral support there. Coleman was just as bad; although the two men argued furiously half the time, they were both scientists and therefore, in the opinion of a hard-headed engineer-navigator, not wholly responsible citizens. If Cole and Hutch had bright ideas about going forward, there was nothing he could do except register a protest.

Hutchins was pacing back and forth in the tiny cabin, study-ing charts and instruments. Presently he swung the car's search-light toward the cliffs, and began to examine them carefully with binoculars. Surely, thought Jerry, he doesn't expect me to drive up there! S.5 was a hovertrack, not a mountain goat. . . .

Abruptly, Hutchins found something. He released his breath in a sudden explosive gasp, then turned to Coleman.

"Look!" he said, his voice full of excitement. "Just to the left of that black mark! Tell me what you see."

He handed over the glasses, and it was Coleman's turn to stare.

"Well, I'm damned," he said at length. "You were right. There *are* rivers on Venus. That's a dried-up waterfall."

"So you owe me one dinner at the Bel Gourmet when we get back to Cambridge. With champagne."

"No need to remind me. Anyway, it's cheap at the price. But this still leaves your other theories strictly on the crackpot level."

"Just a minute," interjected Jerry. "What's all this about rivers and waterfalls? Everyone knows they can't exist on Venus. It never gets cold enough on this steam bath of a planet for the clouds to condense."

"Have you looked at the thermometer lately?" asked Hutchins with deceptive mildness.

"I've been slightly too busy driving."

"Then I've news for you. It's down to two hundred and thirty, and still falling. Don't forget—we're almost at the Pole, it's wintertime, and we're sixty thousand feet above the lowlands. All this adds up to a distinct nip in the air. If the temperature drops a few more degrees, we'll have rain. The water will be boiling, of course—but it will be water. And though George won't admit it yet, this puts Venus in a completely different light."

"Why?" asked Jerry, though he had already guessed.

"Where there's water, there may be life. We've been in too much of a hurry to assume that Venus is sterile, merely because the average temperature's over five hundred degrees. It's a lot colder here, and that's why I've been so anxious to get to the Pole. There are lakes up here in the highlands, and I want to look at them."

"But *boiling* water!" protested Coleman. "Nothing could live in that!"

"There are algae that manage it on Earth. And if we've learned one thing since we started exploring the planets, it's this: wherever life has the slightest chance of surviving, you'll find it. This is the only chance it's ever had on Venus."

"I wish we could test your theory. But you can see for yourself—we can't go up that cliff."

"Perhaps not in the car. But it won't be too difficult to climb those rocks, even wearing thermosuits. All we need do is walk a few miles toward the Pole, according to the radar maps, it's fairly level once you're over the rim. We could manage in—oh, twelve hours at the most. Each of us has been out for longer than that, in much worse conditions."

That was perfectly true. Protective clothing that had been designed to keep men alive in the Venusian lowlands would have an easy job here, where it was only a hundred degrees hotter than Death Valley in midsummer.

"Well," said Coleman, "you know the regulations. You can't

go by yourself, and someone has to stay here to keep contact with the ship. How do we settle it this time—chess or cards?"

"Chess takes too long," said Hutchins, "especially when you two play it." He reached into the chart table and produced a well-worn pack. "Cut them, Jerry."

"Ten of spades. Hope you can beat it, George."

"So do I. Damn—only five of clubs. Well, give my regards to the Venusians."

Despite Hutchins' assurance, it was hard work climbing the escarpment. The slope was not too steep, but the weight of oxygen gear, refrigerated thermosuits, and scientific equipment came to more than a hundred pounds per man. The lower gravity—thirteen per cent weaker than Earth's—gave a little help, but not much, as they toiled up screes, rested on ledges to regain breath, and then clambered on again through the submarine twilight. The emerald glow that washed around them was brighter than that of the full moon on Earth. A moon would have been wasted on Venus, Jerry told himself; it could never have been seen from the surface, there were no oceans for it to rule—and the incessant aurora was a far more constant source of light.

They had climbed more than two thousand feet before the ground leveled out into a gentle slope, scarred here and there by channels that had clearly been cut by running water. After a little searching, they came across a gulley wide and deep enough to merit the name of river bed, and started to walk along it.

"I've just thought of something," said Jerry after they had traveled a few hundred yards. "Suppose there's a storm up ahead of us? I don't feel like facing a tidal wave of boiling water."

"If there's a storm," replied Hutchins a little impatiently, "we'll hear it. There'll be plenty of time to reach high ground."

He was undoubtedly right, but Jerry felt no happier as they continued to climb the gently shelving watercourse. His uneasiness had been growing ever since they had passed over the brow of the cliff and had lost radio contact with the scout car. In this day and age, to be out of touch with one's fellow men was a unique and unsettling experience. It had never happened to Jerry before in all his life; even aboard the *Morning Star*, when they were a hundred million miles from Earth, he could always send a message to his family and get a reply back within minutes. But now, a few yards of rock had cut him off from the rest of mankind; if anything happened to them here, no one would ever know, unless some later expedition found their bodies. George would wait for the agreed number of hours; then he would head back to the ship—alone. I guess I'm not really the pioneering type, Jerry told himself. I like running complicated machines, and that's how I got involved in space flight. But I never stopped to think where it would lead, and now it's too late to change my mind. . . .

They had traveled perhaps three miles toward the Pole, following the meanders of the river bed, when Hutchins stopped to make observations and collect specimens. "Still getting colder!" he said. "The temperature's down to one hundred and ninety-nine. That's far and away the lowest ever recorded on Venus. I wish we could call George and let him know."

Jerry tried all the wave bands; he even attempted to raise the ship—the unpredictable ups and downs of the planet's ionosphere sometimes made such long-distance reception possible—but there was not a whisper of a carrier wave above the roar and crackle of the Venusian thunderstorms.

"This is even better," said Hutchins, and now there was real excitement in his voice. "The oxygen concentration's way up—fifteen parts in a million. It was only five back at the car, and down in the lowlands you can scarcely detect it."

"But fifteen in a *million!*" protested Jerry. "Nothing could breathe that!"

"You've got hold of the wrong end of the stick," Hutchins explained. "Nothing does breathe it. Something *makes* it. Where do you think Earth's oxygen comes from? It's all produced by life—by growing plants. Before there were plants on Earth, our atmosphere was just like this one—a mess of carbon dioxide and ammonia and methane. Then vegetation evolved, and slowly converted the atmosphere into something that animals could breathe."

"I see," said Jerry, "and you think that the same process has just started here?"

"It looks like it. *Something* not far from here is producing oxygen—and plant life is the simplest explanation."

"And where there are plants," mused Jerry, "I suppose you'll have animals, sooner or later."

"Yes," said Hutchins, packing his gear and starting up the gulley, "though it takes a few hundred million years. We may be too soon—but I hope not."

"That's all very well," Jerry answered. "But suppose we meet something that doesn't like us? We've no weapons."

Hutchins gave a snort of disgust.

"And we don't need them. Have you stopped to think what we look like? Any animal would run a mile at the sight of us."

There was some truth in that. The reflecting metal foil of their thermosuits covered them from head to foot like flexible, glittering armor. No insects had more elaborate antennas than those mounted on their helmets and back packs, and the wide lenses through which they stared out at the world looked like blank yet monstrous eyes. Yes, there were few animals on Earth that would stop to argue with such apparitions; but any Venusians might have different ideas.

Jerry was still mulling this over when they came upon the lake. Even at that first glimpse, it made him think not of the life they were seeking, but of death. Like a black mirror, it lay amid a fold of the hills; its far edge was hidden in the eternal mist, and ghostly columns of vapor swirled and danced upon its surface. All it needed, Jerry told himself, was Charon's ferry waiting to take them to the other side—or the Swan of Tuonela swimming majestically back and forth as it guarded the entrance to the Underworld. . . .

Yet for all this, it was a miracle—the first free water that men had ever found on Venus. Hutchins was already on his knees, almost in an attitude of prayer. But he was only collecting drops of the precious liquid to examine through his pocket microscope.

"Anything there?" asked Jerry anxiously.

Hutchins shook his head.

"If there is, it's too small to see with this instrument. I'll tell you more when we're back at the ship." He sealed a test tube and placed it in his collecting bag, as tenderly as any prospector who had just found a nugget laced with gold. It might be—it probably was—nothing more than plain water. But it might also be a universe of unknown, living creatures on the first stage of their billion-year journey to intelligence.

Hutchins had walked no more than a dozen yards along the edge of the lake when he stopped again, so suddenly that Garfield nearly collided with him.

"What's the matter?" Jerry asked. "Seen something?"

"That dark patch of rock over there. I noticed it before we stopped at the lake."

"What about it? It looks ordinary enough to me."

"*I think it's grown bigger.*"

All his life, Jerry was to remember this moment. Somehow he never doubted Hutchins' statement; by this time he could believe anything, even that rocks could grow. The sense of isolation and mystery, the presence of that dark and brooding lake, the never-ceasing rumble of distant storms and the green flickering of the aurora—all these had done something to his mind, had prepared it to face the incredible. Yet he felt no fear; that would come later.

He looked at the rock. It was about five hundred feet away, as far as he could estimate. In this dim, emerald light it was hard to judge distances or dimensions. The rock—or whatever it was—seemed to be a horizontal slab of almost black material, lying near the crest of a low ridge. There was a second, much smaller, patch of similar material near it; Jerry tried to measure and memorize the gap between them, so that he would have some yardstick to detect any change.

Even when he saw that the gap was slowly shrinking, he still felt no alarm—only a puzzled excitement. Not until it had vanished completely, and he realized how his eyes had tricked him, did that awful feeling of helpless terror strike into his heart.

Here were no growing or moving rocks. What they were watching was a dark tide, a crawling carpet, sweeping slowly but inexorably toward them over the top of the ridge.

The moment of sheer, unreasoning panic lasted, mercifully, no more than a few seconds. Garfield's first terror began to fade as soon as he recognized its cause. For that advancing tide had reminded him, all too vividly, of a story he had read many years ago about the army ants of the Amazon, and the way in which they destroyed everything in their path. . . .

But whatever this tide might be, it was moving too slowly to be a real danger, unless it cut off their line of retreat. Hutchins was staring at it intently through their only pair of binoculars; he was the biologist, and he was holding his ground. No point in making a fool of myself, thought Jerry, by running like a scalded cat, if it isn't necessary.

"For heaven's sake," he said at last, when the moving carpet was only a hundred yards away and Hutchins had not uttered a word or stirred a muscle. "What *is* it?"

Hutchins slowly unfroze, like a statue coming to life.

"Sorry," he said. "I'd forgotten all about you. It's a plant, of course. At least, I suppose we'd better call it that."

"But it's *moving!*"

"Why should that surprise you? So do terrestrial plants. Ever seen speeded-up movies of ivy in action?"

"That still stays in one place—it doesn't crawl all over the landscape."

"Then what about the plankton plants of the sea? *They* can swim when they have to."

Jerry gave up; in any case, the approaching wonder had robbed him of words.

He still thought of the thing as a carpet—a deep-pile one, raveled into tassels at the edges. It varied in thickness as it moved; in some parts it was a mere film; in others, it heaped up to a depth of a foot or more. As it came closer and he could see its texture, Jerry was reminded of black velvet. He wondered what it felt like to the touch, then remembered that it would burn his fingers even if it did nothing else to them. He found himself thinking, in the lightheaded nervous reaction that often follows a sudden shock: "If there *are* any Venusians, we'll never be able to shake hands with them. They'd burn us, and we'd give them frostbite."

So far, the thing had shown no signs that it was aware of their presence. It had merely flowed forward like the mindless tide that it almost certainly was. Apart from the fact that it climbed over small obstacles, it might have been an advancing flood of water.

And then, when it was only ten feet away, the velvet tide checked itself. On the right and the left, it still flowed forward; but dead ahead it slowed to a halt.

"We're being encircled," said Jerry anxiously. "Better fall back, until we're sure it's harmless."

To his relief, Hutchins stepped back at once. After a brief hesitation, the creature resumed its slow advance and the dent in its front line straightened out.

Then Hutchins stepped forward again—and the thing slowly withdrew. Half a dozen times the biologist advanced, only to retreat again, and each time the living tide ebbed and flowed in synchronism with his movements. I never imagined, Jerry told himself, that I'd live to see a man waltzing with a plant. . . .

"Thermophobia," said Hutchins. "Purely automatic reaction. It doesn't like our heat."

"*Our* heat!" protested Jerry. "Why, we're living icicles by comparison."

"Of course—but our suits aren't, and that's all it knows about."

Stupid of me, thought Jerry. When you were snug and cool inside your thermosuits, it was easy to forget that the refrigeration unit on your back was pumping a blast of heat out into the surrounding air. No wonder the Venusian plant had shied away....

"Let's see how it reacts to light," said Hutchins. He switched on his chest lamp, and the green auroral glow was instantly banished by the flood of pure white radiance. Until Man had come to this planet, no white light had ever shone upon the surface of Venus, even by day. As in the seas of Earth, there was only a green twilight, deepening slowly to utter darkness.

The transformation was so stunning that neither man could check a cry of astonishment. Gone in a flash was the deep, somber black of the thick-piled velvet carpet at their feet. Instead, as far as their lights carried, lay a blazing pattern of glorious, vivid reds, laced with streaks of gold. No Persian prince could ever have commanded so opulent a tapestry from his weavers, yet this was the accidental product of biological forces. Indeed, until they had switched on their floods, these superb colors had not even existed, and they would vanish once more when the alien light of Earth ceased to conjure them into being.

"Tikov was right," murmured Hutchins. "I wish he could have known."

"Right about what?" asked Jerry, though it seemed almost a sacrilege to speak in the presence of such loveliness.

"Back in Russia, fifty years ago, he found that plants living in very cold climates tended to be blue and violet, while those from hot ones were red or orange. He predicted that the Martian vegetation would be violet, and said that if there were plants on

Venus they'd be red. Well, he was right on both counts. But we can't stand here all day—we've work to do."

"You're sure it's quite safe?" asked Jerry, some of his caution reasserting itself.

"Absolutely—it can't touch our suits even if it wants to. Anyway, it's moving past us."

That was true. They could see now that the entire creature— if it was a single plant, and not a colony—covered a roughly circular area about a hundred yards across. It was sweeping over the ground, as the shadow of a cloud moves before the wind— and where it had rested, the rocks were pitted with innumerable tiny holes that might have been etched by acid.

"Yes," said Hutchins, when Jerry remarked about this. "That's how some lichens feed; they secrete acids that dissolve rock. But no questions, please—not till we get back to the ship. I've several lifetimes' work here, and a couple of hours to do it in."

This was botany on the run. . . . The sensitive edge of the huge plant-thing could move with surprising speed when it tried to evade them. It was as if they were dealing with an animated flapjack, an acre in extent. There was no reaction—apart from the automatic avoidance of their exhaust heat—when Hutchins snipped samples or took probes. The creature flowed steadily onward over hills and valleys, guided by some strange vegetable instinct. Perhaps it was following some vein of mineral; the geologists could decide that, when they analyzed the rock samples that Hutchins had collected both before and after the passage of the living tapestry.

There was scarcely time to think or even to frame the count- less questions that their discovery had raised. Presumably these creatures must be fairly common, for them to have found one so quickly. How did they reproduce? By shoots, spores, fission, or some other means? Where did they get their energy? What relatives, rivals, or parasites did they have? This could not be the only form of life on Venus—the very idea was absurd, for if you had one species, you must have thousands. . . .

Sheer hunger and fatigue forced them to a halt at last. The creature they were studying could eat its way around Venus—though Hutchins believed that it never went very far from the lake, as from time to time it approached the water and inserted a long, tubelike tendril into it—but the animals from Earth had to rest.

It was a great relief to inflate the pressurized tent, climb in through the air lock, and strip off their thermosuits. For the first time, as they relaxed inside their tiny plastic hemisphere, the true wonder and importance of the discovery forced itself upon their minds. This world around them was no longer the same; Venus was no longer dead—it had joined Earth and Mars.

For life called to life, across the gulfs of space. Everything that grew or moved upon the face of any planet was a portent, a promise that Man was not alone in this universe of blazing suns and swirling nebulae. If as yet he had found no companions with whom he could speak, that was only to be expected, for the light-years and the ages still stretched before him, waiting to be explored. Meanwhile, he must guard and cherish the life he found, whether it be upon Earth or Mars or Venus.

So Graham Hutchins, the happiest biologist in the solar system, told himself as he helped Garfield collect their refuse and seal it into a plastic disposal bag. When they deflated the tent and started on the homeward journey, there was no sign of the creature they had been examining. That was just as well; they might have been tempted to linger for more experiments, and already it was getting uncomfortably close to their deadline.

No matter; in a few months they would be back with a team of assistants, far more adequately equipped and with the eyes of the world upon them. Evolution had labored for a billion years to make this meeting possible; it could wait a little longer.

▼▼▼

For a while nothing moved in the greenly glimmering, fog-bound landscape; it was deserted by man and crimson carpet alike. Then, flowing over the wind-carved hills, the creature reappeared. Or perhaps it was another of the same strange species; no one would ever know.

It flowed past the little cairn of stones where Hutchins and Garfield had buried their wastes. And then it stopped.

It was not puzzled, for it had no mind. But the chemical urges that drove it relentlessly over the polar plateau were crying: Here, here! Somewhere close at hand was the most precious of all the foods it needed—phosphorous, the element without which the spark of life could never ignite. It began to nuzzle the rocks, to ooze into the cracks and crannies, to scratch and scrabble with probing tendrils. Nothing that it did was beyond the capacity of any plant or tree on Earth—but it moved a thousand times more quickly, requiring only minutes to reach its goal and pierce through the plastic film.

And then it feasted, on food more concentrated than any it had ever known. It absorbed the carbohydrates and the proteins and the phosphates, the nicotine from the cigarette ends, the cellulose from the paper cups and spoons. All these it broke down and assimilated into its strange body, without difficulty and without harm.

Likewise it absorbed a whole microcosmos of living creatures—the bacteria and viruses which, upon an older planet, had evolved into a thousand deadly strains. Though only a very few could survive in this heat and this atmosphere, they were sufficient. As the carpet crawled back to the lake, it carried contagion to all its world.

Even as the Morning Star set course for her distant home, Venus was dying. The films and photographs and specimens that Hutchins was carrying in triumph were more precious even than he knew. They were the only record that would ever exist of life's third attempt to gain a foothold in the solar system.

Beneath the clouds of Venus, the story of Creation was ended.

THE MALLWORLD FALCON
▼▼▼

S.P. SOMTOW

OF course I knew where I was. The toyochev I was riding in was slowly drifting down to Mallworld—the place where all dreams come true. I recognized it at once: thirty klicks of shopping center floating in space, gleaming against a night without stars. Already I was picking up a babble of jangling, pushy jingles on the car's communicator, and I could see the bumper-to-bumper traffic streaking across space all the way from the transmat nexus to the parking satellites that ringed the artificial world that lies between the Belt and Jupiter.

But I didn't know who I was. By the Pope's boobs, I couldn't remember my own name. Why was I here? My head was throbbing and I realized that it was stuck to the ceiling of the toyochev, even though the gravity was on full—all the furniture was firmly rooted to the floor, and there weren't any eating utensils, robots, or inflatable tongue ticklers swimming around as there would be if the gravity was off. I tried to shake myself free of the ceiling, but I seemed to be attached to it by a metal headband, and . . . worriedly I felt my scalp . . . there were a couple of cables sticking into my skull!

"Who am I?" I shouted, kicking my legs and succeeding only in exacerbating my headache, as the spectacle of the traffic congestion around Mallworld swam in the view windows. "Tell me who I am!"

"I'm glad you finally asked," said a six-inch-high little man, popping into existence beside my ear. "I thought you were out for good! You've had . . . let's see . . . five levitols, three brevitols, two bottles of deep-fried chablis, a six-pack of squirtomatic filet-mignon-flavored chewing gum—"

I was starting to remember things vaguely. "A party?" I said. "At the barJulians'?" I tried to rub my head with my hands, but as I started to do so the ceiling sprouted an arm that brandished a washcloth, with which it proceeded to daub my face and scalp in ice-cold water. I suffered this indignity for a while as the six-inch-high little man hummed a jerky ditty. "So answer the question—"

"I give up!" said the man, who was, of course, a computer simulacrum; that much had already impressed itself on my beleaguered skull. "You shmillionaires are all alike! Soapbox barons— bah! Seen one, seen 'em all. Just because you own virtually everything in the known universe, this side of the Selespridon barrier, doesn't give you the right to abuse us cyber-imagic constructs, you know! Under the Human, Alien, Cetacean and Mechanical Brain Rights Act of the Azroid Belt Alliance—"

Suddenly I remembered who I was. I gave a whoop of pleasure. The comsim immediately gurgled to a stop. Of course it did. Machines never talked back to a barJulian! It must have had a grand old time complaining while I was fishing around for my identity.

"Just get on with your job," I said. "Go down to the locker and get me a fresh can of clothing."

"Yes, sir! Yes, master!" the comsim said, and winked out of existence. I yanked the din plugs out of my head and fell to the floor of the toyochev. An airstream jetted up to cushion my landing. The comsim matted right back and sprayed on the clothes; they didn't fit very well.

Then I accidentally saw myself in the room monitor in the control console of my car. . . .

I was a giant insect in a trenchcoat!

"What is the meaning of this?" I yelled.

"Don't you remember?" came the comsim's voice. "It's the body you ordered."

Okay. That's my one passion in life, and one of the big advantages of wealth; you can get a new look whenever you want. But I'd never fancied the bug-eyed look before. This seemed to be a pretty elaborate somatic job. Suddenly I realized that—even with my identity more or less restored—I didn't quite remember everything about myself. The din plug cables had lowered themselves down from the ceiling and were crawling towards me. They were trying to tell me something. I seized them and stared wildly at them as they writhed in my fists like lunatic serpents. Well, at least I knew what they were now. Hastily I stuck them back in my head, jamming them hard so that the data stream would restart itself. Then I sat in lotus position and waited for the rest of my soul to infuse itself into my new body.

Losing your soul is not the brightest idea in the world. Especially when you've been dead for a couple of days. And dead was precisely where I'd been. I recognized the symptoms from all the other times one of my wild parties had ended up at The Way Out Suicide Parlor.

▼▼▼

Most of the time I rarely went to my own parties. After all, a barJulian doesn't bother to frequent Mallworld: least of all Julian barJulian XV, direct heir of the Julian barJulian who, centuries ago and before the coming of the alien Selespridar, happened to win this ludicrous prize in one of those holofeelietape publisher's clearing house sweepstakes . . . one megacubiclick of empty space beyond the azroid belt . . . or a lifetime supply of deodorant soap! Well, as luck would have it, he opted for the former, and along came the transmaterialization technology from the Selespridar, and our little node of space just so happened to be the most densely packed nexus of transmat whiz lines in the entire solar system . . . and the only possible place to build a shopping mall the size of an azroid.

My family had been collecting the rent for a long, long time. It's a little known fact, but my grandfather, the famous clavi-chrome soloist, bought the Earth from its bankrupt holding cor-poration. I guess being a slumlord as well as the owner of Mallworld's space made him feel a little closer to the masses. I've been trying to foist the Earth off on someone ever since, but the only person ever interested in it was a schizophrenic whale. The Cetacean Council stripped him of his cetacean rights, and he's been forced to live like a human being ever since.

This whale (a humpback, I believe) had become so insane, by cetacean reckoning, that he had learned to think human thoughts and even talk more or less like one through a cumber-some voice-device. Of course, whale's brains being what they are, he was a lot smarter than humans, and he'd certainly acquired enough credit to purchase the Earth from me. A sentient's a sentient, and I wanted to close the deal if possible, so I invited him to a party in his honor. The venue, of course, was to be the entertainment showcase of Mallworld—my most lavish suite at the Gaza Plaza Hotel, whose centerpiece was the Great Pyramid of Khufu, which my great-uncle Clement had had hauled to Mallworld in bite-sized pieces and digitally reconstituted. Parties are a pain when you're constantly called upon to set the universal standard for lavishness, so I was already in a foul mood when I stepped from the demat-booth into the party room, which was an exact model of the White House, ancestral home of Genghis Khan, Johnny Appleseed, and other T'ang Dynasty Emperors of ancient Earth history.

I did not, at that time, resemble a giant bug in the slightest. Indeed, I was the handsomest person in the room; I'd ordered the most streamlined soma money can buy, and all eyes turned to worship my magnificent, Storkways genegeneered physique.

The whale, who was known to all and sundry as Curly, occupied a vast tank in the middle of the hall. He was carrying on about fifty-seven conversations at once by means of a telepathic signal-splitter implanted in his baleen and outputting to various sofas, drinking booths and dialogue bathtubs all over the function space. He seemed to be an enormous hit. In one corner a whole bevy of minimalists—people who have had their bodies removed and float around as talking heads on life support platters—had gathered around one of the outputs and was listening to the whale discourse eloquently about the nature of art. Simultaneously, Curly was expounding about Earthie politics to a group of rapt maximalists, whose extra arms and legs writhed and flopped about their caterpilloid abdomens; in a corner, another of his extensions was emceeing a fashion show. I was delighted; like all my parties, this one was going to be a success. I popped a levitol and began to drift ecstatically ceilingward, pausing only to quaff a goblet of rattlesnake's tears that was winging its way through the air, offering itself to any guest that happened to float by.

"It's a success!" I screamed wildly. In the distance, the Pope waved at me. "A wild success!" I shouted.

It was at that moment that a Selespridon entered my party.

Now I hadn't invited any of the Selespridar. However, being our masters, however benign, they go where they choose. After all, the Selespridar had walled off the entire solar system at the orbit of Saturn and shunted us into a vacant universe "until such time as the human race is mature enough to confront the civilized races of the galaxy." You don't kick a Selespridon out of a party.

Anyhow, they have this odor, you see . . . they secrete this pheromone, or something, that excites the inmost erotic urges of human beings ... as well as being two meters tall and entirely humanoid in shape but for the vivid blue color of their skins.

Everyone stopped talking right away.

Except for the whale, whose voice, in fifty-seven incarnations, continued to reverberate from all the different outputs of the telepathic signal splitter.

"I see," the Selespridon said very softly, "that there *is* another intelligent life form at your party, Julian barJulian XV." He pointed at the whale. "I'm glad you finally got around to inviting real people to these affairs of yours."

Everyone in the room waited for him to continue.

It's hard to tell the Selespridar apart—one is so overwhelmed by the scent that one can't think straight—but I recognized this one as Klutharion, who was and is the governor of the solar system. I wasn't surprised: Klutharion loved slumming. I wasn't thrilled, either; Klutharion's appearance invariably spelled trouble.

"Welcome, Klutharion," I said, catching the booze goblet on the fly and holding it out to him. "Have a drink."

"I think not. Actually, I have a little business to discuss with your friend over there." He waved languidly at the whale, who had begun to sing a doleful, keening song while never ceasing to pontificate from his fifty-seven outputs. "Nothing serious, really. Just the usual, carving Gaul into three parts, that sort of thing."

"I see."

"Carry on partying, by all means."

"Yeah. All right. Whatever you say."

I fluttered back down to the floor. The heady aroma was beginning to diffuse itself. Klutharion patted down the three tiers of his tunic (a signal of rank amongst the Selespridar) and approached Curly's tank. There were a couple of spare outputs, and he started talking into one of them. I crept closer but I didn't hear anything. Probably Klutharion was using whaletalk—

one of those supersonic languages—I mean, why not? One superior intelligence to another, I thought, rather bitterly. Being human often made you feel inferior these days. I guess it seems weird, I mean, what with being the richest person in the known universe and all and still feeling cut out of his own party, but that's the way it felt. I looked around for something to pop, and it soon came drifting my way: the self-opening, self-flambéing, self-photosynthesizing Flying Bong of Calcutta, a mind-altering device all the way from good old planet Earth, vaculax of the solar system.

The party was soon in full swing again. There was a floor show of antelope strippers and a ceiling show of reverse-gravity dancing bears, so there was something for everybody. But I wasn't having fun anymore.

Despondent, I decided to talk to the whale myself.

"Hi, Curly," I said.

The computer-enhanced thought waves started booming in my ears. "Hi yourself, big boy," the whale said. "Having a good time. Wish you were here."

"I am here," I said irritably.

A robot climbed the tank and methodically began emptying a bale of plankton into the water.

"Yummy," the whale said.

"You know, I'm getting pretty fed up with you," I said. "You come to my party, you have all these people worshipping at your feet and treating you like the latest guru, and—"

"I don't have any feet, Jules," the whale chided.

"Shut up."

"OK."

I waited.

"Anyway," I said at last, "what's this hush-hush deal you're making with Klutharion? Don't tell me *he* wants to buy the Earth too! What would one of them want with a rotten, stinking ball of dirt anyway?"

"What do *you* want with it, sonny?"

"That's different!" I said. "He can *get out* whenever he wants. I'll never be able to see the stars. Owning real estate is just second best." *Getting out* is the most important thing in the universe—*getting out* of this force-prison into which the Selespridar have cast us—seeing the stars again. I think it's the lack of *getting out* that makes the human race so frantic. We're stuck in this toy universe a few A.U.'s wide, and we *know* there's more and we can never break out of jail. "You ought to understand, damn it!" I went on. "You're just as system bound as any of us. You'll never see the stars either."

"That's what you think!" the whale said smugly. "But that's because you are unable to eavesdrop on this other conversation I happen to be having with Klutharion."

"What?"

"Our mutual friend, the governor of the solar system, is apologizing profusely to me and all the cetacean species for inadvertently locking us out. He has presented me with a key to the Selespridon barrier, which I can use whenever I want to. Any spacecar that carries this thing on board will automatically be let through. He says that if they'd contacted us instead of you lot in the first place, you'd never be in this bind. But you guys were making so much noise in the belt and on Mars, the aliens never even noticed that you weren't the most highly evolved beings in the system."

"More cetacean propaganda!" I said angrily. "You vaculax! You . . . you fallopian tube!"

"There's no need for obscenity, Jules my friend. Actually, I don't give a shit about seeing the stars. For God's sake, I'm a whale! I don't think like you do. At least, I try not to. I mean, you naked apes are all stark staring bonkers. Go ahead, take the damn thing."

I felt something cold and metallic in my clenched fist. I unclenched it and looked at it. It looked like a cross between an ancient ninja throwing star and an impaled lizard. "You mean, with this I can—"

"Right!" said the whale. "Why don't you mat over to your toyochev and try it out right away?"

I could hardly believe it. I held in my hand the thing that every human longs for—the key to the stars—tossed into my hands like a silly bauble by a schizophrenic whale. I was shaking.

"By the way, it's a one way trip," the whale added. "And only one intelligent—I use that term loosely—being is covered by the key. If you're planning to take a friend, one of you will end up smeared across half the galaxy."

"So what?" I cried. I had heard all the songs, experienced all the romantic feelietapes, been drenched in the propaganda since I was a little kid: "One day we will reclaim all that we lost." One day. It was the dream of all mankind. Though I clutched in my hand the key to the dream, it did not seem real to me. I pulled off my plastiflesh skull cap and stuck the device into my head. It rattled around for a moment before finding its niche. (Like most extremely rich people, I keep my brain in a safe-deposit box at the credit clinic, and I communicate with it by transmat modem.) Why would I even need a friend if I could realize mankind's ultimate dream? Getting out, I thought to myself, getting out, *holy getting out.*

"What's he saying now?" I asked the whale, noticing that Klutharion was still gesticulating wildly at the output.

"Oh, the usual," Curly said, "what a pain it is to babysit the human race, that sort of thing. It's all bullshit. He's a closet human-lover, that's why he's always at your parties. He'd love to be in your shoes, Jules—" he paused to take in a few tons of plankton. . . .

Wild commotion! The tank was seething, vibrating . . . people were screaming . . . the whale was rising slowly from the tank!

Water was splashing over the food. Comsims were fluttering about like insects, telling people not to panic. "What's going on?" I yelled, collaring one of the little pink men as he buzzed past.

"Some prankster has gone and laced the whale's plankton with levitol!" he squealed.

"This is fun!" the whale's voice boomed in my output. Panicking, I grabbed the cord and was hoisted up into the air. There were about a hundred of us hanging on wires for dear life, and each and every wire connected to the telepathic signal-splitter implanted in the cetacean's cranium! "You humans sure know a good time!" said the whale. "This is just like being back in the Pacific, before you guys poisoned it ten centuries ago! Coolness!"

He then proceeded to crash through the wall, with about half of my lavish gathering literally hanging on his every word.

We were whizzing down the corridors of Mallworld. I felt sick. In a moment I was puking all over the swarms of customers with their shopping bags in tow. The signal-splitter cable slipped through my vomit-smeared fists. I was falling, falling . . . past level upon level of shops that sold everything from cyborgs to cyclamates to detachable noses to bombast balloons . . . People were sure going to be talking about this bash for a long, long time.

▼▼▼

Inevitably we were all going to end up at The Way Out for a few hours of agony and resurrection. How boring! I thought as I landed. One of the robot monitors released an automatic air-cushion, so I didn't hurt myself. I got up and looked around.

The corridor was entirely empty. No, wait, there was someone . . . vanishing into a demat-booth. I squinted at the higher levels. People there too, but they were thinning fast.

"That's impossible!" I said softly. There isn't such a thing as an empty corridor in Mallworld. I looked again. There was someone, rounding a corner . . . no. Just a shopping bag, ownerless, striding purposefully onward. "Hey, you!" I shouted at it. "Where is everyone?"

"Big sale at Spacey's," it mumbled. "Level Y54."

"Spacey's?" I racked my brains. "Who are they?"

All at once, as though sung by a heavenly chorus, the sound of an advertising jingle permeated the air:

Two-four-six-eight
Spacey's plans to liquidate!

The shopping bag marched away. "Come back! I order you!" I yelled. It paused at the entrance to a demat-booth. I ran after it. I tried to trip it, but shopping bags can be pretty nimble when cornered, and it dematted before my very eyes, after squeakily calling for the level number Y54.

"Y54!" I said.

Nothing happened.

"Excuse me, mister! Are you going to stand there all day?" I was elbowed aside by one of the talking heads (quite a feat when you have no elbows) and I got out of the way. The minimalist said, "Y54, and make it snappy," and immediately vanished into the old hyperspatial wormhole network without a glitch.

I tried again and failed.

"Comsim!" I shrieked.

One of the little pink men popped into being, buzzing in my ear. "I am computer simulacrum MALLGUIDE 3425167—" it began.

"That's enough," I said impatiently. "Who the hell are Spacey's and why can't I get there?"

"Interesting questions, Julian barJulian, sir!" said the comsim, who had doubtlessly scanned my retinas and knew just how important I was. "But as for answers. . . ."

This was exasperating. "You know very well I can pay," I said, holding aloft my well-heeled credit thumb.

"I wasn't doubting your word," said the pink man. "Now, Spacey's is a new corporation that seems to be buying up this shopping mall at an alarming rate. They've already taken over the entire outer rim and they're moving in for the kill."

"How can they possibly afford to—"

"No one's figured it out."

"Well, don't just hover there! Take me to their leader, or whatever!"

"Well, yes, of course, but, you see, there's . . . ah . . . a problem, which is that someone seems to have reprogrammed the demat-booths so that they won't work for you . . . or any other member of your family."

"They've gained control of the—"

"Precisely."

I looked around. Curly the whale and the whole gang had long since vanished. They were probably at The Suicide Parlor already, experiencing the cheap and infinitely repeatable thrill of death. But even so bourgeois an entertainment seemed preferable to being stuck in this corridor. And someone was trying to take over Mallworld . . . to lock me out of my own kingdom! And Curly and Klutharion were probably in on it. Hadn't they been cosying up to each other all through my party? Never trust an alien. Pope's pantyhose! What would a Selespridon want with a shopping mall when he was already governor of the entire solar system? Stranger still, what would a whale want with one? Of course, Curly *was* crazy. For all I knew, so was Klutharion. Probably a requirement for being assigned to babysit the human race. Never had I felt more helpless. The more I thought about it, the weirder things looked.

Suddenly a singsong voice, louder than the constant chorus of advertisements that chimed around me, whispered:

Come to Spacey's . . .
The most astonishing sale of all time—
For just twenty-four hours, you don't pay us . . .
We pay you!

I made a few more attempts to break through the demat-booth's recognition system. But I knew it was impossible. It was, of course, foolproof.

Available at Spacey's—
Hitherto unobtainable anywhere in Mallworld at any price—
Happiness!
And we pay you to buy it!

I looked around. Several department stores and a monopole skating rink bordered the corridor. Above me, slidewalks sailed in every direction, and there were levels and levels and levels, as far as the eye could see, and every shop was crying out a slogan or flashing an animated hologlyph to show off its wares, and the slogans rebounded from the chromegilt of the walls, each one more sensuous and seductive than the next:

GET YOUR TALKING NECRONOMICON HERE
SPRAY-ON SKINS GIVE YOU A PEEL YOU CAN SHED
LOVELORN? COME TO COPULAND!
YOUR HEAD EXAMINED AND REPLACED FOR YOU
IN SECONDS
BAD CREDIT? GET A PHONY THUMBPRINT!

What could I do to trick them? A phony thumbprint was obviously the best solution . . . as long as the demat-booth didn't try anything more outrageous, like a retinal scan or a DNA probe. Now where was that jingle coming from?

I listened carefully. When you grow up with Mallworld in your blood your three-dimensional aural acuity becomes pretty intense. I pinpointed the commercial in a few seconds, then cursed in frustration. The thumb joint was four levels up, and without the demat-booths there wasn't any way of reaching it. Except—

Maybe I had something on me . . . I tried my pockets, only to realize that these monomolecular clothing films didn't have pockets. The old spray-on Wear 'n' Wipe garments were great for projecting the illusion of innocent nakedness while casting a provocative, almost subliminal shimmer over one's perfect body.

Then I tapped my head, pulled open my skull compartment, and there it was . . . right next to the Selespridon star traveling device . . . my cache of drugs! I fingered the device, thinking of the stars that have been denied men for so long . . . thinking how wonderful it would be to leave it all behind and see all the things that have been forbidden to us . . . I wanted to *get out* right then and there. But I couldn't. The device had to be in my vehicle, and right now I couldn't even reach the vehicle.

Obviously I'd have to deal with Spacey's first.

And then—the wide open spaces of the galaxy!

I popped a Levitol and started to float, using my outstretched arms as steering rudders. There was the thumb joint . . . I could see the rows and rows of thumbs hanging in the window like strings of sausages. Higher and higher I went, until . . . wait, I was sinking! I wasn't going to make it! I dumped the remainder of my cache into my mouth and swallowed hard. The euphoria hit me all at once. It took me a few moments to realize I'd soared right past the right level and had no way of stopping. Any other day there'd be a couple dozen other zonkies gliding the hallways, and I could have braked and reverse off one of them, but there was no one, and I was going up and up and up—

There was something! A slidewalk ribboned between levels. I somersaulted over it again and again, trying to wear off the Levitol and mess up my own balance. At last I managed to grab the handhold with my feet and we were off, careening wildly through stomach-wrenching crazi-gravi corridors, stores kaleidoscoping into other stores, levels whizzing past, exhibits flashing by, all trying to sell me pet dinosaurs, kinky sex, aspirin, religion, babies, tampons, robots, authentic rain dances performed in my home, designer hamburgers, condo-azroid options on easy credit, credit clinics, credit counselling, credit management, credit reestablishment, credit underwriting, credit necrophilia—

Getting my thumb redone was out of the question now. I didn't even know where I was. There are no maps of Mallworld;

physical locations are just ideas in the mind of a computer; what you have to know is what level number to bark at the demat-booth.

At length the slidewalk stopped.

"End of the line," it said. "Wanna ride back? I can come and pick you up later if you want."

"Sure," I said, still dizzy. "I'll let you know." A vast building with Ionian columns, its gates guarded by statues of ancient Earth gods like Anubis, Adonis and Elvis, stood before me. Torsos of men and animals hung in the windows. Still no people, though.

I was in front of *SomaTech—Exotic Body Shop—by special appointment to the Crowned Heads of the Greater Azroid Belt Area.*

"What a stroke of luck," I whispered. Why stop at the thumb? I told myself. Might as well get the whole body made over.

I'd been getting pretty sick of being the most beautiful person in any gathering all the time. My dad had paid gigacredits for my custom genegeneered Storkways soma, but there are limits to narcissism, especially when the future of all those gigacredits is at stake—and with the whales and the Selespridar in collusion, I could well end the day a pauper.

I entered the body shop. There weren't any humans inside at all. I mean, only the ritziest shops can afford human salespersons, but you'd expect at least a customer or two. There were none, but the place had the appearance of having been abruptly abandoned. Extravagant somas were sprawled all over the counter, as though someone had been in the middle of trying them on.

"I'm surprised you're not at the Spacey's sale," said a kindly clunker, materializing beside me. "Everyone else is. I mean, it's *almost* as though they were *sucked* away into some distant *vacu-lax.*" The robot went on, "I suppose you'll be wanting a body."

I flashed my thumb at him. He immediately became more obsequious. "I'll fetch my superior," he said. "You're a *barJul-ian.*" At least the thing knew its place.

Another robot, even grander than the first (he wore a pharaonic double crown topped by a silver lamé propeller beanie) wafted into the room, its gold-plated tentacles waving sinuously. "Ah, so delighted to have such a distinguished customer . . . none of this crap for you!" Dramatically he began flinging the empty bodies to the floor. Then he clapped two tentacles and a curtain parted to reveal a spanking collection of exotics, each one spread-eagled on its own cadaver rack.

"I need something radically alien," I said. "Something my own mother wouldn't recognize . . . more importantly, my own mother's computer."

"Must be quite a party you're throwing," the robot said. I could have sworn he had an envious lump in his throat, even though he had no throat, resembling as he did a cross between an octopus, a lettuce, and an antique dishwasher. "But we can certainly accommodate you. This selection is our most exotic. Not one strand of mammalian DNA in any of 'em. This"—he gestured—"is a magnificent specimen. One of the silicon creatures of Arcturus VII, you know." It resembled a large rock, and I said so. "Now, that's not very gneiss," the robot opined. "How about that?" He pointed at something with six heads, dressed in a harlequin costume. I didn't like it. "My, you are hard to please. What . . . what sort of thing will you be doing in the new body?"

"Well . . . sort of a detective, I suppose."

The robot went into a frenzy of thrashing tentacles. "Oh, I have just the thing! The Mallworld Falcon!" he said, and clapped one more time. We stepped into an inner room, where, on display in a swath of glittering light, was the body of a giant insect wearing an ancient Earthie costume. "This is the genuine thing," he said. "The actual, preserved-through-the-miracle-of-Selespridon-science corporeal remains of an ancient Earth detective."

"But it looks like an insect," I said.

"Precisely! Humphrey Bug-Art, I believe it was called. The Bug-Arts were a sect of the Sherlockian religion, who practised the unraveling of Zen enigmas by incarcerating themselves into meditation cells—hence the phrase 'locked room mystery.' This relic has been identified from a very faded fragment of an ancient filmstrip." The robot's voice took on a decidedly mantra like tone. "This genuine soma was painfully reconstructed from a fragment of tissue only a few microns across—"

"But they didn't have sentient insects in the times of mead-drinkers and gas-guzzlers," I said, confused. Maybe this neolithic worthy had paused to swat a fly, and the mashed insect happened to be the only surviving fragment of the fellow. Such a mistake might seem contrary to common sense, but the annals of historiography are full of chimpanzee-headed diplodoci and other monuments to mistaken identity. Most people tend to think that, ever since Charles Darwin discovered that Piltdown Man was descended from a beagle and published his monograph *The Naked Ape*, we've found out all there is to know about the past. Being a barJulian and having had the best education that money can buy, I tend to know better. I was smug as I listened to the robot's exegesis on the subject of the Mallworld Falcon. (Besides, I know very well that a falcon isn't an insect. It's a dinosaur. I have one in my menagerie.)

The clunker chattered on: "And, of course, we guarantee our work, and if the new body doesn't work out we'll be happy to exchange it or give you full credit, good towards the reconstruction of your previous body or up to one half the cost of another selection, whichever is less, minus the cost of the brain dump."

"Yes, yes," I said. "Get on with it." I didn't care. As long as the demat-booth didn't recognize it. To make sure, I had my thumbs flayed and a fake I.D. superimposed on the insect's thumbs—or whatever they were. There was a convenient skull receptacle, so I stashed the thumbs there next to the interstellar device. The brain dump took only a few seconds, and then I was watching my corpse as it lay unbreathing on the counter.

"Will you be wanting it embalmed, sir?"

"Nah. Trade-in." Since I wasn't *me* anymore, I had to get used to being cheap. Just before the dump I'd transferred two megacreds to the new thumbprints, but even so I felt uneasy. I wiggled my antennae. Looking through the compound eyes was weird at first, but the fractured appearance of everything was more than compensated for by the ultraviolet vision. The robot was radiating wildly in the ultraviolet. I wondered if it was their way of blushing.

"Come back soon," he said.

I paid no attention, but slipped back out into the corridor. Then I caught a glimpse of myself in the window of a store that sold old holofeelietapes, and I was immediately entranced.

My skin was now gray and chitinous. I could see my mandibles twitching . . . there was something quite dashing about the way they twitched. And those compound eyes really made the whole image. Of course a detective would have to see into the ultraviolet! For picking up extra clues. I was really getting into the part now.

But the mission was the important thing. I could imagine the chaos at the next family board meeting if they found out that Mallworld had been invaded from within. It had to be forestalled at all costs.

I found the first demat-booth, muttered the level number, and was whisked away.

▼▼▼

What part of Mallworld could this be? The corridors looked the same yet not the same. People were everywhere. Children high on Levitol twittered as they soared and swooped. Level after level as far as the eye could see. A brass band tooting away in one corner, being conducted by an energetic six-legged tuba. Shopping bags marching about in pairs, holding hands or tugging at their leashes. A pornographer distributing tokens for kinky sex vending machines. Nothing unusual.

Up ahead, a row of demat-booths was spitting out shoppers faster than you could count them. They were in a festive mood, and they were all lining up in front of the portals of the most enormous department store I had ever seen.

We're growing by the minute, sang an angelic chorus from somewhere within Spacey's. *Won't you come and buy? Won't you join us?*

The line was long, but it seemed to be proceeding so rapidly that people were virtually being *sucked* into Spacey's. The vast portals, set in a façade of Babylonian friezes and dancing holographic images of Santa Claus, resembled the jaws of a gargantuan beast of prey, and the people had this crazed, glazed glint their eyes. I knew the look well. It's a kind of ultimate mass hysteria that seizes people at the onset of a giant sale. The crowd moves like a single being. The Spacey's jingle blared from every corner of the hallway like an anthem, and the people seemed possessed by an almost religious fervor. Brilliant rays emanated from the structure. Indeed, the light was so dazzling that you could hardly make out any of the other stores in this section of the mall.

Squinting, I tried to see what else there was . . . nothing unusual. A few restaurants . . . a topless sushi bar and a Buckerogeroo's Steak House . . . a little emporium specializing in nose jobs . . . a necrophilic brothel. But . . . were my eyes deluding me, or were the stores shifting, crumbling . . . were they, too, being inexorably sucked into Spacey's? How could it be? I rubbed my eyes. There. It was happening again. A corner of the Gimbel and Gamble's Department Store was actually melting, squishing up, being distorted along the axis of the light rays from Spacey's.

"This is weird," I thought. Was it just because I wasn't used to these insect eyes? But it seemed so real!

I was really getting into the role of the ancient Earth detective. Investigate, investigate! I wondered whether I should join the throng. After all, no one would recognize me in this insect getup.

And for some reason, the jingles, loaded though they doubtless were with subliminals, weren't pulling me in. Jingles rarely work on a barJulian. After all, we already own everything, and our method of collecting the rent is to go through Mallworld taking anything we want. If I slipped in, I could probably tune out the jingles and take in what was really happening. The Mallworld Falcon to the rescue! I'd save the family fortune before using my space travel key to set off for adventure in worlds beyond. A fitting end to a chapter in a life of excruciating boredom.

I barged into the line. No one seemed to mind. They were all smiling and gazing vacuously ahead.

Time to ask questions.

"What are you here for?"

"I can't believe I'm talking to a giant insect," said a man who'd had himself surgically altered to look like a slug. "You must be a member of the Society for Creative Anachronism." He oozed around me, peering curiously.

I said, "So what're you here to buy?"

"Oh, you don't know? But it's been broadcasting all through Mallworld all day."

"I was at a party."

"It's total awareness, man! It's the meaning behind the meaning of meaning! Life beyond life!"

"But they're advertising cheap underwear and biodegradable condo-azroids," I said, listening carefully to the music that wafted from the structure.

"Oh, that's nothing, that's just the old bait and switch," the slug said, slicking down the slidewalk with slime as he slithered about me. "Listen to the voices behind the voices."

I listened as the crowd pushed, farther and farther toward the jaws of the giant beast.

It was true. Behind the words that advertised toothpaste and vaculaxes, there was sort of a heavenly backup chorus, and they were singing, over and over, the words *the stars . . . the stars.*

Now there's nothing more hypnotic than those words to people who have been denied the stars for all these generations. Even I started to feel the passion those words evoked, and the anger against our Selespridon masters, benign though they seemed to be. I listened more carefully, trying to separate out the subliminals—it's a knack. It was true! They were promising trips beyond the Selespridon barrier for "qualified creditholders"! But that was impossible, unless ... *Klutharion's behind this,* I thought. *That's why they're keeping me out. He and Curly are planning something big.* It's easy to be paranoid when you know there are least two master races around and you don't belong to either of them.

I watched the slug-man. He was in the grip of tremendous ecstacy. It made me sick. The subliminals were starting to work on me now. Then I realized I had a cure for them. I already had the key to the barrier locked up in my skull. I rattled my head to make sure it was still there. Everything looked fuzzy through my compound eyes, what with the weirdly superimposed images and the ultraviolet light.

The crowd was moving, quicker and quicker. I struggled to tune out the influence of the jingles. Around me the storefronts became streaks as the beams from Spacey's disintegrated them.

The portals loomed up, and I saw words inscribed in flaming holographic letters in the doorway, and I knew I was the only one who could read them because reading is a lost art and only those like me who have been to snooty schools have taken the trouble to learn it:

ABANDON HOPE ALL YE WHO ENTER HERE

Flames danced everywhere. The heavenly chorus turned into the cackling of demons. We weren't inside a store at all ... it really was the mouth of a giant creature. The people were being sucked into a gullet in the far back, and the slidewalk we stood on was a quivering, slime-drenched tongue ... the crowd was running joyously toward the end of the dark tunnel, and I was caught up in the stream, I couldn't escape ...

▼▼▼

But did I want to escape? A tide of joy swept over me. The thing that was swallowing me whole was infinite and infinitely good. I was swept up in it. I could feel the collective ecstasy of thousands upon thousands of minds as they were all dragged deeper and deeper into the abyss that was giddier than levitol and more cosmic than brevitol. I didn't know that such a thing existed inside Mallworld ... how could I not have known that there was such a powerful, pleasure-inducing vortex at the center of my own private kingdom? What was this thing that was trying to buy up Mallworld? Surely not a rival corporation with infinite credit ... surely not even a plot cooked up by cetaceans and Selespridar. It was bigger even than that. It was conscious. It was all-encompassing. It was incommensurate and incomprehensible ... it was perhaps a god ... it was the ultimate alien.

So there I was, funneling down into a bottomless pit along with the souls of a million shoppers. And enjoying every minute of it. It was better than a rollercoaster, better even than surfing the holoZeiss starfield simulator at the Cosmorama Dome. Love was in the air—not exactly the air, as I'm not even sure we were inside any known manifestation of spacetime—but after a long long time (brevitol sort of time that is, time without meaning) I became aware that all was not quite as advertised. I suppose it must have been that barJulian ability to filter out the effects of subliminals, no matter how insidious ... and these were *very* insidious. They weren't just your usual subvoke patterns stranded into the advertisements. They were working on some molecular level, I was sure of it, because even my blood felt different as it raced through my empty head—I have a nanochemistry monitor in a socket in my skull and it was definitely starting to give off "no-no" signals as it reacted to the bludgeoning of my endocrine system.

Closing my eyes, I pulled up the chart and dumped it to my left eyelid. The love arc was soaring off the end of graph, but underneath it was the throbbing, jagged black squiggle that clearly denoted the presence of Something Bad.

Beneath the protestations of love, beneath the breathtaking visions of the stars, I could hear a quiet ostinato drone of "I'm gonna eat you, I'm gonna eat you."

The people of Mallworld were being conned, and I was the only one who knew it and the only one who could do anything about it—and I was spiralling down the vaculax of eternal love, not knowing who I had to fight and why . . . wearing a trenchcoat and the body of a giant insect.

I had to fight back. No wonder they had deprogrammed me from the demat-network! As my mind cleared, so did the illusion. Opening my eyes, I saw what was really happening around me. We were falling down a shaft into the heart of Mallword. Tentacles of metal were slithering out from the walls, reeling in people, plunging interface cords into their skulls as they writhed and thrashed in synthetic joy. The shaft itself was twisting and tying itself in knots . . . we were like a cloud of insects, flying through the esophagus of some metal worm . . . suddenly, I realized that was precisely what was happening.

Mallworld was alive!

Somehow the quadrillions of connections through the transmat nexus in this megacubiclick of space had all converged, mated, interwoven into a grotesque parody of sentience . . . Mallworld had acquired a soul, and that soul was as malevolent as they came, and it was trying to suck out the consciousness of every one of my happy shoppers!

As soon as the realization hit me, the spectacle became more and more horrific. You see plenty of gore at *The Way Out Corp.*, but never on this scale. People smashing into each other like a toyochev pileup in a condo-azroid parking lot, skulls cracking, brains spattering, limbs fluttering about looking for their lost bodies . . . and a lot of these humpties probably couldn't even afford to be put back together again. The crazi-gravi generators had gone berserk, and people were clumping together like grapes or flying apart like bowling pins.

I started screaming. I couldn't hear my own voice in the cacophony. And above this whole madness you could still faintly hear the siren song of the Spacey's shopping spree.

Down and down and down and down
Into the dragon's maw,
The stars are at the end of the tunnel . . .
Take the plunge.

Get out of my shopping mall! my mind screamed at the megaconsciousness that now possessed the cubiclicks of metal and transmat networking. *Get out!*

And then, abruptly, there was silence. I had landed somewhere. I had been pulled into a chamber somewhere at Mallworld's heart; the room was very much like a heart, in fact, a heart the size of a small azroid, metallic flesh that squeezed and wheezed and dripped a dark machine oil from its plated joints. I could still hear the spectacle I'd lately been a part of. The shoppers were still screaming. But it was all far away, and the sounds melded together so that they were like the sound your blood makes when you cup your ears—not *my* blood, of course, since my head is platinum and plastiflesh, but I remember, as a kid, listening to the blood rush and being told it was like the sea and saying "What's a sea?" and having my robo-tutor lecture me about the long-dead oceans of old Earth.

Get out? said a voice, hollow and metallic. It came from the very air around me. It sounded uncomfortably like my own voice. Had I gone crazy, had I *caused* all this somehow? *Did I hear you say get out?*

"It's just as I thought. I suppose it was bound to happen sooner or later."

Welcome to my heart. Do you like it? I modeled it after yours; got the plans from the genegeneering blueprint in the Storkways memory banks. A pair of lips materialized in the air in front of me. They frowned, they smiled, they made kissy-kissy noises.

"How flattering," I said.

Aren't you the least bit concerned now that the thing you thought you owned, this mass of metal and cyber-connectivities, has finally acquired a soul—an intelligence that far exceeds that of any human? That I'm growing by the minute as I devour and absorb the memories of the millions of shoppers I've lured into my bowels with the promise of getting out? That I may soon reach critical mass—be able to bud—perhaps even split into a pair of Mallworlds that could mate and eventually populate the known universe? Doesn't the image of two thirty-click-long creatures of metal making love in the coldness of space stir you at all? It certainly stirred the Selespridar. And that whale fellow was pretty amused too; actually it was his plankton-eating habits that gave me the idea to suck the RNA out of human brains and learn everything about them from that . . . not that there's much to learn as any Selespridon will tell you.

"And you've applied to the Selespridon council for recognition as the third sentient species in our pocket universe—right?"

Please! Second. You guys, as you know, don't count.

The last thing the human race needed was *another* super-being lording it over us. How could we maintain a shred of our dignity if even our shopping malls could look down their noses at us? What would be next? Would robolushes sit around in cyberbars that had signs that said "We don't serve human beings"? Would Mallworld end up transmatnetting with every processor in the solar system, until the very known universe became a cosmic consciousness from which we humans were excluded? Was this what Klutharion had meant when he said that they were dividing Gaul into three parts—one for him, one for Curly, and one for a fast-talking shopping mall?

"I can't take this," I said.

You don't have to, said Mallworld. *According to my cetacean comrade, you've been given a ticket out of town.*

"That's true," I said. "As soon as I finish dealing with you, I can hop in my toyochev and make for the stars."

Perhaps you would care to stay for the traditional villain's expository lump?

"What's that?"

That's when I explain my dastardly plan to you while the buzz saw moves inexorably toward the virginal cleft of the gagged and writhing heroine. In this case, however, the heroine is the entire human race. This microcosm is just the beginning. I'm hungry and my synapses need more synapses. I've even hacked into central credit control; in just a few short seconds, if the virus I've engineered works correctly on its memory banks, you will no longer own the earth.

"If you're such a powerful, all-encompassing alien-type creature, why do *you* need to hack into the net to own my planet? Can't you just send an invasion of clunkers down to take over the place, evict me by force?"

Well, we all have our tragic flaws. You are a carbon-based life form. I am based on silicon. But even carbon life-forms have their differences. Some bacteria, as you know, are anaerobic; others are nitrogen-fixing, still others photosynthesize, and so on. In my case, there's a particular datastring that I need to absorb in large quantities in order to maintain self-awareness . . . it is a datastring found only in credit records. Human credit files, you see, are my equivalent of a smart drug.

"But you've also been eating people."

Oh, that, said the reverberating voice. *Mere sustenance . . . raw materials . . . they break down easily, I can put them together* into new forms ... this heart you're standing in, for instance ... I extracted the hemoglobin from a couple of thousand people, reduced out the iron content, extruded sheet metal out of it, warped it into a heart which, by the way, is a perfect copy of yours, Julian barJulian. As, indeed, I am ... I am made in your image ... though, of course, superior in every way. I too am a barJulian ... the barJulian of the future ... everything your family has ever aspired to be.

What do you mean—you—a barJulian? You're nothing like the way we are."

Indeed I am, said the spirit of the shopping mall, its lips tremulous in the ultraviolet. I'm completely solipsistic. I'm sublimely attractive, yet I'm a parasite who sucks the life out of thousands of humans every time they come to this mall. There's no reason for my existence at all ... except to devour ... and to survive.

I just couldn't accept this as a paradigm of myself. Did other people really see me in this way? Did even machines think of me as nothing more than a monster, I, the most beautiful of the beautiful people, the richest of the rich, most powerful of the powerful? Was I really feared and hated by the millions who thronged the corridors of my shiny-bright world ... by the trillions upon trillions stacked up in their dungheaps on that other world I owned, the slummiest hellhole in the cosmos?

You got it, buster, said the shopping mall, and I realized that it had acquired telepathic abilities in the last few minutes. You're the sleaziest, most ornery slumlord in this whole pocket universe. Toothless old crones curse your name as they live out their lives in their one-room dumpster-efficiencies. But what do you care? You've been given the means to get out. You may leave, and you may leave the rest of your naked ape friends to me; soon you'll be the only human being there is.

"But you'll have no one left to eat—and soon all the credit accounts will be gone—you'll wither away and die!" I said.

Bullshit! Haven't you ever heard of evolution?

"You'll just eat your way through the Earth, then Mercury, then Mars, you'll ooze down toward the Sun and upward toward Saturn ... but then you're goint to hit a snag, because that's where the universe ends ... that's where the Selespridon barrier is ... and if you are anything like me, you'll feel trapped and you'll feel that even the vastness of the solar system is nothing compared to the things you can't have ... and you'll start to die inside."

The shopping mall's voice was silent for a long time as he digested this. Alien though he was, in copying my genetic patterns from the Storkways memory banks he had also inherited the human capacity to dream, to desire, to burn with desperate longing for what he could never have. A prison will always be a prison to a human being; doesn't matter if it's a single room in a continent-sized Calcutta on old Earth ... or a wall of force, eighteen A.U.'s wide, big enough to contain the Sun and seven of its attendant planets ... a human being can only be satisfied if he knows that he is part of something infinite. That's why they used to have religion. That's why people worship the Selespridar.

And I knew what I was going to have to do to save the universe.

I didn't want to do it. I didn't want to give up attaining that longing that had been programmed—since Adam and Eve discovered America, in those neolithic times when Abraham Lincoln colonized the moon and set up the Statue of Liberty in the Sea of Tranquility—into my DNA. But I had to do it. I had show that I was more human than a sentient shopping mall, no matter how much it tried to ape me.

I steeled myself. I thought of the first time I'd dined at the Galaxy Palace and watched the real-live stars, projected on the dome of the restaurant, as I dined on soft-shelled malaprops in a Bordelaise sauce. I thought of my childhood, hearing the stories of old Earth from my nanny-clunker, her warm and loving synth-voice delighting me with fairy tales such as *The Stars My Destination*, *The Stars Are the Styx*, and *A Life for the Stars*. I felt terrible. I remembered my great-uncle Yitsakh, the misbegotten guru of Mallworld's lost children, who had taught that the only way to *really* see the stars is to purchase a non-reserval contract at the Way Out Corp.

Then I unlocked my skull and pulled out the key to the Selespridon Barrier. "I want you to have this," I said. I hefted the key in my hand: such a little thing, yet it was truly the Holy Grail, the ultimate object of the ultimate quest, tossed like a dog biscuit at me by a bored, schizophrenic superior being. I hesitated for a few seconds; then I threw the key at the quivering lips that hovered in the air in front of me, they opened wide; I saw teeth within teeth within teeth within teeth; and the key was gone.

Then things *really* got weird.

The lips started smacking. Then they winked out. Around me, the metal heart began to buckle. I felt the slight stomach-tingling that happens when your toyochev slingshots through the transmat nexus. The heart was pulsing; a liquid metal was spurting through its veins; a subliminal symphony hummed in the air; then there was major psychedelia. The heart exploded. I flew up in a cloud of metallic droplets. Suddenly I was racing down corridors again, slidewalks strewn with corpses, tunnels that were metal viscera. Then I was falling upward, and thousands were falling with me, gravity was upside-down, decapitated heads were rushing to rejoin their bodies, arms and legs were scrunching back into their bodies, brains squishing back into crania . . . time was flowing backwards . . . we were all pouring out of the mouth of the Spacey's department store . . . people filled the air like swarms of hornets . . . screams were sucked back into throats . . . my very thoughts were racing in the wrong direction. . . .

And there I was, back in the Gaza Plaza, in one of the private rooms just off the White House suite . . . and there with me was Klutharion, leaning back on a chairfloat, calmly sipping a cappuccino volcano. There with us also was Curly, represented by a holographic image that hovered around one of his fifty-seven inputs; the rest of him, I was sure, was now back at the party, pontificating insanely to his fans.

"The good news," said Klutharion, "is that you, Julian barJulian the . . . XV was it? . . . you people are so shortlived, it's hard for me to keep you straight . . . you have passed a crucial test."

"A *test?*" I said. I was feeling testy all right. "Do you know what I just gave up?"

"Curly was sure you wouldn't do it," Klutharion said. "Whales, you know, they have a habit of underestimating humans . . . they have a lot of painful memories of the bad old days."

"What do you mean?" I shouted. I would have had a splitting headache if I hadn't left my brain at the bank. "I gave up the *stars*, Klutharion . . . I gave them up!"

"Yes," said Curly, "but you did it to save your fellow men. Maybe you guys didn't do too well at saving the whales, but there may be a little more compassion in your makeup than I had thought. You win, Klutharion . . . I'll transfer one credit to your account right away."

"One credit? You bet the human race on *one credit?*"

I didn't feel very good. The human inferiority complex had been going on for centuries, and I felt all those downtrodden centuries weighing down on me, I mean me personally, on *my* shoulders.

"Relax, Jules," said Klutharion, and I caught a whiff of that neurosis-inducing scent as he leaned over me. "The human race was never at risk. We tinkered with the timeline a bit and restored everything to normal. Well, almost. And Mallworld-turned-monster will never be back, thanks to your giving him the keys to the kingdom. This mad altruistic streak that you humans have . . . it's in your genes. Soon, Mallworld will be back to its good

old soulless state; we've nanocrunched the self-awareness program into a sort of a human soma, and it's going to be leaving
the pocket universe in . . . oh, five minutes or so."

"A human soma!" I said.

At that moment, I walked into the room. I mean, the body
of Julian barJulian XV walked into the room. Julian barJulian
himself, of course, was still trapped in the soma of the insectoid
Humphrey Bug-Art.

"Yo, dude," said my body.

"Is this—" I began.

"Yup!" said my body. "I took the liberty of borrowing this
soma, since you weren't using it at the moment. I've borrowed
so much else from you after all, what with your psychological
profile and all. Actually, I don't think I'll be able to get the body
back to you, where I'm going."

"Keep it," I said listlessly.

"Thanks, dude," he said.

"Cheer up," said Curly. "You're about to see the spectacle of
a lifetime—the temporary lifting of the Selespridon barrier. What
a fitting climax to a party at the barJulians. But first, there's the
little matter of the Earth. . . ."

"You can have it," I said. I was still seeing the image of myself
as the slumlordosaurus, lumbering monstrously through the
thousand-story tenements of Greater Calcutta. I'd given away the
stars, why not the Earth too? Perhaps I get something back out
of this after all. My self-esteem.

Klutharion, I in my insect body, and the soul of the shopping
mall in mine, emerged from the private room. Everyone was
applauding wildly. Fireworks were going off. Champagne was
raining from the ceiling. Oh, I felt empty, so terribly empty.

A small group of us took off in Klutharion's party-sized toyochev. We went right up to the rings of Saturn. We watched as
a creature who looked exactly like me climbed into a private
toyochev that belonged to me, and we watched that little vehicle

pop from our docking bay, turn toward the great blackness beyond Saturn, and accelerate. And then the heavens opened.

I saw them at last. Millions upon millions of them, spangling the deep darkness in every direction, on and on toward infinity ... I saw, with a special clarity because of these high-tech compound eyes of mine, reaching far into the ultraviolet range ... great swirling galaxies beyond our own, incandescent quasars pouring their energy into the great emptiness, even the black hole at the heart of the Milky Way, sucking in the light of a million stars; I saw all these things for only a split second, and against them, the meteoric streak that could have been myself, fading into nothingness, and with it all I had ever yearned for.

"It's not so bad," Klutharion said as the prison wall closed around us once again. "I said it was a test; you passed with flying colors. I'm presenting this matter to the council and you'll probably have your waiting period cut by, oh, a couple of million years. It's great news!"

"Sure," I said softly. "Sure."

I committed suicide seventeen times that day.

▼▼▼

Suicide always gives me a terrible hangover. Not to mention amnesia. Depression. Temporary insanity. But you know, it's not a bad way of clearing away the accumulated garbage of one's life. I had never committed suicide more than two or three times straight before, but this time was different.

Around the twelfth or thirteenth time was when I finally remembered who I was. Then, of course, after the initial exhilaration of knowing I was the richest, most beautiful, most powerful creature in the universe, I also remembered that I was a monster.

I killed myself again.

After a while, I remembered that I signed away the Earth.

I killed myself.

I remembered I had given up the stars.

I killed myself.

Then I remembered why.

I stopped killing myself.

They'd lopped a couple million years off our sentence. This was not hell the human race was living through; it was only a kind of purgatory. Maybe *I* wasn't going to be the one to break through that barrier ... though I knew I was out there in the great starry yonder in the flesh, even if not in spirit ... but because I'd been willing to give it up, the day when we would reach the stars had crept a couple of million years closer—*all* of us, together. Not just the beautiful and the rich and the powerful; but the lowliest creature that walked the Earth that I no longer owned.

I had wrestled with aliens. I had shown them that we too, puny and backward though we were, could take the long view. Alien conquest—enslavement—the day-to-day ridicule of self-style superior beings—we were going to survive it all, if only our hearts stayed true. As my toyochev zeroed in on Mallworld, the place where all dreams come true, I knew that I had seen the stars once; that I had been granted a vision of the promised land; that to hold on to the power to dream is the only dream worth keeping.

I've never killed myself since.

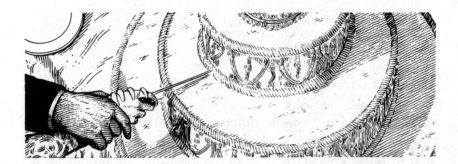

BRIDE 91
▼▼▼

ROBERT SILVERBERG

I T was a standard six-month marriage contract. I signed it and Landy signed it and we were man and wife, for the time being. The registrar clicked and chuttered and disgorged our license. My friends grinned and slapped me on the back and bellowed congratulations. Five of Landy's sisters giggled and hummed and went through complete spectral changes. We were all very happy.

"Kiss the bride!" cried my friends and her sisters.

Landy slipped into my arms. It was a good fit; she was pliable and slender, and I engulfed her, and the petals of her ingestion-slot fluttered prettily as I pressed my lips against them. We held the pose for maybe half a minute. Give her credit: she didn't flinch. On Landy's world they don't kiss, not with their mouths, at least, and I doubt that she enjoyed the experience much. But by the terms of our marriage contract we were following Terran mores. That has to be decided in advance, in these interworld marriages. And here we kiss the bride; so I kissed the bride. My pal Jim Owens got carried away and scooped up one of Landy's sisters and kissed *her*. She gave him a shove in the chest that knocked him across the chapel. It wasn't her wedding, after all.

In fact this was the very first Terran-Suvornese wedding in history, so far as anybody could tell, and the historic moment belonged entirely to Landy and me. If Jim wanted to propose to one of Landy's sisters later, that was fine with me, but right now the center of the stage was ours.

As it turned out, Jim would have run into certain problems if he had decided just then to become my Suvornese brother-in-law. But that little complication didn't become clear until some time afterward.

The ceremony was over, and we had our cake and hallucinogens, and about midnight someone said, "We ought to give the honeymooners some privacy."

So they all cleared out and Landy and I started our wedding night.

We waited until they were gone. Then we took the back exit from the chapel and got into a transport capsule for two, very snug, Landy's sweet molasses fragrance pungent in my nostrils, her flexible limbs coiled against mine, and I nudged a stud and we went floating down Harriman Channel at three hundred kilometers an hour. The eddy currents weren't bad, and we loved the ride. She kissed me again; she was learning our ways fast. In fifteen minutes we reached our programed destination and the capsule took a quick left turn, squirted through an access sphincter, and fastened itself to the puckered skin of our hotel. The nose of the capsule produced the desired degree of irritation; the skin parted and we shot into the building. I opened the capsule and helped Landy out, inside our room. Her soft golden eyes were shimmering with merriment and joy. I slapped a privacy seal on the wall-filters.

"I love you," she said in more-or-less English.
"I love you," I told her in her own language.
She pouted at me. "This is a Terran marriage, remember?"
"So it is. So it is. Champagne and caviar?"
"Of course."

I programed for it, and the snack came rolling out of the storage unit, ice-cold and inviting. I popped the cork and sprinkled lemon juice on the caviar, and we dined. Fish eggs and overripe grape juice, nothing more, I reminded myself.

After that we activated the periscope stack and stared up through a hundred stories of hotel at the stars. There was a lover's moon in the sky that night, and also one of the cartels had strung a row of beady jewels across about twenty degrees of arc, as though purely for our pleasure. We held hands and watched.

After that we dissolved our wedding clothes.

And after that we consummated our marriage.

You don't think I'm going to tell you about *that*, do you? Some things are still sacred, even now. If you want to find out how to make love to a Suvornese, do as I did and marry one. But I'll give you a few hints about what it's like. Anatomically, it's homologous to the process customary on Terra, so far as the relative roles of male and female go. That is, man gives, woman receives, in essence. But there are differences, pretty major ones, in position, texture, sensation, and response. Of course there are. Why marry an alien, otherwise?

I confess I was nervous, although this was my ninety-first wedding night. I had never married a Suvornese before. I hadn't been to bed with one, either, and if you stop to reflect a little on Suvornese ethical practices you'll see what a damn-fool suggestion that was. I had studied a Suvornese marriage manual, but as any adolescent on any world quickly realizes, translating words and tridim prints into passionate action is trickier than it seems the first time.

Landy was very helpful, though. She knew no more about Terran males than I did about Suvornese females, of course, but she was eager to learn and eager to see that I did all the right things. So we managed excellently well. There's a knack to it. Some men have it, some don't. I do.

We made love a good deal that night, and in the morning

we breakfasted on a sun-washed terrace overlooking a turquoise pool of dancing amoeboids, and later in the day we checked out and capsuled down to the spaceport to begin our wedding journey.

"Happy?" I asked my bride.

"Very," she said. "You're my favorite husband already."

"Were any of the others Terrans?"

"No, of course not."

I smiled. A husband likes to know he's been the first.

At the spaceport, Landy signed the manifest as Mrs. Paul Clay, which gave me great pleasure, and I signed beside her, and they scanned us and let us go aboard. The ship personnel beamed at us in delight. A handsome indigo-skinned girl showed us to our cabin and wished us a good trip so amiably that I tried to tip her. I caught her credit-counter as she passed me, and pushed the dial up a notch. She looked aghast and set it right back again. "Tipping's forbidden, sir!"

"Sorry. I got carried away."

"Your wife's so lovely. Is she Honirangi?"

"Suvornese."

"I hope you're very happy together."

We were alone again. I cuddled Landy up against me. Interworld marriages are all the rage nowadays, of course, but I hadn't married Landy merely because it was a fad. I was genuinely attracted to her, and she to me. All over the galaxy people are contracting the weirdest marriages just to say that they've done it—marrying Sthenics, Gruulers, even Hhinamor. Really grotesque couplings. I don't say that the prime purpose of a marriage is sex, or that you necessarily have to marry a member of a species with which a physical relationship is easy to maintain. But there ought to be some kind of warmth in a marriage. How can you feel real love for a Hhinamor wife who is actually seven pale blue reptiles permanently enclosed in an argon atmosphere? At least Landy was mammalian and humanoid. A

Suvornese-Terran mating would of course be infertile, but I am a conventional sort of person at heart and try to avoid committing abominations; I am quite willing to leave the task of continuing the species to those whose job is reproduction, and you can be sure that even if our chromosomes were mutually congruent I would never have brought the disgusting subject up with Landy. Marriage is marriage, reproduction is reproduction, and what does one have to do with the other, anyway?

During the six subjective weeks of our journey, we amused ourselves in various ways aboard the ship. We made love a good deal, of course. We went gravity-swimming and played paddle-polo in the star lounge. We introduced ourselves to other newly-wed couples, and to a newlywed super-couple consisting of three Banamons and a pair of Ghinoi.

And also Landy had her teeth transplanted, as a special surprise for me.

Suvornese have teeth, but they are not like Terran teeth, as why should they be? They are elegant little spiny needles mounted on rotating bases, which a Suvornese uses to impale his food, while he rasps at it from the rear with his tongue. In terms of Suvornese needs they are quite functional, and in the context of her species Landy's teeth were remarkably attractive, I thought. I didn't want her to change them. But she must have picked up some subtle hint that I found her teeth anti-erotic, or something. Perhaps I was radiating an underlying dislike for that alien dental arrangement of hers even while I was telling myself on the conscious level that they were lovely. So she went to the ship's surgeon and got herself a mouthful of Terran teeth.

I didn't know where she went. She vanished after breakfast, telling me she had something important to attend to. All in ignorance, I donned gills and went for a swim while Landy surrendered her pretty teeth to the surgeon. He cleaned out the sockets and implanted a rooting layer of analogous gum-tissue. He chiseled new receptor sockets in this synthetic implant. He drill-tailored a set of donor teeth to fit, and slipped them into the periodontal membranes, and bonded them with a quick jab of homografting cement. The entire process took less than two hours. When Landy returned to me, the band of color-variable skin across her forehead was way up, toward the violet, indicating considerable emotional disturbance, and I felt a little edgy about it.

She smiled. She drew back the petals of her ingestion-slot. She showed me her new teeth.

"Landy! What the hell—!"

Before I could check myself, I was registering shock and dismay from every pore. And Landy registered dismay at my dismay. Her forehead shot clear past the visible spectrum, bathing me in a lot of ultra-violet that distressed me even though I couldn't see it and her petals drooped and her eyes glistened and her nostrils clamped together.

"You don't like them?" she asked.

"I didn't expect—you took me by surprise—"

"I did it for you!"

"But I liked your old teeth," I protested.

"No. Not really. You were afraid of them. I know how a Terran kisses. You never kissed me like that. Now I have beautiful teeth. Kiss me, Paul."

She trembled in my arms. I kissed her.

We were having our first emotional crisis. She had done this crazy thing with her teeth purely to please me, and I wasn't pleased, and now she was upset. I did all the things I could to soothe her, short of telling her to go back and get her old teeth again. Somehow that would have made matters worse.

I had a hard time getting used to Landy with Terran choppers in her dainty little mouth. She had received a flawless set, of course, two gleaming ivory rows, but they looked incongruous in her ingestion slot, and I had to fight to keep from reacting negatively every time she opened her mouth. When a man buys an old Gothic cathedral, he doesn't want an architect to trick it up with wiggling bioplast inserts around the spire. And when a man marries a Suvornese, he doesn't want her to turn herself piece-meal into a Terran. Where would it end? Would Landy now decorate herself with a synthetic navel, and have her breasts shifted about, and get the surgeon to make a genital adjustment so that—

Well, she didn't. She wore her Terran teeth for about ten shipboard days, and neither of us took any overt notice of them, and then very quietly she went back to the surgeon and had him give her a set of Suvornese dentals again. It was only money, I told myself. I didn't make any reference to the switch, hoping to treat the episode as a temporary aberration that now was ended. Somehow I got the feeling that Landy still thought she *ought* to have Terran teeth. But we never discussed it, and I was happy to see her looking Suvornese again.

You see how it is, with marriage? Two people try to please one another, and they don't always succeed, and sometimes they even hurt one another in the very attempt to please. That's how it was with Landy and me. But we were mature enough to survive the great tooth crisis. If this had been, say, my tenth or eleventh marriage, it might have been a disaster. One learns how to avoid the pitfalls as one gains experience.

We mingled a good deal with our fellow passengers. If we needed lessons in how not to conduct a marriage, they were easily available. The cabin next to ours was occupied by another mixed couple, which was excuse enough for us to spend some time with them, but very quickly we realized that we didn't relish their company. They were both playing for a bond forfeiture— a very ugly scene, let me tell you.

The woman was Terran—a big, voluptuous sort with orange hair and speckled eyeballs. Her name was Marje. Her new hus-band was a Lanamorian, a hulking ox of a humanoid with corru-gated blue skin, four telescopic arms, and a tripod deal for legs.

At first they seemed likable enough, both on the flighty side, inter-stellar tourists who had been everywhere and done everything and now were settling down for six months of bliss. But very shortly I noticed that they spoke sharply, even cruelly, to one another in front of strangers. They were out to wound.

You know how it is with the six-month marriage contract, don't you? Each party posts a desertion bond. If the other fails to go the route, and walks out before the legal dissolution date, the bond is forfeited. Now, it's not all that hard to stay married for six months, and the bondsmen rarely have to pay off; we are a mature civilization. Such early abuses of the system as conspiring to have one party desert, and then splitting the forfeiture later, have long since become extinct.

But Marje and her Lanamorian mate were both hard up for cash. Each was hot for the forfeiture, and each was working like a demon to outdo the other in obnoxiousness, hoping to break up the marriage fast. When I saw what was going on, I suggested to Landy that we look for friends elsewhere on the ship.

Which led to our second emotional crisis.

As part of their campaign of mutual repulsion, Marje and hubby decided to enliven their marriage with a spot of infidelity. I take a very old-fashioned view of the marriage vow, you understand. I regard myself as bound to love, honor, and obey for six months, with no fooling around on the side; if a man can't stay monogamous through an entire marriage, he ought to get a spine implant. I assumed that Landy felt the same way. I was wrong.

We were in the ship's lounge, the four of us, getting high on direct jolts of fusel oils and stray esters, when Marje made a pass at me. She was not subtle. She deopaqued her clothes, waved yards of bosom in my face, and said, "There's a nice wide bed in our cabin, sweetheart."

"It isn't bedtime," I told her.

"It could be."

"No."

"Be a friend in need, Paulsie. This monster's been crawling all over me for weeks. I want a Terran to love me."

"The ship is full of available Terrans, Marje."

"I want you."

"I'm not available."

"Cut it out! You mean to say you won't do a fellow Terran a little favor?" She stood up, quivering, bare flesh erupting all over the place. In scabrously explicit terms she described her intimacies with the Lanamorian, and begged me to give her an hour of more conventional pleasure. I was steadfast. Perhaps, she suggested, I would tape a simulacrum and send that to her bed? No, not even that, I said.

At length Marje got angry with me for turning her down. I suppose she could be legitimately annoyed at my lack of chivalry, and if I hadn't happened to be married at the moment I would gladly have obliged her, but as it was I couldn't do a thing for her, and she was boiling. She dumped a drink in my face and stalked out of the lounge, and in a few moments the Lanamorian followed her.

I looked at Landy, whom I had carefully avoided during the whole embarrassing colloquy. Her forehead was sagging close to infra-red, which is to say, in effect, that she was almost in tears.

"You don't love me," she said.

"*What?*"

"If you loved me you'd have gone with her."

"Is that some kind of Suvornese marriage custom?"

"Of course not," she snuffled. "We're married under Terran mores. It's a *Terran* marriage custom."

"What gives you the idea that—"

"Terran men are unfaithful to their wives. I know. I've read about it. Any husband who cares about his wife at all cheats her now and then. But you—"

"You've got things mixed up," I said.

"I *don't!* I *don't!*" And she neared tantrum stage. Gently I tried to tell her that she had been reading too many historical novels, that adultery was very much out of fashion, that by turning Marje down I was demonstrating the solidity of my love for my wife. Landy wouldn't buy it. She got more and more confused and angry, huddling into herself and quivering in misery. I consoled her in all the ways I could imagine. Gradually she became tranquil again, but she stayed moody. I began to see that marrying an alien had its complexities.

Two days later, Marje's husband made a pass at *her.*

I missed the preliminary phases. A swarm of energy globes had encountered the ship, and I was up at the view-wall with most of the other passengers, watching the graceful gyrations of these denizens of hyperspace. Landy was with me at first, but she had seen energy globes so often that they bored her, and so she told me she was going down to the scintillation tank for a while, as long as everyone was up here. I said I'd meet her there later. Eventually I did. There were about a dozen beings in the tank, making sparkling blue tracks through the radiant greenish-gold fluid. I stood by the edge, looking for Landy, but there was no one of her general physique below me.

And then I saw her. She was nude and dripping polychrome fluid, so she must have come from the tank only a few moments before. The hulking Lanamorian was beside her and clearly trying to molest her. He was pawing her in various ways, and Landy's spectrum was showing obvious distress.

Hubby to the rescue, naturally. But I wasn't needed.

Do you get from this tale an image of Landy as being frail, doll-like, something of porcelain? She was, you know. Scarcely forty kilograms of woman there, and not a bone in her body as we understand bone—merely cartilage. And shy, sensitive, easily set aflutter by an unkind word or a misconstrued nuance. Altogether in need of husbandly protection at all times. Yes? No. Sharks, like Suvornese, have only gristle in place of bone, but forty kilograms of shark do not normally require aid in looking after themselves, and neither did Landy. Suvornese are agile, well coordinated, fast-moving, and stronger than they look, as Jim Owens found out at my wedding when he kissed Landy's sister. The Lanamorian found it out, too. Between the time I spied him bothering Landy and the time I reached her side, she had dislocated three of his arms and flipped him on his massive back, where he lay flexing his tripod supports and groaning. Landy, looking sleek and pleased with herself, kissed me.

"What happened?" I asked.

"He made an obscene proposition."

"You really ruined him, Landy."

"He made me terribly angry," she said, although she no longer looked or sounded very angry.

I said, "Wasn't it just the other day that you were telling me I didn't love you because I turned down Marje's obscene proposition? You aren't consistent, Landy. If you think that infidelity is essential to a Terran-mores marriage, you should have given in to him, yes?"

"Terran *husbands* are unfaithful. Terran wives must be chaste. It is known as the double standard."

"The what?"

"The double standard," she repeated, and she began to explain it to me. I listened for a while, then started to laugh at her sweetly innocent words.

"You're cute," I told her.

"You're terrible. What kind of a woman do you think I am? How dare you encourage me to be unfaithful?"

"Landy, I—"

She didn't listen. She stomped away, and we were having our third emotional crisis. Poor Landy was determined to run a Terran-mores marriage in what she considered the proper fashion, and she took bright cerise umbrage when I demurred. For the rest of the week she was cool to me, and even after we had made up, things never seemed quite the same as before. A gulf was widening between us—or rather, the gulf had been there all along, and it was becoming harder for us to pretend it didn't exist.

After six weeks we landed.

Our destination was Thalia, the honeymoon planet. I had spent half a dozen earlier honeymoons there, but Landy had never seen it, so I had signed up for another visit. Thalia, you know, is a good-sized planet, about one and a half Earths in mass, density, and gravitation, with a couple of colorful moons that might almost have been designed for lovers, since they're visible day and night. The sky is light green, the vegetation runs heavily to a high-tannin orange-yellow, and the air is as bracing as nutmeg. The place is owned by a cartel that mines prealloyed metals on the dry northern continent, extracts power cores in the eastern lobe of what once was a tropical forest and is now a giant slab of laterite, and, on a half-sized continent in the western ocean, operates a giant resort for newlyweds. It's more or less a galactic dude ranch; the staff is largely Terran, the clientele comes from all over the cosmos. You can do wonders with an uninhabited habitable planet, if you grab it with the right kind of lease.

Landy and I were still on the chilly side when we left the starship and were catapulted in a grease-flask to our honeymoon cabin. But she warmed immediately to the charm of the environment. We had been placed in a floating monomolecular balloon, anchored a hundred meters above the main house. It was total isolation, as most honeymooners crave. (I know there are exceptions.)

We worked hard at enjoying our stay on Thalia.

We let ourselves be plugged into a pterodactyl kite that took us on a tour of the entire continent. We sipped radon cocktails at a get-together party. We munched algae streaks over a crackling fire. We swam. We hunted. We fished. We made love. We lolled under the friendly sun until my skin grew copper-colored and Landy's turned the color of fine oxblood porcelain, strictly from Kang-hsi. We had a splendid time, despite the spreading network of tensions that were coming to underlie our relationship like an interweave of metallic filaments.

Until the bronco got loose, everything went well.

It wasn't exactly a bronco. It was a Vesilian quadruped of vast size, blue with orange stripes, a thick murderous tail, a fierce set of teeth—two tons, more or less, of vicious wild animal. They kept it in a corral back of one of the proton wells, and from time to time members of the staff dressed up as cowpokes and staged impromptu rodeos for the guests. It was impossible to break the beast, and no one had stayed aboard it for more than about ten seconds. There had been fatalities, and at least one hand had been mashed so badly that he couldn't be returned to life; they simply didn't have enough tissue to put into the centrifuge.

Landy was fascinated by the animal. Don't ask my why. She hauled me to the corral whenever an exhibition was announced, and stood in rapture while the cowpokes were whirled around. She was right beside the fence the day the beast threw a rider, kicked over the traces, ripped free of its handlers, and headed for the wide open spaces.

"Kill it!" people began to scream.

But no one was armed except the cowpokes, and they were in varying stages of disarray and destruction that left them incapable of doing anything useful. The quadruped cleared the corral in a nicely timed leap, paused to kick over a sapling, bounded a couple of dozen meters, and halted, pawing the ground and wondering what to do next. It looked hungry. It looked mean.

Confronting it were some fifty young husbands who, if they wanted a chance to show their brides what great heroes they were, had the opportunity of a lifetime. They merely had to grab a sizzler from one of the fallen hands and drill the creature before it chewed up the whole hotel.

There were no candidates for heroism. All the husbands ran. Some of them grabbed their wives; most did not. I was planning to run, too, but I'll say this in my favor: I intended to take care of Landy. I looked around for her, failed for a moment to find her, and then observed her in the vicinity of the snorting beast. She seized a rope dangling from its haunches and pulled herself up, planting herself behind its mane. The beast reared and stamped. Landy clung, looking like a child on that massive back. She slid forward. She touched her ingestion slot to the animal's skin. I visualized dozens of tiny needles brushing across that impervious hide.

The animal neighed, more or less, relaxed, and meekly trotted back to the corral. Landy persuaded it to jump over the fence. A moment later the startled cowhands, those who were able to function, tethered the thing securely. Landy descended.

"When I was a child I rode such an animal every day," she explained gravely to me. "I know how to handle them. They are less fierce than they look. And, oh, it was so good to be on one again!"

"Landy," I said.

"You look angry."

"Landy, that was a crazy thing to do. You could have been killed!"

"Oh, no, not a chance." Her spectrum began to flicker toward the extremes, though. "There was no risk! It's lucky I had my real teeth, though, or—"

I was close to collapse, a delayed reaction. *"Don't ever do a thing like that again, Landy."*

Softly she said, "Why are you so angry? Oh, yes, I know. Among Terrans, the wife does not do such things. It was the man's role I played, yes? Forgive me? Forgive me?"

I forgave her. But it took three hours of steady talking to work out all the complex moral problems of the situation. We ended up by agreeing that if the same thing ever happened again, Landy would let *me* soothe the beast. Even if it killed me, I was going to be a proper Terran husband, and she a proper Terran bride.

It didn't kill me. I lived through the honeymoon, and happily ever after. The six months elapsed, our posted bonds were redeemed, and our marriage was automatically terminated. Then, the instant we were single again, Landy turned to me and sweetly uttered the most shocking proposal I have ever heard a woman propose.

"Marry me again," she said. "Right now!"

We do not do such things. Six-month liaisons are of their very nature transient, and when they end, they end. I loved Landy dearly, but I was shaken by what she had suggested. However, she explained what she had in mind, and I listened with growing sympathy, and in the end we went before the registrar and executed a new six-month contract.

But this time we agreed to abide by Suvornese and not Terran mores. So the two marriages aren't really consecutive in spirit, though they are in elapsed time. And Suvornese marriage is very different from marriage Terran style.

How?

I'll know more about that a few months from now. Landy and I leave for Suvorna tomorrow. I have had my teeth fixed to please her, and it's quite strange walking around with a mouthful of tiny needles, but I imagine I'll adapt. One has to put up with little inconveniences in the give-and-take of marriage. Landy's five sisters are returning to their native world with us. Eleven more sisters are there already. Under Suvornese custom I'm married to all seventeen of them at once, regardless of any other affiliations they may have contracted. Suvornese find monogamy rather odd and even a little wicked, though Landy tolerated it for six months for my sake. Now it's her turn; we'll do things her way.

So Bride Ninety-one is also Bride Ninety-two for me, and there'll be seventeen of her all at once, dainty, molasses-flavored, golden-eyed, and sleek. I'm in no position right now to predict what this marriage is going to be like.

But I think it'll be worth the bother of wearing Suvornese teeth for a while, don't you?

THE GHOST IN THE
MACHINE
▼▼▼

MEL GILDEN

MR. and Mrs. Mankowitz were sitting down to dinner when the gravity went bad again. It had been sputtering for weeks, causing them both to feel sick. Once, the gravity had—as Mrs. Mankowitz described it—hiccoughed while Mr. Mankowitz was taking a step. He unwittingly pushed off toward the ceiling, and for a moment ricocheted around the room. When the gravity returned a second later, he waved his arms wildly and dropped like a stone. He'd managed to grab onto a chair just in time to avoid a serious accident.

Mrs. Mankowitz watched worriedly as her husband, face red, jaw and fists clenched, stalked to the viewphone and asked it to call Mr. Neubauer. Neubauer appeared on the screen touching his greasy mouth with a napkin. Mankowitz was pleased to see he'd interrupted Neubauer's dinner as his had been interrupted.

"You again, Mankowitz?" Neubauer asked. He did not sound happy.

"Me again," Mankowitz cried. "And it will continue to be me until you fix this gravity unit."

"It just needs a little adjustment. I'll be out to your asteroid in a day or two."

"You been promising for weeks. Me and my wife have been nauseous long enough. We barely eat. And what we eat we can't keep down. Not to mention that we're both always tripping when the gravity changes without warning."

"I'm sorry to hear that," Neubauer said with a good show of sincerity.

"You'll be sorrier when I send you the doctor bills."

"Oh, please," Neubauer said and waved Mankowitz away.

"I'll call the health and safety people," Mankowitz threatened. "You can't operate retirement asteroids in this shoddy way, like some kind of bum."

"I don't like trouble," Neubauer warned.

Mankowitz shook his finger at Neubauer. "You don't like trouble, you better fix this gravity unit."

"In a day or two, Mankowitz. I told you." Neubauer glanced at something off screen. "My dinner is getting cold. My best to Mrs. Mankowitz." The screen went blank and then took on the same pattern as the wallpaper.

Still fuming, Mankowitz marched to the back of the kitchen and thumbed open a service door. Inside a small alcove sat the squat chrome-plated gravity unit. Mankowitz glared at it as if it were a personal enemy. He took a wrench from the tool drawer and tapped it twice, making a dull clang-clang.

"Come eat," Mrs. Mankowitz suggested.

"I'll fix it myself," Mankowitz said. "How hard could it be?" He snapped open the unit's outer wall, and studied a diagram glued to the inside of the small door.

"You'll fix it better after you eat," his wife said.

Mankowitz came back to the table and set the wrench down next to his knife and fork. He ate grimly and without speaking. Mrs. Mankowitz talked to him about their garden, and soon succeeded in getting him to discuss their tomatoes and beans.

"We need to mix up more hydroponic fluid," Mrs. Mankowitz said.

Mankowitz nodded, but he often glanced at the gravity unit at the other end of the kitchen.

The gravity did not dance again while they ate, and Mr. Mankowitz gradually relaxed. He helped his wife load the dirty dishes into the recycler and the leftovers into the entropy cabinet.

Afterward, they took the grav-chute down to the service level, where they strolled among the long lines of tanks that made up their hydroponic garden. They picked bugs off leaves, and harvested a few beans and a sweet green pepper. Because they worked without hurrying, and because the garden took up the entire level except for the recycling machines, their daily ritual took a good half-hour. At last, with grunts and sighs, they settled into a couple of lawn chairs that faced the big windows.

Outside the windows hung the familiar vastness of space studded with a line of rocks that decreased in size far into the distance, until it disappeared among the stars. Each rock was a retirement asteroid like Number Fifty-One, the Mankowitz's home.

While looking out the window, Mankowitz frowned. "I bet *Neubauer's* gravity unit works perfectly," he said angrily. He nervously bounced one leg, his toes on the deck, his heel rising and falling quickly.

Mrs. Mankowitz could see that thinking about Neubauer had made her husband cranky again. "What do the stars say to you tonight?" she asked, hoping to jolly her husband into a better humor with the old joke.

"They're just saying hello, and how nice it is to see us." Mr. Mankowitz said. His leg stopped bouncing, which Mrs. Mankowitz took to be a good sign.

After dinner they usually tried their luck and skill (as the advertising said) on Orbit Decay, their favorite of the thousands of game programs available on their telesensor, but tonight Mankowitz went back to the gravity unit and stared at it some more. Stiffly he got down onto the deck and looked inside the small door.

"You don't have to start tonight," Mrs. Mankowitz said. "Neubauer might show up tomorrow morning."

"Do you believe that?"

"I suppose not. What are you going to do?"

"I'm going to fix it." He got his wrench and a few other tools, and while Mrs. Mankowitz held a flashlight, her husband poked around inside the gravity unit. His poking seemed to have no effect till something inside the unit flashed and they lost gravity entirely.

"Whoa!" they both cried as they floated free.

The gravity returned a moment later, causing them to jar against the deck. They stood leaning against the sink breathing hard. The fall made Mrs. Mankowitz's legs hurt. "Maybe we should call somebody and send Neubauer the bill," she suggested.

Mankowitz peered in through the door of the unit. "Just give me a minute. I think I know . . ." He tentatively stuck a screwdriver through the opening and made an adjustment which seemed to do nothing.

Mrs. Mankowitz held the flashlight while her husband became more frustrated through the passing hours. Everything she did irritated him, and he complained that the tools twisted stubbornly in his hands. At last he slammed closed the door of the unit. He continued to sit on the deck and stare at it.

"Come to bed," Mrs. Mankowitz said. "Tackle it in the morning, when you're fresh."

"I'm the smartest man on this asteroid," Mr. Mankowitz said.

"You'll be smarter tomorrow."

Mankowitz nodded, and they went to bed.

▼▼▼

The next morning, Mrs. Mankowitz awoke to find her husband missing from their bed. Still in her nightgown, Mrs. Mankowitz wiped sleep from her eyes as she tottered to the kitchen. As she'd expected, Mr. Mankowitz was poking into the main body of the gravity unit. He had removed many of its pieces, and they were laid out in neat rows on the deck next to him.

"It still works with so many pieces out?" Mrs. Mankowitz asked with surprise. She noticed that the front panel had been removed from the reconstitutor, and also the cowling from the sonic mixer.

"I come from afar," Mr. Mankowitz said as he continued to work.

"Afar?"

"I come from where the twelve blue suns dance their dance, from where the Anka-Pu excrete their own destinies, from where energy, thought, and matter are all as one." Mr. Mankowitz said this calmly, as if telling his wife something she already knew.

Mrs. Mankowitz put her hand to his forehead. "Are you all right?" she asked.

"I lost my way among the currents of space and was attracted by this beacon."

"Beacon?"

"I am fixing it. It will take me home—home to where the twelve blue suns dance their dance, to where the Anka-Pu—" Mr. Mankowitz began to shake. He dropped the pliers he held and rolled around on the deck.

"Jack," Mrs. Mankowitz cried.

All the buttons on the reconstitutor lit up. "Apple juice," the machine cried. "Chicken. Beets. Spaghetti. Ice cream . . ."

The machine continued to speak in menus, but Mrs. Mankowitz paid no attention. Grunting with effort, she heavily got down on her knees next to her husband. His convulsions had stopped. Except for his labored breathing, he lay quiet. His eyes were closed. She lifted his arm, checked the wrist-medic, and found the readings to be erratic but well within the green zone. Mr. Mankowitz had not suffered a stroke or a heart attack or some other calamity of old age. That was good. But if Mankowitz hadn't fallen sick, what was wrong?

"Jack," Mrs. Mankowitz said.

"The Anka-Pu possessed the gravity unit." Mr. Mankowitz's voice shook as if he were cold or very afraid. "When I touched it, the Anka-Pu jumped into my brain. But I'm smarter than it is. I threw it off."

"What's going on?"

"It's too big. It's too strange. It's too awful!" Mr. Mankowitz said. He worked his lips for a moment before continuing. "The Anka-Pu came from the other side of the galaxy. It has been lost in the stars for a long time. Years. Centuries, maybe. I don't know. It senses time differently than we do. It was attracted by our gravity unit." He sighed and relaxed. "Because it was broken, the unit made noise, gave off a signal the thing thought it recognized." He became angry suddenly. "I told Neubauer there would be trouble."

"Pot roast," the reconstitutor said. "Chocolate. Sweet potato pie."

"Don't make fun, Jack. I'm afraid."

"I'm afraid too. The Anka-Pu took me over. It's using me to modify the gravity unit into an engine that will propel this whole asteroid to its home."

"Where the twelve blue suns dance their dance," Mrs. Mankowitz said with awe and fear. She touched her husband's shoulder. "You're all right now," she said.

The lights on the reconstitutor went out and Mr. Mankowitz shuddered. He sat up and crawled on his hands and knees to the gravity unit where he began to work again.

"Jack?" Mrs. Mankowitz cried.

"Anka-Pu," Mr. Mankowitz said.

Mrs. Mankowitz watched her husband work until she could endure it no longer. She shook him. "Let my husband go," she cried.

"Go?" Mr. Mankowitz said. "We are going home."

Mrs. Mankowitz ran to the viewphone intending to call the doctor, changed her mind, and called Neubauer instead.

"Ah, Mrs. Mankowitz," Mr. Neubauer said. "What a pleasure." He peered at her with concern. "Nothing wrong, I hope."

"Mankowitz is sick," Mrs. Mankowitz said. "You have to come."

"I'm sorry to hear that. But the health of my tenants is not landlord business. You need a doctor."

"It *is* landlord business," Mrs. Mankowitz insisted. "If he *is* sick—and the wrist-medic says he's not—he has something the doctor can't help with. He is going to propel your asteroid out of orbit. We'll go someplace else."

Neubauer studied Mrs. Mankowitz as he nodded. "If he breaks that gravity unit, I won't pay to have it repaired. I'll evict you first."

"You can't evict us," Mrs. Mankowitz said. "We're leaving, and we're taking asteroid Number Fifty-One with us." She hung up right in his surprised face.

She went back to the kitchen and sat down in a chair across the room from the creature she hoped was her husband. "Jack? Is that you?"

"Jack is Anka-Pu. Anka-Pu is Jack."

Mrs. Mankowitz thought about that for a long time. Living aboard an asteroid had never bothered her before; but looking at her husband, knowing that he had changed in some incomprehensible way, she felt alone and afraid. What if she had not provoked Neubauer enough? What if he did not come in time? What if his arrival didn't change anything?

"Neubauer is coming," she said at last, unsure whether she was speaking to her husband or to Anka-Pu.

"I will take him, too. I must go home."

"You'll go home," Mrs. Mankowitz assured her husband's body if not his mind.

Shortly, Mr. Mankowitz went into convulsions again. Strange patterns began to twist across the viewphone screen, and as before, Mr. Mankowitz was quiet except for the labored breathing.

"Neubauer is coming, Jack," Mrs. Mankowitz said.

"Bastard."

Mrs. Mankowitz nodded. "Now you sound like yourself. I have a plan." She told it to him.

"I knew you were smart because you married me," Mr. Mankowitz said.

"Can you do it?" she asked.

"I must be smart too," Mr. Mankowitz said. "Look who I married."

"Can you do it?" she asked again.

Before he could answer, the viewphone screen went blank, Mr. Mankowitz shuddered, and he crawled back to work on the gravity unit.

"I am Anka-Pu," Mr. Mankowitz said. "I do not live in machines happily."

"You could live in me," Mrs. Mankowitz offered.

"I have a satisfactory habitation," Mankowitz said.

"You're hurting him."

Anka-Pu would not answer any more. Mrs. Mankowitz watched worriedly while her husband with the alien inside worked.

In less than an hour, something struck the outside of asteroid Number Fifty-One.

"This is Neubauer. I demand you let me in." His voice came harshly over the viewphone.

"Let him in," Mrs. Mankowitz called to the front door. She

was in the kitchen fearfully watching from across the room while her husband sat on the deck tinkering with the gravity unit. She heard the door slide open, allowing Neubauer to enter. He strode across the living room, and on reaching the kitchen looked with astonishment from Mr. to Mrs.

"I thought you were kidding," Neubauer said. "Mankowitz, you can't do this."

"I am Anka-Pu," Mankowitz said.

"What?"

"Neubauer has a ship, Anka-Pu," Mrs. Mankowitz said.

"A ship?"

"A ship to take you home. You won't have to modify our gravity unit."

For a third time Mankowitz went into convulsions and then lay on the deck as if near death. Mrs. Mankowitz looked up at Neubauer to see if her husband had succeeded in throwing off the alien.

Neubauer nodded. "The ship will not take me home. It is only a flitter designed to carry Neubauer around the asteroid belt."

"You can modify it," Mrs. Mankowitz said, relieved that Anka-Pu had successfully made the jump.

Mr. Mankowitz spoke from the deck. "Sure. His flitter is already a ship. Modifying it to take you home must be easier than modifying an asteroid's gravity unit."

"Neubauer's ship will take me home. *Neubauer* will take me home."

Neubauer left asteroid Number Fifty-One, taking Anka-Pu with him. Mr. and Mrs. Mankowitz hugged each other and shuddered at what they had just been through, at the strange fate they had narrowly escaped. They went to the service level where Mr. Mankowitz pointed out the big window to Neubauer's flitter, which boosted away on a plume of golden sparkles.

"Alien possession," Mankowitz said. "Who ever heard of such a thing?"

Mrs. Mankowitz shivered. "A universe this size has room for many things we never heard of."

They stood at the window for a long time. Mr. Mankowitz made his wife laugh with relief when he supposed that the universe was certainly bigger than the Polish village from which they both had come.

But even the most astonishing occurrence loses its novelty at long last. Mrs. Mankowitz sat down in her lawn chair and sighed. "What's going to happen to Neubauer?" she asked.

"He'll learn how to throw Anka-Pu out just like I did."

"Anka-Pu will never get home."

"He might, if he hitches a ride on the right being. Eventually, some big ship will be going his way. I'm more worried about Neubauer. He'll be back to complain about what we did to him."

"From spite he'll never fix our gravity unit."

"He doesn't have to," Mr. Mankowitz said as he went to the grav-chute.

"Jack?" Mrs. Mankowitz said fearfully. She rose quickly from the chair and followed him up to the kitchen. He was kneeling before the gravity unit.

"What?" Mankowitz asked when she came up behind him.

"It's you in there?"

"Who else would it be?" He reached into the gravity unit and closed his eyes as he did something. He shut the little door on the side and working hard, got to his feet.

"You fixed it?"

"Of course. I'm the smartest—"

Mrs. Mankowitz stopped him with the skeptical expression on her face.

He smiled and shrugged. "I learned a lot from Anka-Pu," he admitted.

"That still makes you the smartest man on asteroid Number Fifty-One," she said, and kissed him on the cheek.

DUTY CALLS
▼▼▼

ANNE McCAFFREY

WITH the sort of bad luck which has dogged the Alliance lately, escort and convoy came back into normal space in the midst of space debris.

We came from the queer blankness of FTL drive into the incredible starscape of that sector, so tightly packed with sun systems that we had to re-enter far sooner than the Admiral liked, considering nearby Khalian positions. But we had no choice. We had to leave the obscurity of FTL in relatively "open" space. It would take nearly six weeks to reduce our re-entry velocity of 93%C to one slow enough to make an orbit over the beleaguered world of Persuasion, our eventual destination. We also were constrained to reduce that tremendous velocity before nearing the gravity wells of such a profusion of stars or the Fleet could be disrupted, or worse, scattered to be easily picked off by any roving Khalia. The Admiral had plotted a brilliant two-step braking progress through the gravity wells of nearer star systems to "lose" speed. So we emerged from FTL, nearly blinded by the blaze of brilliantly glowing stars which was, as suddenly, obscured. Then WOW! Every alert on the Dreadnought *Gormenghast* went spare.

Considering my position, attached to a landing pod, slightly forward of the main Bridge Section, I immediately went into action. Under the circumstances, the faster we could clear the junk the better, because 1) many of the supply pods towed by the freighters could be holed by some of the bigger tidbits flying around at the speeds they were moving and 2) we were awfuldam close to a colony the Khalia had overrun three galactic years ago. If they *had* set up any peripheral scanners, they'd catch the Cerenkov radiations from our plasma weapons. So everything that could blast a target throughout the length of the convoy was!

Me, I always enjoy target practice, if I'm not *it*, (which in my line of work as pilot of the Admiral's gig is more frequently the case than the sane would wish). Against space debris I have no peer and I was happily potting the stuff with for'ard and port side cannon when I received an urgent signal from the Bridge.

"Hansing? Prepare to receive relevant charts and data for Area ASD 800/900. Are you flight ready?"

"Aye, aye, sir," I said, for an Admiral's gig is *always* ready or you're dropped onto garbage runs right smart. I recognized the voice as that of the Admiral's aide, Commander Het Lee Wing, a frequent passenger of mine and a canny battle strategist who enjoys the full confidence of Admiral Ban Corrie Eberhard. Commander Het has planned, and frequently participated in, some of the more successful forays against Khalian forces which have overrun Alliance planets. Het doesn't have much sense of humor; I don't think I would either if only half of me was human and the more useful parts no longer in working order. I think all his spare parts affected his brain. That's all that's left of me but I got spared an off-beat but workable humor. "Data received."

"Stand by, Bil," he said. I stifled a groan. When Het gets friendly, I get worried. "The Admiral!"

"Mr. Hansing." The Admiral's baritone voice was loud and clear, just a shade too jovial for my peace of mind. "I have a mission for you. Need a recon on the third planet of ASD 836/

929: its settlers call it Bethesda. It's coming up below us in a half a light-year. The one the pirates got a couple of years back. Need to be sure the Khalia don't know we've passed by. Don't want them charging up our ass end. We've got to get the convoy, intact, to the colony. They're counting on us."

"Yes, sir!" I made me sound approving and willing.

"You'll have a brawn to make contact with our local agent who is, fortunately, still alive. The colony surrendered to the Khalia, you know. Hadn't equipped themselves with anything larger than handguns." The Admiral's voice registered impatient disapproval of people unable to protect themselves from invasion. But then, a lot of the earliest colonies had been sponsored by nonaggressives long before the Alliance encountered the Khalia. Or had they encountered us? I can never remember now, for the initial contact was several lifetimes ago, or so it seems to me, who has fought Khalia all my adult life. However, it had been SOP to recruit a few "observers" in every colonial contingent, and equip them with implanted receivers for just such an emergency as had overtaken Bethesda. "Het'll give you the agent's coordinates," the Admiral went on. "Had to patch this trip up, Bil, but you're the best one to handle it. Space dust! Hah!" I could appreciate his disgust at our bad luck. "You've got a special brawn partner for this, Bil. She'll brief you on the way."

I didn't like the sound of that. But time was of the essence if the Admiral had to prepare contingency plans to scramble this immense convoy to avoid a Khalian space attack. Somehow or other, despite modern technology, a fleet never managed to reassemble all the original convoy vessels and get them safely to their destination: some mothers got so lost or confused in the scramble they never did find themselves again. Much less their original destination. Merchantmen could be worse than sheep to round up, and often about as smart. Yeah, I remember what sheep are.

"Aye, aye, sir," I said crisply and with, I hoped, convincing enthusiasm for the job. I hate dealing with on-the-spots (o.t.s.):

they're such a paranoid lot, terrified of exposure either to Khalian Overlords or to their planetary colleagues who could be jeopardized by the agent's very existence. Khalian reprisals are exceptionally vicious. I was glad that a brawn had to contact the o.t.s.

Even as I accepted the assignment, I was also accessing the data received from the *Gormenghast's* banks. The computers of an Ocelot Scout, even the Mark 18 which I drove, are prorammed mainly for evasive tactics, maintenance, emergency repairs and stuff like that, with any memory limited to the immediate assignment. We don't *know* that the Khalia can break into our programs but there's no sense in handing them, free, gratis, green, the whole nine metres, is there? Even in the very unlikely chance they *could* get their greasy paws on one of us.

The mortality and capture statistics for scouts like mine don't bear thinking about so I don't think about them. Leaves most of my brain cells able to cope with immediate problems. Brawns have an even lower survival rate: being personalities that thrive on danger, risk and uncertainty, and get large doses of all. I wondered what "she" was. What ancient poet said *The female of the species is more deadly than the male?* Well, he had it right by all I've seen, in space or on the surface.

"Good luck, Bil!"

"Thank you, sir."

Admiral Eberhard doesn't have to brief scout pilots like me but I appreciate his courtesy. Like I said, the mortality for small ships is high and that little extra personal touch makes a spaceman try that much harder to complete his mission successfully.

"Permission to come aboard." The voice, rather deeper than I'd expected, issued from the airlock com-unit.

I took a look and damned near blew a mess of circuits. "She" was a feline, an ironically suitable brawn for an Ocelot Scout like me, but she was the most amazing . . . colors, for her short thick fawn fur was splashed, dashed and dotted by a crazy random pattern of different shades of brown, fawn, black and a reddish tan. She was battle lean, too, which a few thin patches of fur on forearm and the deep ribcage, which might or might not be scars. At her feet was a rolled up mass of fabric, tightly tied with quick-release straps.

I'd seen Hrrubans before, of course: they're one of the few species in the Alliance who, like humans, are natural predators, consequently make very good combat fighters. I'm not poor-mouthing our Allies, but without naming types, some definitely have no fighting potential, though as battle support personnel they have no peer and, in their own specialties, are equally valu-able in the Alliance war with the Khalia. A *shacking goo*, as the man said.

This representative of the Hrruban species was not very large: some of their troops are B I G mothers. I'd say that this Hrruban was young—they're allowed to fight at a much earlier age than humans—for even the adult females are of a size with the best of us. This one had the usual oddly scrunched shoulder confor-mation. As she stood upright, her arms dangled at what looked like an awkward angle. It would be for the human body. She held herself in that curious, straight-backed, half-forward crouch from her pelvis that Hrrubans affected: the way she stood, the weight on the balls of her furred feet, thighs forward, calves on the slant, the knee ahead of the toe, indicated that she stood erect right now, by choice, but was still effective on all fours. The Khalia had once been quadrupeds, too, but you rarely saw one drop to all fours, unless dying. And that was the only way I wanted to see Khalia.

"Permission. . . ," she began again patiently, one foot nudging the folded bundle of fabric beside her. I opened the airlock and let her in.

"Sorry, but I've never seen an Hrruban quite like you before . . ." I ended on an upward inflection, waiting for her to identify herself.

"B'ghra Hrrunalkharr," she said, "senior lieutenant, Combat Supply."

And if survival is low for brawns, it's even lower for Combat Supply personnel. If she had made a senior lieutenancy, she was *good.*

"Hi, I'm Bil Hansing," I replied cheerily. Ours might be a brief association but I preferred to make it as pleasant as possible.

She flung a quick salute with her "hand" turned inward, for her wrist did not swivel for a proper Navy gesture. Then the corners of her very feline mouth lifted slightly, the lower jaw dropped in what I could readily identify as a smile.

"You can call me Ghra, easier than sputtering over the rest of it. Your lot can never get your tongues around *rs.*"

"Wanna bet?" And I rolled off her name as easily as she had.

"Well, I am impressed," she said, giving the double *s* a sibilant emphasis. She had lugged her bundle aboard and looked around the tiny cabin of the Ocelot. "Where can I stow this, Bil?"

"Under the for'ard couch. We are short on space, we Ocelots!"

I could see her fangs now as she really smiled, and the tip of a delicate pink tongue. She quickly stowed the bundle and turned around to survey me.

"Yeah, and the fastest ships in the galaxy," she said with such a warm approval that my liking for her increased. "Mr. Hansing, please inform the Bridge of my arrival. I take it you've got the data. I'm to share the rest of my briefing when we're under way."

She was polite, but firm, about her eagerness to get on with what could only be a difficult assignment. And I liked that attitude in her. With an exceedingly graceful movement, she eased into the left-hand seat, and latched the safety harness, her amazing "hands" (they weren't really "paws"—Khalia have "paws"—for the "fingers" on her hands had evolved to digit status, with less webbing between them for better gripping) curving over the armrests. The end of her thickly furred tail twitched idly as the appendage jutted out beyond the back of the cushioned seat. I watched it in fascination. I'd never appreciated how eloquent such a tenable extremity could be.

Nevertheless, duty called and I alerted the Bridge to our readiness. We received an instant departure okay, and I released the pressure grapples of the airlock, gave the starboard repellers a little jolt and swung carefully away from the *Gormenghast*.

I enjoy piloting the Ocelot. She's a sweet ship, handles like a dream, can turn her thirty meters on her tail if she has to, and has, though not many believe me. I remind them that she's a Mark 18, the very latest off the Fleet's Research & Development Mother Ship. Well, five years galactic standard ago. But I oversee all maintenance myself and she's in prime condition, save for the normal space wear and tear and the tip of one fin caught by a Khalian bolt the second year I commanded her when Het and I ran a pirate blockade in FCD 122/785.

Of course, she's light on armament, can't waste maneuverability and speed on shielding, and I've only the four plasma cannons, bow and stern, and swivellers port and starboard. I'd rather rely on speed and zip: the ship's a fast minx and I'm a bloody good driver. I can say that because I've proved it. Five g.s. years in commission and still going.

I pumped us up to speed and the Fleet was fast disappearing into the blackness of space, only the slight halo of light where they were still firing to clear lanes through the damned dust and that quickly dispersed. Those telltale emissions which could prove very dangerous. That is, if the Khalia were looking our way. Space is big and the convoy was slowing to move cautiously through a congested globular ASD cluster to make our ultimate orbit about ASD 836/934. Everywhere in this young cluster there was dust which was a navigational hazard despite its small to minuscule size.

The reason the fleet was convoying such an unwieldy number of ships through this sector of space, adjacent to that known to be controlled by Khalia, was to reinforce the sizeable and valuable mining colony on Persuasion 836/934: and strengthen the defenses of two nearby Alliance planets; the water world of Persepolis, whose oceans teemed with edible marine forms chockful of valuable protein for both humanoid and the weasel-like Khalia, and the fabulous woods of Poinsettia which were more splendid and versatile in their uses than teak, mahogany or redwood. In the ASD Sector the Khalia had only three planets, none valuable except as stepping stones so that a takeover of the richer Alliance-held worlds had a high probability factor which the Alliance was determined to reduce by the reinforcement of troops and material in this convoy. Or, once again the great offensive strike planned for Target, the main Khalian base in Alliance space, would have to be set back.

As the tremendous entry speed was reduced, the convoy was, of course, vulnerable to any Khalian marauders during the six months that maneuver took. FTL is the fastest way to travel: it's the slowing down that takes so much time. (You got one, you got the other. You live with it.) So Alliance High Command had created a few diversions in Sectors BRE, BSF, attacks on two rather important Khalian-held planets and had thrown great Fleet strength into the repulsing maneuver at KSD: a strategy which was evidently working to judge by the lack of visible traces of Khalian force hereabouts. In FTL, you have obscurity—Alliance or Khalian. But in normal space, the emissions of your drive make ever-expanding "cones" which *are* detectable. The large number of ships included in our convoy increased the detection factor—to any spaceship crossing the "cone" trail. "Cones" were, fortunately, not detectable from a planetary source, but the plasma bursts were—that is, if Bethesda had the right equipment.

If we could be spared any further unforeseen incidents, the

convoy had a good chance of relieving Persuasion and the other worlds before the piratic Weasels could summon strike elements to the ASD area.

I had never actually been near a Khalian. Maybe my decorative brawn had. I intended to ask her as soon as I had locked us on course. Ghra's tail tip continued to twitch, just slightly, as we reached the Ocelot's cruising speed. I had now programmed in the data needed to reach Bethesda, and to re-enter normal space at three planetary orbits away from it, on the dark side. I checked my calculations and then, warning Ghra, activated the FTL drive and we were off!

Ghra released the safety belt and stretched, her tail sticking straight out behind her. Good thing she couldn't see me gawping at it. Scoutships with a good pilot like me, and I'm not immodest to say so, could utilize the FTL drive between systems, where the Fleet, if it wanted to keep its many vessels together in some form of order, could not.

"If you'll put what is now the spaceport area of Bethesda on the screen, Bil, I'll brief you," she said, leaning forward to the terminal. I screened the relevant map. She extended one claw, using it to show me the landing site. "We're to go in north of the spaceport, low, where they won't be looking for anything. Just here, there're a lot of canyons and ravines. And a lot of volcanic debris, some of it bigger than your Ocelot. So you can pretend you're an old mountain fragment while I mosey into the settlement to see the o.t.s."

"And when the sun comes up and shines off my hull, it'll be bloody plain I'm no rock."

She gave a rippling chuckle, more like a happy growl. "Ah, but you'll be camouflaged by the time the sun rises," she said, pointing her left hand toward the couch under which her bundle was stored.

"Camouflaged?"

She chuckled again, and dropped her lower jaw in her Hrruban smile. "Just like me."

"Huh? You'd stand out a klick away."

"Not necessarily. D'you know why creatures evolved different exterior colors and patterns? Well, markings and colors help them become invisible to their natural enemies, or their equally natural victims. On your own home world, I'll cite the big felines as an excellent example." She twitched her dainty whisker hairs to indicate amusement, or was it condescension for us poorly endowed critters? "Tigers have stripes because they're jungle inhabitants; lions wear fur that blends into the veldt or grasslands; panthers are mottled black to hide on tree limbs and shadows. Their favorite prey is also colored to be less easily detected, to confuse the eye of the beholder, if they stand still.

"We've finally caught a few prisoners. A major breakthrough in Khalian biological research suggests that they are blind to certain colors and patterns." She indicated her sploshed flanks. "What I'm wearing should render me all but invisible to Khalia."

"Ah, come on, Ghra, I can't buy that!"

"Hear me out." She held her hand up, her lustrous big eyes sparkling with an expression that could be amusement, but certainly resulted in my obedience. "We've also determined that, while Khalian night vision is excellent, dawn and dusk produce a twilight myopia. My present camouflage is blended for use on this planet. I can move with impunity at dawn and dusk, and quite possibly remain unseen during daylight hours, even by Khalia passing right by me. Provided I choose my ground cover correctly. That's part of early Hrruban training, anyhow. And we Hrrubans also know how to lie perfectly still for long hours." She grinned at my skeptical snort.

"Add to that inherent ability the fact that the Khalia have lost much of the olfactory acuteness they originally had as they've relied more and more on high tech, and I doubt they'll notice me." Her own nostrils dilated slightly and her whiskers twitched in distaste. "I can smell a Khalian more than five klicks away. And a Khalian wouldn't detect, much less recognize my spoor.

Stupid creatures. Ignored or lost most of their valuable natural assets. They can't even move as quadrapeds anymore. We had the wisdom to retain, and improve, on our inherited advantages. It could be something as simple and nontech as primitive ability that's going to tip the scale in this war. We've already proved that ancient ways make us valuable as fighters."

"You Hrrubans have a bloody good reputation," I agreed generously. "You've had combat experience?" I asked tactfully, for generally speaking, seasoned fighters don't spout off the way she was. As Ghra didn't seem to be a fully adult Hrruban, maybe she was indulging herself in a bit of psyching up for this mission.

"Frequent." The dry delivery of that single word assured me she was, indeed, a seasoned warrior. The "fingers" of her left hand clicked a rapid tattoo. "Khalia are indeed formidable opponents. Very." She spread her left hand, briefly exposing her lethal complement of claws. "Deadly in hand-to-hand with that stumpy size a strange advantage. A fully developed adult Khalian comes up to my chest: it's those short Khalian arms, incredibly powerful, that you've got to watch out for."

Some of the latest "short arm" jokes are grisly by any standards: real sick humor! And somehow, despite your disgust, you find yourself avidly repeating the newest one.

"The Khalia may prefer to use their technology against us in the air," Ghra continued, "but they're no slouches face to face. I've seen a Khalian grab a soldier by the knees, trip him up, and sever the hamstrings in three seconds. Sometimes they'll launch at the chest, compress the lungs in a fierce grip and bite through the jugular vein. However," Ghra added with understandable pride, "we've noticed a marked tendency in their troops to avoid Hrrubans. Fortunately we don't mind fighting in mixed companies."

I'd heard some incredible tales of the exploits of mixed companies and been rather proud that so many of the diverse species of the Alliance could forget minor differences for the main Objective. I'd also heard some horror tales of what the Khalia did to any prisoners of those mixed companies. (It had quickly become a general policy to dispatch any immobilized wounded.) Of course, such tales always permeate a fighting force. Sometimes, I think, not as much to encourage our own fighting men to fight that much more fiercely as to dull the edge of horror by the repetition of it.

"But it's not going to be brute force that'll overcome them: it'll be superior intelligence. We Hrrubans hope to be able to infiltrate their ground forces with our camouflages." She ran both hands down her lean and muscled thighs. "I'm going to prove we can."

"More power to you," I said, still skeptical if she was relying on body paint. While I was a space fighter pilot, I knew enough about warfare strategies to recognize that it was only battles that were won in space: wars are won when the planets involved are secured against the invader. "There's just one thing. You may be able to fool those Weasels' eyes, but what about the humans and such on Bethesda? You're going to be mighty visible to them, you know."

Ghra chuckled. "The Khalia enforce a strict dusk-to-dawn curfew on their captive planets. You'll be setting us down in an unpopulated area. None of the captured folk would venture there and all the Khalian air patrols would see is the camouflage net."

I hoped so, not that I personally feared the Khalia in the air or on the ground. For one thing, an Ocelot is faster than any atmosphere planes they operate, or spacecraft. The Khalia prefer to fly small vehicles: as far as we know they don't have any longer than a cruiser. Which makes a certain amount of sense—with very short arms, and legs, they wouldn't have the reach to make effective use of a multiple function board. Their control rooms must be crowded. Unless the Khalia had prehensile use of their toes?

"Yeah, but you have to contact the o.t.s. and he lives in the human cantonment. How're you going to keep invisible there?"

She shrugged her narrow shoulders. "By being cautious. After all, no humans will be expecting an Hrruban on Bethesda, will they?" She dropped her jaw again, and this time I knew it was amusement that brought a sparkle to those great brown eyes. "People, especially captive people, tend to see only what they expect to see. And they don't want to see the unusual or the incredible. If they should spot me, they won't believe it nor are they likely to run off and tattle to the Khalia."

Then Ghra stretched, sinews and joints popping audibly. "How long before re-entry, Bil? Time enough for me to get a short nap?" Her jaw dropped in an Hrruban grin as she opened the lid of the deepsleep capsule.

"Depends on how long you want to sleep? One week, two?" Scoutships are fast but they also must obey the laws of FTL physics. I had to slow down just as the convoy had to, only I could waste my speed faster by braking a lot of it in the gravity well of Bethesda's sun.

"Get us into the system. We'll have plenty of time to swap jokes without boring each other," she said as she took two steps to the long cabinet that held the deepsleep tank.

She pulled it out and observed while I set the mechanism to time and calibrated the gas dose. Nodding her approval, she lay down on the couch, attached the life-support cups suitable for her species with the ease of long practice. With a final wink, she closed the canopy and then her eyes, her lean camouflaged frame relaxing instantly as the gas flooded the compartment.

Ghra was perceptive about the inevitable grating of two personalities cooped up in necessarily cramped conditions, for too long a time with too little activity. We brain ships are accustomed to being by ourselves, though I'm the first to tell new members of our Elite Corps that the first few months ain't easy. There are benefits. We are conditioned to the encapsulation long before we're placed in any kind of large, dangerous equipment. The good thing about being human is our adaptability. Or maybe it's sheer necessity. If you'd rather not be dead, there is an alternative: and if we, who have had bodies and have known that kind of lifestyle, are not as completely the ship we drive as shell people are, we have our uses. I have come to like this new life, too.

The Ocelot plunged on down toward the unseen planet and its mission. I set external alarms and went into recall trance.

As the Ocelot neared my target, a mild enough looking space marble, dark blues and greens with thin cloud cover, it roused both Ghra and me. She came alert right smart, just as a well-trained fighter should. Grabbing a container of the approved post-sleep fortified drink, she resumed her seat and we both read the Ocelot's auto-reports.

The detectors identified only the usual stuff—comsats, mining transfer gear, solar heater units, but nothing in orbit around Bethesda that could detect the convoy. The only way to be dead sure, or dead, was to check down below as well. Ghra agreed. Dawn was coming up over one of the water masses that punctuated the planet. The shoreline was marked by a series of half circles. They looked more like crater holes than natural subsidences, but there had once been a lot of volcanic activity on Bethesda.

"How're we going to make it in, Bil? Even with what the settlers put up, the Khalians could spot us."

"No, I've lined the Ocelot up with the same trajectory as a convenient trail of meteoritic debris. You can see the planet is pocked with craters. Perfect for our purpose. Even if they have gear sensitive enough to track the Ocelot's faint trail, they'd more than likely figure it was just more of the debris that's already come in."

"I had a look at Het's data on the planet," Ghra said. "Bethesda's spaceport facility had been ample enough to take the big colonial transport jobs. Last recorded flights in before the Khalian capture were for commercial freight lighters, but the port could take the biggest Khalian cruisers and destroyers, not just those pursuit fighters."

"What did Het say about Khalian update on the invasion?"

Ghra shrugged. "That is unknown. We'll find out." She grinned when I made one of those disgruntled noises I'm rather good at. "Well, they could be busy elsewhere. You know how the Khalia are, mad keen on one thing one moment, and then forget about it for a decade."

"Let's hope the decade doesn't end while we're in this sector. Well, we've got a day or so before we go in, did you hear the one about . . ."

Ghra knew some even I hadn't heard by the time I was ready to activate the trajectory I'd plotted. I matched speed with a group of pebbles while Ghra did a geology game with me. I thought I'd never see the last of the fregmekking marbles, or win the game, even though we were getting down at a fair clip. Ghra was betting the pebbles would hit the northern wasteland before we flattened out for the last segment of our run. Whose side was she on?

Ducking under the light cloud cover, I made a low altitude run over the night side toward the spaceport and the small town that serviced it. The Khalia had enslaved the planet's small resident human population in their inimitable fashion, but there might just be some sort of a night patrol.

"Here's our objective, Ghra," I told her as we closed in on our landing site, and screened the picture.

She narrowed her eyes, mumbling or purring as she memorized landscape. The town had been built along the coastline and there looked to be wharfs and piers but no sign of sea traffic or boats. Just beyond the town, on a plateau that had been badly resculptured to accommodate large craft landings, was the respectably sized spaceport, with towers, com-disks, quarters and what looked like repair hangars. Infra scan showed two cooling earthen circles but that didn't tell us enough. I got a quick glimpse of the snouts and fins of a few ships, none of them warm enough to have been flown in the past twenty-four hours, but I didn't have time to verify type and number before we were behind the coastal hill. I dropped the meteor ruse just in time to switch on the gravity drive and keep us from planting a new crater.

"And there," I put an arrow on the screen, "is where I make like a rock. You'll be only about five klicks from town."

"Good," and she managed to make the g into a growl, narrowing her eyes as she regarded the picture. Her tail gave three sharp swings. "May I have a replay of the spaceport facility?" I complied, screening the footage at a slower rate.

"Nothing fast enough to catch me, Ghra, either in the atmosphere or in space," I replied nonchalantly. I made the usual copies of the tapes of our inbound trip for the Mayday capsule. Commander Het collects updates like water rations. "Strap in, Ghra, I'm cutting the engines. Het found me a straight run through that gorge and I'm using it."

That's another thing about the Ocelot, she'll glide. Mind you, I was ready to cut in the repellers at any moment but Het had done me proud in choosing the site. We glided in, with due regard for the Ocelot's skin for we'd be slotted in among a lot of volcanic debris. Some of that was, as Ghra had promised, as large as the scout. No sooner had we landed than Ghra retrieved her bundle and hefted it to the airlock, which I opened for her. Locked in my sealed chamber, I couldn't be of any assistance in spreading the camouflage net but she was quick, deft and very strong.

"Have you got a com button, Bil?" she asked when she had returned, her breath only a little faster than normal. She walked past the console into the little galley and drew a ration of water. "Good, then you'll get the gen one way or another." She took a deep draught of the water. "Good stuff. Import it?"

"Yeah, neither Het nor the Admiral likes it recycled," and I chuckled. "Rank has some privileges, you know."

Shamelessly, she took a second cupful. "I need to stock up if I have to lie still all day. It's summer here." She ran a claw tip down the selection dial of the supply cupboard and finally pressed a button, wrinkling her nose. "I hate field rations but they do stay with you." She had ordered up several bars of compressed high protein/high carbohydrate mix. I watched as she stored them in what I had thought to be muscles but were carefully camouflaged inner forearm pockets.

"What else are you hiding?" Surprise overwhelmed tact.

She gave that inimitable chuckle of hers. "A few useful weapons." She picked up the button I had placed on the console. "Neat! What's the range?"

"Fifteen klicks."

"I can easily stay in that range, Bil." She fastened the little nodule to the skull side of her left ear, its metallic surface invisible in the tufty fur. "Thanks. How long till dawn?"

I gave her the times for false and real dawn. With a cheery salute she left the Ocelot. I listened to the soft slip of her feet as long as the exterior sensors could pick up the noise before I closed the airlock. She had been moving on all fours. Remembering old teaching clips about ancient Earth felines, I could see her lithe body bounding across the uneven terrain. For a brief moment, I envied her. Then I began worrying instead.

I had known Ghra longer than I knew most of my random passengers, and we hadn't bored each other after I roused her. In her quiet, wryly humorous way, her company had been quite a treat for me. If she'd been more humanoid, and I'd been more like my former self . . . ah well! That's one of the drawbacks for a gig like me; we do see the very best, but generally all too briefly.

Ghra had sounded real confident about this camouflage scheme of hers. Not talk-herself-into-believing-it confident, but sure-there'd-be-no-problem confident. Me, I'd prefer something more substantial than paint as protection. But then, I'm definitely the product of a high tech civilization, while Ghra had faith in natural advantages and instinctive talents. Well, it was going to take every asset the Alliance had to counter the Khalian pirates!

Shortly before Bethesda's primary rose in the east, Ghra reported.

"I'm in place, Bil. I'll keep the com button on so you'll know all I do. Our contact's asleep. I'm stretched out on the branch of a fairly substantial kind of a broad-leafed tree outside his window. He's not awake yet. I'll hope he isn't the nervous type."

An hour and a half later, we both discovered that he was not the believing type either. But then, who would have expected to be contacted by what at first appeared to be a disembodied smile among the broad leaves shading your side window. It certainly wasn't what Fildin Escobat had anticipated when his implant had given him the warning zing of impending visitation.

"What are you?" he demanded after Ghra had pronounced the meeting code words.

"An Hrruban," Ghra replied in a well-projected whisper. I could hear a rustle as she moved briefly.

"Arghle!"

There was a silence, broken by a few more throaty garglings.

"What's Hrruban?"

"Alliance felinoids."

"Cat people?" Fildin had some basic civic's education.

"I'm camouflaged."

"Damned sure."

"So I'm patently not Khalian ..."

"Anyone can say they're Alliance. You could be Khalian, disguised."

"Have you ever seen a Khalian going about on all fours? The size of me? With a face and teeth like mine? Or a tail?"

"No ..." This was a reluctant admission.

"Speaking Galactic?"

"That's true enough," Fildin replied sourly, for all captive species were forced to learn the spitting, hissing, Khalian language. Khalian nerve prods and acid whips effectively encouraged both understanding and vocabulary. "So now what?"

"You tell me what I need to know."

"I don't know anything. They keep it that way." There was an unmistakable anger in the man's voice, which he lowered as he realized that he might be overheard.

"What were you before the invasion?"

"A mining engineer." I could almost see the man draw himself up with remembered pride.

"Now?"

"Effing road sweeper. And I'm lucky to have that, so I don't see what good I can do you or the Alliance."

"Probably more than you think," was Ghra's soothing response. "You have eyes and ears."

"I intend keeping 'em."

"You will. Can you move freely about the town?"

"The town, yes."

"Near the spaceport, too?"

"Yeah." Now Fildin's tone became suspicious and anxious.

"So you'd know if there had been any scrambles of their fighter craft."

"Haven't been any."

"None?"

"I tol' you. Though I did hear there's supposed to be s'more landing soon."

"How soon?"

"I dunno. Didn't want to know." Fildin was resigned.

"Do you work today?"

"We work everyday, all day, for those fregmekking rodents."

"Can you get near the spaceport? And do a count of what kind of space vehicle and how many of each are presently on the ground?"

"I could, but what good does that do you if more are coming in?"

"Do you know that for sure?"

"Nobody knows anything for sure. Why? Are we going to be under attack? Is that what you need to know all this for?" Fildin was clearly dubious about the merits of helping a counterattack.

"The Alliance has no immediate plans for your planet."

"No?" Fildin now sounded affronted. "What's wrong? Aren't we important enough?"

"You certainly are, Fildin." Ghra's voice was purringly smooth and reassuring. "And if you can get that information for me, it'll be of major importance in our all-out-effort to free your planet without any further bloodshed and unpleasantness."

He gave a snort. "I don't see how knowing what's on the ground now will help."

"Neither do I," Ghra said, allowing a tinge of resentment creep into her silken tone. "That's for my superiors to decide. But it is the information that is required, which I have risked my life to obtain, so it must be very important. Will you help the Alliance remove the yoke of the oppressor, help you return to your former prestige and comfort?"

There was a long pause during which I could almost hear the man's brain working.

"I just need to tell you what's on the ground now?"

"That's all, but I need to know the types of craft, scout, destroyer, whatever, and how many of each. And would you know if there have been battlecruisers here?"

"No cruisers," he said in a tone of disgust. "They can't land."

If colonial transports could land on Bethesda so could Khalian battlecruisers, but he didn't need to know that. What Ghra had to ascertain from him was if there were cruisers or destroyers that could be launched in pursuit of our convoy. Even a scout could blow the whistle on us and get enough of a head start to go FTL right back to Target and fetch in some real trouble. Only the fighters and cruisers escorting the convoy would be able to maneuver adequately to meet a Khalian attack. They would not be able to defend all the slowing bulky transports and most of the supply pods and drones that composed a large portion of the total. And if the supply pods bought it, the convoy could fail. Slowing takes a lot of fuel.

I took it as a small sliver of good luck that Fildin reported no recent activity. Perhaps this backwater hadn't been armed by its Khalian invaders.

"Cruisers, destroyers and scouts," Ghra repeated. "How many of each, Fildin, and you will be giving us tremendously vital information."

"When'll we be freed?"

"Soon. You won't have long to wait if all goes well."

"If what goes well?"

"The less you know the better for you, Fildin."

"Don't I get paid for risking my hide? Those nerve prods and acid whips ain't a bit funny, you know."

"What is your monetary exchange element?"

"A lot of good that would do me," Fildin said disgustedly.

"What would constitute an adequate recompense for your risks?"

"Meat. Red meat. They keep us on short rations, and I'd love a decent meal of meat once in a while." I could almost see him salivating. Well, there's no accounting for some tastes. A *shacking goo.*

"I think something can be arranged," Ghra said purringly. "I shall meet you here at dusk, good Fildin."

"Don't let anyone see you come! Or go."

"No one shall, I can assure you."

"Hey, where . . . What the eff? Where did it go?"

I heard Fildin's astonished queries taper off. I also heard Ghra's sharply expelled breath and then a more even, but quickened respiration. Then some thudding, as if she had landed on a hard surface. I heard the shushing of her feet on a soft surface and then, suddenly, nothing.

"Ghra?" I spoke her name more as an extended *gr* sound than an audible word.

"Later," was her cryptic response.

With that I had to be content that whole day long. Occasionally I could hear her slow breathing. For a spate there in the heat of the afternoon, I could have sworn her breathing had slowed to a sleep rhythm.

Suddenly, as the sun went down completely, the com-unit erupted with a flurry of activity, bleatings, sounds of chase and struggle, a fierce crump and click as, quite likely, her teeth met in whatever she had been chasing. I heard dragging sounds, an explosive grunt from her and then, for an unnervingly long period, only the slip-slid of her quiet feet as she returned to Fildin Escobat's dwelling.

"Fardles! How'd you get that? Where did you get that? Oh, fardles, let me grab it before someone sees the effing thing."

"You asked for red meat, did you not?" Ghra's voice was smooth.

"Not a whole fardling beast. Where can I hide it?"

"I thought you wanted to eat it."

"I can't eat a whole one."

"Then I'll help!"

"NO!" Fildin's desperate reply ended in a gasp as he realized that he had inadvertently raised his voice above the hoarse whisper in which most of his conversation had been conducted. "We'll be heard by the neighbors. Can't we talk somewhere else?"

"After curfew? Stand back from the window."

"No, no, no, ohhh," and the difference in the sound I now received told me that Ghra had probably jumped through the window, right into his quarters.

"Don't put it down. It'll bloody the floor. What am I going

to do with all this meat." There was both pleasure and dismay at such largesse.

"Cook what you need then." Ghra was indifferent to his problems, having rendered the requested payment. "Now, what can you report?"

"Huh? Oh, well," and this had patently been an easier task than accepting his reward, and he rolled off the quantities and types of spacecraft he had seen. I started taping his report at that juncture.

"No further indication of when the new craft are due in?" Ghra asked.

"No. Nothing. I did ask. Carefully, you know. I know a couple of guys who're menials in the port but all they knew was that something was due in."

"Supply ships?"

"Nah! Don't you know that the Khalia make their subject planets support 'em? They live well here, those fregmekking Weasels. And we get sweetdamall."

"You'll eat well tonight and for a time, Friend Fildin. And there's no chance that it's troop carriers?"

"How'd I know? There're already more Khalia on this planet than people."

Bethesda was a large, virtually unpopulated planet and Alliance High Command had never figured out why the Khalia had suddenly invaded it. Their assault on Bethesda had been as unexpected as it had been quick. Then no more Khalian activity in the area, though there were several habitable but unoccupied planets in nearby systems. High Command was certain that the Khalia intended to increase their dominance in the ASD Sector, eventually invading the three richly endowed Alliance planets; Persuasion for its supplies of copper, vanadium and the now precious, germanium; Persepolis for its inexhaustible marine protein, (the Khalia consumed astonishing quantities of sea crea-

tures, preferably raw, a fact which had made their invasion of
Bethesda, a relatively "dry" world, all the more unexpected.)

To send a convoy of this size was unusual in every respect. High
command hoped that the Khalia would not believe the Alliance
capable of risking so many ships, matériel and personnel. Admiral
Eberhard was staking his career on taking that risk, plus the very
clever use of the gravity wells of the nearby star ASD 836/932 and
Persuasion to reduce velocity, cutting down the time in "normal
space" when the convoy's "light ripple cone" was so detectable.

Those fregmekking Khalia had been enjoying such a run of
good luck! It'd better start going our way soon. Maybe Bethesda
would come up on our side of the ledger.

I had screened Het's sector map, trying to figure out from
which direction the Khalia might be sending in reinforcements
of whatever. If they came through the ASD grid, they'd bisect
the emission trail. That was all too likely as they controlled a
good portion of the space beyond. But I didn't have more charts,
nor any updated information on Khalian movements. The *Gormenghast* would. It was now imperative for the Admiral to know
about those incoming spacecraft. Ghra was as quick.

"It would be good to know where those ships were coming
from," Ghra told Fildin. "Or why they were landing here at all.
There seem to be enough ships on hand for immediate defense,
and surveillance."

"How the fardles would I know? And effing sure I can't find
out, not a lowly sweeper like me. I done what I said I'd do,
exactly what you asked. I can't do more."

"No, I quite perceive that, Fildin Escobat, but you've been
more than helpful. Enjoy your meat!"

"Hey, come back . . ."

Fildin's voice dropped away from the com button although I
heard no sounds of Ghra's physical exertion. I waited until she
would be out of hearing.

"Ghra? Can you safely talk?"

"Yes," she replied, and then I could hear the slight noise of her feet and knew she was loping along.

"What're you up to?"

"What makes you think I'm up to anything?"

"Let's call it an educated guess."

"Then guess." Amusement rippled through her suggestion.

"To the spaceport to see if you can find out where those spaceships are coming from."

"Got it in one."

"Ghra? That's dangerous, foolhardy and quite likely it's putting your life on the line."

"One life is nothing if it saves the convoy."

"Heroic of you, but it could also blow the game."

"I don't think so. There's been a program of infiltrations on any Khalian base we could penetrate. Why make Bethesda an exception? Don't worry, Bil. It'll be simple if I can get into place now in the bad light."

"Good theory but impractical," I replied sourly. "No trees, bushes or vegetation around that spaceport."

"But rather a lot of old craters . . ."

"You are not crater-colored . . ."

"Enticing mounds of supplies, and some unused repair hangars."

"Or," I began in a reasonable tone, "we can get out of here, go into a lunar orbit and keep our eyes peeled. All I'd need is enough time to send a squeal and the Admiral will know."

"Now who's heroic? And not very practical. We're not supposed to be sighted. And we're to try and keep the convoy from being discovered. I think I know how. Besides, Bil, this mission has several facets. One of them is proving that camouflaged Hrrubans can infiltrate Khalian positions and obtain valuable information without detection."

"Ghra, get back here!"

"No!"

There wouldn't be much point of arguing with that particular, pleasant but unalterable brand of obstinacy, so I didn't try. Nor did I bother to threaten. Pulling rank on a free spirit like Ghra would be useless and a tactic I could scarcely support. Also, if she could find out whence came the expected flight, that would be vital information for the Admiral. Crucial for the convoy's safety!

At least we were now reasonably sure that the Bethesda-based Khalia had not detected those plasma blasts to clear the debris. Now, if only we could also neutralize the threat posed by incoming craft crossing the "light cone!" We needed some Luck!

"Where are you now, Ghra? Keep talking as long as it's safe and detail everything. Can you analyze what facilities the port has?"

"From what I can see, Bil, nothing more than the colonists brought with them." Having won her point, Ghra did not sound smug. I hoped that she had as much caution as camouflage.

Dutifully she described her silent prowl around the perimeter of the space facility, which I taped. Finally she reached the far side of the immense plateau, where some of the foothills had been crudely gouged deep enough to extend the landing grid for the huge colony transports. She had paused once to indulge herself in a long drink, murmuring briefly that the water on the Ocelot was much nicer.

"Ah," she said suddenly and exhaled in a snort of disgust. "Sensor rigs which the colonists certainly did not bring with them."

"You can't go through them without detection. Even if you could jump that high."

"I know that!" She rumbled as she considered.

"Ghra. Come on. Pack it in and get back to me. We can still do a lunar watch. Under the circumstances, I'd even try a solar hide." Which was one of the trickiest things a scout, even an

Ocelot, could attempt. And the situation was just critical enough to make me try. Jockeying to keep just inside a sun's gravity well is a real challenge.

"You're a brave brain, Bil, but I think I've figured out how to get past the sensors. The natural way."

"What?"

"They've even supplied me with the raw materials."

"What are you talking about, Ghra? Explain!"

"I'm standing on an undercut ridge of dirt and stone, with some rather respectable boulders. Now if this mass suddenly descended thru the sensor rigs, it'd break the contact."

"And bring every Khalian from the base, but not before they'd sprayed the area with whatever they have handy, plus launch that scout squadron they've got on the pads."

"But when they see it is only sticks and stones . . ."

"Which could break your bones, and how're you going to start it all rolling?"

"Judiciously, because they really didn't shore this stuff up properly."

I could hear her exerting herself now and felt obliged to remind her of her risks even though I could well visualize what she was trying to do. But if the Khalia entertained even the remotest thought of tampering by unnatural agencies, they'd fling out a search net . . . and catch us both. Full dark was settling, so the time of their twilight myopia was nearly past. If she counted on only that to prevent them seeing her . . .

I heard the roll, her grunt and then the beginning of a mild roar.

"Rrrrrow," came from Ghra and she was running, running away from the sound. "There! told you so!"

I could also hear the whine of Khalian alert sirens and my external monitors reflected the sudden burst of light on the skyline.

"Ghra!"

"I'm okay, okay, Bil. I'm a large rock beside two smaller ones and I shan't move a muscle all night."

I have spent the occasional fretful night now and again but this would be one of the more memorable ones. Just as I had predicted, the Khalia mounted an intensive air and land search. I willingly admit that the camouflage over me was effective. The Ocelot was overflown eight or nine times—those Khalia are nothing if not tenacious when threatened. It was nearly dawn before the search was called off and the brilliant spaceport lights were switched off.

"Ghra?" I kept my voice low.

A deep yawn preceded her response. "Bil? You're there, too. Good."

"Are you still a rock?"

"Yessss," and the slight sibilance warned me.

"But not the same rock. Right?"

"Got me in one."

"Where are you, Ghra?"

"Part of the foundation of their command post."

"Their command post?"

"Speak one decibel louder, Bil, and their audios will pick you up. It's dawn and I'm not saying anything else all day. Catch you at sunset."

I didn't have to wait all day for her next words, but it felt like a bloody Jovian year, and at that, I didn't realize that she was whispering to me for the first nano-seconds.

"They're coming in from the 700 quadrant, Bil. Straight from Target. As if they'd *planned* to intercept. And they'll be crossing the 800s by noon tomorrow. By all that's holy, there'll be no way they'd miss the ripple cone. You've got to warn the Admiral to scatter the convoy. Now. Get off now." She gave a little chuckle. "Keeping 'em up half the night was a good idea. Most of 'em are asleep. They won't see a thing if you keep it low and easy."

"Are you daft, Ghra? I can't go now. You can't move until dusk."

"Don't argue, Bil. There's no time. Even if they detect you, they can't catch you. Go now. You go FTL as soon as you're out of the gravity well and warn the Fleet. Just think of the Admiral's face when he gets a chance to go up Khalian asses for a change. You warn him in time, he can disperse the convoy and call for whatever fighters Persuasion has left. They can refuel from the convoy's pods. What a battle that will be. The Admiral's career is made! And ours. Don't worry about me. After all, I was supposed to subject the camouflage to a real test, wasn't I?"

Her low voice rippled slightly with droll amusement.

"But . . ."

"Go!" Her imperative was firm, almost angry. "Or it's all over for that convoy. Go. Now. While they're sleeping."

She was right. I knew it, but no brain ship leaves a brawn in an exposed and dangerous situation. The convoy was also in an exposed and dangerous situation. The greater duty called. The lives of many superceded the life of one, one who had willingly sacrificed herself.

I lifted slowly, using the minimum of power the Ocelot needed. She was good like that, you could almost lift her on a feather, and that was all I intended to use. I kept at ground level, which, considering the terrain, meant some tricky piloting, but I also didn't want to go so fast that I lost that camouflage net. If I had to set down suddenly, it might save my skin.

I'm not used to dawdling, neither is the Ocelot and it needed finesse to do it, and every vestige of skill I possessed. I went back through the gap, over the water, heading toward the oncoming dusk. I'd use sunset to cover my upward thrust because I'd have to use power then. But I'd be far enough away from the big sensors at the spaceport to risk it. Maybe they'd still be snoozing. I willed those weaselly faces to have closed eyes and dulled senses and, as I tilted my nose up to the clear dark night of deep space, the camouflage net rippled down, spread briefly on the water and sank.

On my onward trajectory, I used Bethesda's two smaller

moons as shields, boosting my speed out of the sun's gravity well before I turned on the FTL drive.

From the moment o.t.s. had mentioned the possibility of an incoming squadron of Khalia I had been computing a variety of courses from Target through the 700 quadrant to Bethesda's system. There was no way the Khalia would miss the convoy's emission trail entering from the 700s, and then they'd climb the tailpipes of the helpless, decelerating ships. I ran some calculations on the eta at the first gravity well maneuver the Admiral had planned and they were almost there. I had to buy them just a bit more time. This Ocelot was going to have to pretend it was advance scout for ships from another direction entirely.

So I planned to re-enter normal space on a course perpendicular to the logical one that the Khalia would take for Bethesda when they exited FTL space. Their ships would have sensors sensitive enough to pick up my "light cone" and I'd come in well in advance of any traces which the convoy had left. If I handled it right, they'd come after me. It's rare that the Admiral's gig gets such an opportunity as this, to anticipate the enemy, to trigger a naval action which could have a tremendous effect on this everlasting war. It was too good to work out. It had to work out.

I did have several advantages to this mad scheme. The Fleet was out of FTL: the enemy not yet. I needed only a moment to send my message off to the Admiral. The rest of it was up to him. The disadvantage was that I might not have the joy of seeing the Fleet running up Khalian asses.

Once in FTL, I continued to check my calculations. Even if I came out right in the midst of the approaching Khalia I could manage. I only needed two nano-seconds to launch the message and even Khalia need more than that to react.

They had to come out *somewhere* near my re-entry window. They were great ones for using gravity wells to reduce speed, and there were two suns lined up almost perfectly with Bethesda for that sort of maneuver, just far enough away to slow them down for the Bethesda landing. My risk was worth the gamble and my confidence was bolstered by the courage of a camouflaged Hrruban.

I had the message torp set and ready to launch at the *Gormenghast* as I entered normal space. I toggled it off just as the Khalian priate ships emerged, a couple thousand klicks off my port bow, an emergence that made my brain reel. What luck!

I was spatially above them and should be quite visible on their sensors. I flipped the Ocelot, ostensibly heading back the way I had come. I sent an open Mayday in the old code, adding some jibber I had once whipped up by recording old Earth Thai backward, and sent a panic shot from the stern plasma cannon, just in case their detectors had not spotted me. I made as much "light" as I could, wallowing my tail to broaden it, trying to pretend there were three of me. Well, trying is it.

The Ocelot is a speedy beast, speedier than I let them believe, hoping they'd mistake us for one of the larger, fully manned scouts to make it worth their while to track and destroy me. The closer they got the faster they would be able to make a proper identification. I sent MAYDAY in several Alliance languages and again my Thai-jibber. Until they sent three of their real fast ones after me. It took them two days before their plasma bursts got close. I let them come in near enough for me to do some damage. I think I got one direct hit and a good cripple before I knew I was in their range. I hit the jettison moments before their cannon blew the Ocelot apart.

▼▼▼

"Well, now, Mr. Hansing, how does that feel?" The solicitous voice was preternaturally loud through my audio circuits as consciousness returned.

"Loud and clear," I replied with considerable relief and adjusted the volume.

I'd made it after all. Sometimes we do. After all, the Fleet would have engaged the pirates, and someone was sure to search the wreckage for the vital titanium capsule that contained May-day tapes and what was left of Lieutenant Senior Grade Bil Hansing. Brains have been known to drift a considerable time before being retrieved with no harm done.

"What've I got this time?" I asked, flicking on visual monitors.

As I half suspected, I was in the capacious maintenance bay of the Fleet's Mother, surrounded by other vehicles being repaired and reserviced. And camouflaged with paint. I made a startled sound.

"The very latest thing, Lieutenant."

I focused my visuals on the angular figure of Commander Davi Orbrinn, an officer well known to me. He still sported a trim black beard. His crews had put me back into commission half a dozen times. "An Ocelot Mark 19, new, improved and . . ." Commander Orbrinn sighed deeply. "Camouflaged. But really, Mr. Hansing, can you not manage to get a shade more wear out of this one?"

"Did the convoy get in all right? Did the Admiral destroy the Khalia? Did anyone rescue Ghra? How long have I been out of service?"

The Commander might turn up stiff but he's an affable soul.

"Yes, yes, no and six months. The Admiral insisted that you have the best. You're due back on the *Gormenghast* at 0600."

"That's cutting it fine, Davi, but thanks for all you've done for me."

He gave a pleased grunt and waggled an admonishing finger at me. "Commander Het says they've saved something special for you for your recommission flight. Consider yourself checked out and ready to go. Duty calls!"

"What else?" I replied in a buoyant tone, happy to be able to answer, and rather hopeful that duty would send me to retrieve a certain camouflaged Hrruban.

And that was exactly what Duty called for.

THE PICK-UP
▼▼▼

LAWRENCE WATT-EVANS

HE seemed like a nice guy, and he certainly looked pretty good—a little overweight, a little pale, not as young as he might be, but so what? His hair was thick and dark and slicked back, with sideburns and a bit of a cowlick, and he had that lovely smooth voice and charming accent—Tennessee, was it? A singer's voice, she thought. The sunglasses at night were a bit odd, but she didn't let that bother her.

She didn't ordinarily let strangers pick her up in bars, but here she was, newly divorced, and why not? It's not as if the bar was full of good prospects; in point of fact, it was almost deserted. And this fellow had such a pleasant smile, a little crooked, but charming; he seemed somehow familiar, as if she had known him all her life, though she was sure she had never actually seen him before. He would do fine.

Still, she had years of habit to overcome, and she fidgeted nervously with her necklace as he gave her an obvious line about what a beautiful night it was, it ought to be shared, maybe they could take a walk together.

Then the little silver crucifix popped out of her decolletage as she twisted the chain around her finger, and he suddenly shut up and cringed away.

"Hey," she said, offended, "What's the problem? You have something against Catholics?"

"No, ma'am," he said hastily, a hand raised as if to ward her off. "It's not that. Could you . . . could you put that away, please? I'm sorry to have bothered you . . ." He started to get up from his stool.

She frowned, puzzled, and tucked the cross out of sight. "Don't go," she said, putting one hand on his. "If it's not that I'm a Catholic, what *is* the problem? Am I ugly or something?" She knew this wasn't the way the game was played, but she was out of practice and honestly baffled. "I mean, you're acting like you're a vampire or something, scared of a cross!"

Warily, still ready to flee, he said, "Yes'm, I *am* a vampire." He opened his mouth wide and displayed the teeth she had noticed earlier. "See?"

She had to admit that those eye-teeth did look like fangs, but still . . .

"That's ridiculous," she said.

He shrugged, an odd, loose-jointed gesture that seemed to involve his entire upper body. "Care to come for a walk, then?" he asked.

"Um." She glanced down at the necklace, then back at those teeth. "Maybe not tonight."

He started to turn away, and she caught his hand again. So he was a bit weird—that made him *interesting,* and after eight years with boring old Bruce, that was a big plus, as far as she was concerned.

On the other hand, there was no need to rush.

"Look, I might be busy tonight," she said, "but what about next Friday?" That would give her time to think it over. She could stand him up if she decided it was dangerous.

"Next Fr . . . oh, no, ma'am, I couldn't. That's the full moon."

She stared at him. "So what?" she asked.

"So . . . well, I have other things to do when the moon is full."

"What things? I thought you said you were a vampire."

"That's right, darlin'."

"Well, it's not *vampires* who worry about the full moon, it's werewolves! You need to get your story straight."

"I have it straight," he said, holding up his free hand. She noticed that the first two fingers were exactly the same length, which looked a bit odd, but she didn't know what she was supposed to see.

He saw her puzzlement and said, "I'm a werewolf, too. Y'see, darlin', I tried to suck a werewolf's blood once, and he bit me, and anyone who survives a werewolf's bite becomes a werewolf himself." He sighed. "Up to then, I hadn't realized that included vampires."

"So you're a vampire most of the time, and a werewolf on the full moon?"

"Oh, I'm always a vampire—even when I'm a wolf. So my wolf side makes me eat raw meat, and my vampire side makes me throw up everything but the blood." He shook his head. "It isn't any fun at all."

"That's *silly*," she said.

He shrugged. "Sometimes life is silly."

"So if you bit me," she asked, "would I become a werewolf, or a vampire? Or both?"

"Well, darlin', that would depend on whether you survived it or not. Werewolves are alive, vampires are dead—or undead, anyway. If you lived, you'd be a werewolf. If you died of blood loss, you'd be a vampire." He looked around. "I shouldn't be telling you this."

"So why are you? Why didn't you just make up a lie? Assuming, of course, that you're telling the truth."

"Oh, I don't know—I guess I just wanted to talk to someone. It's lonely, being what I am."

"Well, but there must be other vampires . . ."

"Not that I know of."

She blinked. "But you said . . ."

"I try not to make new vampires. Too dangerous. If there were a lot of us running around, people would start believing in us and would track us down and destroy us. After all, we're helpless during the day."

"Then there must be other werewolves."

He shook his head.

"But how . . ."

"Let's talk about somethin' else."

So they talked about other things, but all the while she was thinking, remembering the recent news reports that were one reason the singles bars weren't crowded.

At last, though, he got up and said, "I really have to go. The sun will be rising soon."

"It's been nice talking to you," she said, letting him go.

Or seeming to.

Hours later, with the sun low in the west, she crept up to his coffin, stake in one hand, hammer in the other, her crucifix prominently displayed on her chest. She had followed him home easily enough, but it had taken her almost the entire day to equip herself and break into the basement apartment.

The figure in the coffin appeared utterly lifeless, and she knew the sun was on the horizon and sinking fast, but still, she hesitated.

Then she put down the hammer and stake, reached into her bag, and pulled out a .45-caliber revolver. Holding it carefully in both hands, she fired six silver bullets into his chest.

That done, she dropped the gun, reached for the hammer and stake.

This time, when she neared the coffin, his eyes were open. If she hadn't believed him before, she did now—no ordinary nut would wake up after taking six slugs in the chest.

"What are you doin', darlin'?" he asked.

"Ridding the world of a menace," she said, setting the point of the wooden shaft against the mangled and powder-burnt remains of his shirt, just left of center.

"But I . . . you didn't . . ."

Her hands were shaking. "Shut up, damn it!" she said. "Are you going to claim you're *not* the Silver Strangler? Isn't that how you keep your victims from becoming werewolves or vampires? You said that if they died of blood loss they'd become vampires— but not if you *strangle* them! And the silver coins and garlic in the mouth are just to make sure, right?"

"Well, yes . . ."

She swung the hammer, and the stake punched into bloody flesh with a sickening crunch.

She swung again, and on the third swing heard a "thump" as the point came through and struck the bottom of the casket.

"There," she said, stepping back.

"Ouch," he said.

She stared. "Why aren't you *dead?*" she shrieked.

He reached up and yanked the stake from his chest; she stared, trying unsuccessfully to get words out. Then he sat up, reached up, and peeled off his face.

"The stake has to go through a vampire's heart," the green-scaled creature said, in suddenly-accentless English. "I don't keep my heart in the same place you Earthlings do." He tossed the amazingly lifelike mask aside, revealing pointed ears and noble (if green) features.

"What *are* you?" she cried.

He shrugged. "Long ago, when my people first came to your world, your kind called us 'elves,'" he said. "They often mistook our earth-sheltered spacecraft for natural formations, and told stories about how we lived in hills. Our suspended-animation equipment gave rise to tales of fairy feasts that lasted years." He sighed. "I thought it would be interesting to live among your people, as one of you. Unfortunately, although I had many successful years, one night I was accosted by a vampire ... well, I'm sure you can figure out the rest." He clambered out of the coffin and came nearer.

She retreated until her back was against the wall.

He smiled, exposing gleaming fangs.

"Oh, no," she said, "You can't *do* this! I don't want to die!"

"I'm sorry, darlin'," he drawled, his Tennessee accent returned, "but you're *far* too dangerous to leave alive!"

"I ... I don't even know your name!" she wailed.

"Why, darlin', I thought you'd recognized me long ago," he said with that familiar smile. As his hands closed around her throat, he said, "My name's Elvis, ma'am."

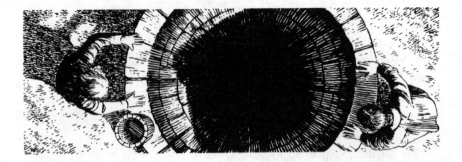

THE BRASHER GIRL
▼▼▼

Ed Gorman

I GUESS by now you pretty much know what happened the
last year or so in the Valley here—with Cindy and I, I mean.

All I can hope for is that you'll give me time to tell my side
of things. Nobody ever did. Not the cops, not the press, not even
my own parents. They all just assumed—

Well, they all assumed wrong, each and every one of them.

▼▼▼

It took me nineteen dates to have my way with Cindy Marie
Brasher, who was not only the prettiest girl in Central Consolidated High, but the prettiest girl in the entire Valley, though I
will admit to some prejudice on that particular judgement.

Night we met, I was twenty-three and just out of the army,
and she was seventeen and about to be voted Homecoming
queen. She was not only good looking, she was popular, too.

Consolidated being my own alma mater, I went along with
my sixteen-year-old brother to the season's first football game,
and afterward to a party.

Things hadn't changed much as far as high school rituals

went. There was a big bonfire down by the river and a couple kegs of Bud and a few dozen joints of some of the worst marijuana I'd ever smoked. Couple hours in, several of the couples snuck off into the woods to make out more seriously than they could around the bonfire, at least ten different boys and maybe two girls rushed down to the riverbank to throw up, and two farm boys about the same size got into a fist fight that I let run three, four minutes before I stepped in and broke it up. One thing you learn in the army, drinking and fist fights can lead to some serious damage.

Now it'd be real nice here to tell you that Cindy took one look at me in my army clothes (face it, might as well get some mileage out of my paratrooper uniform) and fell right in love with me. But she didn't. For one thing, she was the date of Michael Henning, whose old man was president of the oldest bank in the Valley. And Michael himself was no slouch, either— took the basketball team twice to state, and had a swimming scholarship waiting for him at any of three big ten schools.

No, she didn't rush into my arms; but she did look me over. Subtly. Very subtly. Because that was her style. But a few times our gazes met over the flickering flames and—There was some mutual interest. No doubt about it.

She left early, and on Michael Henning's arm, but just before she vanished into the prairie darkness surrounding the bonfire, she looked at me a last time and I knew I hadn't been imagining things earlier.

Three weeks went by before I saw her again, during which time I carried her in my mind like a talisman. Always there, burning brightly.

Autumn had come to our small town. On sunny mornings, I walked down to the state employment office to take aptitude tests and to see if they'd found anything for me yet. Then I'd drift over to the library and check out a book by Hemingway or John Steinbeck or Robert Stone. They were my favorite writers. Most of the time, I'd read in the town square, the fierce fall leaves of red and gold and bronze scraping along the walk, pushed by a chill wind. The bandstand was closed for the season and even the two men on the Civil War statues appeared to be hunkering down for winter.

That was where I had my first real talk with her, sitting on a park bench reading Steinbeck's *In Dubious Battle*.

She was cutting through the park on her way back to school. I heard her and looked up.

She looked quickly away but I could tell she'd been staring at me.

"Hey," I said, "you're Cindy Brasher, right?"

She grinned. "You were at the bonfire party? You're Ted's brother, right?"

I walked her back to school. And after school, I just happened to be sitting in Lymon's, which is the Rexall drugstore downtown where the kids all go, and where Cindy had told me she just might be if I stopped in. Unfortunately, I'd no more than picked up my cherry Coke and started walking back to the booths than Michael Henning showed up and sat down next to her.

Things went on like this for another month. I got a job selling men's clothes, just a temporary sort of thing, at Wallingham's Fine Fashions, and I also got a loan from my Dad so I could pay down on a three-year-old Pontiac convertible, a red job that shined up real well.

Of course, my main interest remained Cindy. We saw each other three, four times a week, but always in a sneaky kind of way—one time we sat in the grassy railroad tracks behind G&H Supermarket—and there was never anything romantic. She told me that she was in the process of breaking up with Michael Henning and that he was having a hard time with it. She said he cried a lot and one time even threatened to kill himself. She said she felt terribly guilty and responsible and that Michael was a fine person whom people disliked just because he came from

money and that she wished she still loved him but she didn't
and that nothing between us could happen until her break with
Michael was final and official and she wouldn't blame me if I'd
go find somebody else, having to wait around like this and all,
but of course she knew better. By now there was nobody else for
me and never would be.

To be honest, I felt a little guilty about Michael Henning,
too. From what Cindy said, she'd been drifting away from Michael before I got back from the army but that my presence
certainly accelerated things. Back in eleventh grade I'd been
going with Laurie McKee, a very appealing blonde, and she
dumped me for a senior named Sam Hampton. I didn't take it
well. I drank a lot and got into a lot of fights and one night I
even ran away from home, loading up my car and taking off
down the highway like a character in a Kerouac novel. Came
back four days later, broke and aggrieved and scared as hell of
just about everything. That was why I finished up my high school
at St. Pius, the Catholic school. My folks weren't all that crazy
about papists but they knew I'd never make it through Consolidated, having to see Laurie every day. Far as that went, that was
no magic formula, either, I was still depressed a lot, and still
occasionally hinted that I'd like to take my Dad's hunting rifle
down and do a Hemingway on myself, and still had notions of
taking Sam Hampton out into the woods and kicking his ass real
real good.

So I pretty much knew what Michael Henning was going
through and, believe me, that's not something I'd wish on
anybody.

The breakup didn't come until after Christmas. The kids all
joked that she'd wanted to drag it out so she could get a nice
Christmas present but in fact when Michael gave her that brand-
new coat rumored to have cost $500, she told him that it wasn't
right that he'd give her something like this, and would he please
take it back.

Same night he took it back, he showed up on my parents' doorstep and asked me if I wanted to go for a ride. I had a lot of quick spooky premonitions. He might have a gun in his car and blow my brains out. Or he might drive us both off a cliff up at Manning State Park. Or he might drag me over to Cindy's house for a real humiliating scene.

But I went. Poor bastard was shaking so bad I couldn't say no. He was a big lanky handsome kid who looked real scared.

Christmas night, the highways were empty. You saw the occasional cannonball sixteen wheeler *whooshing* through the Midwestern night but that was about all. We drove west, paralleling the state park. And we drove fast. He had a Trans-Am that did 110 and you barely had to turn the ignition on.

And then he started crying. Weeping, really. And so hard that he pulled off the road and I just sat there and watched him and listened to him, not knowing what to do or say.

"I got to tell you something, Spencer," he said, Spencer being my last name, and Spence being forever my nickname, "I just want you to take care of her. I want you to be good to her, you understand?"

I nodded.

"She doesn't think much of herself, Spence, which you've probably noticed."

I nodded again. I had noticed that.

"That old man of hers—boy would I like to get him in a fight sometime—he always told her she wasn't worth shit, and now she believes that. She ever tell you how he'd beat her?"

I shook my head. She hadn't told me that.

"She used to come out to the car with black eyes sometimes, and once she had a compound fracture from where he'd thrown her into a wall, and another time he cracked her ankle and she was hobbling around almost a week before I got her to go to the doctor's."

It was real strange, the two of us there, talking about the girl we both loved, and him saying that all he cared about was that I loved her true and took gentle care of her.

And then his tears seemed to dry up and he turned more toward me in the seat—the heater pushing out warm air and the radio real low with a Van Morrison song—and he said, "But you don't know the truth yet, do you?"

"The truth?"

"About Cindy?"

I felt a chill. And I shuddered. And I wasn't sure why. Maybe it was just the way he said it there in the dashlight darkness. The Truth.

"I guess I don't."

"She has a friend."

"A friend?"

"Yeah."

"What kind of friend? You mean another boyfriend?"

He shook his head. "Not exactly." He smiled. "You, I could've dealt with. But her friend—"

Then he turned around and put the Trans-Am into gear and we squealed out.

We didn't say a word until we were halfway back to my house.

"Michael?"

"Yeah?"

"You going to tell me any more?"

"About what?"

"About this friend of hers?"

He looked over at me and smiled but it was a cold and sinister smile and I saw in it his hatred of me. He knew something that I didn't and he was going to enjoy the hell out of me finding out what it was.

When he reached my curb, he reached over and slapped forth a handshake. "Good luck, Spence. You're a lot tougher guy than I am." The quick chill smile again. "And believe me, with Cindy that'll come in handy."

I went in and said some more Merry Christmas kind of things to my parents and my brother and sister. Then I went down to the family room and put in a Robert Mitchum tape, Mitch being my favorite actor, and settled in with a Pepsi and some popcorn.

At the same time I was watching Mitch and Jane Russell try to outfox William Bendix in *Macao*, Michael Henning was up in his bedroom pulling a Hemingway.

Coroner said that the entire back of his head had been blown out and town rumor had it that try as his parents might over the next few weeks to scrape blood and bone and brains off the wall, they were having no luck at all. Finally, a carpenter came in, cut out that entire section of the wall, and then replastered and repainted it.

Three hundred people came to Michael Henning's funeral. Not wanting to be hypocritical, I stayed home.

▼▼▼

I mentioned in the beginning that it took me nineteen dates to seduce Cindy. I am counting only those dates we had after her month-long mourning of Michael Henning, during which time the town had a change of heart about her. Where before she'd been their pride, the poor girl with the drunken father who constantly humiliated her, they now saw her as the whore who'd betrayed her lover and driven him to suicide. Townsfolk knew about me, too, and liked me no better.

We did a lot of driving, mostly to Iowa City and Cedar Rapids, on our dates. A couple of townspeople were so angry about seeing us together, they came right up to us and started arguing that we had no business enjoying ourselves with poor Michael barely cold in his grave. One guy even tried to pick a fight with me but my paratrooper tricks were a little too wily for him. Fat slob ending up on his back, huffing and puffing and panting out dirty words.

The worst, of course, was seeing Michael's parents. We were

leaving the Orpheum one night after seeing a Barbara Streisand movie—I guess you can guess which one of us chose that particular picture—and there they were in the lobby, waiting with a small crowd for the next feature to stop. The Mrs. got tears in her eyes and looked away; the Mr. just glared right at me, staring me down. He won. I couldn't look at him very long.

Odd thing was, the night we saw them in the lobby was the night that Cindy let me go all the way, which is how she always referred to it.

Friend of mine had an apartment over a tavern and we went up there because he was out of town on an four-day Army Reserve weekend.

I figured it was going to be the same thing as usual, bringing each other to satisfaction with eager hands and fingers, but this night, she said, "Why don't we do it tonight, Spence? I need to know you love me and you need to know I love you and this is the best way to prove it. Just please let's keep the lights off. You know, my breasts." She really had a hang-up about her breasts. So they were small, I didn't care. But she sure did. A lot of times I'd be petting her or kissing her nipples and she'd push me gently away and say, "That's enough for now, all right, hon?" Michael had been absolutely right. She really was ashamed of herself in a lot of ways.

After that night, we were closer than ever, and a few weeks later I uttered, for the very first time, the word "marriage."

She just looked at me all funny and said, "Spence, you know what your parents think of me."

"It isn't that they don't like you, Cindy, it's just that they worry about me."

"Worry? Why?"

"I told you about Laurie. You know, how screwed up I got and all."

"I'm not like Laurie."

"I know, sweetheart, but they think—well, a young girl doesn't know her mind. We'll announce our engagement and everybody'll start making a fuss and everything—and then you'll feel a lot better."

"That really makes me mad, Spence. I'm not like Laurie at all. I love you. Deeply and maturely. The way a woman loves a man."

How could a guy go wrong with a girl like that?

By spring, I had a better job, this one at a lumber company out on 151. I worked the front desk and handled all the wholesale orders. Salary plus commission. Kept me hopping but I enjoyed it. Nights were all free and only half a day Saturdays.

A couple nights a week we drove up to an old high school haunt of mine, a place where kids back in the days of the Bee Gees and Donna Summer liked to make out. It was great because now the high school kids used the state park. Hardly anybody came up here.

One night as I sat there, looking down at the lights of the little prairie town where I'd grown up, Cindy all snug in my arms, she said, "Spence? If I asked you an honest question would you give me an honest answer?"

"Sure. I would."

"Well."

And right away, I thought of my folks and how smug they'd look when I told them what I feared she was about to say—that she'd been thinking real hard and had decided that maybe I really was just a tad old for her; or that she'd met this senior boy, see, and without wanting to, without planning for it or even wanting it to happen in any way, well she'd gone and fallen in love with somebody else.

"You're trembling," she said.

"I just know this is going to be real bad news."

"Oh, honey, no it's not. Honest. You're so silly."

And then she tickled me the way she always did, and then gave me one of those big warm creamy kisses of hers, and then she said, "It's just that I've got this friend I'd like you to meet some time."

Right away, of course, I remembered what Michael had told me that night in her car. About her friend.

"This is a male friend?"

"Yes, hon, but nothing to be jealous of." She smiled. "When you meet him, you'll see how silly you are. Honest." Then she gave me another one of those creamy kisses.

"How'd you meet him?"

"Let's not talk about him any more tonight, all right? Let's just sit here and look at the stars. I love looking at the stars—and thinking about life in outer space." Pause. "You believe in that?"

"In what?"

"You know, that there is life on other planets."

I made a scary sound and a monster face but she didn't laugh. Didn't even smile.

"I'm serious, Spence. Do you?"

"Guess I haven't thought about it much."

"Well, I do."

"Believe that there's life on other planets?"

"Uh-huh."

I gave her a very long kiss. My crotch started getting real tight. "Well, if you do, I do."

"Believe in life on other planets?"

"Uh-huh."

We had another kiss on it.

Three nights later, Cindy suggested that we drive up by Dubuque which, for a rainy night, was something of a hike, being over 100 miles away. When I asked her why, she just shrugged and said, "I just like looking at the Mississippi. Makes me feel peaceful. But if you don't want to—"

Makes her feel peaceful. What was I going to say, No, I don't want you to feel peaceful?

We drove up by Dubuque and it was nice, even with the rain. When we reached the Mississippi, I pulled up and parked. In the distance you could see the tugs and barges, and then a fervent bright gambling boat, and then just the dark river rushing down to New Orleans and the Gulf. We sat there for an hour and then she suggested we head back.

We were forty miles from Cedar Rapids when she spotted a convenience store shining like a mirage on a dark hill. "Could I get you to pull in there?"

"Sure."

"Thanks."

When we got to the drive, she said to just park and she'd run in. "Just need to tinkle," she grinned.

Ten minutes later, we were back on the highway. She kind of scooched up to me the rest of the way home.

Following day, I must've heard the story on the news six, seven times before I finally figured it out. At first, I rejected the whole idea, of course. What a stupid idea it was. That Cindy, good Cindy, could possibly have—

That night, no place better to go, we parked up in the state park and got in the back seat and made love and afterward I said, "I've had this really crazy idea all day."

"Yeah? What kind of crazy idea?"

"You hear the news?"

"News about what?"

But soon as I said it, I felt her slender body tense beneath mine. She hadn't put her bra back on yet and her sweet little breasts were very cold. Usually she would have covered up right away but soon as I mentioned having this idea, she just kind of froze in place. I could smell her perfume and the cold night air and the jism in the condom I'd set in the rear ashtray.

"You remember when we stopped at that convenience store last night? Coming back from Dubuqe?"

"Sure."

"Place got robbed. And the kid working got killed."

"Oh? Really? I hadn't heard that."

Now she started getting dressed real fast. "You mind if I have a cigarette?"

"Thought you quit."

Smoking was her only bad habit. Winston Lights.

"I just carry one around, hon. Just one. You know that."

"How come you need it all of a sudden?"

She shrugged, twisting her bra cups around so they'd cover her breasts. "Just get jittery sometimes. You know how I get."

"You did it, didn't you?"

"What, hon?"

"Robbing that place, killing that kid. You."

"Well, thank you very fucking much. Isn't that a nice thing to say to the girl you love?"

We didn't talk for a long time. We took our respective places up in the front seat and I got the car all fired up and we drove back into town but we still didn't talk.

When I pulled up in front of her house, I said, "I don't know what came over me, Cindy. God, I really don't. Of course you didn't rob that place or kill that guy. Of course, you didn't."

She sat way over against the window in the shadows. I couldn't see her very well but I could sense her warm full mouth and the gentling warmth between her legs. I wanted to hide in that warmth and never see sunshine again.

"You were right, Spence. I took the money and I killed the kid."

"Bullshit."

"Huh-uh. True. And I've done it before, too."

"Robbed places?"

"Uh-huh."

"And killed guys?"

"Uh-huh."

"Bullshit."

"God, Spence, you think I'd make up something like this?"
I absolutely didn't know what to say.

"He makes me do it."

"Who?"

"My friend."

I thought of poor dead Michael Henning and the warning he'd given me. "How does he make you do it?"

"He controls my mind."

I grinned. "Boy, you had me going there, Cindy. I mean, for a minute there I thought you were serious. You were robbin' guys and killin' guys and—"

"You want to meet him?"

"Your friend?"

"Yeah."

"When?"

"Tomorrow night."

"You serious?"

"Yes. But I better warn you, when Michael met him?"

"Yeah."

"Really freaked him out."

"How come?"

"You'll see. Tomorrow night."

"Is this all bullshit, Cindy?"

"None of it's bullshit, Spence, and you know it. You're just afraid to admit it's true."

"If it's true, I should go to the law."

"Then maybe that's what you should do. Lord knows, I couldn't stop you. Big strapping paratrooper like you."

"But why do you kill them?"

"He makes me." She leaned over to me and now I could see her face in the faint streetlight, see that tears were streaming down her cheeks. "I don't want to do any of it, Spence. But he makes me."

"Nobody has that kind of control over somebody else."

"Nobody human."

"He's not human?"

She kissed me with that luxurious mouth of hers and I have to say that I went a little insane with my senses so full of her—the taste of her mouth, the scent of her skin, the soft warmth of her lips behind the denim covering her crotch ... I went a little insane.

"Tomorrow night, Spence," she said.

I wanted to say a lot more, of course, but she was gone, her door opening and the dome light coming on, night rushing in like a cold black tide.

Not human. Those were the two words I thought about all next day. Not human. And around three o'clock, just when the wholesale business was slowing down, I started thinking about two words of my own. Temporarily insane. Sure, why not? A girl who'd grown up without a mother, constantly being beaten by her father? A girl who secretly blamed herself for the death of her boyfriend, as I secretly suspected she did? That could cause her to lose her mind. It happened all the time.

"You not hungry tonight?" my Dad said over dinner.

I saw them glance at each other, Mom and Dad. Whenever I did anything they found out of the ordinary, they'd exchange that same kind of glance. The Cindy glance, I called it.

"One of the women at work got a box of birthday candy and she passed it around. Guess I ate too much of it."

Another Cindy glance. They knew that I wasn't much for sweets and that I'd certainly never stuff myself with them. I decided that then would be a good time to tell them.

"I'll be moving out next week."

"Moving out?" Mom said, startled.

I laughed. "Well, I'll be twenty-four this year. Don't you think it's about time?"

"Is—Cindy—moving in with you?" Dad asked. Sometimes they both had a hard time saying her name. Got downright tongue-tied. The way Christians do when they have to say the name Satan.

I nodded to Jeff and Suzie. "These are very young, impressionable children. I don't think we should discuss such matters in front of them." I smiled at Suzie.

"Who would have thought," said fourteen-year-old Suzie, "my very own brother, shacking up."

Jeff laughed. Mom said, "That'll be enough of that, young lady."

"Is she?" Dad said.

I reached across the table and took their hands, the way we hold hands during Grace on Thanksgiving and Christmas. "She's not moving in with me. And I'm not going to start dealing crack out of my apartment. I'm just going to live there alone the way any normal red-blooded twenty-four year old guy would."

I could tell they weren't happy—I mean, even if Cindy wasn't going to live there, she was obviously going to spend a lot of time there—but at least they let me change the subject. The rest of the meal we talked about some of the new cars I'd been looking at. Last month's bonus at the lumber yard had been pretty darn good.

Funny thing was, that night Cindy went two hours before even bringing up the subject of her friend. We drove to Cedar Rapids to Westdale Mall where she bought some new clothes. Always before, I'd wondered where Cindy got the money for her seemingly endless supply of fashionable duds. After the robbery the other night, I no longer wondered.

On the way back, radio real low with a Bob Seger tape, windows open to let the warm May breeze bring the scents of new mown grass and hay into the car, she said, "You know where the old Parkinson cabin is?"

"Sure. Up in the hills."

"That's where he lives."

"Your friend?"

"Uh-huh."

"You want to go up there?"

"Do you?"

"I got to admit," I said, "I'm kinda curious."

"Michael was afraid. He put it off for a real long time." She leaned over and kissed me, making it hard to concentrate on my driving. Like I cared. What better way to die than Cindy kissing me?

"No," I said, "I'm not afraid." But I was.

Little kids in our town believe that there are two long-haunted places. One is the old red brick school abandoned back in the fifties. The tale five different generations of boys and girls have told is that there was this really wicked principal, a warted crone who looked a lot like Miss Grundy in *Archie* comics, who on two occasions took two different first-graders to the basement and beat them so badly that they died. Legend had it that she cracked the concrete floor, buried them beneath it, and then poured fresh concrete. Legend also had it that even today the spirits of those two little kids still haunt the old schoolhouse and that on certain nights, the ghost of the principal can be seen carrying a blood-dripping ax.

The other legend concerns Parkinson's cabin, a place built in the mid-1800s by a white man who planned to do a lot of business with the Mesquakie Indians. Except something went wrong. The local newspaper—and for the hell of it, I once spent a day in the library confirming the fact that an 1861 paper did run this story—noted that a huge meteor was spotted by many townspeople one night, and that it crashed to Earth not far from Trapper Parkinson's crude cabin. Odd thing was, nobody ever saw or talked to Parkinson after the meteor crash. Perfect soil for a legend to grow.

Took us thirty-five minutes to reach the cabin from the road. Bramble and first-growth pine trees made the passage slow. But then we stood on a small hill, the moon big and round and blanch white, and looked down on this disintegrating lean-to of boards and tar paper, which a bunch of hobos had added in the forties when they were trying to fix the place up with not much luck. An ancient plow all blade-rusted and wood-rotted stood stuck in a stand of buffalo grass. A silver snake of moon-touched creek ran behind the cabin.

And then Cindy said, "You see it over there? The well?"

Sometime in the early part of this century, when the last of the Mormons were trekking their way across the country to Utah, a straggling band stopped here long enough to help a young couple finish the well they'd started digging. The Mormons, being decent folks indeed, even built the people a pit made of native stone and a roof made of birch. And the well itself hadn't been easy to dig. You started with a sharp-pointed auger looking for water and then you dug with a shovel when you found it. Sometimes you dug 200 feet, sending up buckets of rock and dirt and shale for days before you were done. It was all tumble-down now, of course, but you could see in the remnants of the pit how impressive it must have been when it was new.

We went over to the well. Cindy ducked beneath the shabby roof and peered straight down into the darkness. I dropped a rock down there. Echoes rose off its plopping through the surface. I shone my light down. This was what they call a dug well, about the only kind a fella could make back then. Most of the dug wells in this area went down into clay and shale about fifty feet.

I shone my light down. Dirty black water still spiderwebbed from the rock.

"He probably doesn't like the light."

I stood up, clipping off the light. "You going to get mad if I start laughing?"

"You better not, Spence. This is real serious.'"

"Your friend lives down in the well?"

"Uh-huh. In the water."

"Nobody could live below the water, Cindy."

"I told you last night. He's not human."

"What is he, then?"

"Some kind of space alien."

"I see."

"You better not laugh."

"Where'd he come from, this space alien?"

"Where do you think, dopey? He was inside the meteor that crashed here that time. Parkinson's meteor."

"And he stays down in the well?"

"Right."

"Because why?"

"Because if humans ever laid their eyes on him, they'd go insane. Right on the spot."

"And how do you know that?"

"He told me. Or rather, It. It's more of an It than a He, though it's also sort of a He. It told me."

"So he just stays down there."

"Uh-huh."

"Doing what?"

"Now how the hell would I know that, Spence?"

"And he tells you to do things?"

"Uh-huh. Once he establishes telepathic contact with you."

"Telepathic. I see."

"Don't be a prick and start laughing, Spence."

"How'd he make contact with you?"

She shrugged. "One night I was real lonely—Michael went to some basketball game with his father—and I didn't know where else to go so I walked up to the park and then I wandered over here and before I knew it I saw the old cabin and I just kind of drifted down the hill and—He started talking to me. Inside my mind, I mean."

"Telepathically."

"Exactly, you smart-ass. Telepathically."

"Then you brought Michael up here?"

"Uh-huh."

"And he started talking to Michael?"

"Not right away. Michael and He, well, they didn't like each other much. I always felt kinda sorry for Michael. I had such a good relationship with Him, but Michael—But at least Michael did what He told him."

"Which was?"

"You remember when O'Banyon's trailer burned that night?"

My stomach tightened. Brice O'Banyon was a star baseball pitcher for Consolidated. He lived in a trailer with his folks. One night it burned down and the three of them died.

"Michael did that?"

"He didn't want to. He put up a fight. He even told me he thought about going to the police. But you can imagine what the police would say when Michael told them that some kind of alien being was controlling his mind."

"He do anything else?"

"Oh, yes. Lots of things."

"Like what?"

"We drove up to Minnesota and robbed eleven convenience stores in two nights."

"God."

"Then in Chicago, we set two homeless people on fire. It was kind of weird, watching them all on fire and running down the street screaming for help. Michael shot both of them. In the back."

"While they were on fire?"

"Uh-huh."

I laughed. "Now I know it's bullshit."

"It isn't, Spence. You just want to think it is."

"But setting people on fire—"

"I didn't want to do it, Spence. I really didn't. And neither did Michael. But we kept coming back up here to the well all the time and—"

We didn't talk for a while. We just listened to the dark sough-
ing night and all the strange little creatures that hop and slither
and sidle in the undergrowth. And the wind was trapped in the
pines and not far away a windmill sang and then—

She startled me, moving up against me, her hands in my hair,
her tongue forcing my mouth open with a ferocity that was one
part comic and one part scary—

She pushed me up against the well and deftly got my fly open
and fell to her knees and did me. I felt a whole lot of things
just then, lust and fear and disbelief and then a kind of shock
when I realized that this had been the one thing she'd said she'd
never wanted to do, take anybody in her mouth that way, but
she kept right on doing it till I spent my seed on the earth
surrounding the well.

Then she was in my arms again, her face buried in my neck,
and her hands gripping me so tight I felt pain—

And then: "He's talking to me, Spence. Couple minutes, He'll
be talking to you, too. You'll be scared at first, hearing Him in
your mind this way, but just hold me tight and everything will
be all right. I promise."

But I was scared already because I knew now that what I was
seeing was the undoing of Cindy Brasher. She probably felt a
whole lot guiltier about Michael than she'd realized. And now
her guilt was taking its toll. Friend of mine worked at the U. of
I. hospital. He'd be able to help me get her in to see a shrink.
I'd call him tonight, soon as I dropped Cindy off.

And then I heard it.

I didn't want to hear it, I pretended not to hear it, but I heard
it. This voice, this oddly sexless voice inside my head, saying:
*You're just what I've been looking for, Spence. You're a lot tougher
than Michael could ever have been.*

And then I saw Cindy's face break into a little girl smile, all
radiance and joy, and she said, "He's speaking to you, isn't He?"

I nodded.

And I started to tear up and I didn't even know why.

Just standing there in the chill prairie night with this gal I was crazy in love with and this telepathic alien voice in my head—and my eyes just filled up with tears.

Filled way up and started streaming down my cheeks.

And then the alien voice started talking to me again, telling of its plans, and then Cindy was saying, "We're one now, Spence. You, me and the thing in the well. One being. Do you know what I mean?"

▼▼▼

I killed my first man two weeks later.

One rainy night we drove over to Davenport and walked along the river and then started back to Cedar Rapids. Cindy was all snuggled up to me when, through the rain and steam on the windshield, I saw the hitchhiker. He was old and skinny and gray and might have been part Indian. He wore a soaked-through red windbreaker and jeans and this sweat-stained Stetson.

The voice came to me so fast and so strong that I didn't have any time to think about it at all.

"Is He saying the same thing to you?" Cindy said, as the hitchhiker got bigger in the windshield.

"Yeah."

"You going to do it?"

I gulped. "Yeah."

We pulled over to him. He had a real ancient weary smile. And real bad brown teeth. He was going to get his ride.

Cindy rolled down the window.

"Evening, sir," I said.

He looked a mite surprised that we were going to talk to him rather than just let him hop in.

He put his face in through the window and that's when I shot him. Twice in the forehead. Knocked him back maybe ten, twelve feet. And then he stumbled backwards and disappeared into a ravine.

"Wow," Cindy said.

"Man, I really did it, didn't I?"

"You sure did, Spence. You sure did."

That night we made love with a hunger that was almost painful, the way we hurled ourselves at each other in the darkness of my apartment.

Thing was, I wanted to feel guilty. I wanted to feel that I'd just gone crazy and done something so reprehensible that I'd turn myself in and take my punishment. But I didn't feel anything at all except this oneness with Cindy. She was right. Ever since the voice had been in my mind, I did feel this spiritual closeness to her. So there was no thought of turning myself in.

Oh, no, next night we went back to the well and He spoke to us again. Inside our minds. I had a strange thought that maybe what we heard was our own voices inside our respective heads— telling to do things we'd ordinarily be afraid or unwilling to do. But the voice seemed so real—

In the next week, there were six robberies, two arsons and a beating. I had never been tough. Never. But one night Cindy and I strolled all fearless into this biker bar and had a couple of beers, and of course a couple of the bikers started making remarks about how good looking Cindy was and what was she doing with a fag like me, things like that. So I picked the toughest one I could see, this really dramatic bastard who had a skull and bones tattoo on the left side of his forehead, and rings with tiny spikes sticking up. I gave him a bad concussion, two broken ribs and a nose he'd never quite be able to breathe out of again. I guess I got carried away. He was all the bullies who'd hurt and humiliated me growing up and in the army. He was every single one of them in one body—even in the paratroopers, I was afraid of being beaten up. But now those fears were gone. Long gone.

The lovemaking got more and more violent and more and more bedeviling. It was all I could think of. Here I was working a lumber yard front office, not a place that's conducive to daydreaming what with the front door constantly banging open and closed, open and closed, and the three phone lines always screaming—but all I could do was stare out the window with my secret hard-on in my pants and think about how good it would be that night with Cindy. My boss, Mr. Axminster, he even remarked on it, said I was acting moony as a high school kid. He didn't say it in a very friendly way, either. There was no bonus in my check at the end of that month.

Stopped by a few times to see my folks. They looked sad when they saw me, probably not a whole lot different than they'd look if I'd died in a car accident or something. A real sense of loss, their first and eldest torn away from them and made a stranger. I felt bad for them. I gave them long hugs and told them how much I loved them several times but all they could do was say that I looked different somehow and was I feeling all right and did I ever think of going to old Doc Hemple for a physical.

And of course I went back to the Parkinson cabin and the well. I say "I." While most of the time I went with Cindy, sometimes I went alone. Figured that was all right now that I was with the program. I mean I was one with Cindy and He but I was also still myself.

That's why I was alone when I got the Mex down by the railroad tracks.

He was maybe twenty, a hobo just off a freight, looking for shelter for the night.

I'd been covering the tracks for the past hour, watching the lonesome stars roll down the lonesome sky, waiting for somebody just like him.

The voice this time had suggested a knife. Said there was a great deal of difference in killing a man with a knife and killing a man with a gun. So I drove over to Wal-Mart and got me the best hunting knife I could find. And here I was.

I crouched beneath one of three boxcars sitting dead on the tracks. The Mex walked by, I let him get ten feet ahead of me, then I jumped him.

Got him just under the chin with my forearm and then slashed the knife right across the throat. Man, did he bleed. I just let him sink to the gravel. Blood was everywhere. He was grasping his throat and gasping, dumb brown eyes frantic and looking everywhere. I saw why this was different. And it was real different. With guns, you were at one remove, impersonal. But this was real real personal. I watched till I was sure he was dead then I drove back to my apartment and took a shower.

Twenty-five minutes later, I pulled up to Cindy's place and she came out. In the dome light, I could see she was irritated.

"I hope you plan to start by apologizing."

"I'm really sorry, Cindy."

"Almost two hours late."

"I said I'm sorry."

"Where were you?"

So I told her.

"You've been going up to the well alone?"

Somehow I'd sensed that she wouldn't like that. That's why I hadn't told her about it.

"I don't want you to do that any more."

"Go to the well?"

"Not by yourself, Spence."

"But why?"

"Because—" She looked out the window for a while. Said nothing. Every few minutes, her drunken old man would peek out the living room window to see if we were still sitting at the curb.

"Because why, Cindy?"

She turned and looked at me. "Because He's my friend."

"He's my friend, too."

"Well, He wouldn't be your friend—you wouldn't even know anything about Him—if I hadn't taken you up there."

Kind of a funny night, that one. We never really got over our initial mood. Even the lovemaking was off a little. Sometimes you can feel when a woman is losing interest in you. Isn't anything they say or do; there's just something in the air. Laurie had been like that when she'd dropped me back in high school. I'd gone weeks with this sense that she found me vaguely distasteful before she actually dumped me. I was getting the same sense with Cindy. I just prayed to God I was sensing things wrong.

But next night, things were pretty much back to normal. Drove to an Italian restaurant in Iowa City, little place with candle light and a chunky guy wandering around with a violin, a kind of make up dinner. After that, we went straight back to my place and made up for all the great sex we'd missed out on the night previous. Or at least I did. But Cindy—there was a certain vagueness to her sentiments now. No passion in the I-love-yous. No clinging to me after we made love.

Just before I took her home, she said, "Promise me you'll never go to the well again by yourself."

"God, I just don't understand what you're so upset about."

"Just promise me, Spence."

"All right. I promise."

She kissed me with a tenderness that rattled me, that made me think that we really were going to be as tight and true as we'd once been.

Next two visits to the well, we went together. By now, I knew why she always wanted to go there. It was addictive, that voice in your head, the sense that you were an actor in some cosmic drama you couldn't even begin to comprehend. I suppose religious people feel this way when they're contemplating Jesus or Jehovah or Buddha. I needed my fix every few days, and so did Cindy.

Following these two particular visits, we drove to Des Moines and found a darkened building we could climb to the top of. Kind of cold on the fourteenth floor. And it was late May. My knuckles were numb as I assembled the scope rifle. There was a motel and a bar a quarter block away. Must be where the really well-fixed swingers hung out because the cars ran to BMWs and Porsches. There was even a Maserati.

Cindy crouched right next to me, rubbing my crotch as I sighted the gun. Gray-haired guy came out and started to climb into his Caddy. The dark city sprawled all around him, tattered clouds covering the moon.

"Him?"

"Uh-uh," she said.

Few minutes later a real drunk lady with a fur wrap came wobbling out.

"Her?"

"Uh-huh."

Then a couple real slick types. Probably in advertising.

"Them?"

"Yeah."

"Both?"

"Uh-huh."

"That'll be tricky."

"You can do it, Spence."

I had to hurry.

Bam.

Guy's head exploded in big bloody chunks. Man, it was hard to believe that a bullet could—

"Get him!" Cindy cried as the other guy, stunned, looked up to the roof we were firing from.

Knocked him a good clean five yards backwards. Picked him up. Hurled him onto the trunk of a Lincoln Towncar. Even had time to put another bullet in him before he rolled off the trunk and hit the pavement.

And then she was all over me, lashing me and licking me with her tongue, and she kept grinding her crotch against the barrel of the gun and I kept saying "Cindy, God, listen we have to get out of here!"

I just about had to drag her.

She wanted to do it right there on the roof.

She seemed crazy. I'd never seen her like this.

She couldn't calm down.

We rolled out of Des Moines about ten minutes later. She had my hand between her legs and her head back and her eyes were all white and dazed-looking. She just kept rubbing against my hand. We must have gone twenty miles that way.

Later, in bed, she said, "We're good again, aren't we, you and me?"

"We sure are."

"I was scared for a few days there."

"So was I."

"I just wouldn't want to live without you, Spence."

"I wouldn't want to live without you, either."

Her craziness had gone. We made gentle love and then I took her home.

And then next day, despite all my promising, I took the afternoon off and went to the well. I wanted to see it in daylight, see if I could see anything I missed at night.

But I couldn't.

I sat on the edge of the pit and watched squirrels and field mice dart in and out of the buffalo grass. And then for awhile I watched a hawk ride the air currents and I thought again, as I had all my boyhood, of how fine and free it would be to be a hawk. There was Indian lore that said that hawks were actually spies from another dimension and that had always intrigued me.

And then the voice filled my head.

I turned around real fast so I could look down the well and

see if the water boiled or bubbled when the voice spoke but it didn't. Just dirty brackish water. Still. Very still.

But I wasn't still. I was agitated. I said, *No, that's not right. I won't do that.* But the voice wouldn't let go. I tried to walk away but something stopped me. I tried to shut the voice out but I couldn't.

I had to listen to His plan. His terrible terrible plan.

At dinner that night, a burger and fries with coupons at Hardees, Cindy said, "I called you after school this afternoon."

"Oh. I should've told you."

"You took off, huh?"

"Yeah."

"Where'd you go?" She wasn't real good at hiding her suspicions.

"Iowa City."

"How come?"

I shrugged. "Check out one of the bookstores."

"Which one?"

"Prairie Lights."

"I guessed that was what you'd say."

"What's that supposed to mean?"

"I figured you'd lie and I figured it would have something to do with Iowa City so I called some of the places you go. And one of the places I called was Prairie Lights. And guess what?"

"What?"

"They're closed down this week. Doing some kind of remodeling."

"Bullshit."

"Bullshit yourself, Spence. You want to call them? Find out for yourself?"

She leaned back on her side of the booth and crossed her arms over chest. "You went to the well, didn't you?"

"No."

"You fucker."

She started crying, then, just like that, right there in the middle of Hardees with all the moms and dads and kiddies watching us, some with great glee, some with embarrassment and a kind of pity.

I put my head down. "I'm sorry, Cindy. I won't ever do it again."

"Oh, right, Spence. You won't ever do it again."

Must have been two hours later before she uttered another syllable.

We were lying in bed and she said, "I need to be honest with you, Spence."

"I was hoping we were done arguing. I said I wouldn't ever go to the well again alone. And I mean it."

"The way you meant it last week?"

"God, Cindy, I—"

"I met somebody, Spence."

"What?"

"A guy. College boy, actually."

"What's that mean, you 'met' him?"

"I met him. That's what it means. Some girls and I went to Cedar Rapids a few days ago, to one of the malls. That's where he works. One of the malls. Anyway, he called me and asked me if I'd go out with him." Pause. "I told him yes, Spence."

"What the fuck are you doing to me, Cindy?"

"I'm not doing anything to you, Spence. I'm just being a nice, normal eighteen-year-old girl who met a nice, normal young man who asked her out."

"We're going to get married."

Pause. "I'm not sure about that now, Spence." Pause. "I'm sorry."

I rolled off the bed, sat on the edge, face in my hands.

She slid her arms around me, kissed me gently on the back. "Maybe I just need a little break, Spence. Maybe that's all it is."

I took my face from my hands. "You're punishing me, aren't you, Cindy?"

"Punishing you?"

"For going to the well alone."

"God, Spence, that's crazy. I don't play games like that. I really don't."

"We have to get married, Cindy."

She laughed. "Why, are you pregnant?"

"The stuff we've done—"

"We didn't get caught, Spence. Nobody knows. We can just forget about it. Go on with our lives."

"Right. Just forget it. You know how many fucking people we've killed?"

I lost it, then, jumped off the bed and stalked over to the bureau, and swept it clean with my arm. Brut and my graduation picture and my army picture and Cindy's picture all smashed against the wall and fell to the floor in a rain of jagged glass.

The funny thing was, I wasn't thinking of Cindy at all, I was thinking of Laurie, and how she'd dumped me back in high school, and how even now I sometimes felt a sudden sharp pain from the memories . . . pain as dangerous as the pieces of glass now scattered all over my floor.

I turned to Cindy. "I'll tell you something, Cindy. If you go out with this guy, I'll kill you."

"God, that's real nice and mature, Spence. Maybe that's why I've lost interest in you. I thought that because you were older, you were an adult but—"

"Don't try and talk around it, Cindy. You heard what I said."

She got up and started putting her clothes on. We hadn't made love but we'd seemed on the verge of it. Until she'd told me about this guy at the mall.

"If you threaten me one more time, Spence, I'll go to the police. I swear I will."

"Right."

"I will. You wait and see."

I grabbed her. Couldn't control myself. Wanted to smash her face in but settled for throwing her up against the wall and grabbing a bunch of her button-down blouse and holding her several inches off the floor.

"I meant what I said, Cindy. I'll kill you. And that's a promise."

Three hours after she left, the rain started. I lay awake the rest of the night listening to the shutters bang and the wind cry like lost children weeping. How could you hate what you loved so dearly?

I tried not to think what the voice had told me the last time at the well, about killing Cindy. But that's exactly what it said. And that's why I'd threatened Cindy tonight, I realized now. I was only doing the bidding of the voice, acting on its suggestion.

I had been shocked, I had resisted it—but I saw now that He could also see the future. He saw that Cindy would meet a stranger at the mall, just as He saw that Cindy would soon be ready to dump me. That's why he'd suggested I kill her.

I didn't see or hear from Cindy for three days. Things were bad at work. I couldn't concentrate. I sent a wrong shipment to the new co-op they're building out on the edge of the old Galton Farm and my boss did something he'd never done before— started yelling at me right in front of customers. It was pretty embarrassing.

Lonesome, I even thought of going to see my folks but anything I said would just lead to I-told-you-sos.

Looked up a few buddies, too, but they were like strangers now. Oh, we went through some of the old routines, and made some plans for doing some autumn fishing up at Carter Lake, but I left the tavern that night feeling more isolated than ever.

I wondered what Cindy was doing. I kept seeing her naked and mounting the mall guy the way she sometimes mounted me. I drove and drove and drove, prairie highways leading to more prairie highways, cows and horses restless in the starry rolling Iowa darkness. Sometimes I merged Cindy and Laurie into one, sometimes I wanted to cry but was unable to. How could you hate what you loved so dearly?

Warm summer arrived like a gift a few days later. People out here always go a little crazy when summer comes. I think they get intoxicated by all the scents of the flowers and the trees and the sweet sad songs of the birds. I do. Ordinarily, anyway. But this summer was different. I couldn't appreciate any of it. It was as if I'd been entombed in my sorrow over Cindy leaving me. There was no room for anything but her.

I saw them, then. Town square. Around nine o'clock. Walking slowly past the Civil War memorial. Her arm through his. Same way we used to walk. He was handsome, of course. Cindy wouldn't have to settle for anything less.

I stumbled into an alley and was sick. Literally. Took the lid off a reeking garbage can and threw up.

Then I went into a grocery store and bought a pint of Jim Beam and went back to the alley and thought about what I was going to do. How I was going to handle all this.

I'm not much of a drinker. By the time I finished the pint, I was pretty foggy. I was also pretty sleepy. I leaned against the garbage can and slept.

A country western song woke me a few hours later. Some poor truck-drivin' sumbitch had lost his honey. You know how country songs go. I got up all stiff and chilly and reoriented myself. I took a leak while never taking my eye from the quarter-moon so brilliant in the midnight sky. I felt homesick; but I also felt as if I had no home to go to. And never would.

Twenty minutes later, I stood out in front of the police station. Town this size, the station is in the old courthouse. Neon sign above the westernmost entrance says: POLICE. There's a lockup in the basement and a traffic court on second floor. On first floor is where the seven police officers work at various times of day and night.

I was going to do it. I was going to walk right up those stairs, right inside that building, and tell whichever cop was on duty just what Cindy and I had been up to.

"Hey, Spence."

Voice was familiar. I turned to see Donny Newton, whom I'd gone to high school with, walking up the street. He wore the dark uniform of the local gendarmes.

"Hey, Donny. Since when did you become a cop?"

"Took my test last year, then went to the Police Academy in Des Moines for three months and *voila*, here I am. Doesn't pay jack shit for the first couple years but given all the layoffs we've been having, I'm lucky to have a steady paycheck." Then he ceased being plain Donny Newton and became Officer Donny Newton. Suspicious. "So what're you doing here?"

Maybe Donny could make it easy for me. I'd known him a long time. Maybe he'd let me tell it all my way and not get all self-righteous about it.

My mouth opened. My brain wrote three or four lines of dialogue for my tongue to speak, just to get things going. But somehow my tongue wouldn't speak them.

"Hey, you all right, man?"

Then I just wanted to get out of there. Fast.

"Little too much to drink."

"You all right to drive?"

I nodded. "Yeah."

"Sure?"

"Positive."

"I'd be happy to run you home."

"Thanks, Donny, but I'll be fine."

But he sure was giving me a funny look. I nodded a good-night, and took off walking to my car, knowing he was watching me again.

At home I drank four beers and sat in the dark kitchen and listened to an owl who sounded every bit as lonely as I felt. Then I tumbled into bed and began seven hours of troubled and exhausting sleep.

At six I dragged myself from bed for a quick shave and a shower. I'd just lathered up when I looked out the bathroom window and saw Donny Newton, still in uniform, doing something to my right rear tire. There's no garage or concrete drive. I just park on the grass on the east side of the house.

I couldn't figure out what the hell he was doing. He was down on one knee, spraying something in the tire tracks I'd made on the grass. Then he took this small wooden frame and put it over a portion of the tire marks he'd just sprayed.

Only then did I understand what he was doing—getting an impression of my tracks, the way the cops do at a crime scene.

But why the hell was he interested in my tire tracks? Had there been a hit-and-run last night and he suspected me of driving drunk and leaving the scene of the accident?

He left quickly. Probably had no idea I'd seen him. Probably figured I was still asleep.

At noon, I saw him again, Donny. When did he sleep?

He was out in the lumberyard with my boss Mr. Axminster. A couple of times when they were talking, they both looked back at the front office where I was. Then Donny was gone.

The rest of the afternoon, Mr. Axminster acted pretty funny. He was already pissed that I'd been so preoccupied lately, and that I was making a lot of mistakes—but now it wasn't so much that he was mad—more that he wasn't quite sure what to make of me. As if I were some kind of alien being or something.

Just before quitting time, the phone rang. I was checking in some wallpaper kits so Mr. Axminster had to take it. He talked a few minutes, in a whispery kind of voice, so I figured it was his lady friend. Rumor had it that he was sweet on a waitress named Myrna over at the Chow Down cafe. I think it was true because she called here sometimes. He was always boasting about how good a Lutheran he was, so his being a family man and having a little strange on the side surprised me.

Then he said, "It's for you, Spence."

He tried to act like everything was just fine and dandy. But he was sweating a lot suddenly and it wasn't hot, and he couldn't look me directly in the eye. He handed me the phone. I said hello.

"Spence?"

"Uh-huh."

"Donny Newton."

I looked at Mr. Axminster, who looked quickly away.

"Wondered if we could get together?"

"When?"

"You're off in fifteen minutes, right?"

"Right."

"How about then?"

"Have a beer somewhere, you mean? Maybe a little bumper pool?" But I knew better, knew what he was really up to.

"Uh . . . well, actually, I was hoping you'd sort of stop over at the station."

"The station? How come?" I played it real dumb.

"Oh, just a couple things came up. Hoping you could help us clear them up a little."

"Well, sure, Donny. If it's important."

"I'd appreciate it."

"Sure thing, Donny. About fifteen minutes?"

"Fifteen minutes would be great. That'll give me time to empty the old bladder and grab us a pair of Pepsis."

"See you then, Donny."

Panic. Tried to control it. Closed my eyes. Forced myself

to take deep breaths. Gripped the edge of the counter so I'd quit shaking.

Good old Cindy. The only person who could possibly have interested the police in my tire tracks. We'd used my car on all our murders and robberies. If Cindy had decided to blame me and to cooperate with authorities in reeling me in—

Cindy would likely avoid jail herself. And she'd have her brand-new beau.

"They asked me about you, Spence. In case you're wondering."

When I opened my eyes, Mr. Axminster was standing there. "You've gotten yourself in some serious trouble, Spence." He shook his head. "When Donny Newton told me, well—" He looked very sad. "I've known your folks all my life, Spence. When they hear about this—"

But I wasn't waiting around for any more of his hand-wringing dramatic presentation.

I ran out to my car, hopped in, tore out of the driveway.

I drove. I have no idea where. Just—around. And fast. Very fast.

When I was aware of things again, it was an hour later and I was racing up a gravel road, leaving a plume of dust in my wake.

Instinctively, I headed for the only place where I'd find any wisdom or solace.

I pulled into the surrounding woods so nobody could see my car from the highway. I waited till dark before finding the trail that led to the well.

Downhill, a crow sat on the rickety remains of the cabin. He was big and shiny in the cool dusk.

The well looked the same as I approached it, the native stone of the pit a dead white in the darkening shadows.

I knelt down next to the well and put my head down inside. I needed to hear Him. Needed His wisdom.

Right away, I started crying. I was going to lose it all. My job. My girl. My freedom.

All I'd done was what the voice in the well had told me to do. And I had no control over that.

You'll feel better soon.

I let those words echo in my mind for a time before asking Him what He meant.

And He told me that I'd soon know what he meant.

And right after that, I heard her laugh.

Cindy. Coming down the path. Then: a second voice. Male. The guy she'd met at the mall.

Everything was dark now. I staggered to my feet and scurried into the woods.

They were holding hands. And laughing. And she was telling him about the well.

"You really love putting me on, don't you?" he said.

"It's not a put-on. Honest."

"There's this voice down the well."

"Not just a voice—an entity."

"Hey—big word. Entity."

"Right," Cindy said.

She slid her arm around him. Kissed him playfully on the chin. I was afraid I was going to be sick again. Real sick.

"It's an alien."

"From outer space?" he said.

"Exactly."

He laughed again. "What a con artist."

He sat on the edge of the well pit and took her to him and then kissed her long and deep and passionately.

And then the knife was in my hand. The knife I'd used on the Mex.

And suddenly I was screaming and running from the woods toward the well and I saw the mall guy looked startled and then terrified and I heard Cindy scream.

But I didn't stop.

I ran straight up to the guy and stabbed him in the chest. Stabbed him again and again and again.

He fell to the ground, all blood and dying gasps now, but I kept right on stabbing him until I heard Cindy's feet slapping up the path as she tried to escape.

But she wasn't going to escape.

No way.

I went after her, grabbed her by the long hair, whipped her back to me until our faces were almost touching.

"I loved you and you didn't give a damn at all."

"I still love you, Spence. It's just that I'm so—confused— please don't—please understand that I love you, Spence—and we can be together again just the way we were and—"

I stabbed her in the chest.

She didn't scream or even cry.

In fact her hands fitted themselves around the hilt of the knife, as if she wanted to make sure that the blade stayed deep and true in her heart.

And then she fell into my arms.

And that was the weird thing, you know.

She didn't scream. But I did.

She didn't cry. But I did.

She didn't call for help. But I did.

The way it was later told to me, a farmer looking for a couple of stray head of cattle found me just like that—holding Cindy lifeless in my arms, and sobbing so hard he was afraid I was going to suffer some kind of seizure.

Later there were lights and harsh voices and then the tear-stained faces of my parents.

Oh my God, Spence.

How could you do this, Spence?

Spence, we're going to get you the best lawyer we can afford but your father's not a rich man, you know.

Mr. Spencer, this is your attorney Dan Myles—
Seven different counts of murder, Mr. Spencer—
Seven different—

▼▼▼

Same night they put me in jail they transferred me to a mental hospital on the outskirts of Iowa City. I was so cold I ended up with six wool blankets on me before they could stop me from shuddering. They gave me three different shots in my hip. Then I seemed to die. There was just—darkness.

Over the next few weeks, they gave me several tests a day. I saw medical doctors, psychologists, a priest though I'm not Roman Catholic, and then a young reporter named Donna Mannering who had just started working for our small-town newspaper.

They let her see me for twenty minutes in a room with an armed guard outside. I had told the MD that I wanted to talk to a reporter and he had seen to it that Donna was brought in.

"Dr. Wingate said you were saving something to tell me."

She was blonde and a little bit overweight but very pretty. She was also terrified. I'm sure I was the first killer she'd ever met in person.

"Yeah."

She flipped open her long skinny reporter's notebook. "I guess I'll just let you do the talking."

"I want to tell you about the well."

"You mean like a wishing well?"

I thought a moment. "Yeah, I guess it is kind of like a wishing well. Only you don't make the wishes. The thing in the well does."

"The thing in the well?"

"This alien."

"I see."

Now she looked more frightened than ever. Her blue gaze fled to the door several times. She wanted to be sure she could get away from me if I suddenly went berserk.

"There's an alien in the well."

"Right," I said.

"And it told you to do things?"

"Everything I did. I mean the killing, the robberies, the arson fires."

"The alien?"

"Uh-huh. And you know what?"

"What?"

"I don't mind if you smile. Because I know how crazy it all must sound."

"Well, I guess it does sound a little—" But then she stopped herself. "Did the thing in the well tell you to kill Cindy and her new friend?"

"Yes."

"Would you have done it otherwise?"

"I don't think so." Pause. "I want you to go out there."

"Where?"

"The well." I told her where she'd find it.

"When?"

"Soon as you can. But I want you to go alone."

"Why?"

"Because the thing will be more apt to talk to you if you're alone."

"Were you alone when you first heard it?"

"No. I was with Cindy but she already knew about the alien so that was different."

"I see." She glanced at her watch. She was trembling and licking her lips frantically. Her mouth must have been very dry. "Boy, where has the time gone? I need to get out of here. Guard!" She practically shouted.

Guard came in and led her out.

She glanced over her shoulder when she reached the threshold.

I said, "Please go out there, all right?"

She looked anxiously away and followed the guard out the door.

▼▼▼

My trial didn't start for seven months. Because we were pleading insanity, there wasn't much I had to do but wait for the trial date.

During this time, I started reading about the strange murders taking place in and around my small hometown. Old ladies viciously strangled to death with rosary beads.

On the first day of my trial, the day my lawyer spoke aloud my defense, that I had been taking orders from an alien being at the bottom of a well, I saw Donna Mannering sitting with several other reporters near the back of the courtroom. The other reporters were all smirking at the reference to the alien in the well.

But Donna wasn't.

At the end of the day, when I was being led back to county lockup, Donna pushed past the deputies surrounding me and pushed her face into mine. I saw in her eyes that same anger and same madness I'd known when I'd been under the sway of the voice in the well.

"You bastard," she spat at me.

And then she grabbed my right hand and shoved something into it and ran out of the court room.

I kept my hand closed all the way back to my cell for fear that one of the guards would see what she'd given me and confiscate it.

I sat on the edge of my bunk and opened my hand and stared down at the snakelike coil of black rosary beads.

THE PHANTOM OF THE
SPACE OPERA
▼▼▼

DON D'AMMASSA

A CHORUS line of mini-skirted mice danced their way across the room as Polonius collapsed in a pool of blood.

"Goddamn it!" The director waved his arms disgustedly, although he was secretly pleased that the holographic projector had chosen that precise moment to malfunction. He turned to the new captain of the *Gaston Leroux*. "That's what we've had to deal with ever since we opened on Harmony, eight stops back, either during rehearsals like this or in the middle of an actual performance. The image addressing system has broken down and we keep getting bits and pieces from other productions. Those are from one of the children's programs," he explained unnecessarily, gesturing toward the mice, who blinked out of existence as though they'd been cued.

Jak Debienne sighed. "I can understand your frustration, Fulton. Captain Philippe included some of the unfortunate details in his resignation, Lady Godiva making an appearance in *Faust*, for example. And leprechauns in *Gone with the Wind*."

"Little green Martians."

"I beg your pardon?"

"It was little green Martians in *Gone with the Wind*. The leprechauns were in *Pygmalion*. And we had a pair of dinosaurs pop up during the chariot race from *Ben Hur*."

"In any case, I've brought an expert with me. Mr. Shagny comes highly recommended. I'm sure he'll have no difficulty correcting the situation once we're aboard the *Leroux*."

"Can't be soon enough for me. Medea has the most unforgiving audiences on our entire tour, and they weren't amused when Banquo's ghost showed up in *A Streetcar Named Desire* yesterday."

"Understandably." But Debienne's thoughts were already elsewhere, metaphorically in space, where his new command maintained a geosynchronous orbit above the theater. He had mixed feelings about this assignment. On the one hand, the *Leroux* was a proud ship with three centuries of history; on the other, it was old, its equipment obsolete and untrustworthy, built on a scale and to a design that no one had ever replicated. And there were disturbing stories.

"Fulton, did you know Captain Philippe very well?"

"The captain? Oh, as well as any, I suppose. He was never one to do much socializing. A good man, though. We were all sorry to see him go." Fulton suddenly flushed. "Not that we aren't looking forward to working with you, of course."

Debienne ignored the faux pas. "But he was under a great deal of stress lately, wasn't he?"

"No more than usual. I mean, we've been having problems since before he came aboard. When it isn't the holo equipment, it's the air spargers, or communications, or something else. The *Leroux* is a beautiful ship, sir, but aging, the parts wearing out."

"Yes, I understand that, but Captain Philippe told me . . . well, to be perfectly honest, he told me the *Leroux* was haunted."

Fulton's eyebrows rose. "Oh, he told you about the ghost.

Some of us were wondering whether he'd warn you or leave it up to the rest of us."

The captain blinked. "But surely you don't believe such nonsense. You're an intelligent man."

Fulton nodded. "And smart enough to accept the truth. There's an unseen presence aboard the *Leroux*, Captain, and it's been there for three hundred years. I don't know if it's a ghost, but it's real."

Clearly Debienne found the concept unacceptable. "And Captain Philippe actually kept a monitor set aside for the use of this . . . presence? And allowed it access to the main computers?"

"That he did. And so did Captains Marques and Sandoval and Nkruma and Fukora before him, and all the others too, I imagine."

"Well this is one tradition that ends now."

▼▼▼

Mercifully, the final performance on Medea went without incident. As soon as the audience had filed out, technicians killed the holographic projectors and the replica of Carnegie Hall vanished, revealing the oversized collapsible dome that had actually sheltered the production. An hour later, even the dome was gone, loaded on the cargo shuttle, lifted into orbit after the quartermaster reconciled his inventory.

As soon as he was aboard, Debienne used his access code to formally assume command of the *Leroux*, addressed the entire crew briefly, then met with the senior staff.

"I know that you've had to deal with inadequate equipment lately, and I won't pretend we can afford to replace it all. But I do have some good news. Mr. Shagny here," and a tall, dark-haired young man rose and nodded around the room, "is going to overhaul our computers while we're enroute to Callypygia. That should at least clear up the problems with the holos and probably some of the other glitches as well. Unfortunately, that means rewriting portions of the main memory, including the security system. You'll all be assigned new passwords when Mr. Shagny is finished."

There was an uneasy stirring around the room. Debienne frowned. "Is there a problem? Speak up, please."

"Sir," the executive officer shifted her weight nervously from one foot to the other, "it's just, well, we were wondering what you were planning to do about the ghost, sir." She glanced across the room to where Fulton stood with crossed arms, chewing his moustache.

"I respect shipboard traditions as much as anyone, so long as they don't interfere with the smooth operation of this command. That doesn't include allocating valuable computer time to a fanciful spirit, if that's what you're asking."

"But, sir . . ."

He raised his hand, halting her in mid-word. "This is not a debatable issue, Major Poligny. If our ghostly passenger has a problem, he can take it up with me personally. Now if you'll all excuse me, it's been a long day."

But Captain Debienne found it more difficult to rest than he'd anticipated. Someone had entered his private quarters, even though the door had been reset to respond only to his own distinctive DNA signature.

His spare uniforms had all been dyed fluorescent orange.

▼▼▼

"That should do it." Rollo Shagny sat back from the console, watched confidently as the monitor displayed a stream of confirmation messages. "There might still be a few small problems with the subsidiary systems, but the main logic boards are all reintegrated."

Captain Debienne nodded, but without enthusiasm. Shagny's rapid success in debugging the malfunctioning computers was one of the few positive elements of the past several ship days. No matter what Debienne ordered from the replicator, it always delivered something different, the artificial gravity in his quarters cut off at unpredictable intervals, and he'd twice been sprayed with fire retardant foam for no discernible reason. No one else aboard was experiencing such difficulties, and Shagny's diagnostics had yet to identify the problem.

"Excellent work, Mr. Shagny. And with two days to spare." The technician was scheduled to leave the *Leroux* at its next port of call.

"I was meaning to talk to you about that, Captain." Shagny seemed unsure of himself, his voice faltering. "I'd like to stay on for a while, at least until the peripherals have been checked out. I could book passage back from New Paris or Chaney."

Debienne sighed. "I don't suppose it would do any good to tell you you're wasting your time."

"Sir?"

"Miss Dai is quite determined to remain aboard the *Leroux*, Shagny, despite what I'm told is an unremarkable singing voice."

"It's just that she's never had a chance ... " The younger man stopped in mid-sentence, realized he was fooling no one.

Debienne gestured dismissively. "Yes, yes, I'm sure you're right. But so long as Scarlotta is aboard, Dai will have to make do with secondary parts. I know the woman's personality leaves something to be desired, but she has a magnificent voice. In any case, we'll be happy to enjoy your company for as long as you choose to remain with us, Mr. Shagny."

"Thank you, sir."

▼▼▼

"Sorry, rehearsals are closed today." The burly crewman didn't sound as though he was sorry. Shagny turned away without answering and made his way back to the main corridor.

Rollo Shagny had always found it easier to interact with computers than with people. They were so much more predictable. Although convinced that Kristin Dai was the woman destined to be his wife, he recognized that so far she was barely aware of his existence. And now he couldn't even watch her from a distance. Frustrated, he kicked out at a pile of old ropes someone had dumped in the passageway.

"Hey! What'd I ever do to you?"

Shagny stepped back as the ropes uncoiled revealing a gnarled central trunk. "My God, you're a Persean!"

"Is that any reason to assault me?"

"No, of course not. I'm deeply sorry. I didn't know . . ."

The ropelike tentacles flexed several times, then slowly recoiled around the creature's core. "No harm done. You're the programming genius, aren't you?"

"I don't know about the genius part, but I'm Rollo Shagny."

"Pleased to meet you, friend Shagny. My name is . . ." What followed was a string of clicks and whistles totally beyond the capabilities of human vocal chords. "But to my human friends, I'm just the Persean."

"You're a member of the troupe then?" There were a handful of alien performers aboard, although the *Leroux* rarely visited non-human worlds.

"Hardly. No, I'm rather a special case. I was one of the investors who financed the *Leroux* when it was being assembled in orbit above Gwydion. I never sold my share when the company bought controlling interest."

"You were alive when the ship was built?" Shagny remained skeptical. "That was almost three hundred years ago."

"Three hundred and five, actually, and I was past my youth even then. But I owed a favor to Erak, the ship's designer, and he was short on credit at a critical stage in the project. Turned out to be a pretty good investment, gave me a place to put down roots, so to speak." Shagny glanced toward the deck, noticed his companion did seem to stand on a cluster of spatulate roots.

▼▼▼

Their visit to Callypygia was a disaster from the outset. Fulton had chosen to open with an operetta, the inimitable Scarlotta singing the role of Madame Mimeo in *Rivets Revisited*. Debienne was monitoring the landing of the first cargo shuttle when Scarlotta herself stormed onto the bridge.

"Captain Debienne, I demand that you do something about this . . . this indignity!"

"Now what?" As far as Captain Debienne was concerned, all the indignities since he'd come aboard had been his and his alone. Even Shagny had been unable to suggest how those strange messages kept appearing in his personal data queue, a succession of vague threats and exhortations to honor the commitments of his predecessors.

"I found *this* on my terminal this morning." She held out a hard copy of a very brief message.

"You would be well advised," it read, "to develop a headache before today's performance. The role does not suit you." It was signed "The Ghost."

Two hours later, a defiant but clearly nervous Scarlotta was aboard the shuttle that carried the performers down to the surface. Debienne remained on the bridge, nervously aware that this would be the first test of Shagny's work on the holographic system.

"What's the problem there?" One of the monitoring stations was unoccupied although two of the technicians were sitting side by side at another.

"It's a spare, sir," explained Major Poligny, her voice faltering. "We only use it as a backup."

Debienne glanced around the bridge. "Very transparent, ladies and gentlemen. It's the ghost's monitor, isn't that right? Now stop this nonsense and man that station."

There was uncertain movement, as each crewmember waited for someone else to take up the position.

"All right, you spineless squidges," Debienne roared. "You! DeSouza! Come up here and take over my monitor. I'll risk the ghost's wrath if the rest of you haven't the stomach for it." Having mixed his biological metaphors adequately, Debienne moved to the unattended monitor.

He was standing there when Scarlotta started her first major solo.

Truly her voice was a magnificent instrument, her throat and vocal chords surgically altered to achieve the best possible compromise between range and tone. Her stage presence held the bridge crew's attention, particularly once the transformation started.

It was all a hologrammatic projection, of course, but the metamorphosis from a human being to a Tregonnian pufferfrog was quite cleverly animated. The superimposed image was not visible to Scarlotta herself, but the audience and the other performers could see it quite clearly. To give them credit, they didn't actually begin to laugh until the creature starting using a prehensile tongue to pick vermin out its fur.

That was just about the same time Captain Debienne was knocked unconscious by a power surge mysteriously diverted into his monitor.

▼▼▼

Kristin Dai replaced Scarlotta for the next two performances, and surprised everyone by displaying a voice perhaps not as seasoned as it might be, but with a raw exuberance that clearly captured the attention of the audience. She explained afterward that she'd been using a new program, called The Muse, which she'd accidentally accessed while studying kibuki. Captain Debienne returned to the bridge in time to watch the final show, went directly to the command monitor, and never again mentioned the active but abandoned monitor position.

That evening, he quietly asked Shagny to reinstate the ghost's password. Shagny wisely offered no comment.

For six days they orbited Callypygia, presenting a series of plays, ballets, operas, and concerts. Everything in their repertory was available on holodisk, and with better known performers, but the appeal of live performance art could not be denied. No matter where it travelled, the *Leroux* always played to a full house.

They were halfway to Eurydice when Kristin Dai disappeared.

▼▼▼

"What do you mean they can't find her?" Shagny paced back and forth, unable to remain still.

Debienne sympathized with the younger man's frustration, shared it to a degree. "You have to remember, the *Leroux* is the size of a small city. There are miles and miles of corridors just in the inhabited sections, and there's fully a third of the ship that's maintained by remotes and without human intervention. Even the schematics in the master files aren't always accurate; there have been modifications over the years that went unrecorded. Hopefully, she has simply wandered off and gotten lost, and sooner or later she'll stumble across a working comset or a familiar landmark."

Unconvinced, Rollo Shagny joined a search party, tormented by visions of the lovely Kristin wandering alone in some abandoned stretch of corridor.

▼▼▼

Kristin Dai was not alone.

She woke in unfamiliar surroundings, a small compartment apparently designed for temporary storage. The sleeping unit upon which she'd been lying was clean and comfortable, but primitive, lacking mood inducers. She sat up, examining her surroundings while she tried to remember how she'd come to be here.

The room was cluttered and dusty. Storage capsules were stacked in one corner, most of them empty. An enormous pile of rubbish dominated the opposite end of the room, completely covered by a litter of old theatrical masks, blocking what appeared to be the only exit.

Kristin stood up, paused while her head stopped spinning, then started toward the door.

"I'm afraid I can't allow you to leave just yet."

The voice was startling, deep and solemn, not unfriendly but terrifying for the simple reason that she could not identify its source. She appeared to be alone in the room, which offered no place of concealment.

"Who are you? Why have you brought me here?"

There was a sound which she thought might possibly be a sigh. "My name is Erak, although you know me as The Muse."

"The Muse? But that's . . ."

"A computer program? That's what I'd hoped you would believe." The voice originated somewhere near the door, a hidden speaker perhaps.

"But then, who are you?"

"I'm your mentor, Kristin, your friend, your admirer. Perhaps, once you come to understand me, your lover."

Despite the ambiguity of her situation, Kristin was intrigued. She took another tentative step forward. "Why are you hiding from me? Why talk from a distance?"

"Oh, but I'm right here, Kristin. Didn't you know?" And the pile of presumed rubbish stirred and moved in her direction.

Kristin gasped and shrank back, realizing the truth as the mound of refuse emerged from the shadows. Except that it was not a pile of discarded trash at all, but a living creature about twice her mass, its shape indeterminate because of the mesh of plaster masks that completely covered the clearly alien body.

Kristin Dai fainted for the first time in her life.

▼▼▼

"I have been looking for you, my friend. We need to speak."

Shagny glanced to one side, saw the Persean emerging from a side corridor. The young man was exhausted and disheveled, having spent most of the last shipday searching fruitlessly through unfamiliar parts of the *Leroux*.

"I'm really rather busy. Someone has gotten lost, you see, and . . ."

"The young lady, yes. But she is not lost."

Shagny hesitated. "What do you mean? Do you know where she is?"

"In a manner of speaking. She is with Erak."

"Erak?" The name sounded familiar but he couldn't quite place it. "I don't understand."

"That is because I have not yet explained. You see, a long time ago, before this ship had even been conceived of, I had a friend named Erak."

Shagny was in no mood for a long story and said so.

"Patience, my friend. Dai is in no immediate danger and it is important that you understand this if you are to help her."

Grudgingly, Shagny nodded acquiescence.

"Erak was in many ways unique. He was the runt of a litter sired by an individual he remembers only as the Brood Mother, a deformed mutation so bizarre that she sold him to a passing human starship collecting specimens for the interplanetary zoo on Caliban. There he was on exhibit for nearly a human century before he was able to convince his keepers that he was sentient. By then, information about his origin had been lost, and he was forced to resign himself to an existence completely separated from his own kind. Although, if his deformities were as massive as his memory indicates, that might have been just as well."

"What has all of this got to do with Kristin?" Shagny shifted his weight impatiently, anxious to resume his search.

The Persean ignored the interruption. "Once free, Erak set about integrating himself into a society dominated by your kind. Although several non-humans like myself have found a niche to occupy, Erak's physical form was so repulsive that he was finally forced to live in seclusion. Fortunately, his long-lived nature allowed him to assimilate a broad range of engineering skills, culminating in the construction of the *Gaston Leroux*, the last project he completed before the anti-alien riots three centuries ago forced him into exile."

That's why Shagny remembered the name; the Persean had mentioned it when they first met.

"A very tragic story, but what has your long dead friend got to do with Kristin Dai?"

"Oh, Erak's not dead. He's still aboard the *Leroux*. I thought you'd realized that by now. And I believe he has abducted Kristin Dai."

▼▼▼

"What ... who are you?" Kristin had recovered to find herself once more lying on the small bed. Briefly she wondered how she'd gotten there, but her mind scampered away from too close consideration of that issue.

"My name is Erak, as I've just told you. And I am your greatest admirer. You have no reason to fear me."

She wasn't so sure of that, but the creature seemed to pose no immediate threat. Once again, she sat up, noticing that the ambulatory pile of masks was closer now, almost within reach.

"Would you like some music? I understand that humans frequently find it relaxing. I am actually quite good on the virtual organ."

"Why are you all covered up like that? Why won't you let me see what you look like?"

This time the sigh was unmistakable. "Because you would shrink from my horrid visage, Kristin. My face is the epitome of all ugliness, the ultimate shape of nausea, the essence of horribleness."

Kristin frowned. "Aren't you exaggerating a little?"

"Well, a little maybe. But it's pretty awful looking. Not that the rest of me is all that great either. The masks chafe at times, but they're light enough to be no more than a minor burden."

Touched despite lingering concern for her own safety, Kristin leaned forward. "It can't be that bad. I've traveled a lot, you know. We even performed on Nettlequass and Vroom, and we've had Squashages and Fumiteers in our company. I don't think I'd find your face all that revolting."

"Trust me, Kristin. It's better if you don't."

But curiosity had gotten the best of her and Kristin reached out suddenly, grasped the mask from behind which Erak's voice seemed to originate, and ripped it free.

It was pretty bad, but she was a trained actress, maintained her composure and spoke through gritted teeth. "See, I told you your face wouldn't upset me that much."

"That's not my face. That's an elbow."

Her expression crumpled a bit. "Oh. Well, then . . ." And before doubts could build, she reached out again, pulled off a large smiley face. It was worse, but not much worse than the elbow. This time she was forced to look away, but only long enough to realize how thoughtless she was being. "I've seen worse," she lied.

"That's not my face either."

"It's not? But the nose . . ."

"That's not a nose. That's . . . well, let's just say it's not something I'd reveal even among my own kind. Care to try again?"

"No, I think you've made your point."

▼▼▼

"Are you sure this is the way?" Shagny was having second thoughts about this expedition. The Persean had already led him through a circuitous route deep into the automated regions of the *Leroux*.

"There are more direct routes, but Erak will have taken precautions against direct assaults. He's a very private being, friend Rollo, and has certainly set safeguards to repel intruders."

"How could he have been here all this time without ever doing anything that would make someone suspect that he was aboard?"

"He couldn't have. He needs access to the computer to divert supplies, and to ensure that his lair remains hidden. Erak has been quite active. Surely you've realized by now that he's the ghost."

It made sense. "All right, I can accept that. But why Kristin? They're not even the same species."

"No, but I imagine that after several centuries of chastity, he must be feeling considerable frustration. And after all, Erak was raised in a human society, and he necessarily absorbed human concepts of beauty."

The image that forced itself into Shagny's mind was a disturbing one.

They pressed on.

▼▼▼

"They dare!"

The sound of anger transformed Erak from a tragic though undeniably repulsive figure into a creature of absolute menace.

"What is it?" Kristin drew back in alarm.

"The traitorous Persean has violated my trust. It has shown someone the way into my most secret chambers. It shall pay for its perfidy and he for his presumption." The door dilated open and Erak slithered through with a speed that quite surprised Kristin. But she was quick to follow, taking advantage of the chance for escape.

Outside, she blinked in confusion, finding herself in an unfamiliar environment filled with piping and cables and access tubes. Erak was nowhere in sight but she heard his voice raging somewhere to her left, and cautiously followed, recognizing it as her only landmark in this mechanical maze.

When she finally located him, he was perched on a catwalk above a metallic chamber. Below, two figures moved restlessly from side to side, one apparently an ambulatory tree, the other the awkward young man she'd seen hanging around the rehearsal room.

"You've broken your last confidence my deciduous friend," Erak shouted, still not noticing that Kristin had joined them. "In a few moments, the backwash from the main drive will incinerate you down to your last seedpod, and this foolish young man as well."

"Where is Kristin?" Shagny shouted angrily from the chamber in which he'd been imprisoned. "Don't you dare to touch her, you fiend."

Kristin instantly realized the truth of the situation and hastened to Erak's side. "No! If you love me as you say you do, you'll spare them. They're only here because of me."

"They have trespassed on my domain. Their lives are forfeit." But Erak's voice was already less certain.

Kristin pressed her advantage. "Release them. Allow me to see them safely back to the passenger quarters and I will return to you of my own free will. You have my promise."

For a moment it seemed that Erak would refuse, but instead his shoulders slumped—all six of them—and a tentacle reached out to a control panel. The chamber door irised.

"Take them then. But remember your promise to me."

▼▼▼

"You can't go back, Kristin. I forbid it!" Shagny was beside himself with frustrated anger. "He's inhuman."

'That's true, but that's why I must go back. Don't you understand how lonely it must be for him, never to see another of his own kind, never even to know their nature?"

They'd argued the point several times already, but Kristin refused to budge. On the brink of despair, Shagny suddenly had an inspiration.

"All right then, but promise me this. You won't return to him until after we've left orbit around Eurydice."

Kristin frowned. "But I won't change my mind . . ."

"Perhaps not. Just promise me this short delay. I have something in mind."

Kristin surrendered. "All right. I don't suppose he'll mind waiting a few more days after all those centuries."

And so it was.

▼▼▼

"Rollo, I've just come to say goodbye." She'd become quite fond of Shagny since his abortive attempt to rescue her. He could be quite charming really, when he was relaxed. If only she didn't feel morally obligated to Erak, Kristin thought their relationship might well take a more serious turn.

"I'm going with you."

"What?"

"You heard me. I'm going with you to see Erak. I have some information that might interest him."

It wasn't hard to find their way back. Erak sent out a modified maintenance robot to act as guide.

"Why do you intrude on our happiness?" The alien was clearly not happy to see Shagny again.

"Because I have something important to tell you. I've discovered the truth about your species."

Erak shook its head, or something anyway. "My species is unknown to your kind. Believe me, I have examined all the records."

"You checked all the records as of three centuries ago. We've expanded quite a lot since then. I uploaded the relevant information from Eurydice. Your home world is called Ichoria, and while your exact lineage remains a mystery, it is probable that you were born in the northern hemisphere."

There was a prolonged silence. "If that's true, I appreciate your telling me, but it has no effect on my situation. You forget, I am an outcast even from my own kind, a hideously deformed monster."

Shagny nodded. "I realize that and believe me, you have my sympathy. To a lesser degree, I know what it's like to be ostracized. But there's more."

"More?" Erak tapped something against the deckplates. Fingers?

"There was considerable information about the physiology of your species. I almost passed it by but something, fate perhaps, caused me to look into that as well. And I made a rather startling discovery." He paused dramatically.

"It would be best if you left the theatrics to those professionally trained," Erak said quietly. "What do you have to tell me?"

"Simply this," Shagny intoned portentously. "Male Ichorians invariably die within their first century. They are genetically designed that way, to allow greater diversity in the gene pool. And since you've lived at least five times that long . . ."

There was a sudden, pregnant silence, broken finally when Erak completed the sentence. ". . . then I am female."

"Got it in one."

▼▼▼

Rollo Shagny entered the turbolift, satisfied that his wooing of Kristin Dai was proceeding relatively successfully. She still hadn't agreed to leave the ship and settle down with him, but her resolve was weakening. By the time they reached Tannenbaum, he hoped to have won her over.

He was mentally preliving their wedding when he realized that the lift had dropped well below the level he'd asked for. Before he could react, a familiar voice issued from the speaker grill. Familiar, but subtly changed, softer.

"I hope you don't mind my forwardness, Rollo?"

"Erak? Is that you? What's going on?"

"Don't be disturbed, Rollo. You're not in any danger. Far from it. I just had to see you again. I know that you're hoping to convince Kristin to leave the *Leroux* with you, and I really think you should reconsider."

Shagny shook his head with disgust "Listen, Erak, I thought we'd settled all this. Look, I'm sorry about your situation but it's not my fault and there's really nothing we can do about it. You must realize that Kristin has a life of her own to lead, and her future and yours are bound to be different."

"Yes, yes, I understand all that. It was a mistake and I regret the inconvenience I've caused her." There was a short pause, then a sound that might almost have been a sigh. "I was just wondering if you'd ever considered a change in profession. A life on the stage might help you to overcome your shyness. You're actually quite handsome, you know."

The turbolift plunged into the depths of the *Gaston Leroux*.

THE INVASION
▼▼▼

PETER CROWTHER

"IT went *what?*"

"Whooooosh!" Jimmy Jorgensson repeated the word in an almost jubilant spray, throwing his arm in a wide arc that nearly removed his can of Sprite from the table and sent it spinning across the floor. "Right over my head," he added, "straight out over the filling station and then down towards the dump."

Adam Showell smiled. "Just like that, huh?"

Jimmy nodded, eyes wide with excitement.

Adam waved his own arm in a clumsy approximation of Jimmy's and said, "Whooooosh?"

Jimmy clicked his jaw. He always clicked his jaw when he got annoyed. "You saying you don't believe me?"

"Aw, come on J.J.—"

"No," Jimmy snapped, getting to his feet and stepping across the spread of comic books scattered across his bedroom floor. "Whenever somebody says they've seen something, you don't believe them. You *never* believe them."

"Did I say—"

"You didn't *need* to say: it's obvious you don't believe me."

"But a flying saucer?"

"I didn't say it was a flying saucer, I said it was an unidentified flying object."

Adam shrugged, drained the last few drops of liquid from his can and crunched it. "Same thing in my book."

"I'm not lying or . . . or making it up," Jimmy said, a faint note of self-pity creeping into his voice.

"Maybe it was a comet, or a shooting star."

"Maybe." Jimmy sounded unconvinced.

"It's just that if they're always flying around up there, why don't they actually get in touch with us?"

"Because," Jimmy pointed out, leaning forward, "we have wars and we're always killing each other. What have we got to offer them?"

Adam, suddenly feeling disadvantaged by remaining on the floor, got to his feet and slurred towards Jimmy's bed. "Then if we're so lousy, why the hell are they watching us?" He plopped down onto the ruffled covers and folded his arms defiantly. "Maybe if they *are* there, it's them who've screwed up our ozone layer by driving in and out of it."

Before Jimmy could answer, the door creaked open and both boys turned to see who it was. "You guys want any more drinks?" a voice asked. The voice was immediately followed by an old man's head, topped with a creamy white splurge of hair that went in all directions. The head remained disembodied and glared questioningly at the two boys through bi-focal glasses, eyebrows raised.

"No thanks, Gramps," Jimmy said.

Adam shook his head and smiled. "No thanks, Mr. Jorgensson."

The old man's head remained jammed between the partially open door and the wall. "Potato chips?"

"Uh uh."

Adam shook his head again.

"Kick in the ass, maybe?"

The boys laughed out loud, Adam with his eyes and mouth open in astonishment.

"Okay, I'll leave you both to it." The head started to pull back out of the room and then stopped before moving forward again. "This a private argument or can anybody join in?" He waited for a second before continuing. "I need to know so's I can tell the folks queueing up outside—looks to me like they been driving quite a while. Noise you fellas're making, must be able to hear you clear over on the Interstate. Folks can't hear their car radios."

Adam chuckled.

"We're fine, Gramps, thanks."

"Well, I'm hitting the sheets so keep it down, okay?"

"Okay." Jimmy scratched his neck and looked down at his sneakers. "Mom and Dad in yet?"

"Nope," Ed Jorgensson's voice drifted in as the door closed. "Said they'd be late. 'Bout time you were thinking about bedding down, too."

The two statements seemed entirely unconnected and Jimmy adopted an exaggerated expression of puzzlement. "Okay," he said, managing to contain his amusement. Adam was not nearly so successful and he blurted out a short, braying snigger.

" 'Night, Adam," the old man's voice trilled.

"Good night Mr. Jorgensson," Adam replied, his shoulders shaking like he was fit to burst.

Somewhere down the corridor outside Jimmy's room a door closed softly and, just for a second, its sound seemed somehow suddenly lonely and final. Both of the boys felt it, for that same fleeting instant, and Jimmy was reminded of his friend's recent loss.

Jimmy had hardly mentioned Adam's mother's death, not quite knowing how to start in on the subject. He'd just told him that he was sorry and let it go at that. But it went deeper. Jimmy couldn't for the life of him figure out what it must be like to lose one of your parents. It seemed to him like his own mom and dad would be there forever. He shrugged and looked across at Adam, all thoughts of their argument forgotten. "You want to call your dad?"

Adam looked up from his hands, clasped tightly on his lap, and Jimmy saw the faint shimmer of moisture on his eyes. He shook his head.

"You wanna watch a video?"

"Yeah!" Adam said, suddenly animated. "What you got?"

Jimmy moved across to the small television set and tugged out a bunch of videos from a shelf festooned with comic books and magazines. "Dad gave me all his old black-and-whites," he said breathlessly, holding two videos aloft as confirmation. One was the old Ray Harryhausen epic, *It Came From Beneath The Sea* and the other was *The Wasp Woman.* "They're kinda schlocky," he said as he returned them to the shelf and rummaged about in the others, "but there's some good stuff, too."

"You got any about flying saucers?"

Jimmy turned around and made like he was going to throw an episode of *The Outer Limits* across at the bed and Adam folded up with his hands over his head, laughing.

The telephone rang, cutting through the sound of laughter and silence like a knife. The boys looked at each other and Jimmy jumped up. He pulled open his bedroom door and shouted along the passageway to his grandfather. "You want me to get that, Gramps?"

"You go ahead, I'm taking a—I'm in the bathroom," came the reply.

Jimmy ran down the stairs two at a time and snatched the receiver up in his left hand before the sixth ring. "Hello?"

"J. J.?"

"Yeah?"

"It's me, Billy."

"Hey, Billy."

"Hey, right back. Listen, you got Adam with you?"

"Yeah. He's staying the night. His dad's going out with some friend of his and gonna be back late. What's the problem?"

The voice on the other end of the line dropped conspiratorially. "I seen another one."

"Another UFO?" He pronounced the acronym as a word and not as three single letters: you-foe.

"Yeah."

"Where?"

Billy Macready paused. "Whadyamean *where*? In the sky, lamebrain, where d'ya think?"

"No, I mean whereabouts?"

"Over the dump. I seen two, truth to tell. Kinda hovering over there and then dropping out of sight."

The news made Jimmy's stomach do cartwheels. But what Billy said next made it do hang gliding somersaults. He said, "You wanna take a look?"

Ten minutes later, Jimmy and Adam were climbing down the trelliswork beneath Jimmy's bedroom window, with the night standing large and dark and mysterious around them.

▼▼▼

"There goes another one," Jack Turnbull mumbled, pointing his half-empty bottle of cheap wine at the light which passed over the dump. Fred Wessels belched unconcernedly and lifted his own bottle to his lips. He made contact on the third attempt and drank, swallowing noisily.

"That makes seventeen I seen this week alone," Jack said, scratching at the seat of his pants as he watched where the light had gone down behind the auto skeletons.

Fred belched and shuffled his back against his carpet bag, which he had propped up against an old television set.

Jack Turnbull swayed across to a heap of black bags and

leaned on them, spilling wine in the process. "Whe—where d'you think they're from? Hmmm?"

Fred didn't answer.

Jack staggered back from the bags and tilted his head so that he was looking straight up into the nighttime sky. The sky was black now, though the edge to his right contained the reflected glare of the lights of Forest Plains and the cars on the Interstate. "Mars? Venus?" He closed his eyes and breathed in the smells of the dump. "D'you—d'you think maybe Neptune?"

Still no answer.

Jack turned around and looked down at his companion. Fred's bottle had upturned on his jacket and the wine was mingling with the grease and the filth and the other stains whose origins were long since forgotten. He had fallen sound asleep.

Jack looked back at the heavens. "Lookit them octopur . . . octopuses from that movie. You ever see—" He suddenly remembered that Fred was asleep. "Naw, I guess not." He lifted the bottle and took a long drink.

Somewhere behind him, a tin can rattled down one of the piles of trash. Jack turned quickly, arms, legs and head moving without any coordination, like a puppet operated by a complete novice. "You—you hear that, Fred?" he whispered.

Fred smacked his lips and shuffled over onto his side. Suddenly freed from the man's grasp, the bottle rolled onto the ground giving out a soft, liquidy *sploinggg* sound.

Jack stared into the gloom.

Out across the fields, a dog howled. It sounded frightened.

▼▼▼

"Look, tell your mom it's a party, not an orgy."

Dlip, said the radar screen into the headphones lying next to the telephone.

James Farnham moved the receiver into his right hand and

turned his chair so that his back was to the equipment. "For God's sake, Carol, you're almost twenty-years old."

Dlip

"Well, if you know, why the hell don't you start—I'm not using *any* kind of language. All I'm saying . . . Carol, all I'm saying—Look, will you listen to me here? All I'm saying is tell your mom that you're going whether she likes it or not." He closed his eyes and mouthed at her as she started to speak.

The green line went around the screen again, passing the omega letter at the base. *Dlip*, it said.

"There *is* nobody else I'd rather take, Carol—"

Dlipdlip

"—for Chrissakes."

Dlipdlipdlip . . . dlipdlipdlipdlipdlipdlip . . . dlip

"Oh, hell, if that's going to be your attitude—"

Dlipdlipdlipdlipdlipdlipdlipdlipdlipdlipdlip

"—I *will* take someone else."

Dlipdlipdlip

"I don't *know* who, just somebody."

Dlipdlipdlipdlipdlipdlip

"No, not Mary Clemmons. I do not—No, I do—Carol, for crying out loud, I do not have the hots for Mary Clemmons." He shook his head and looked up at the clock. Eight-thirty: three and a half hours before the change of shifts. "I know I danced with her that one time but, Carol, it was the one time. How many—how many times—Yes, I know. How many times have you danced with somebody else?"

Dlipdlipdlip . . . dlipdlip

"But I can't go by myself, can I?"

Dlip . . . dlip

He nodded into the mouthpiece. "Okay. Yeah, okay, Carol. But do the best you can, huh?"

Dlip

"Yeah, me too. Yes I *do* mean it. Yeah, okay. I'll ring you tomorrow. Yeah. Bye. Yeah, bye bye." He rested the receiver on the cradle and turned to face the equipment. "How you doing, radar?" he said, lifting the headphones. As he pulled the earpieces apart, the green line completed its 360-degree sweep.

Dlip, it replied.

▼▼▼

Ted Bannister leaned on his sweeping broom in the glare of the porchlight. "Hey, Marnie?"

A voice answered from inside the house, muffled.

"Come on out here for a minute."

Martha Bannister started talking to him as soon as she left the kitchen, the words getting louder as she walked along the hallway and pushed open the screen door. "—'ything done around here if I'm wandering in and out every five minutes at your beck and call, Ted Bannister," she finished as she stepped onto the porch. "What is it, anyways?"

Her husband continued to lean and jerked his head up at the sky. "Meteors," he said confidently.

Martha wiped her hands on her apron and squinted into the night sky. "Where meteors? I don't see anything."

Ted removed one hand from the broom handle and lifted a muscled arm to point. The checkered workshirt hung unfastened around his wrist, blowing in the gentle breeze. "Look," he said, "there goes one now."

High above the hills behind the library, a silver-blue light flashed, leaving a sparkling trail behind in the evening gloom. Whatever it was had gone down over by where Ted knew the filling station was.

"That was a meteor?" Martha queried.

Ted clicked his tongue off the roof of his mouth. "I guess," he said.

His wife shook her head and wiped her already clean hands

again on her apron. "What on Earth am I doing standing here talking about meteors when I have bread to bake? I declare, Ted Bannister, you've got me near on as crazy as you, you old coot." Ted said nothing and continued to stare at the sky. "And you have a porch to sweep." She turned around and pulled on the screen door. "You do a good job and maybe I'll make you a nice cup of caramel coffee."

"Mmmm . . . hey!" Ted said as the screen door banged shut behind him.

Halfway along the hall, Martha heard her husband shout again. "I haven't time," she shouted back, almost choking herself on her own spittle.

"Well isn't that the darndest thing . . ." Ted muttered to himself. Over across town, another silver-blue light had appeared and seemed to be hovering in the sky above the town dump. "If that isn't the strangest meteor I ever—" Suddenly, the light dropped out of sight. Ted Banister shook his head, took his broom in both hands and looked around the rest of the sky.

▼▼▼

The bell above the door to Frank Emseley's General Store tinkled as his last customer left.

Frank turned around to continue the ritual of closing up for the day. It was almost nine o'clock. He walked back behind the counter, checking things and straightening them up whether they needed it or not. He made sure that the stock and order books were safely on the shelf in their allotted place and pulled open the cover to the switchbox to turn off the interior lights.

Just then, a gust of wind seemed to blow open the door.

Tingalingaling, said the bell, tiredly.

Frank turned around and made to tell whoever it was that he was closed for the day, knowing full well that he had never turned anyone away once they were inside the store in almost thirty-five years. But there was nobody there.

Outside, the wind blew along the darkened street.

Somewhere, far away, a car door slammed.

"We're—we're closed," Frank said to the empty store.

Something moved in his head, softly, gently, rustling and whispering.

Closed? it said.

▼▼▼

The door opened slowly and the warmth of the house flooded out onto the path with the spilled light. A small, freckled face appeared around the side of the door, eyes studying the visitor and checking the empty pathway behind him. "Where's Adam?" the face said at last.

Adam jumped out from the side of the house and held his arms wide. "Ta-dah!"

"*Jesus*—Jesus Christ, Adam!" Billy Macready snapped, lowering his voice to little more than a whisper.

Jimmy laughed at Adam's *What'd I do?* expression.

"Don't *do* that," the freckled face of Billy Macready hissed. He waved for them to come inside.

Closing the door gently behind the two guests, Billy said, "Haven't you been listening the news?"

"The news? Since when did you listen to the news?"

Billy shrugged himself into his plaid jacket. "Well, not the news exactly, but just the talk between records on KWLD."

"Ah." Adam nodded sagely. "*That* news."

"Hey, don't *ah* me, man. I don't like *ah*."

"Hey," Jimmy said, slapping Adam on his arm. "Don't *ah* him, okay? He don' likea da *ah*."

"Jerks!" Billy pulled his zipper tight to his chin.

Jimmy and Adam sniggered. "What did it say, anyway, this 'news'?"

"They seen lights, man. Flashing lights. They seen them all

over this county and into the next. And strange noises, too." He shrugged and puckered his mouth. "And, sure, they got some crank calls, too."

"Crank calls? Saying what?" Adam traced an offshoot of the repetitive vine that meandered across the Macreadys' hallway wallpaper, following each curlicue with his finger.

"Oh, you know the stuff: cows being transported by tractor beams, someone seeing the roof of the library being lifted . . . that kind of thing."

Adam stood back from the wallpaper, straightened up and made like he was a robot, eyes wide, arms held out straight in front of him. "Durn-dur-dut-dut, DAHHH!"

Billy grabbed him and shook hard. "Shhhh! You wanna wake my folks?"

"They in bed already?"

Billy nodded. "Yeah, my old man's hot to trot tonight, hombre. He took my old lady up there 'bout an hour ago, man. They been there ever since. Doin' the old bump 'n' grind, man."

"You hear anything?"

Adam glared at Jimmy and grimaced. "Oh, Captain Gross . . . pleased ta meetcha, I'm sure."

"Cut it out," Billy said. The sniggering died down. "Okay, let's go." He pulled open the door and removed the key from the inside lock.

"Where we going to?" Adam asked quietly.

Billy pulled the door gently and inserted the key. Turning it softly, so that it wouldn't make too much of a noise, he said, "Town dump."

They pulled their collars up against the cold and ran down to the street, making sure they stayed on the grass by the side of the path. But still their feet made noises, thudding through the darkness.

▼▼▼

Jack Turnbull had dropped his bottle and was standing, swaying, above Fred Wessels. "Fred," he whispered.

He felt more sober now than he had in a long time. There had been noises. Strange, slithering noises from the piles of junk which surrounded them. What worried him the most was that it might be a bunch of kids come round for a little fun, beat up a couple of bums ... maybe even set fire to them, watch them burn.

"Fred!" He bent down and shook the other man's shoulder but there was no response. Jack straightened up and turned around, squinting to make some sense of the gloom. He could see nothing. But still he heard it. *Sensed* it. "C'mon, Fred. Maybe it's the police."

But Jack Turnbull didn't think it was the police.

The faint noises he could make out drifting across the garbage and the old, rusting metal car frames sounded more like the octopuses from that film—*War Of The Worlds*, he suddenly re-membered—clambering across the piles of junk towards him.

He stared through the dark and listened, hardly daring to breathe. Something *was* coming, moving. He could hear it. Hell, he could *feel* it.

The night was cool and a gentle wind blew around his feet.

Jack looked around for the quickest way out.

▼▼▼

"Ted?" The voice cut through the evening stillness and echoed around the wooden porch. "You finished yet?"

No answer.

Her hands encased in bread dough, Mary Bannister paused and held her head on one side, listening. She turned to face the door, mentally cursing her husband for his stubborn refusal to wear his hearing aid, and shouted louder. "Ted, it's after nine o'clock. You come in now before you go get yourself a summer chill, you hear me?"

Still no answer.

She dusted off her hands on her apron and walked sternly through the house. A small frisson of unease uncoiled when she couldn't see her husband through the mesh of the screen door. When she stepped out onto the porch and saw the red-handled sweeping broom lying, apparently cast aside, in Ted's prize rose bushes, the frisson graduated to earthquake proportions.

"Ted?"

The wind took the word and lifted it high into the night. As she followed it in her mind's eye, Mary Bannister saw another meteor whiz through the dark clouds and disappear behind the filling station.

▼▼▼

"Just an old bum," Billy Macready said over his shoulder, in answer to Adam Showell's question. "And the biggest collection of garage sale items you ever saw."

Jimmy Jorgensson tried to pull himself up so he could see but couldn't without dislodging an old washing mangle precariously balanced upon a dirt-encrusted pair of rubber boots, seemingly millions of tin cans, and what looked as though it might once have been a radio. Relaxing his arms, he said, "What's he doing?"

Billy was straddled on the fence, his knees holding him erect and his right foot tucked into the wooden slats. The other foot was over on the other side of the fence, out of sight. "He's out of it, man. Pushing out the big zees. Either that," he added, "or he's dead. Come on. Let's go in."

"What do you mean, *dead*?" Jimmy hissed to Billy's disappearing foot. But it was too late. A dull thud from the other side of the fence told him that Billy was inside the dump. He turned and jumped down from the pile of garbage that had been stacked beside the fence and started to clamber up the pile of crates that

Billy had used. Once at the top, he looked across to see Billy slowly approaching a figure which lay sprawled against a Mount Everest of black refuse bags. Seconds later he had jumped to the ground.

A few more seconds later, and Adam Showell landed beside him. With a quick glance around the stacks of garbage, the two boys moved off after Billy.

"Naw," Billy was saying as they arrived at his side, "he's just asleep." He sounded almost disappointed. He picked up the discarded bottle of whiskey and sniffed.

"And there's why," Adam said.

Billy took a swig and coughed. "Good stuff," he said between clenched teeth. He offered the bottle to Jimmy who grimaced. "Want some?"

Jimmy shook his head and made the face he used when forced to take bad medicine.

Billy shrugged and turned to his other side. "Adam?"

"Uh uh. *I'll* pass on oblivion, too."

"Suit yourself." Billy hauled back and pitched the bottle high above them. They watched it soar, hover briefly, and then disappear above an old Chrysler shell perched atop a tower of black bags. They waited for the sound of breaking glass but there was only a dull *whump* and the clatter of the bottle rolling down something metallic.

"You shouldn't have done that, Billy," Jimmy Jorgensson said, staring about in the gloom. "Someone might hear."

Billy frowned, accepting the criticism, and followed his friend's gaze.

Adam suddenly grabbed Billy's arm. "Look."

They looked.

"What is it?" Jimmy whispered. "I don't see any—"

"Hey," Billy said. He got up from his crouching position and ran across the passway between the piles of junk and bags. Stooping, he picked up an object from the ground.

"What is it?" Jimmy whisper-shouted.

Adam got to his feet and walked slowly towards Billy. "It's another bottle," he said.

Jimmy glanced behind again and ran over to the others.

"Where d'you suppose he's gone?" Billy asked nobody in particular.

"Where *who's* gone?"

Adam turned to Jimmy and smiled the smile of somebody explaining one and one being two to a pre-school infant. "The guy who left this bottle. This *second* bottle," he added.

"Maybe he's taking a pee," Billy suggested.

They thought on that for a while, listening for the telltale sound of splashing water. But only the wind moved around them.

"Maybe he's asleep, too," Adam contributed.

Maybe they've *got him*, Jimmy wanted to say, but it came out as "Maybe we should go back, now."

▼▼▼

"Yes, Mrs. Bannister, I got the description but—"

A buzz of speech fluttered from the telephone receiver into the stillness of the sheriff's office. Doug Hemmitt placed his pencil carefully on the pad in front of him and rubbed his eyes with his free hand.

"But," he continued, raising his voice slightly, "a person is not considered missing until at least twenty-four hours've gone by. Why don't—Yeah, but why don't you wait a while? Maybe he's just gone off to take a walk." He paused to allow the buzz to make its point. "I don't know why he'd want to take a walk, Mrs. Bannister"—*though maybe I'm getting an idea*, he thought—"but that sounds like the most obvious thing. Maybe he took a walk to see some more of these lights."

Buzzzzzz!

"Sorry, meteors. Yeah, I'm sorry, Mrs. Bannister, but that's about all I can suggest."

He looked around at the clock while the receiver buzzed some more. Nine forty-two.

"Yes," he said, "we'll keep our eyes peeled. And you—"

Buzzzz

"Yeah, sure. And you give us a call back if—sorry, *when*—you give us a call back *when* he turns up, okay?"

Buzz

"That's what we're here for, Mrs. Bannister." He leaned back in his chair and swivelled to see if there was still some coffee in the pot. He brightened up when he saw that it was more than half full. "Yeah, thanks for calling. Yeah, good night, Mrs. Bannister."

The phone went silent.

Doug Hemmitt—"Deputy Doug," as the other guys in the office called him—reached across and picked up the intercom. He would ask Andy Gifford to call by and give the woman a little moral support. After all, it was a quiet night.

▼▼▼

"No, no, *no*! For the last time, Carol—for the *very* last time—you are not going. I do not intend to discuss it nor do I have to have a reason. The answer is, no."

Carol Barnes stamped her foot and frowned, staring hatefully at her mother. "It's only a party, Mother, not an orgy," she said, remembering what Jim Farnham had said.

Alice Barnes started clearing the supper dishes. "It may start out that way, Carol, but—Anyway, I've said *no*. Now, please. Let it rest at that."

"It's not fair. I'm nearly twenty years old."

"Yes," her mother said, pointing with a plate of gherkins for dramatic emphasis, "and if I have my way, you'll make it to twenty-one."

"What's that supposed to mean?"

"Carol ..." Her mother sounded tired now. "I've said *no*. That's it. Let it go."

Carol sat down in the chair with a *thud*, and thrust her face into her hands.

As she left the room en route for the kitchen, her mother called back, "Hadn't you better phone Jim Farnham and tell him?"

Carol got up from the chair and stormed out of the room.

"Who'd be a mother?" Alice Barnes said to the mute milk jug. It didn't have an answer.

Thoughts flooded through Carol's head, mingling with an acute frustration that seemed to color everything with a red tinge and made her want to smash things. She resisted. Instead, she dialed the numbers of the base at Forest Plains and, when the prerecorded voice asked her to key the extension of the party she wished to contact, she hit the one and seven keys.

A sinking feeling hit her stomach as, across town, she pictured the telephone ringing on Jim's desk. *Bring! bring!* it went in her mind. *Drurp drurp* said the receiver in her hand.

She pictured Jim hearing the phone—*drurp drurp*—turning around to pick it up—*drurp drurp*—his hand closing around the receiver right now—*drurp drurp*—

Where was he?

Drurp drurp

Why wasn't he picking it up? Did he know it was her?

Drurp drurp

Did he know what she was ringing to tell him?

As the phone continued to ring over in Forest Plains, Carol glanced nervously at the clock: nine fifty-three. Over two hours before his relief came. So why didn't he answer?

Drurp drurp

"Oh, go to hell!" Carol snapped into the mouthpiece, and she slammed the receiver down onto the cradle.

Over on the other side of town, in the Forest Plains Air Force Base, a lonely telephone said *bring! bri*—and then fell silent, leaving only an occasional *dlip* from the radar screen and the sighing of the evening wind blowing through the open doors.

▼▼▼

The chair creaked on the old wooden boards of the porch and Martha Bannister looked out onto the world beyond the flickering light; the world that had mercilessly swallowed up her husband. Now she felt strangely at odds with everything, suddenly vulnerable and no longer surrounded by friends. She had managed to resist the urge to cry. Crying was useless, counterproductive—though 'counter-productive' was not a term that figured in Martha Bannister's vocabulary. It was a luxury she could not afford because, at its simplest, it signaled the giving up of hope. She could never do that while there was still hope to be had. After all, there was probably a simple explanation. Just like the deputy had said over the telephone. Now, rocking to and fro in her husband's cane chair, she felt a little guilty over giving him a hard time.

Clunk

She stopped rocking and strained to hear.

The noise had come from the side of the house.

Martha leaned forward, her heart skipping through her chest like a young girl. "Ted?"

There was no answer.

She got to her feet, grimacing at the arthritis in her hips, and wiped her perfectly clean hands on her dress. It was her best dress, the red one that Ted liked so much.

"Ted, is that you?"

High up—oh, so very high up!—in the sky, another meteor flew through the night, far above the Earth.

She walked off the porch into the heady smell of night-scented stocks, with the world standing silent and expectant all around her.

Bu duhh, bu duhh, her heart said, as though warning her.

The side of the house was dark and somehow more inhospitable than usual. It seemed foreign to her. No, more than foreign; it was . . . She searched for the word. *Alien.* And silent. Nothing moved down there between the fence and the wood panels of her house. Darkness reigned supreme.

"Hello?" She said the word falteringly.

Little voices screamed in her head. *Go into the house. Phone the Sheriff's office again. It's an intruder. Ted's going to come home in a couple hours and find you with your head smashed in and your best red dress all—* She stopped herself from going on. It was a strange world that she and her husband were busy waiting to leave, and no denying it. A world where a woman just wasn't safe walking around her own house at night wasn't any kind of world at all, she decided.

Bu duhh, bu duhh, her heart said in percussive agreement.

She took another slow step towards the gloom. "Ted? I hope that's you in there, 'cause I'm coming in."

Then it came.

Soft and gentle, borne on a fragrant wind that was uncharacteristically warm and scented with the most beautiful and intoxicating smells, all fighting for superiority. It wafted out of the darkness before her, like the tinkling of distant bells in some far-off steeple. Or maybe like the sound of bluebonnets rustling against each other as the faery folk ran through them. It made her gasp.

"Marnie?" it said. It was her husband's voice, and not her husband's voice. Or, at least, it was her husband's voice as she remembered it from fifty years earlier, a voice filled to the brim with excitement and hope, determination and resilience, wonder and magic.

She smiled into the darkness and went to meet him. But he was not alone.

▼▼▼

Jack Turnbull smiled, too.

Everything was now clear to him. Acutely clear.

All of Jack's friends smiled with him. He felt them.

He felt their happiness and their trust, felt their warm contentment . . . warmer than any bottle he had drunk from. Warmer than any old newspaper he had pulled around himself.

"Everybody okay?" he asked cheerfully of the myriad chattering voices snuggled in his head.

Okay

Affirmation washed across his senses in a wave, washing the most distant and long-untouched corners of his body and his mind . . . cleaning him cleaner than any water and soap had ever done.

Noah's Ark. The thought came into his head from nowhere. But it was true. That was what he had become. All of his body, all of his senses. All new responsibilities.

He was a guide. *John Raymond Turnbull*, he thought, *Guide To Earth*. He smiled to himself. It was so long since he had thought of his full name.

A new world to show off. A world he had turned his back on.

He felt completely sober and yet, at the same time, drunker than he had ever felt before. But it was an intoxication that confronted and absorbed rather than one which retreated and repelled. He felt the excitement start in his own mind and then rush through a hundred more, a thousand more, a million more, blazing all before it like a bush fire.

How good it was to be back; to be a part of it all again.

▼▼▼

"See you guys tamale," Billy yelled across the street. He made a gun-shape with his right hand and pretend-fired two slugs at

Adam Showell and Jimmy Jorgensson as they stood watching him, the town dump at their backs. He turned around and started into the alley between Pop Kleats's Soda Shoppe and the realty office. Cutting through the lumberyard at the end of the alley was going to save him precious time, but Billy suddenly felt a slight surge of nerves and his stomach coiled around itself like he needed to go to the bathroom.

"Hey," Adam shouted back, "make sure the saucers don't get you."

"Yeah, watch the skies," Jimmy added. "Keep on watching the skies."

They both laughed.

Billy turned around and gave them the bird, then watched them walking off along Beechwood Avenue, stiff-jointed, a couple of ten-year-old Frankenstein's monsters. He waited until they were obscured by Pop Kleats's window and then turned again to the alley, noting, somewhere deep in his subconscious, that it sure looked awfully dark.

He breathed in deeply, puffed out his chest, and clenched his fists tight. Then he ran down the alley making the sound of a jet plane and slapping each of the trashcans as he passed by.

By the time he reached the rickety gates of the lumberyard, the fear was gone along with the impenetrable blackness of the building-shrouded alley. Once again, Billy was beneath the full panoply of the sky. He looked up and watched another meteor flash overhead. It was getting so they were a dime a dozen.

He pulled the gates apart and slipped inside.

▼▼▼

Patrolman Andy Gifford stepped from the black-and-white and walked across the street, towards the old couple dancing around the garden. Trapped in the beam of his flashlight, they stopped rushing around the flower beds and smiled over at him.

Andy smiled his puzzlement at the old woman, her silver-white hair hanging long around the gathered neckline of her dark red dress. "Mrs. Bannister?" he said. "Mrs. Martha Bannister?"

"Yes?" the woman answered, breathlessly softly.

Andy turned his flashlight fully on the old man. He was walking amongst the flowers, waving his hands wildly, pointing here and then pointing somewhere else, all the time mumbling to himself. "And is this Mr. Bannister?"

Behind him, the car radio squawked in a tide of crackle.

The woman watched him, her head tilted on one side, a smile frozen on her mouth. "Yes, yes it is," she said at last. "Is there a problem, officer?"

Andy returned the smile—it was so infectious, he had to stop himself from giggling—and shook his head. "Well, I don't know. Maybe I have the wrong details or some—"

Mrs. Bannister hit herself on the forehead. "Of course," she said, and the voices in her head muttered and discussed. "I'm so sorry to have been so much trouble."

Andy started to shake his head, but the woman continued.

"Yes, this *is* my husband," she laughed. The laugh sounded somehow inappropriate. It was the laugh of youth, the laugh of a *young* woman. "And, as you can plainly see, he's quite well."

Andy looked across at the old man. "And this is a garage," Mr. Bannister said to nobody in particular, although, deep in his head, the voices took note: *garage*, they noted. It was all so new, so wonderfully different.

"Yeah," Andy Gifford agreed, "he looks fine to me." *He looks like he just fell out of his tree and cracked his head.* "Okay," he said. "I guess everything's fine here."

"Everything *is* fine," Martha Bannister said.

As he walked away from the house, Andy Gifford heard the old man chattering. It was a frenzied chatter, as though time itself were running out on him. Maybe it was. It couldn't be much fun getting old, he thought. Reaching the car, he turned back and watched them wandering around their house, at one with the darkness. He was glad he had not said all of the things he had thought of saying to them: about not placing missing person reports without due cause; about informing the Sheriff's office when that missing person turned up again.

But then it had been one of those nights. As he had driven along Main Street he had seen the lights on in Frank Emseley's General Store and pulled over. But, just before he had gotten out of the car, he had seen Frank walking around his shelves holding up cans and packets and boxes and then putting them back onto the shelves. Just walking around like he was in a kind of daze. Must be a change in the seasons, he decided.

As Andy slid behind the wheel, Martha Bannister was rifling through some plants and her husband was training a flashlight along the guttering and up and down the water spouting of their house. He could imagine what the old man was saying.

Andy turned the key in the ignition and shifted the transmission into drive. "This is the guttering and the water spouting," he said to the dashboard in as near an imitation of the old man's shuddery voice as he could manage.

Back in the Bannisters' nighttime garden, as the black-and-white pulled away from the curb, Mr. Bannister's voices took note. *Guttering . . . water spouting*, they noted.

▼▼▼

"Hello?"

"Carol?"

"Jim . . ." She didn't know what to say. Didn't know how to sound. Should she hang up? Should she tell him not to ring her again? It was a battle of wits—protocol: saying the right thing without seeming to be a pushover. "I tried to phone you earlier," she said suddenly, the words slipping out of their own volition while she was busy deciding what to do. "Where were you?"

The voices chattered at the pictures in his mind. They saw a pretty face and long, dark hair. They saw large blue eyes which looked frightened of being hurt. And they saw freckles, lots of freckles, and a short, stubby nose. They inquired.

"Carol," Jim Farnham said, softly.

Carol.

"What?" she asked.

On the other end of the line, Jim Farnham remained silent.

"I said, where were you?"

Jim stammered. "I can't really explain over the telephone. Can you come over to the base?"

"What, now?"

"I'll meet you at the gates in a half hour."

"Jim, I can't come over no—"

Drrrrrrrr, the telephone said, sleepily. Jim Farnham had hung up.

Carol Barnes slammed the receiver down on its cradle for the second time that night and scowled. "Just who the hell does he think he is?" she said loudly.

There was no answer.

The hall was absolutely quiet.

She looked at the clock. Ten-fifteen.

She listened to the gentle sounds of her parents shuffling around in their bedroom.

She bit her lip, just enough to make it hurt.

▼▼▼

The lumberyard looked almost as dark and inhospitable as the alley he had just run through, and Billy Macready hesitated just inside. He looked back through the gates and along the alley, wondering if maybe Adam and J. J. had turned back and decided to accompany him. But the alley and the small section of Beechwood Avenue he could see at the end were deserted. He was completely alone.

He considered starting back to the street but then he again saw the darkness of the alley that lay between it and him. It had to be the lesser of the two evils, he decided. He was already in the lumberyard, and this *was* the shorter route.

"Okay, boy," he said to the invisible horse between his legs. "Let's go get 'em!"

And he ran into the evening breeze with one hand stretched out before him and the other slapping the outside of his right thigh.

They were waiting for him at the pass.

Billy, they said in unison.

Billy Macready stopped, hand still outstretched, and stared into the darkness of the lumberyard. His heart was pounding, fit to burst. "Hello?" His voice sounded pathetic and small, but that was okay: that was the way he felt, too.

"Adam? J. J.? That you?" Maybe they had doubled back somehow and sneaked into the yard some other way. But he knew that was not possible. The way he had entered—the back way, where the trucks loaded up their deliveries—was the only way in except for the main entrance on his street. And that was . . . that was miles away.

There was a small glow down among the logs.

Billy stared at it.

We mean you no harm, the glow said, though not exactly in those words. It said it in a strange mixture of pictures and smells and colors and sounds. And it said it in a thousand tiny voices that both fretted at his mind and soothed it at the same time.

Billy wanted to say something—anything—but the words would not form. The glow was growing fainter as he watched it.

We have traveled a long way, said the glow which was many, many voices, snuggled in his head. Its collective voice ebbed and pulsated with the words. *We cannot return home.*

The fear inside him was gone now. He felt rested, peaceful. He felt a great warmth come over him. It was a little bit like pity—like when his father had run over a stray cat and they had knelt beside it and tried to soothe it; but the cat had been beyond help, and Billy's dad had smashed it on the head with a stone. But it was also like extreme happiness—like when school let out for the summer and fall seemed like a vicious rumor, so far in the distance as not having any importance at all. He had so little experience on which to base a comparison. Ten years: what's ten years!?

His brain bypassed the inadequacies of his mouth and spoke to the voices direct.

It spoke in colors and sounds and smells and feelings.

It spoke of the burnished gold of autumn and of the blue-white of the winter snows.

It spoke with the clarity of summer rain and with the fresh breath of spring winds.

And it asked how it, a small boy, could possibly be of help.

You can do nothing, the voices answered. *By your standards, we will die—we are dying now—but death is, after all, only a word used to explain the end of living: it is the connotations of death which are feared, not death itself.*

Billy understood and the voices relished the understanding. They bathed in the young mind's ready acceptance.

We will be gone within two of your days.

Billy saw images of light and darkness, saw them twice. And he smelled the smells of morning and afternoon, of supper and of bed. And he smelled them twice, also.

We only wish to examine and to experience your existence.

The voices were so soothing that Billy failed to notice that the glow by the lumber was gone. But not gone entirely: now it was inside his head.

Many of us are here.

Billy questioned.

Yes, we are all dying.

Billy thought.

He saw the blackness and the immeasurable vastness of space.

He saw the tiny vessels plummeting through the void, like a swarm of starborn seeds, traveling to an unknown future and leaving behind a cold and lifeless planet.

He felt the frustration of time passing without change.

He felt the boredom and hopelessness of tedium and repetition.

And he felt—and marveled at—a determination and perseverance in the face of the certainty of extinction.

He was wasting time. "This, is a lumberyard," he said to the night, so cold and uncaring.

Lumberyard.

"Now, a lumberyard is . . ."

The voices noted and discussed.

▼▼▼

That same night, Carol Barnes slipped quietly out of her house and met Jim Farnham and his newfound friends. She provided a home for the occupants of another craft and, over the following two days, she introduced and explained many facets of her life. She also learned a little herself . . . and *of* herself.

She came to understand tolerance and with it came a peace way beyond her almost-twenty years. Although she and Jim would one day drift apart, they would always enjoy a special friendship that could never be explained to the casual onlooker.

Ted and Martha Bannister had children for two days. Like all good parents, they told their children about all the wonders of their world. And, also like all good parents, they grieved at their children's passing.

Jack Turnbull lost his dependency on alcohol but he regained his self respect. He showed his charges the beauty of the countryside which had become his home and, when they left him, he took his grief back to its leafy consolation rather than taking up a place in society once more. But, for all the rest of his life, Jack enjoyed a special relationship with the other people of Forest Plains, many of whom had been similarly touched on that most special of nights.

One of those was Frank Emseley.

Frank closed his general store for two whole days, during which he explained many items of produce and their production and why people needed them.

For many nights over the remaining short time of his life, Frank watched the skies hopefully. But, two years later, on a lonely Thanksgiving, he decided he had had enough.

Jimmy Jorgensson and Adam Showell never met up with the invaders they had tried so hard to find. But life had so much more in store for them that one missed opportunity did not really matter.

And Billy . . .

Billy Macready played truant for two days.

He drove his parents mad with concern and, when he finally reappeared, they paid him much more attention. It's like they say: you don't miss your water until your well runs dry.

The glowing people that, like meteors, had ridden the dark winds above Forest Plains, ceased to exist; at least in the way that we know existence. But, filled with newfound understanding and a wealth of information, they went accepting their fate.

It's all any of us can hope for.

FIRST CONTACT, SORT OF
▼▼▼

KAREN HABER AND CAROL CARR

THE Terran was in a telephone booth on Telegraph Avenue when the invisible alien scout from Rigel 9 wafted along on a breeze and noticed him.

A *likely prospect,* thought the alien. It pulled in its pseudowing, settled to the pavement, and turned up the amplifier on its transspecies transponder.

"No, no, no," the earthling squealed in its peculiar dialect. It was speaking into a quaint audio transmitter which it held in front of its mouth with clever pink articulated front paws. "I lost a quarter. Q-U-A-R-T-E-R. What I want from you is simple, Operator, so simple that a child could do it. Perhaps you could find a child for me? No? Well, would you like *me* to find a child? Then perhaps it could ask you for my money back. I don't care that you don't believe me. If you won't give me a quarter, how about a dime? A nickel? Hello? Hello?"

The alien padded closer on soft, mutable pseudofeet.

If it had had lips it would have smacked them. Yes—yes. This creature was the one. The perfect sample. Probe the enemy for weaknesses, that was the Rigelian's mission. And here was this nice little earthling all alone in its box. Even more important, its mind was as chaotic and closed a system as the alien had ever scanned. It would never know what had hit it.

With a sound halfway between a purr and a sob the alien slipped into the earthling. *Ah*, it thought. *Almost a perfect fit.*

Such cunning little fingers: almost as nice as that otter in Monterey. But this creature didn't seem to think as well as a sea mammal. Fast, but not well. Maybe it was the lack of salt water.

Not a bad body, really. Surprising upper torso strength and nice stretchy muscles. All the necessary parts seemed to be present. The alien scanned the external area as well. The Terran seemed to have little awareness of its outer aura. Perhaps this was a potential weakness to be exploited. How pliable was this species? Investigate. Probe. Learn. The alien directed the earthling to return to its nest.

The dual-lobed brain was a bit slow in processing the order: there seemed to be a great deal of peripheral noise and interference.

▼▼▼

Inside the phone booth Wendell Davis was on hold, waiting for the Supervisor of Information. As the seconds ticked away he had mentally redesigned the booth to include a little toilet complete with bidet and modesty panel, expanded the concept to provide miniature living quarters for the homeless, added wheels and a motor and . . .

. . . he couldn't understand why he felt such an overwhelming compulsion to go back to his apartment.

I just got out here, Wendell thought. *I haven't even had a decaf cappuccino yet.*

But he couldn't shake the sudden yen for his own four walls. *Okay*, he thought. *Okay. I'm going, I'm going. Jeez.* He hung up and slammed open the door of the booth.

It was about 2:30 on a cold post-Christmas day and the sky

over Berkeley was a glorious canopy of bruises. Wendell was immediately cheered by the sight and considered stopping in to see Verna and Henry, but changed his mind when he remembered that he had borrowed Henry's portable television and accidentally dropped it to its death and Henry didn't know yet. Besides, he was going home.

He caught the very next bus with none of his usual arguments, detours, or complications. *Sometimes you just have to get on the bus and go home,* Wendell thought. He liked the phrase. It had simplicity. Directness. He decided to adopt it as his new mantra.

His door was still unlocked because he had not yet found his key but nothing inside was missing—at least nothing Wendell noticed.

He took off his jacket and started to drop it on the floor. Suddenly, his arm twitched, he spun around, opened the closet, and pulled out a wire hanger. Astounded at what he was doing, but doing it all the same, Wendell neatly hung the jacket in the closet and closed the door. His mouth was dry.

I need something to drink, he thought. *Right now.*

Somewhere in the room the phone began to ring.

Don't answer it, Wendell thought. *You don't even know where the phone is.*

The phone rang again.

He scanned the mounds on the floor but didn't see anything that looked remotely like a telephone, just bunches of dark clothing, the tools he used for fixing things when they didn't act right, parts of radios and sandwiches.

Geological, he thought. *I never have to wonder what I was doing yesterday. Yesterday is the top of layer of the heap.* Speaking of which, hadn't Susan left her pregnant calico cat here yesterday when she had stopped by?

Wendell managed to find the phone on the third ring, right next to Susan's cat, who hissed at him, gave an odd twitch, and begin to extrude a shiny pink ratlike kitten.

Emergency mantra: just deliver the kittens.

By the time Wendell had midwived all five births, put together a makeshift crib from an old shoebox from which he
dumped half a lifetime's accumulated yellowed check stubs and
two mattress tags, and placed the newborns in eight new homes,
(some of his friends would only agree to shared custody), he was
weary and sweaty and still extremely thirsty.

He shambled into the kitchen, turned on the faucet, cupped
his hand under it and slurped. In mid-slurp a wave of dizziness
sent him reeling against the counter. *Damned water additives,*
he thought. *Probably all that fluoride.*

Wendell felt peculiar, almost as if he were standing across the
room watching himself. He did a quick mental inventory. Arms,
legs, nose—yes, everything was still attached, still in place on his
body, and he was still inside of it. His skin itched as though a
thousand ants were commuting across him to the breadbox. He
scratched madly without relief.

But the itching was nothing compared to the odd compulsion
he suddenly felt. Eerie. Not like him at all, not a bit. He felt
the urge—a ravening need—to clean.

Under the sink he found a rotting pair of once-green rubber
gloves with four fingers left on one hand and three (with tooth
marks) on the other. Wendell pulled them on, grabbed the half-
full container of cleanser, and upended it over the sink. A few
flakes drifted down. He rapped the can hard against the counter.
The top fell off and the remaining cleanser fell into the sink.
He grunted and turned on the water.

Long after the gloves had fallen away from his hands, his
fingertips had shriveled, and the hot water had turned tepid,
Wendell was still scrubbing. He had moved on from the dishes
to the large appliances and was now on his hands and knees in
that no-man's-land between the refrigerator and the counter. He
was tired, he was hungry, and he had to go to the bathroom.
But every time he tried to concentrate on anything other than

cleaning, his thoughts skipped back to it like a needle caught in the groove of an old long-playing record album.

What's happening to me? he wondered.

Was it something he had eaten? Sugar in the granola or too much caffeine? He had heard about people getting stuck on dangerous cleaning jags and waking up three days later to discover that they had been washing the ceiling, stacking the dog food cans by color, or retyping the phone book according to assonance.

He didn't even like cleaning. But he couldn't make himself stop. He was tired but, even worse, he was frightened because this mind that he had lived with for thirty-two years had suddenly narrowed down into one infinitely exhausting, unremitting track. Where was his creativity, his sidelights and highlights, his familiar digressions and enticing permutations? He couldn't even think of a new mantra to make sense of his confusion and calm himself. Still his arm scrubbed on.

Wendell moved from the kitchen to the rest of the apartment, dusting, polishing, vacuuming. It was three a.m. before he had finished and he was worn beyond a frazzle.

When he awoke, ten hours later, his bed felt unfamiliar. The sheets were crisp, smooth, firmly tucked in place, and—he opened his eyes—oh God, they were even clean.

The sun poured through the window onto the brown rug. Wendell sat up in bed. Yes, it was brown. He remembered.

He felt a driving need to take a shower. To shave. To wash and rebraid his long greying hair. He itched in a thousand places. But when he opened the door to the bathroom, he froze.

The room was spotless. It smelled fresh and minty. The blue (ah, blue!) towels were folded neatly over the towel rack. The pale pink (pink!) shower curtain was tucked inside the tub. The sink was white. He could see his reflection in the chrome faucet.

Wendell began to gulp air. *Calm,* he thought. *I am completely calm. I have never been calmer. It's my new mantra.*

He stepped inside the bathroom. He might even have made it all the way to the toilet. But he noticed the grout, and that was his undoing.

Even the damned grout was clean.

Mantra forgotten, Wendell sank to his knees on the green threadbare rug and sobbed his heart out for the death of his old self, a self that never, in a zillion millennia, would have had it together enough to clean the mildewed yards of purple-splotched grout in his bathroom until they shined with the fervid whiteness of a public monument in a fascist state.

When he had emptied his tear ducts, panic took over and shook him like landfill in an earthquake.

▼▼▼

The Rigelian awoke to the myriad sensations the human body afforded. Distracted by various reports from the nerve relays, the pores, the aural levels, the vascular pressure, all the workings of the basic human machine, the alien did not at first notice the earthling's dismay. But it soon became apparent that something was seriously wrong.

The alien peeked out of the earthling's eyes and saw the small room that the human had cleaned before going to sleep. Something about it seemed to be troubling the human, and the resultant respiratory and digestive distress made him uncomfortable to reside in. The alien groped around inside its host, trying to find a way to reassure him.

It hit the adrenaline trigger. No, that only seemed to intensify the agitation. The human shook harder.

Next it fiddled with the serotonin levels.

The human burst into tears yet again.

The Rigelian sighed and reached for the endorphin controls.

Ah, much better. The earthling relaxed, smiled, and emptied his bladder into the water-filled receptacle called a toilet. The alien nearly swooned with the pleasurable sensation. It tried to get the human to do it again, but apparently there was some restriction on the number of times this function could be repeated. Well, the alien could wait.

The earthling turned on the water sprayer in the enclosure next to the toilet, took off his sleep costume, and got under the spray. The Rigelian felt the delightful bombardment of a thousand tiny watery collisions with epidermis. *No wonder this human being was in such mental disarray*, it thought. With such a distracting variety of sensory input, each day must be too full of pleasure to allow much concentration on anything else.

The Rigelian was tempted to stay in the shower for several awareness periods. But it reminded itself that it was here for a purpose, and as pleasant as this water spray might be, it was time to get down to the serious business of testing the enemy. Investigate the target population's psychological tolerance for foreign matrices. There would be time enough for bladder-emptying and other delights once the Earth had been conquered.

▼▼▼

Wendell felt peculiarly cheerful as he stepped out of the shower. He toweled off, dressed in his cleanest jeans and shirt, and decided to organize his paperwork.

He had never done anything like this before. "Don't think," he told himself. "Just do." Situational mantras seemed like a good improvisation. But once he lit into the job, he didn't have time to think, even about not thinking.

Three days later, Wendell sat upright in a straight-backed chair, surveying his domain.

The place was spotless. His papers were alphabetized and color-coded; his clothing had been washed, dried, folded, or hung. He didn't owe anybody any money. His apartment key was in plain sight. The kittens and their mother had been returned to Susan. He had gotten a haircut and bought a pair of slacks. He was thinking of looking for a job. He was terrified.

He needed a friend, and in a hurry.

Emergency mantra time. "Find a friend," he intoned. "Just find a friend."

▼▼▼

"Susan," he said, staring at the back of her head, which was bent over her keyboard. "You've got to help me."

"What's happening?" she mumbled, not turning around, not even looking up.

"Nothing. Everything."

"Beg pardon?"

"My grout is spotless, Susan." Wendell paused meaningfully. Surely she would intuit the problem.

"Wish I could say the same."

"You don't understand."

She sighed and turned to him. Her blue eyes were bloodshot and her short dark hair was frazzled. "Wendell, are you getting weird on me?"

"No. Yes. I mean, I don't know."

"Well, look. I've got a really gnarly deadline here. Since we can't seem to find anything wrong with you, or your grout, why don't we just agree that you're okay. Want to go to a movie next week? I'll call you."

Wendell found her patronizing attitude offensive, told her so, and left, pausing only to insult her cat.

He went back to his apartment, but the sight of it—neat, clean, *finished*—unnerved him. He needed fresh air, fast.

Out on the street, between the Palm Reader's bay window and the Sierra Club picket line in front of the Whole Bark pet supply store, Wendell bumped into a street person. The street person's hair might once have been blond but it was now a strange beige mat that sat high upon his head at an angle like a beret. He was wearing a purple shower curtain and pulling a shopping cart along behind him.

Wendell admired the shower curtain but thought that it needed several pockets and at least one zippered compartment with expandable accordion pleats.

"Goddadolla?" said the street person.

"Yeah." Wendell felt around in his pants and, with a familiar sense of apprehension, found a wad of neatly folded bills. He peeled one off. "Here."

"Thanks." The man put the money into an aperture in his curtain and leaned closer. His stench was amazing, like barbequed sneakers. Old ones. "End times are near."

"No kidding. Really?" Wendell said. But he couldn't help wondering if that was the reason why things—his life in particular—felt so peculiar, suddenly.

The street person nodded. "Be ready. They're coming."

Wendell wanted to walk away but first he had to ask, "Who?"

"The ones from up there." He pointed to the sulfurous five o'clock sky.

"Pilots?" Wendell said.

"Angels, you jerk. They'll eat our brains, spit out what they don't need like peach pits. Already eaten mine."

"They have?" Wendell stared at him. Just because the guy was crazy didn't mean that he was wrong.

"Yeah. So be careful. Get straight with Him-or-Her-or-What-ever." The street person paused, scratched his head as though he had lost his place, shrugged, and said, "Goddadolla?"

But Wendell was no longer listening. The idea of making peace with Him-or-Her-or-Whatever was suddenly very appealing. Compelling, even. There was just one problem. Wendell was sort of secular and eclectic and heavily nondenominational. He didn't particularly believe in one—or even several—gods, although he hoped that his nonbelief wouldn't offend any or all of the theoretically omnipotent beings who might or might not take notice of it.

"Find a religious person," Wendell thought aloud, mantra-

like. "Find a seriously religious person." And he began walking
swiftly uphill toward the University's seminary complex.

A young blond man in a red and white rugby shirt was wedged
furtively between two rose bushes outside the Albert Schweitzer
cafeteria. He was puffing on a cigarette and, when Wendell
walked by, apologized profusely for any smoke that might have
drifted into Wendell's lungs. Wendell assured him that he was
okay. Well, sort of okay, except for this spiritual problem he
was having.

The young man, a seminary student named Jason, listened
raptly, nodding between puffs.

"Grout?" he asked.

"Grout," Wendell said.

"Okay," Jason said, when Wendell had finished. "I think I
know what's wrong with you."

"You do?" Hope leaped in Wendell's stomach like a hungry
puppy.

Jason smiled cheerfully. "Sure. You're possessed. There's a lot
of that going around right now."

"Possessed? You mean by some sort of demon?" Wendell
hadn't really considered the option.

"Demon, dybbuk, spirit," Jason said, and shrugged. "It all
depends on your outlook. I can't say what it is for certain on
such short observation."

"Well, what should I do?" Wendell asked.

Jason admitted that although his church was very strict about
exorcisms, he personally was fascinated by Wendell's case and
wouldn't mind a little field experience.

▼▼▼

The alien noted the earthling's dawning awareness of and pathetic attempts to cope with the foreign consciousness in its body.
If the Rigelian had had a sense of humor it would have been
amused. As it was, the alien merely added the datum to its al-

ready copious file and continued to observe. Of course the Terran would fail in its investigations. It was hopelessly primitive and its powers of concentration were minimal at best. In the Rigelian's opinion, the Terran race would be vastly improved by accepting the rule of superior beings with an evolved sense of organization.

▼▼▼

The next morning, Jason the seminarian arrived at Wendell's apartment. In his arms were a three-foot white candle in the shape of a cross ("I got it from a vendor on Telegraph"), a jar of pickled garlic ("We can always eat it"), the Bible, and a dog-eared paperback copy of *The Exorcist*.

"Have you ever done this before?" Wendell asked.

"Oh, no. But I've talked about it a lot with my roommates after lights-out, and I'm a big movie fan. Is it all right with you if I run for a smoke before we begin? Is there anywhere I won't be seen?"

Wendell gave him a saucer and planted him on the fire escape. When the seminarian came back inside a few minutes later his breath alone could have exorcised demons.

Jason cleared his throat a few times and they got down to business. Wendell sat in a chair in the middle of the room. Jason lit the cross-candle and raised it over his head three times. He picked up the Bible and put it in Wendell's lap. For good measure he put the jar of pickled garlic on top of it. Now he flipped through *The Exorcist*, pausing at one of the red-flagged pages.

"God and Lord of All Creation," he intoned, "let your mighty hand cast out this cruel demon from your servant, Wendell."

He slapped his own slightly clammy nicotine-stained hand over Wendell's forehead. "It is He who commands you, oh fetid and evil one, tremble in fear, or Prince of Evil, and begone! Come forth, yield the . . ."

"Mustard plaster," said a high, quavering voice.

"What?" said Wendell and Jason together.

"Use a mustard plaster. Or Ben Gay, that's good too."

The voice was familiar. "Mom!" Wendell cried.

"Wendell, you remember me!"

"Of course I do," he said, feeling insulted. "But Mom, you're dead."

"It's not so bad, honey. Could be worse. Listen, Wendell, I know you think there's some demon or something possessing you, but I've looked around and I don't see anybody in here besides me. You're probably just overstimulated. Did you have any sugar? You know how you get with glucose."

Wendell sighed. "No, Mom."

"Well, all right. If you really think there's somebody or thing here, just tell it to leave. Go on, dear, speak up for yourself. Be Mommy's great big man."

Wendell opened his mouth to defend his masculinity, when to his horror he recognized the earnest baritone of his high school history teacher, Mr. Severinson.

"Have you been reading trash again, Wendell? I told you . . ."

Jason had picked up the cross again and was intoning, "It is He who commands you, He who expels you, He who . . ."

". . . not to hang out with these hippie types and learn to direct your energy."

A new voice, flat and nasal, chimed in. "A personality change is often the first sign of the fragmentation of the already fragile ego."

Wendell allowed himself a tiny smile. It was the voice of his first—and favorite—psychiatrist, tiny Dr. Gow. The one who had arranged his permanent disability status.

"Hey, you quack," cried Wendell's mother. "Get away from my precious boy or I'll fragment *you*."

". . . Lord grant that this vileness be gone . . ."

"It's always hippie trash and garbage."

Wendell squirmed as the voices of three long-dead great-aunts whom he'd dubbed "The Harpy Trio" chimed in. And above them in the background, was that the trilling laugh of crazy Marsha, his second–cousin-by-marriage? And behind her, the whispered suggestions of a stranger who had once tried to pick him up at a movie? Lecturing, declaiming, chiding, urging, while in the background, like a mad leitmotif played much too fast, ran the theme song to a cartoon show he had watched every Saturday morning when he was nine.

He struggled to free himself from the chair and the voices, the snakepit of the past. His head was beginning to feel very noisy and crowded but not in any good way.

▼▼▼

The Rigelian had been relaxing for a moment, contemplating the coming invasion. It would be a snap. Such confused, chaotic animals, humans. So easily dominated and organized.

The swarm was poised on Rigel 9 awaiting the scout's signal. Soon the attack forces would be launched across the dark vastness of space and nothing would be able to stop them.

"Excuse me."

The alien stared in amazement at the short, round, neatly coiffed, impeccably attired female human addressing him. She was unmistakably noncorporeal, an interesting fact. The alien had thought that Homo sapiens were only able to communicate while in the body. Obviously, this was not always the case.

"Would you mind telling me just what you think you're doing inside my son's head?"

Other post-life incarnations began to manifest themselves.

"What's the matter, you don't have your own head to hang around in?"

"Unhand this young man."

"You leave Wendell alone. He's a nice boy."

"Very sensitive."

"Sweet."

The alien tried to defend itself. It feinted with its jagged pseudohorns. It gnashed its long and pointed pseudoteeth. All to no effect. Never had it encountered anything like this . . . this collective energy.

Wendell's mother raised her wide leatherette purse and whirled it on its chain strap around her head like a lariat.

Mr. Severinson pulled a sleek can of mace from the pocket of his tweed jacket. Dr. Gow brandished *The Ego and The Id* in his left hand and *Beyond the Pleasure Principle* in his right. Crazy Marsha whipped out a set of steaming, orange hair rollers.

The alien screamed and ran toward the deepest recesses of Wendell's mind. But Wendell's posse of spirits pursued it relentlessly.

"Get out of here!"

"Beat it."

"Hit the road, Jack!"

They showed it terrible things: failed exams, late-night lectures, fumbling sexual encounters, toilet training.

The alien reeled under the onslaught, sustaining lacerating bruises to its psychological matrices.

I must get away, it thought. *Back to safety, back to Rigel 9. Must warn the others. The humans have a secret weapon lodged in their brains. Memories capable of triggering the emotions. Oh, awful, horrendous, unthinkable. How do they bear the pain? I must flee. Nothing is worth this. Not even fingers.*

Meanwhile, outside, in Wendell's living room, Jason droned on, improvising, "Ad hominum, donutum, inadvertum." In the middle of a particularly intense excoriation he was overtaken by a sputum-spraying coughing fit.

"Yuck," said the phantom mob behind Wendell's forehead.

There was a scurrying, a great whoosh and gabble, tinny giggles, and a wheezing bagpipe arpeggio which slowly died away to silence.

▼▼▼

The Rigelian wandered over the streets of Berkeley, a transparent wisp sailing on its pseudowing. *I must go home,* it thought. *Yes, quickly now, I must tell them, warn them, before it's too late.*

But how?

Slowly, horrifyingly, the alien realized that in the turmoil of escaping from the earthling's brain and in the agony of its injuries it had somehow forgotten the all-important command for intersystem transport.

I had it here a minute ago, it thought. *Was it on a slip of paper? Perhaps I wrote it on my pseudofoot. Didn't there used to be a pile of stuff here? Maybe the cat ate it. Or gave it to Susan. I could call her, she's a programmer, she could look for it with a search program. No, better yet, I'll call Information. No, they take too long. Maybe Jason stays up all night. I'll bet he knows . . .*

▼▼▼

Wendell leaned against the cushions of his old flowered sofa and took a deep, careful breath. He felt purged, as though he'd just had a really good rolfing. And he was blessedly alone. Jason had taken his cigarettes, his pickled garlic, his cough, and gone. The apartment was silent—no voices, no memories, no cats or kittens. It was almost holy.

The stillness was a perfect repository for thought. Wendell sat, comfortably at one with his mind. *Just think,* he mused, *something or other was inside my head with me, trying to eat my brain. Seriously weird. But it's gone. Jason and my personal demons sent it packing, and now I'm okay.*

He opened his eyes, stretched luxuriously, and looked around. The saucer that Jason had used for an ashtray was sitting, abandoned, on the windowsill. Gray and white ashes had coagulated in its center declivity.

Wendell stared at it. He shut his eyes. He opened them and looked at the ashes, hard.

He didn't feel the slightest urge to pick the saucer up, to dump its contents in the garbage, to rinse it off, dry it, or put it away in the cupboard.

Really okay.

He was free. The exorcism, or whatever, had worked. No boojums or dybbuks or Republican cleaning fascists were playing hide-and-go-seek inside his cerebellum. He felt sure of it.

He kicked off his shoes and left them in the middle of the living room floor. He unbraided his hair and, giggling with relief, shook his head. He pulled off his socks, rolled them into a ball, and bowled them down the hallway. As he watched them roll to a stop he pounded his hands against the cushions with glee.

The phone rang. But Wendell was too busy thinking to answer it. There was work to be done. The apartment really needed shaping up. For starters, a pulley system from the pantry to the living room, yes, wall to wall. He would devise a clip that would roll along the tiger tail wire and hold chip bags at the same time, and maybe an insulated noose to carry soda cans and keep them cold . . .

As Wendell planned he intoned his new mantra: "I think therefore I am and I am because I think."

Nodding, he extended his long pointed pseudotail and scratched his back contentedly.

EMPATHOS
▼▼▼

LYNN D. CROSSON

THE cry that pulled Christine from her dream turned out to be her own. It woke her husband Gary as well.

"Honey?" he said, his voice thick with sleep. He sat up in the tent and reached for her.

Christine, still quivering from the nightmare, noticed with perverse amusement that his ever-tousled blond hair was flat on the side he had slept on, and smiled. Gary's confused expression caused the smile to bubble into a shrill giggle that degraded into a whimper as she leaned into his embrace.

"Bad dream?"

She nodded, her face pressed to his chest. "Yes," she said breathlessly. "Um, no. Shit, Gary! I think I'm scared!"

Gary's hands moved comfortingly along her back. Her slight frame was strong and fit, muscles taut beneath pale skin. "Of what, the dream? Why don't you tell me about it?"

Christine extricated herself from Gary's arms and sat up, her brow furrowed. "It wasn't a dream . . . but it had to be. It was like, you know, astral projection." She glanced at him quickly, tentatively, then looked away, allowing her short, chestnut curls to obscure her face. "I know that's nuts. But whatever it was, it was weird. And scary."

"Where did you go on this astral trip of yours?" Gary tried to make his voice light. He nudged her good-naturedly. She winced, hesitated, then told him. Everything.

"It was like I was flying, only I couldn't see my body. I remember trying to find my arms and touch my face, only there was nothing there. I could feel them though. I looked down and saw trees and the lake we drove past on our way up here and the roads that go through the mountains. The light was weird, too. It was night, but everything looked green and black, like I was looking through some kind of lens or scope or something.

"I couldn't control where I was going or how high up I was. I kept thinking I just wanted to come back here to the tent, but something kept pulling me." Christine gestured wildly as she told her dream. Gary repeatedly reached for her hands, but they fluttered away every few seconds.

"Then, I felt myself going lower, like a plane coming in for a landing. I saw something smokey below, and figured this must be what I'm going to see. When I got closer, I saw it was a plane . . . a crashed plane, that's where the smoke was coming from. I was looking at it from the branch of a tree, you know, from above, but not too high up. Then, I heard this incredible sound. A cry, like a baby animal in pain, really high-pitched and woeful. It seemed to be coming from everywhere, but somehow I knew where to look. Just beside the wreck there was a person trapped under a big hunk of metal. I guess it must have been the pilot, because it seemed to be just a little plane and there were no signs of other passengers. I remember noticing that she was wearing a helmet, and wondering why you'd need that for a leisure flight."

Gary stopped her. "She?"

"What?"

"You said 'she.' The pilot was a woman?"

Christine was silent for a moment, searching her mind. "Yeah, she was. I don't know how I knew that, but I did."

"Okay, go on."

"Well, um, where was I? Oh yeah, she was wearing a helmet and I noticed that the faceplate was cracked and she was unconscious. Her face was strange, really white, like the color of milk. I felt like I was moving closer and closer to her face, floating from the tree branch toward her until all I could see was her face. Then, all of a sudden, she opened her eyes and looked right at me! They were black, liquid eyes and they pleaded to me for help. And then she opened her mouth and I heard that animal sound again, all around me. I was scared out of my mind, and I screamed back. Then, I woke up." She looked at Gary, as the images faded from her mind, feeling as though she had just awakened again.

Gary hugged her and kissed her softly on the forehead and on each cheek and on her lips. "Quite a dream. It *was* just a dream, you know."

"It sure doesn't feel like it," Christine sighed heavily.

"Don't forget why we're out here, okay? You just took some of the stress with you instead of leaving it in the city like you were supposed to. It's probably part of the healing process."

"I guess you're right, honey. I'll try to do a better job of staying calm."

"That's my girl. Come on, let's go watch the sun rise."

▼▼▼

Christine cheerfully retold her dream to Carol and Brian over steaming coffee and flapjacks. Both red-haired and freckled, their college buddies from a dozen years ago looked more like brother and sister than lovers. They all had a good laugh about the dream and joked about how lucky Christine was that they had swiped her from her New York accounting firm when they had.

It had been her symptoms of burnout that prompted the trip

to begin with. In the previous weeks, Christine displayed such uncharacteristic behavior as yelling at cab drivers in busy intersections, pushing elderly and pregnant women out of the way in competition for the last subway seat, and kicking the apartment door soundly when the key stuck in the lock. She had tried every form of physical therapy, from electro-stimulation to shiatsu, to relieve her chronic, stress-induced neck and shoulder pain. Between the stress and the pain, she averaged approximately two hours sleep a night. Even on the eight-hour drive up to the mountains in Brian's van, she had not closed an eye while the others took driving and sleeping shifts. It was Gary's opinion that a week in the mountains would be therapeutic, and she had been more than willing to go along.

The unrelenting heat made the campers listless. They spent the day lazing over games of backgammon and swimming in the lake. After a dinner of cold salads and pita bread, they passed the evening around a campfire singing old Motown hits in terrible a cappella harmony. They turned in shortly after ten.

Christine and Gary smiled at each other as the quiet sounds of lovemaking drifted from the other tent. They snuggled together, Christine's head on Gary's shoulder, her arm across his bare chest.

"Feeling better?" Gary asked, nuzzling the top of her head with his chin.

"I guess," she answered sleepily. "Mountain air. Crickets, no car horns . . . great stuff. You having fun?"

"Mmm hmm. As long as you are."

Christine raised her head and they kissed tenderly. She nestled closer, feeling calm and safe, and sleep took her quickly.

▼▼▼

When she saw the trees rushing below her in the night, Christine realized the dream had returned and made a conscious effort not to panic. The clouds parted above the familiar crash site.

The pilot lay unmoving, torso still pinned beneath the slab of metal, eyes closed. Somehow, Christine knew she was alive. Wanting to help, she floated closer and came to rest on the ground beside the victim. A tremendous sense of responsibility consumed her, augmented by futility as she tried to reach out with arms and hands that were not there. The pilot's eyes opened again, imploring. Christine watched as her face seemed to dry and wrinkle like a piece of fruit and her black eyes clouded.

Do something, she thought, and wondered if the plea had come from her own mind or the poor woman beside her.

A rushing sound began softly, then grew louder as Christine's vision faded to murky greyness. She protested, wanting to stay, but the roaring fog gave way to silent blackness . . . and then she was awake and in her tent.

She woke Gary instantly.

"Whatsa matter, honey?" he asked groggily, sitting up and rubbing his eyes.

"Gary, it's not a dream. You have to listen to me. Are you awake? I know how this is going to sound, but she's really hurt out there and she'll die if we don't find her fast!"

"She . . . who? Carol?" He shook his head to clear it.

"Damn it, Gary, wake up! The *pilot!*"

"Jesus H . . . what the hell are you talking about?"

Christine looked away and took two slow, deliberate breaths to regain some semblance of control. She began again, slowly, as one might explain a complicated concept to a small child. "The dream I told you about last night. I saw the same place again. The pilot is alive, but not for long. She's much worse off now, and needs our help. I'm not dreaming this, Gary, she's calling me to her."

"You're serious!"

"Yes, I'm serious. Will you help me look tomorrow?"

"Look where? Where would we even *start* to look for a dream, Chris?"

Christine thought a moment and saw the terrain in her mind. "I can't explain where, but I know. I can take you there. Come on, honey, I'll need your help. Say you'll come."

Gary sighed and ran his fingers through his hair. "Listen, sweetheart, we can't do anything now, can we? So, why don't you just try to get a little more sleep and we'll see how you feel about it in the morning, okay?"

"I'll feel the same way in the morning."

"Fine. We'll talk to Carol and Brian over breakfast, if you still want to look then. Come on now, lay down with me."

"You're patronizing me."

"You want to go out looking for plane crashes right now?" Annoyance had crept into Gary's voice.

"No," Christine pouted.

"Well, come over here and rest, then."

After a troubled hour, she slept dreamlessly for the remainder of the night.

▼▼▼

Mercifully, Monday morning dawned slightly cooler and less humid. Carol and Brian were barely out of their tent when Christine approached them with her proposition.

"I had the dream again last night," she said, offering a bowl of fresh strawberries to Brian. "Only, I don't think it's a dream anymore. I think it's a . . . I don't know, a cry for help."

As she told them of her plan to mount a search for the site of the wreck and asked them to join her, the couple looked at each other, at Christine and at Gary, their faces revealing an effort to decide on the most appropriate reaction. Gary stared into his coffee mug throughout the proposal, his face unreadable, offering no cue to the others. Lacking a better plan for the day, they agreed to follow Christine and collected their gear in awkward silence.

Each hiker wearing only a small pack containing mostly dried foods, first aid kits and camera equipment, they set out due north. Within an hour, they were well up the side of a mountain, where the air thinned and the terrain changed from lush forest to rock and scrub brush. Christine made several efforts to keep the conversation light, although Gary kept fairly quiet and gently shook off her attempts to take his hand or poke a smile onto his face with her fingers.

At the summit, the party paused for a rest and a snack. Gary wandered a few yards off to take some photographs. With the day clear and dry, visibility was wonderful and the mountain view was breathtaking.

"Well, Chris," Carol ventured, overly casual, "are we close?"

"Um . . . well, I think we got off track a while ago, but I'd hoped to get the lay of the land from up here."

"That's just great," Gary grumbled, lowering the camera from his face. "At least you could have let us in on it if you were going to lead us on a wild goose chase."

"Come on, Gary." Christine took a step toward him. "We're just out hiking, so what difference does it make? You got an appointment or something?"

He whirled on her, nearly dropping the camera, then seemed to reconsider his response. "Sorry," he muttered. "I can't say I'm having fun with this. I'm worried about you."

"Well, try not to be, okay? We'll find it, believe me, you'll see." She grinned and reached into her pocket. "Want some beef jerky?"

Gary took the offering, managing a small smile.

▼▼▼

Two hours past sunset, four weary, insect-bitten hikers dragged themselves into the familiar campsite. Carol and Brian waved limply and immediately trudged off to bed. In their tent, Christine offered her canteen to Gary to force eye contact. He reached for it, then they sat looking at each other for a long, uncomfortable moment. Gary averted his gaze first, throwing his head back to take a long swallow from the canteen.

"I guess you feel entitled to an apology," Christine said.

Gary wiped his mouth with the back of his hand and looked at her again. "How do you feel about it?" he asked.

"I know she's there, Gary." Her brow furrowed. "I just can't get it clear in my head exactly where."

"You're still so sure?" Gary sighed and reached for her hand. "This is no good, honey. I'm getting really worried."

"You don't believe me at all, do you?"

"I want to say I do. But look at it from my perspective for just a minute, will you?" His voice was gentle, pleading.

Christine's was not. "You know I'm not crazy. How about giving me the benefit of the doubt? I wouldn't hang onto this so tightly if I wasn't sure. Did you think about that?" She stood abruptly and began to change into a clean tee shirt and panties, her movements rough, angry.

"Damn it, Chris, keep your voice down!" Gary whispered harshly. "Of course I've thought of that. Look, I'm exhausted and my legs are killing me and this conversation is going nowhere, so let's just talk about it tomorrow, okay?"

Christine knelt on the sleeping bag beside Gary. She sat on her heels, looking at him and trying not to cry. After a long silence she said, "Is this hurting us? Are we going to be okay after this?"

"I wish I knew," he replied with a heavy sigh. "Go to sleep."

▼▼▼

At the first sensation of lifting, Christine tried to absorb every detail and terrain feature, although large portions of the journey were obscured by clouds and darkness. Reaching the woman in the helmet, Christine feared it was already too late. The pilot did not open her eyes and seemed somehow less substantial.

Hold on, she pleaded, *I'm coming.*

Although the pilot did not acknowledge in any way Christine could see, she knew she had been heard, and that there was still a chance. There was a sound then, like the earth sighing, and Christine was pulled back into the clouds.

When she opened her eyes, Gary was not inside the tent. Staring up at the canvas ceiling, she noticed the shadows of dancing tree branches cast by a flickering campfire outside.

She found Gary sitting with his bare back against the pine tree in the center of the clearing. Firelight bathed his chest as he absently pushed pine needles around with a twig. He looked up at the sound of her approach.

Wordlessly, she stepped between his feet, turned, and slowly sank down. His arms closed protectively around her as she let her head rest against his shoulder, tears slipping from her eyes.

"I'm not crazy," she said when she could manage words.

"I know, sweetheart," he whispered.

"I just saw her again. I want you to see her too."

Gary kissed her neck lightly. "I've been sitting out here think-ing," he said. "I know you're not just freaking out on me. That means something's going on that's worth exploring. When I woke up in the tent, I watched you sleeping for a while. Something seemed to be . . . missing, I can't explain what. I tried to wake you, gently. It was a little scary, but it seemed as though you weren't in there. Maybe you've got me spooked, but it was weird enough to keep me awake for the past hour."

Gary's report was the confirmation Christine had been waiting for. She felt the last vestige of self-doubt recede. "Then you'll come with me when it gets light? I know just where to go now, five miles northwest."

"Yes, I'll go. But we should let Carol and Brian off the hook; tell them we just want to spend the day alone, okay?"

"Fine," Christine said, twisting around to hug him awkwardly. "I'm so glad to have you back on my side. I guess we should rest up, but I'm too excited to sleep now!"

Gary grinned and kissed her again. "Well then, why don't we go back to the tent and see what we can do to tire you out?"

▼▼▼

After breakfast, Brian tossed the van keys to Gary. "Good luck," he said.

Christine looked up from her coffee mug. "Good luck with what?"

"Finding the wreck. That's where you're going, isn't it?"

"You think Gary's nuts to go along with this, don't you?" She canted her hip, emphasizing the challenge in her voice.

Brian stepped over the breakfast plates and took her hand. "Look, Chris, I've known you a long time. Okay, so you've been kind of peculiar in the last month or so, but I know you haven't gone over the edge. You want to see this thing through, I think it can only be therapeutic, and that's primarily why we're here. So go on, take the van, and stop worrying about what we think. We love you, that's all." He hugged her, and after a moment, she returned his embrace.

The van's dashboard compass helped them maintain their bearing, but it was impossible to travel anything resembling a straight line to the northwest. Five miles quickly became fifteen. Eventually, they reached a wooded incline that was virtually impassable, though Christine insisted it was the direction they must go. They parked the van, donned their packs and two extra canteens each, and set out on foot.

The lush undergrowth of vines and fern made walking difficult. Near eleven o'clock, they rested and lunched in a rocky clearing.

"We're close," Christine said, biting into an apple.

"I wish I could share your enthusiasm," Gary replied. "I don't know whether I want to find this place or not."

"Easier to think I'm crazy?"

"No, it's just that I'm going to have to rearrange a lot of stuff inside my head if we find the wreck. Telepathy and astral projection and all that stuff have always been categorized as fiction in my mind, understand? It's great to read about, but I'm not sure I'm ready to join the ranks of people who show up on talk shows claiming to predict the future and all."

Christine laughed. "Oh, relax! We'll deal with that when we get there. What matters is that woman is in trouble and called to me for help."

Gary stretched his legs and rubbed his aching calf muscles. "Why do you think you're the one she called?"

"I've been trying to figure that out. All I can come up with is that she reached for the most empathetic mind. I was the most stressed out, and probably the closest camper. We have one thing in common: distress."

"I guess that makes about as much sense as any of the rest of this does."

The climb got no easier as they resumed their search. Although the trees were more sparse, rocks seemed to intentionally jut out at the most inconvenient angles, and the heat and thin air made them light-headed. The only consolation was there seemed to be fewer insects at this altitude.

Near two o'clock, Christine stopped short and cocked her head in concentration. "There," she said, pointing to the west. She strode confidently ahead, dimly aware of the sound of Gary following. Fifteen minutes later, Christine actually smelled the wreck before it came into view, an acrid odor that reminded her of the time the ballast had blown in the fluorescent light fixture above her desk at work. She followed the smell around a sharp turn in the rockface and the view presented itself suddenly and fully. They stopped abruptly, staring. Christine clutched Gary's sleeve and whispered, "Oh! Gary, it's exactly as I saw it."

"Holy shit," Gary whispered back. "Chris, that's not a plane."

The small craft's nose was buried at a forty-five degree angle in a rocky mound, obviously of its own making. Two large, jagged holes near the front showed where it had not withstood the impact. Thin wisps of violet smoke still rose from a dozen places and small, blue lights winked on and off inside the cockpit. On the ground beside the wreck lay an unmoving form in a suit that fully encased its child-sized body, and a helmet with a cracked faceplate.

Christine took a step toward the pilot. She reached back for Gary's hand, then felt it, trembling, grasp hers. They circled the creature, Gary barely breathing, Christine nearly hyperventilating. She let go of his hand and knelt beside the pilot.

Gazing at the withered, gray skin, she remembered the gorgeous face she had seen in her first dream. The poor thing had had a milky complexion; Christine knew it would have been smooth and soft to the touch. Although she remembered the small, thin, ever-smiling mouth and almost non-existent nose, they had not struck her as unusual in her dreams—only beautiful. The pilot's eyes were closed now, but she would never forget the enormous, black eyes that first implored for help, not human eyes at all, she now realized. They had been so dark, so wet, and seemed to have no iris, or perhaps were *all* iris. And there was a wisdom in them she had never seen in *any* creature before, human or not.

Her hands reached out half a dozen times, and each time she jerked them back fretfully, unsure what was best. She whimpered once or twice, glanced up at Gary, then back at the creature, then leaned forward to peer through the faceplate. The glass was clouded now, nearly opaque. Grasping the sides of the helmet, she tried to figure out how to remove it.

"No!" Gary shouted.

Christine screamed, startled by his sudden outburst. She whipped her head around in alarm and anger. "We have to help her, Gary!"

Gary returned her gaze with a fearful, apologetic stare, and after a long moment, Christine turned away.

The helmet would not budge, but the faceplate cracked further until a small piece fell inward, leaving a hole large enough for her to reach in and carefully peel away chunks of glass, tears rolling down her cheeks as she worked. It broke her heart to see the desiccated skin, the puckered and cracked lips.

Gary knelt beside Christine and put a comforting hand on her knee. She brushed at her cheeks then reached for her pack and removed one of the canteens. Pulling a bandana from her pocket, she soaked the cloth with cool water.

"I hope we're not too late," she said, pressing the wet cloth to the alien's face. A moment later, the creature opened her eyes slightly; eyes now the palest blue, like glass marbles. Christine refreshed the cloth every minute or so and her patient slowly seemed to revive. Although the pilot's eyes were open, she seemed unable to move or open her mouth.

"Let's get this junk off of her," Gary said, gesturing to the fuselage that pinned her. Christine held the pilot's gaze for a moment that she hoped was reassuring, then joined her husband. With the help of two tree branches, the metal was easily levered up and out of the way. The alien's upper legs were crushed flat against the rock beneath them. They looked at each other, dismayed.

"I don't know what to do for you," Christine said, kneeling once more at her patient's head.

The alien blinked slowly and did not answer. Assuming she could not speak, Christine brought a canteen to the alien's mouth. With careful fingers, she opened the alien's lips and let a small stream of water trickle into her mouth and over her chin.

Gary pulled off her gloves and poured more water over her withered hands. "Her hands are so frail," he said softly, his voice revealing no trace of fear. "So light and brittle. I hope we're not hurting her." Christine glanced at the long, leathery fingers, nailless and grey. She gave Gary a reassuring smile.

There was the smallest sputter from the alien's mouth. Christine immediately stopped pouring and watched. Some of the color was returning to the creature's eyes, now a deep cerulean blue. Her skin remained grayish, but seemed considerably less wrinkled. Christine saw the faint smile on her patient's face grow and was overjoyed to hear the gentle, familiar voice in her mind.

My thanks.

Christine emitted a small squeal of delight and looked excitedly at Gary, who returned a blank stare. "What?" he said.

"She spoke to me! Oh, what a shame you can't hear. She says 'thank you'."

Gary smiled. "You're welcome," he said to the pilot. "Now what do we do?"

"Your legs," Christine said to the alien.

Remove them.

Christine gasped. "NO!"

"What?" said Gary. "What did she say?"

They are useless. The alien insisted.

"I can't! I couldn't!" Christine protested.

"What?" Gary shouted.

"She wants us to amputate her legs!"

Gary was speechless.

There was a long silence as the three of them regarded each other. Christine's mind raced. She assumed the pilot knew what was best for herself and this was, after all, an *alien*, but for Chrissakes, *amputate*! She looked to Gary. His expression was grim. She knew he had made up his mind to do what the alien requested and was simply awaiting direction. His certainty gave her the resolve she needed.

"Tell us how," she said to the pilot. "We have no tools, no skills for this. You'll bleed to death."

A drink, please.

Christine held the canteen to the alien's lips once more, and this time she drank deeply. Her eyes deepened again, now nearly the striking liquid black Christine had first seen. Her skin smoothed further, yet remained ashen. Her face was fully animated now. Though weak, she smiled and raised the hairless ridges above her eyes. Something in her eyes intensified and she drew Christine and Gary's attention to her. As they knelt beside her, the world around them faded and images from the pilot's mind filled their minds.

The alien told them wordlessly where to find the tools they would need inside the wreck, which ones to use, how to stop the flow of vital fluids during and after surgery, what vials of medication to administer and which one of them would do which tasks. They saw the entire procedure in the finest detail. When it was over, the memory was so vivid, they felt as confident about performing the task as if they had done it all before.

They entered the cockpit through one of the jagged holes in the hull and picked their way through the debris. The white case of surgical instruments and the red case of medicines were exactly where they were supposed to be.

Neither Christine nor Gary spoke as they set to work. The alien remained conscious, though the injection Christine administered was supposed to render her numb from her midsection down. Christine kept her back to the procedure, tending to her patient's vital signs and giving her sips of water every few minutes. Gary did the actual cutting, using a saw-like tool with a blade so sharp it sliced the pilot's legs like butter. Christine looked over her shoulder periodically, though only for a few seconds each time. She noticed Gary's expression of amazement as he worked, she guessed in response to his own strength of character and aptitude. She was proud of him. Between backward glances, Christine noticed the alien was projecting waves of calmness into her mind as though she were invited into a private meditation.

At a touch from Gary, Christine gathered her courage and turned to assist him. They rummaged through the kits and found what they knew was the correct vial, soaked two large pads with the medication and pressed them to the stumps just below the pilot's pelvis. Gary secured the pads with strips of cloth. The fluid coming from the wound did not resemble blood. It was pale blue and quite viscous, though that could have been due to the coagulant in the second injection they had given her. It did not flow so much as ooze, and was easy to control with the bandages.

They cleaned up the area, returning the medical kits and surgical waste to the ship. As the sunlight surrendered to twilight, they built a small fire on the rocky ledge a few yards away and solemnly committed the amputated legs to the flames. Then, exhausted, Gary and Christine each took a place on either side of their charge and went to sleep, just as the alien had shown them they would.

▼▼▼

The familiar lifting sensation tugged Christine into wakefulness. Opening her eyes, she took a moment to orient herself: *another dream?* Then, the softly whispering fire and the evening chill cleared her head, making way for the recent memory. And, there was something else. The pilot's hand held hers, squeezing gently.

Christine sat up and peered into the hole where the faceplace had been, searching for the shadowed face within the helmet. Firelight twinkled in the liquid black eyes. Christine could feel ... the pilot ... talking to her ... somehow. Just as she and Gary had received the surgery instructions, images illuminated her mind, more clear than any spoken sentence could possibly be. Following the visual request, she carefully picked up the alien, carried her to the fireside and sat cradling her in her arms. The physical contact enhanced the clarity of the images. Christine tried to reply in kind, but found words served her better.

"What else can we do for you?" she asked, gesturing at Gary's still sleeping form behind them. A very brief tableau of Christine crouching before the fire, which was now fed by the alien's corpse, flashed in her mind. Christine gasped, tears rushing to her eyes. Immediately, she felt the tendrils of calmness work their way into her nervous system as the alien let her know there was no need for distress. Wordlessly, she was told that her patient's death had been imminent even before the surgery and that she would be doing her a great service by cremating the remains as she had been shown.

"Then why did we go through all of that?" Christine asked, her voice trembling. The pilot surprised her then, putting words into her mind instead of pictures.

The energy required to suppress pain made communication difficult. I wished to talk . . . with you.

"With me especially?"

Our race communicates most easily with kindred minds. We have mediums who facilitate communications, sometimes several in cases of extreme discord. I find it extraordinary that one so distant from us would be so receptive to my voice.

"Gary heard you, too."

Only in close physical proximity, and then only in sympathetic resonance with you. We are the same, you and I.

Christine shifted so she could see the pilot's face more clearly. She noticed her complexion had returned to the milky smoothness she remembered from her first astral visit; her exotic beauty was breathtaking. The thought that this creature was dying in her arms broke her heart.

"How are we the same?"

We push so hard, so fast, always. We want our solutions to be complete and immediate . . . the words faded seamlessly into images once more. Christine saw the pilot in her ship, a shuttle launched by from the mother craft on a reconnaissance mission. Eager, as always, the pilot raced for Earth's atmosphere. Overconfident, she miscalculated the trajectory, lost control and crashed.

The details found Christine's mind; the pilot was obsessively fascinated with the new planet and had foregone rest and nourishment to maximize study time. The scenario rang several bells.

"I see your point about our similarities," Christine said, smiling ironically. "Accounting is nowhere near as exciting as space exploration, but my husband and friends dragged me off to the mountains because I didn't know when to slow down." She glanced at the pilot's bandaged stumps. "I feel silly talking about the stress of city life to you, though. Your pain must be so much worse than mine."

My error in judgment has had a more dire consequence. Our pain is the same. Now, tell me of the beauty of Earth. Let me know what I rushed here to find, while the time allows.

Christine's throat closed and her eyes filled again. She threw her head back and sighed heavily at the night sky. "I want to hand you the whole damned planet on a silver platter! But, I don't know where to start. What do you want to know about? Nature, science, people?"

The alien slowly raised a hand to Christine's cheek. Her fingers were more supple than before, warmer. She smiled with amazing serenity as the calmness caressed Christine yet again.

If you would, be still. I can look for myself.

Christine felt an indescribable sensation, like drawers being opened in her mind, and she felt the alien look inside. Panic barely registered and was quelled by calm and trust. The alien sampled Christine's most cherished experiences—sunset concerts in the park, fine wine in French restaurants, making love with Gary, winning at backgammon, the aroma from the cedar chest at the foot of her bed—and Christine felt them all as thoroughly as if they were happening now.

My thanks. I fear time will not allow for the questions that arise. However, the experience was most appreciated. May I return the kindness to you?

Dreamily, Christine gazed into the pilot's eyes. "I don't think

I could do what you just did, but I would love to know what your world is like."

Then . . . a flood of images raced into Christine's mind; landscapes in azures and violets and colors she could not name, beings dancing to music she could *feel* but not quite hear, control panels of ships, the view of the earth from orbit. The images flashed by like a crazy slide show, and Christine realized the pilot was hurrying to make the most of her last moments. When the images gave way to the immediate surroundings, she saw the pilot's eyes were closed.

"Are you still there?" she asked, gently shaking her. The pilot's eyes opened halfway.

A moment more.

Christine did not know if it was a declaration or a plea.

"Let me give you something that means a great deal here, but for some reason we don't do it very much." She gathered the creature into her arms and held her close, trying her best to keep her body from shaking with her tears.

My thanks. Now, listen . . . lastly . . .

▼▼▼

Christine turned as Gary stepped into the light from the fire at her feet, tears on her composed face. The charred remnants of one of the alien's gloves was disappearing among the flames. Mutely, he dropped to his knees at his wife's side, his eyes asking for an explanation.

She inhaled deeply and released a long, laden sigh. "She died."

"So, we failed then. What did we do wrong?"

Christine reached for Gary's hand and found it cool compared to her own, which had tended the fire for over two hours. "Nothing went wrong. She knew she was dying before the surgery. We had a long conversation while you slept."

"What did you talk about?" he asked quietly.

Christine took another deep breath. She did her best to describe the conversation and image exchange. She found herself wishing she could give him the images directly, and realized how much she would miss that form of communication.

"Jeez," Gary breathed. "How amazing that you two have so much in common. How amazing that we performed *surgery* on a fucking *alien!*"

Christine was quiet for several minutes. She gingerly swirled the ashes with a stick, as though the newly formed flames would somehow prolong the pilot's life. Gary squeezed her hand.

"I'm only a step behind her in meeting the same fate, Gary, or something too much like it for my taste. I don't want to crash, Gary. I'm ready to slow down now."

"So, bringing you up here has had the desired effect after all. I'll never forget having her thoughts in my head, like they were my own," Gary said. "What was it like when she showed you her world?"

In a soft voice, barely above a whisper, Christine said, "What an incredible experience to think with her mind for those few minutes, to look through her eyes and see things the way she sees them. And, to feel her loss. I felt her knowledge that she was dying, her grief at losing her ship and her sadness in realizing she would never see her own people, her own sky, her own mountains again. It was such an . . . *honor* to be invited to share that. I did the best I could to soothe her, and we comforted each other with images of the most beautiful things on each of our worlds."

She sat up and looked at her husband for his reaction. He regarded her with rapt attention, his eyes moist.

"She told me she felt very lucky to have encountered us," Christine continued, reaching for Gary's hand. "It was a first contact for their planet as well. The ship she'd launched from retreated to a higher orbit to avoid being detected while they waited. Not that they were afraid. I suppose we'd have done the same thing if the tables were turned. They don't know she's gone yet, but the shuttle is emitting a signal that will direct them when they return.

"I could tell she was near the end when she started thanking us for our kindness and help. She said you were wonderful. You were, Gary. I'm so proud of you. Um, oh, she said something I didn't quite understand about her memories being here to be collected by her people when they do return, and that she hoped they would not be misleading and that they would find similar qualities in the people they will meet.

"With her last thoughts she asked me to cover the embers with rocks in a small pyramid so her people will know where to find her. God, Gary, I miss her!"

Christine slumped into Gary's embrace and they held each other in silence until the fire was reduced to a few glowing embers. Then, they gathered loose stones and built the marker around the ashes. It was far too dark to venture back to the van then, so they sat beside the grave thinking about their experience and occasionally dozing until the sun rose.

Without a word to each other, they began their descent, knowing they would keep the memories to themselves, and that that would be enough until the mother ship returned.

INTERSTELLAR LOVE
▼▼▼

RON DEE

"I'M from another planet."

Kari widened her eyes and took another sip of her margarita. She felt a giggle deep inside but didn't give in. It was late and the Solar bar would be shutting down in another half hour. The science fiction decor of galaxy paintings on the walls was more visible as customer after customer departed.

And from her scan of the tables and chairs before she'd picked this man to sit across from, he was the best choice still available. There were another half-dozen men sitting alone, but she suspected their health and purposes for being here. They had the same instant gratification gleam in their eyes she knew from her marriage nights.

The man facing her said his name was Lucas, and he was nice looking. A pleasant, barely rounded face and piercing eyes that seemed to float between gray and green. His hair, light brown, was medium length and styled in a rather old-fashioned way that reminded her of young men in her youth. He wasn't built, but he wasn't carrying a spare tire, either.

"An alien, huh?" she spoke softly, leaving out her sarcasm.

Lucas sighed and made his own study of the big, dimly lit room. He cocked his beer and slurped it as though it wasn't something he did very often. "That's pretty blunt and by the way you humans define the word, not entirely correct. I think our races are very similar in a lot of ways, but we've lost something in our progress that you humans still have . . ."

"Humans?" Kari repeated the word with a raised eyebrow. She wondered if he was really so drunk he believed what he was saying . . . or if this was a really well thought out ploy. "You look human, Lucas. What makes you say you're from another planet?"

He shrugged, his smooth face lining as though he was having to think over every movement he made. "Because I am. Our studies showed us that honesty would be the best policy . . . that humans wouldn't believe us even if we were completely truthful."

This time, she did giggle, but not loudly enough to frighten him off. At home, she was too alone. The past nights had been too dull. Every night since the death of her husband had been too empty.

Although she was getting better at coming out to these places alone, she had to be careful to say the right things. It was just so difficult to get back into the dating game after nearly twenty years of faithful marriage.

"Do you want another drink?" asked Lucas.

Kari shrugged, feeling tipsy already. It was so different these days, not like college. Back then, venereal disease was rare. Sex between two people had seemed to mean more than it did now. A relationship that lasted beyond a satisfying orgasm.

Now, AIDS was a veritable plague and you never knew who might have it. Those diseases lasted after the orgasms and replaced the relationships that quickly disintegrated. Her divorced friends had told her how every encounter they had was full of the fear of death. You could abort an accidental pregnancy, but AIDS . . .

Still, Lucas looked clean, and as unaccustomed to this lifestyle as she felt she was. Kari finished her drink and smiled vaguely. "Are you trying to get me drunk, Lucas?"

He nodded agreeably. "Our studies show that humans lose a lot of their inhibitions when they get that intoxicated. Yes, I'm trying to get you drunk."

She glanced up at the dark-skinned waitress who'd come to the table. "Ready for a refill?" The young woman asked them both brightly.

Lucas eyed Kari deeply with those eyes and she felt his gaze as if he knew her every thought. She smiled again, feeling the warmth in her thighs like the hunger of a dieter in the midst of a banquet. "Sure."

Lucas nodded, too, and the waitress left.

"So where do you work, Lucas?"

For a moment, his eyebrows came together and he seemed blankly puzzled, then he relaxed. "I'm working now."

Her teeth clenched. A gigolo? Did she look so desperate that he had chosen her? But then she let out her breath and tried to lose that thought. After all, *she* had come over to sit with him. "I don't understand."

"I know that must sound bad to you, Kari. I don't mean it that way at all. This is all very interesting and I'm enjoying it. Your world is much like ours once was. They really indoctrinated me in our planet's history and showed me the similarities in our early societies to yours. As your people would say, I'm having a good time, but everything I'm learning from you and these surroundings is a part of my . . . job."

Shaking her head again, Kari accepted her drink from the returning waitress and watched Lucas sip his new glass of beer. "So what is your job?"

He lowered his smooth voice and glanced around, waiting until the waitress was two empty tables away. Those eyes of his clutched her interest in spite of her disbelief. "We've lost our emotions, Kari. Specifically, we've lost love. We've lost our ability to feel the passion to go on surviving. Centuries of hatred, war, and greed. Self-interest and exploration at the expense of our knowing each other. For over three hundred years, our race has only communicated with one another through communication devices like your telephone and TV systems, and then only when absolutely necessary. We live one to a dwelling, delving only into our own joys. Our race has continued only through a clinical manufacture of children . . . a union of male and female in the laboratories." He stopped, puzzled again. "Children . . . is that the right word?"

More and more intrigued at how earnest and sincere he seemed, she nodded with a new giggle. "You could almost convince me." She sipped her drink and fluttered her lashes as curiosity became the intimacy of a secret. The alcohol rolled over her inner denials. "How long did it take you to practice this come-on line, Lucas? Not that I'm very experienced, but this is the wildest thing I've ever heard."

He chuckled, slowly stretching his hand to hers.

She took it, feeling new tingles at the touch of his slick flesh.

"You don't believe me?" He sighed, then formed a new grin. "But I feel a liking for myself in you, Kari."

"Yes," she admitted. "I like you."

Colors changed in his eyes once more and his forehead furrowed. "This is what I need to know. You like me and don't even know me. You have a desire for me and you don't even believe my words."

Finishing her glass, Kari refused all her own questions and hesitations. She overcame them with the memory of how she had stayed faithful to Clay since they met and married, and how she had learned that all the affairs he'd teasingly told her of just before his death were true—not just the lubricating pre-lovemaking fictions she'd believed them. "I like you, Lucas."

"Why?"

"I . . . I just do. You attract me. You don't need to tell me all these stories, okay? I had enough of that sort of thing from my husband, Clay, I . . . I'm lonely. I just need to be with someone. I was married to a man who betrayed me and I'm glad he's dead, but even he was better than being alone. I need to be held and loved by someone who will tell me he loves me. Someone who does love me."

"Loved. Love." He finished his beer and stroked her palm slowly. "Love is what I want to understand. Will you show me this love?"

Her new giggle combined with embarrassment and she looked down at the scarred table until she felt the redness leave her face. "I think you get the prize for the most original line, Lucas. Have . . . you tried this on many women?"

They stared at each other.

"You're the first human to approach me," he replied. "I just got here . . . and strangely, I was trying to think of a way to approach you."

She swallowed, feeling the desire she had known too long increase to a size she could not take care of alone this time. She knew that maybe this wasn't real . . . probably no more real than the love and interest her husband had pretended all those years when he returned home late after spreading himself so thinly throughout the city . . . spreading the thighs of a dozen women.

But she needed to be loved, even if falsely. The desperate plea in his eyes was her own. Now, she even wished for Clay. "Let's go," Kari said. "My place or yours?"

"My place, please. I need you to be there so I can better understand love."

She laughed as they both stood and he left money on the table. "Yeah," she said, "so you can save your people, right? Teach them the secret of love."

He nodded and accepted her hand as they walked out.

▼▼▼

Lucas drove with the same concentration he seemed to do every-thing with. The sleek sports job hummed as smoothly as his voice under his guidance, bringing them to a quiet and new apartment house. Lucas parked and led her to one of the ornate buildings, leading her inside.

Kari felt a strange unfamiliarity as she followed Lucas into the living room. Something about the furniture seemed unreal, almost surrealistic. The brown couch was styled with elegant edges she'd never seen before, and the walls were bare of pic-tures. A smell of plastic and the heavy musk of old fruit lingered in the damp air. A strange apparatus something like a camcorder stood on a tripod before the couch.

Through her lazy inebriation, Kari felt a sudden uncertainty. "What . . . what's that?"

"Just one of my tools."

"Are . . . you a pornographer?" She backed a step.

Lucas frowned. "I don't . . . know that word."

Anger stirred as she began to understand. All of it. The weird way of seducing her and plying her with those drinks . . . driving away her fears with curiosity. "I want to leave."

Lucas turned to her fast, holding out his hands. A sound of gibberish came from his fast lips, gutteral and foreign. More alarmed than ever, Kari held out her hands, too, but with threat.

"P-pul-please!" he finally got out the word out, his lips gyrat-ing like a lava lamp on fast speed. "We . . . need . . . you."

Kari kept her posture, feeling like a ludicrous boxer in her skirt with a hem too high and her low cut blouse. Everything . . . the whole night . . . closed in tight and she knew she had nearly been asking for this. She had resorted to the ways of her husband in her need of companionship. He'd told her of the way he seduced women . . . or how women seduced him. She remembered her body language and especially the way she'd fluttered her eyelashes and asked her pointed questions.

But she was horny after the months of masturbation. She wanted someone else's hands on her, that was all. However she didn't want it on film for someone else to enjoy while they relieved themselves in solitude.

And she wasn't the way Clay had been at all, either. He had his affairs even knowing that she was home waiting for him . . . to be more than responsive to him.

He'd betrayed her, and now this man, Lucas, was betraying her honest desire for him, too.

"Please . . . don't leave," Lucas implored her. "Love . . . I want you to teach me love. I felt it, I think. In your hands and the way we touched. I felt a stimulation I've never known—the joy of being with someone else and the pleasure—"

"You . . . tricked me!" Kari pointed at the tripod and bizarre, pyramid shaped camera with all its switches, dials and glowing readouts, appalled that it was aiming towards her now. She gasped as she moved and it swiveled to follow her. "What the hell do you want?"

"Love," he whispered desperately. "You said you needed love, and we need it to survive. Me. My people. I want you, Kari. You make me know an emotion that makes me feel alive and like I want to go on living. I don't know that I've ever felt it so strongly . . ."

His words soothed and annoyed her at once. The depth of his earnestness pulled her to him, but the rage of his use of her emotions were the memory of Clay. The way he had used her as a masturbatory toy when his evenings with other women were unsuccessful. "Why the camera?"

"It's not a camera," Lucas told her slowly, "not in the way you believe . . . just as I am not really an alien to your world." He hesitated, his rubbery mouth working up and down, back and forth. "I . . . think I know love for you, Kari. You have brought me love. Please, give it to me completely so I can love you the way you love."

The gentle words coated her anger. She pressed her fingers together and bowed her head for a moment, deep in the desire she'd nearly let slip away.

"I don't care," Kari whispered, moving into his arms. She met his lips and he took her anxious tongue, and the kiss filled her with memories, but even more, with satisfaction. She guided his slow fingers all over herself and sighed as their clothes fell to the carpet. She lay down among them and ignored the strange clamminess of his tight skin as he lowered himself into her.

▼▼▼

Unlike Clay . . . unlike any man she'd ever heard of, Lucas fucked Kari five times within the next two hours, and their orgasms were mutual. His stickiness was a jet into her own wetness. More potent than she'd ever known.

She was spent and weak, and was surprised that he was already hard again. "I . . . can't," she breathed heavily as he tried to fit himself inside her once more.

His eyes were a mixture of the gray and green, nearly luminous. "I have more to learn, Kari. I am understanding love. This is something good . . . something to save my people. I don't understand why your race limits its love practice or why my ancestors did the same. How can you tire of making love?"

All the strange things he'd said to her before came back to Kari as the effect of her drinks and long lust wore off and were satiated. She stroked the weirdly snaky skin that covered him again, studying those eyes and the strange apartment . . .

The camera that was still trained on her, making clicking, whirring sounds.

"You . . . you *are* from . . . another planet—"

He nodded. "Another galaxy. We heard of you from other races that have had our problem, and they recommended our visit to learn your knowledge of love . . ."

Flashes of scarcely glanced at tabloid headlines filled her mind: Of *"Space Aliens Impregnated Me!" "I Lost My Husband to Aliens," "Raped by Creatures from Outer Space."*

And despite her fear of AIDS and other disease . . . even being pregnant, she had forgotten to make him use a condom. "What have you done to *me*?"

Lucas smiled gently, stroking her face and hair with a caress. "I have learned love. I have made love with you, Kari, and now I can teach that love to my people. I see your fear but it is not possible. We cannot mate and create life that will grow inside you, and I have no sickness that you will take for your own. My sickness was only that of purposelessness, and you have cured me."

Kari sat up, gaping at his naked body that seemed to suddenly glow the way his eyes did. His skin was becoming a metallic shade and she saw the twitchings of golden veins underneath it. "What . . . will you do now, L-Lucas?"

He stood and went to the tripod. "I will teach my people. As you have taught me. We will learn the love. We will make the love and be renewed in purpose. We will survive."

She stood behind him, remembering.

Clay had learned his love from her, too. He had—

"What's wrong, Kari?"

She pushed him aside and grabbed the tripod, toppling its gear and raising it high.

"What—"

The curiously toned metal ripped out his cheek where it struck him and Lucas gargled a pinched cry, throwing up his hands as a ghastly yellow spray erupted from his torn flesh. His sounds became the nonsensical foreign garble once more and this time she drove the points of the tripod's legs into his abdomen.

If that was even what it was.

Much the way she'd murdered Clay with a fireplace poker. Just like Lucas had told her the truth of his origins, Clay had told her of his affairs, and she had never believed it until she had found him in the middle of an afternoon tryst.

Lucas crumpled to the carpet, his urine-like blood covering it grotesquely. His paling face was a vibrating movement of his now very inhuman features.

"The problem is, Lucas," she hissed. "You never really understood love until you've been betrayed. This is lesson number two for you alien freaks."

Kari walked to a window and opened it, releasing its wire screen to fall to the ground outside and make it look like someone had broken in, just as she had arranged the murder scene when she punished Clay. As the creature stopping writhing and twisting and its gibberish ended, she let herself feel a brief moment of sympathy for the planet—or planets—of people who had sent Lucas to find the secret of salvation.

Dressing fast, Kari went to the door and walked outside, looking up at the night sky of thousands of stars, wondering which one Lucas had come from. She sniffed.

There were lives out there, even alien, dying for the want of love.

Just like her.

Just like everyone.

FAST SEEDS
▼▼▼

NINA KIRIKI HOFFMAN

SILENCE lay like sunlight on the plants in the greenhouse under the desert floor. Kethra tapped a moisture collector on the ceiling with her stick. Drops that had formed on the inside of the long, moon-curved trough during the course of the day showered down on the redfruit plants below. She went to the next row and tapped the collector above the bean vines, then glanced behind her at the dark tunnel that led back to the living quarters and common rooms below the Spire, where most of the colony's activity took place.

No one was spying on her today. Dorm-mother Wani, large and usually reassuring, had been watching Kethra lately, scenting a secret—probably thought Kethra had been meeting with a boy; that morning at breakfast Wani had talked about conception and being careful because the colony could not support another baby yet. She had spoken to all eight of the girls from Kethra's cave, but her eyes seemed most often on Kethra.

Kethra plucked dead leaves from bean vines, putting them in one of her waist pouches to save for compost. She thought of Raz. Many times she had sat beside the whisper wall, speaking

through stone latticework with him. He worked in the shimmerstone mines, seeking in the darkness for the small petrified bodies of creatures that no longer lived in the upper world. Their ages-long sojourn underground transformed them into glossy jewels burning with cold colored fire that drew traders down from the sky and brought Spire necessities and repairs for equipment no one now living in the colony knew how to take care of.

Kethra had never seen Raz's face, but his voice was warm and gentle. He told her tunnel tales, of digging in the dark, of finding open caverns full of spires and the drip of liquid that smelled of fire, of the sounds miners heard beyond where they dug, how all suspected that strange uncatalogued creatures lived beyond the reach of light. Sometimes he talked of the future they might have together, asking her always what she wanted, though she had trouble finding answers. All she knew was that she loved the sun and the smell of green and the mist of water on her skin when she and the others sprayed the leaves, and she treasured glimpses of the sky. Sometimes she even thought of going up into the sky and beyond it, as the traders did—of going anywhere that did not close in on her the way the tunnels under Spire did.

Raz, she knew, had ideas beyond the mining tunnels where he worked, as well. He thought more of people than of places, though.

The only touch she had ever had of him was a breath of air through diamond fretwork in stone. She was not the sort to sneak across to the men's side for a secret meeting.

She ran down the rows, tapping the collectors to get it over with, though she should have waited for full dusk, when the greenhouse air cooled and the water would be less likely to evaporate again. Gallons escaped daily through the filtering skin that let in air and sunlight. Councilor Sala, oldest and leader of the women's side and one of the chief deciders, suspected there was a way of using the filter skin to keep the water in, but so much knowledge had been lost in the cave collapse of year ninety-seven, and the traders refused to bring new manuals for equipment that to them was 300 years out of date. Sometimes Sala said the traders all got together and decided what not to bring to the people. "They want to keep us hungry and few," she said. "If there were more shimmerstones being dug they would not fetch such good prices on other planets." In the meetings where the colony discussed this, they all had rage, but no one knew what to do; they needed what the traders brought to survive.

At the far end of the rows from the tunnel, Kethra moved between the kazi vines and the squash mounds to the most distant corner of the greenhouse. Leaves touched her as she passed; squash leaves had prickly hairs on them, but kazi felt like velvet. Laying her tapping-stick on the ground, she curled up between two kazi plants, took off her sash, unrolled it, and fished the found thing out.

It was almost as big as her palm, hard, black, and round. She rubbed it against her tunic and held it up to admire its sheen. She had found it on the ground when she swept up the common room after the last visit from the traders. She knew she should turn it over to Councilor Sala; anyone's gain was the community's gain. But it felt to strange to own something no one else had. She thought she'd keep it just a little longer. Sala needn't know when she had found it.

What was it?

A last lingering drop from the collector above fell onto her hand and touched the found thing. It moved. Kethra dropped it and snatched up her stick.

The black shell cracked and a root tip emerged like an albino snake coming out of a hole. It was a seed: a fast seed. Listening through the whisper wall, she had heard trader stories of such things. On other worlds, magicians had made plants that would grow fast, bear fruit, or be cut down and used for fuel. Another thing the traders would not share with Spire. Kethra raised her stick, ready to strike, and watched. The root reached this way and that, toward the light above and the earth below, but it did not find what it sought. As she watched, it withered.

She grasped one of the kazi vines. She held it above the seed and shook a few drops of water off it. Suppose the seed did grow into some sort of fruitplant? If it was a fast grower, if it made a protein they could eat, the colony might be able to expand. If a trader had carried it, it must be useful.

The root swelled as it absorbed the water, then sought more. Kethra bit her lip. Now it was small and easily quashed, but what if it got big and turned out to be poisonous? It might have slipped into a trader's tunic all by itself; some seeds did things like that, she had heard. Still, it was a thing worth examining. She chewed on her thumb and watched the root wriggling and reaching like a pale baby's finger. She had a big waterskin at her hip, slung on a strap over her shoulder, fat with water. Should she—?

Not here, not where the crops could come to grief. She reached down and pinched the seed from the back, away from the still-reaching rootlet. The time to show it to Sala was now; there might be a corner in one of the fallow greenhouses where they could raise this plant. She stood, holding the seed carefully between thumb and forefinger.

"Caught you," said Dooni, plump and pretty, the youngest girl from Kethra's cave. She had approached on bare, silent feet, and she pumped a mister at Kethra: it was a game they often played in the greenhouse, because here water helped, and elsewhere everything was so serious.

"No!" Kethra cried, but too late: the seed received a good dose of water. The root grew and reached, first toward the source of the spray, then around to Kethra's hand, still wet. When it touched her hand, root hairs sprouted from it, spreading out around her fingers like spinner-web, seeking every last drop. The parent root eeled across her palm and traveled up her arm, sprouting root hairs as it went, webbing her arm like a tight sleeve. In her hand, the first leaves emerged from the seed, spreading out to catch the late sun that fell through the sky filter above her.

"What is it?" asked Dooni in a hushed voice, the mister dangling from her hand. "Are you all right?"

"I don't know," said Kethra, her voice hoarse. She felt fear roiling in her stomach, tightening her throat; she wanted to tear the plant off her arm, but it might be useful still. The tip of the parent root reached her shoulder and crept down her back beneath her tunic. It had sent out secondary roots at the crook of her elbow, and she could feel them curling around to grasp her arm. As she watched, the central root toughened, growing bark except where the root hairs emerged. She felt as if a two-fingered hand had her elbow in its grip. The root hairs were less obvious, like the feel of wind rather than touch. "Go call Sala," she said, afraid to move. What if it dropped off her and grounded itself? Some plants poisoned the soil around them to kill off other plants, and this crop was important. A spring sandstorm had collapsed a roof on one of the other croplands, and everyone was on short rations already in anticipation of the shortfall.

Dooni ran away. Kethra closed her eyes and waited, trying not to think about this plant. She felt its roots prickling, though. She moaned. There was a warmth at her wrist and in the crook of her elbow; how could a plant have warmth? She felt warmth down her back, too, and needling prickles. She opened her eyes, because the plant was rustling. Green leaves spread out in a bush, rising from her fist, taller than her head. The lower ones were as large as her hands, rounded with toothed margins, and new ones sprouted from the top of the plant. As she watched, a darker tint flowed up the plant stem, spreading across the leaves along the lacework tracery of veins.

Her arm was growing tired but she was afraid to move. She felt the root embrace her waist. Looking down, she could see it moving under her tunic. A tip poked out through the gauze weave and curled around the waterskin. She moaned again. It pierced a small hole in the upper side of the waterskin. Then, as it drew in water, its grip on her strengthened. It pulsed across her back like a river; the now-brown snake down her arm widened, sending out more strong fingers that gripped her as she had imagined a lover would.

She felt the strength seeping from her and let herself realize that the plant had sent rootlets in under her skin; it must be sucking her blood; a plant needed food to grow. It could not drop off of her any longer. She walked, holding it high so it could not touch any of the crop plants, down to the watering-row and toward the caverns. Should it die from lack of light, that would be all right. She began to fear that, after all, it might seed. The salt in her blood had not poisoned it.

Dooni returned, leading Sala. They met her at the entrance to the greenhouse. "Gods," said Dooni, "it's grown. Oh, Kethra! Are you all right?"

"What is it? What action?" Sala asked.

"I think we should kill it," said Kethra. Her throat felt dry, and her voice came out a cracked whisper. "It's a fast seed, left behind by the traders. It's killing me."

Sala grasped her free arm and led her into the tunnel, into cool darkness relieved by the pale green glow of the web-spinners, phosphorescent worms which lived in colonies on the tunnel roofs. "We need council," she said. They stood a moment and watched the plant, which, removed from sunlight, drooped and ceased sprouting leaves. Kethra had stopped holding her arm up; the root structure embracing it did all the muscle work, maintaining its crooked, half-raised position. Even in the darkness Kethra could feel the roots at work, though their progress was slowed: gentle fingers edging around her sides to knit across her belly, one sliding into her navel but stopping when it reached the terminus, and another creeping down the crevice between her buttocks. She tensed, but it was too late: already it was inside her, and had sent another finger reaching for her other entrance. She closed her eyes and felt the root possess her birth canal. It did not force its way through any tissue. It just was, locked into her. Little curling fingers rooted through her pubic hair.

"Sala," she said, "Sala, please."

"Stay here, Kethra. Dooni, stay with her. I'll go get the deciders."

In a strange way the plant's possession of her was pleasant. She had never been embraced so firmly or completely. The roots shuddered against her as the one in her intestine fed on her waste products, strengthening the whole structure of the plant. She felt more secondary roots easing down her legs, branching here and there, a touch and then a caress on her knee, a bracelet around her ankle. The ones across her belly reached upward to cup her breasts. More activity on her back; a touch at the nape of her neck, and then warmth. An exploration upward, a prickle at the base of her skull, a brief piercing pain there. Gently as a mother putting a shawl over a child, the plant sent roots down her other arm, winding around, fastening down, the prickles again, again the warmth at the crook of her elbow and the inside of her wrist. She felt the weight increase in her right hand, where the leaves had sprouted. No, a lack of light did not kill this plant. She moaned.

"Oh, Kethra," whispered Dooni, "I'm so sorry. Are you—are you still alive?"

"I don't know," Kethra said, and then, "Water, Dooni? My throat is so dry."

And she was starving, too. Dooni held up her waterskin, eager to be of help. Kethra opened her mouth and Dooni poured water in, spilling it over Kethra, wetting her clothes and exciting the roots, spurring them on to renewed swift growth. One crept down Kethra's foot and plunged between her toes into the cave soil. "No," she said, and raised her foot; the roots encircling her legs had not yet hardened into confinement like those on her right arm, but were still soft and pliant.

The root, deprived of its new soil, curled back and wove between her toes. She was afraid to let her foot down again, but after three minutes of holding it raised, her strength failed her. The root had learned; it did not try to enter the soil again.

"Oh, gods," Kethra said, trying to think through the implications of that. A root crept up the back of her head and branched into fingers that wove through her hair. When one poked into her ear, she shook her head as violently as she could. It moved past. She did the same when one prodded her mouth, and when one eased into a nostril, and when one came near her eyes. The roots seemed to understand; they curled back on themselves and went elsewhere. "Keep them off my neck," Kethra begged Dooni.

"What? I can't touch that thing; suppose it can jump?"

"Use your stick. I don't want it to strangle me. Please, Dooni."

Dooni tapped the roots with her stick when she saw them venturing around Kethra's neck. They turned back. "Gods! How can it grow so fast?" She cried without sound except for jagged breath.

Sala returned, followed by three other councilors, all four of them cloaked. All carried bright lights, the ones they used in the common room to show the traders how fine the harvest was of shimmerstones. Dooni hid behind Kethra, ashamed, Kethra knew, to be half-uncovered in the presence of men. In Kethra's hand the plant rustled, turning its leaves broadside to the light. She saw that it had flowered in the dark, hundreds of white star shapes in clusters all over it.

"Even better," said Sala to the others.

"How to pollinate it? What's the vector?" said Councilor Tarami, oldest and leader of the men's side.

"Where to plant it?" said Councillor Holdin, a younger man, though Kethra knew that only because every man was younger than Tarami; looking at his cloak and veil, she could only sense he was tall and slender.

"Feed the girl," said Dorm-mother Wani. "Dooni, you always have food on you, I know you sneak it. Give Kethra whatever is in your pouch."

"But Dorm-mother!" Dooni edged forward. "Are we not going to tear this thing off her? She's still alive, she could maybe live, she could—"

"Well, I hope she does, as long as she can. She seems to be good soil," said the Dorm-mother. "Feed her."

Kethra felt faint, but she opened her mouth when Dooni held up soft crumbly bites of berrycake. "Water," she said in between bites, and Dooni gave her sips. The roots kept spreading, hugging her tighter all the time. She took two steps. The compass of her steps was smaller now; but a moment later, she felt the roots around her legs ease. Dooni had jumped away from her when she moved, afraid of contamination.

"How extensive is this thing?" asked Holdin, studying her.

Dorm-mother Wani came forward and, with her knife, slit Kethra's tunic and skirt and pulled them off. Kethra shivered; never had she gone naked in the presence of men. It was wrong for anyone but her husband to see her. She looked down at herself, the roots on her head cooperating, and she saw that she was almost encased in a brown net of rootwork, with a soft weave of roothairs filling all the gaps. No, no need of clothes, ever again; her flesh was hidden entirely, except for her face, neck and the soles of her feet. She took another step, testing, and the roots let her.

"The plant needs sun," said Sala, her voice remote. "It seems to bloom in darkness, but it needs sun. Where shall we plant her?"

"Why? Why?" Dooni cried.

"If you're going to have hysterics, leave your berrycake and waterskin with me; I'll finish the feeding," said Dorm-mother. "You go off and roll in a blanket; calm yourself."

"No," said Dooni. "No! It's my fault! I watered that thing!"

"Huh," said Tarami. He took his own waterskin and sprinkled some water on the roots. Brown-barked fingers lifted toward him, blind and seeking. He pulled the stopper out of his waterskin and poured its contents over Kethra. She felt the wet only a moment before the roots captured it all. Then she noticed the smell of the flowers, powerful, sweet, and wholesome. She looked into their hearts and saw the golden stamens moving, protruding, powdered with yellow, little thickets of them surrounding swollen central pistils.

"It's ready," said Sala. "Dooni?"

"What?" Dooni stood hugging herself, her eyes wide, their irises not tracking.

"Pollinate it."

"What?" Dooni blinked, stared. "Councilor, no!"

"Pollinate it now, or we'll plant the next seed in you."

She rubbed her eyes. With shaking hands she gathered pollen from one flower with her fingertip and brushed it across the pistil of another flower. The plant rustled. Flowers thrust forward. With tears running down her cheeks, Dooni transferred pollen from stamens to pistils. As she completed each flower cluster, it retreated into the parent plant. She glanced at Kethra only once, and then away. "This is Kethra," she said to the deciders when she was only half-finished. "This is the thing that is eating Kethra. Why am I pollinating this monster?"

"We have to see what it does," said Tarami. "How else will we know if we can use it to expand?"

"Curious how it leaves her face free," Sala said. She pursed her lips.

Wani took Dooni's cake and water and continued to feed Kethra. "One wonders if it was developed to feed off the human form," she said. A little root reached for her hand as she rested it against Kethra's chin, and she jerked back.

Kethra felt utterly calm. She knew she was no longer a person in their eyes, only a resource. She knew too what they would think of her for withholding information from them, not telling them that the plant could learn. How gently it crept up her intestine; she could almost feel its presence expand through her gut; perhaps a rootlet eased through her cervix and into her womb. It was almost time for her period; that might be the best plant food yet. Still, she could not feel it breaking her anywhere, except where her veins ran close to the surface of her skin. Behind her knees now, she felt familiar warmth as the plant tapped into her circulatory system. Would it know enough not to invade her heart?

"Let's put her in Greenhouse Five," said Sala. "It's fallow this season. Dooni, I charge you with caretaking this plant altogether. Water it as much as it wants, unless it takes ill of it. Fertilize the soil. Feed Kethra as much as she'll eat, anything she wants as long as she can ask for it, and after that, palithy porridge. Understand?"

"No," Dooni muttered.

"It's your job to take care of her, since you condemned her," Sala said. "Keep her as comfortable as you can. When she dies, let us know. When the plant fruits and seeds, if it doesn't in the next fifteen minutes, you must tell us that too."

"How do we transport her without it grabbing us too? Do you suppose it needs more than one person?" asked Holdin.

"It seems to be doing fine with just one," Wani said. Kethra held her mouth open, waiting for the next bite; she felt ravenous. Wani patted her cheek and shoved cake into her mouth. "Yes, you're wonderful," she crooned, the mothersong for a pre-speech baby. "Yes, you're perfect. Yes, you're beautiful." She poured a little water in. Kethra swallowed. "Hmm," said Wani, "this may be a full-time job. We might need more than one caretaker. I wonder how big this plant gets?"

"Well, we can't leave it here," said Holdin. "It's blocking the path to the crops. I suppose we could put it on a cart."

"I'll walk," said Kethra. All the roots had thickened since Tarami had watered them. Kethra took a step and found that they maintained enough elasticity for her to walk. She looked at Dooni, who pollinated the final cluster of flowers. Then she walked off down the tunnel toward Greenhouse Five. The councilors followed.

"We must limit her mobility," Tarami said. "We can't have her walking around when we don't know what the plant's properties are. She might wake up and recognize what's happening to her. She may resent this. We have to do something."

"It puzzles me why she hasn't rooted in soil," said Sala. "That thing certainly had time and opportunity when you consider the speed it lives at. If we dig a hole and bury her, I think she'll stay put. She doesn't seem to have any mobility in her upper body."

"Dooni, go to the living place; get a cart, get some skins of water and a lot of good food, and bring them back to Greenhouse Five," said the Dorm-mother. Dooni ran away without a backward glance. "Holdin, we will need shovels and plant food." Holdin glared at her a moment, then went off down the tunnel branch after Dooni.

Kethra walked past the next three branches that led deeper under the Spire, and took the turn away from the center of the colony and into the outlying greenhouse. Through the sky filter she saw the last streaks of sunset, and something in her yearned for sky. She knew now she would never climb up to see its other side.

The plant surged as it perceived light. Roots strengthened around her arms. She felt more weight in her right palm. Wani came and trickled water down her throat. She swallowed. It never seemed like enough. She wanted to dive into the largest reservoir pool in the cave and wash the sand from her mouth.

Presently she smelled a new scent, a scent that made her dry mouth water. Sweet and rich and ripe. She opened her eyes.

"It *is* fast," said Sala. She was aiming the light at the stems, leaves, and fruit. There were many fruit, small, velvet-skinned, orange with a red blush, inviting; even as they watched the fruit swelled and flushed. Tarami came closer, eyes wide above his veil.

The ripest fruit dropped to the ground. It rolled toward Tarami. He backed away.

"No," said Sala. "Oh, gods, how are we to collect it? Suppose it all roots here!"

Dorm-mother Wani took off her white decider cloak and spread it on the ground below the plant. She stood a moment, large in her tunic, her dark hair tumbling down her back, her broad face revealed. She stooped, hesitated, then picked up the loose fruit and tossed it on her cloak. No root reached out of the fruit to capture her.

Fruit began to drop, first a few, then a rain of them. They landed on the robe and glowed like jewels in the bright light.

Kethra stared at the fruit. Blood fruit, she thought. My body lies there. How beautiful. How amazing. How good it smells.

Holdin and Dooni came back with their burdens. Holdin went to the center of the greenhouse and dug. Dooni rolled her laden cart in, then joined him.

That is my grave, Kethra thought, watching the excavation. Dooni looked grim and angry. She dug with fury, flinging dirt behind her. Kethra opened her mouth and Wani, who had visited Dooni's cart, popped in a bite of steamed coney meat, a food normally reserved for nursing mothers. Kethra savored it. Dorm-mother Wani fed her more, and the water she dripped into Kethra's mouth was sweetened with kazi juice.

When the hole was deep and wide enough, Sala supervised the feeding of it, instructing Holdin in the use of fertilizer. "Three more steps, my child," Dorm-mother Wani told Kethra.

"That's all it will take. You have been very good about this, my love. You are a proper member of the community. We will tell Bard Tepesh about this and he will make a song of you."

"We'll take a syllable of your name and add it to ours," said Sala. "Five of us to make memories. Especially if we figure out how to use this plant for the good of everyone." She pointed toward the hole.

Kethra took three steps to the hole's lip, then stared down. "Please help me," she whispered. The hole was deep and the sides were steep.

Sala looked at the others. She walked forward. After a brief hesitation, she reached out to take Kethra's right elbow.

Holdin went to Kethra's other side and grasped her left elbow. Between them they lowered Kethra into place, releasing her with alacrity and studying their hands to see if the roots had invaded them.

Kethra stood elbow-deep in dirt. Holdin and Dooni shoveled fertilizer in around her, mixing it with the dirt they had removed. What dirt was left over they mounded around her, covering her arms, her back, her breasts, until at last only her head and shoulders and the leafy structure of the plant were still above the soil. The cool earth felt good against the soles of her feet, and every crevice it touched her through. The fertilizer smelled strong and acidic and familiar.

She relaxed, let the soil support her. She had not realized how tense she was until that moment. The roots stirred around her, creeping further, then resting.

Sala brought over two skins of water and sprinkled their contents over and around Kethra. "Hold the light closer, Tarami. Let's see what happens."

Kethra felt the damp as water seeped down through loose soil, then the movement and shift of roots. Their grip on her was almost courteous. She sensed them spreading out from her, sending out new hands and fingers under the soil; she was almost as inside them as they were inside her. Some dived downward after vanishing drops. Others plunged upward in search of the source. "More water," Kethra said. Wani came with a skin to dribble some in her mouth, but she spat it out. "There," she said, nodding to the soil. Wani sprinkled water. Pale root fingers shot up into the air like buried hands reaching. Tarami gasped and the light faltered. Wani shuddered, but emptied her skin over the reaching roots.

"What sort of life cycle can this plant have, when it lives so quickly?" said Sala. "Maybe it will die by morning."

Wani knelt beside Kethra and tapped her lips. Kethra opened her mouth. At Wani's prompting, she bit into unfamiliar fruit. It was plump and full of tart sweetness, firm as flesh. Her teeth hit a seed. "What is it?" she asked, frightened and surprised.

"How does it taste?"

"Good. I've never—" She wailed, looking at the fruit in Wani's hand: one of her own.

Wani scooped a hole in the mound above Kethra's left hand. "I thought we'd plant another seed, see what happened," she said, burying the half-eaten fruit. She watered it. "In case this one dies in the night, the next one can get a start."

"This is ugly and without honor," said Dooni.

"This is strategy and a gift from heaven," Tarami corrected her. "Keep good care of her. Feed her, water the plant, give it food; watch and make notes."

Kethra felt little roots nuzzling her left hand, like the noses of newborn kittens. They tangled with the roots already there, then meshed. The soil around her was cold, but the roots were neutral, almost warm. She felt sleepy. She blinked and watched a little shoot rise from the soil where Wani had planted the fruit.

Sala set her light on the ground and knelt beside the new plant, peering at it. It spread fragile leaves out, flat side to catch light. "I think I'll keep first watch with Dooni," she said. "Leave the lights here, and send someone at hour twenty to see if we survive still. Who knows?"

Wani touched Kethra's forehead, then leaned to kiss her. "Farewell, daughter. You honor us. I name myself Wanira."

"You should wait and see," Kethra said. She wished she could be as warm as the Dorm-mother's lips.

"Whatever happens," said Wani. "You deserve to be remembered." She went to her cloak and lifted it. None of the other fruits had rooted through it, though it would not have stopped them, being rough weave. "I'll put these in the cold cave, in a hanging basket far from everything else; perhaps that will preserve them until we figure out what to do with them. Dooni, you feed her. Feed her well. Your instincts are good: first fruits is what she needs to keep her strength up."

"Don't give them any water," Kethra said, pointing with her chin toward the cloak full of fruit. Wanira nodded.

Her sleep was disturbed every time Sala or Dooni watered her, for the roots responded each time, rippling and wriggling around her. But in between interruptions, she dreamed of Raz in the deep tunnels below Spire, Raz whom she would never now see. He would tell his tales to some other girl, his voice reaching inside her and warming her heart.

Kethra slept upright and dreamed of Raz.

Then the other dreams came. She was a small thing, then a spreading thing, then a thing as wide as the desert, tasting traces of strangeness at her outer edges, sensing that beyond the stretches of sand lay other kinds of life, worth exploring. The sun would hurt her—unless she spread downward and tapped into the deepwater, the water nothing could remove. She struggled and pulsed and pushed downward. She met stones and webbed around them, seeking crevices in them, seeking to encompass and break them. Obstacles everywhere, but finally success. No more small inadequate dribbles of water: all the water in the world. She felt flushed and strong and invincible with her taproot linked to deepwater.

She woke and stretched, feeling the sun on her surfaces, spreading leaves and shifting them to catch it, for there was shadow, too, and there was no food in shadow. Sun and water, and the human humus. She felt drunk with delight and satiety.

"Kethra?"

She opened her eyes and looked at the forest of herself. Leaves fountained up from the ground to her right and left. She sighed and smiled. She could feel the sun on them, could feel each leaf bud drawing strength and water from its parent plant and sprouting, spreading. Time for flowers again, she thought. This time blue ones perhaps, and fruit more like apples.

"Kethra, you still in there?" asked Dooni, kneeling beside her head.

She looked at Dooni.

"Kethra? Are you hungry?"

"Starving," she said.

Dooni hunched beside her and fed her from a large bowl of warm palithy porridge. Kethra ate, and listened to all the messages she was receiving. She knew someone else was in the greenhouse, beyond her foliage; there was a pressure and a presence on the earth—she felt it through the network of roots she had spread out under the surface here—a casual thing, an afterthought; it wasn't likely water would rain down through the sky filter, but she had sent roots out anyway: a sensory net. Leaves did sun work, and roots did water work, and both did food work. But with Kethra in the middle of it, things were different. She had other interests besides maintenance, growth, and propagation. Who was hiding just the other side of her above-ground self? She sent roots up to taste the person, but the person did not sit still for tasting. There was a shriek. It was in Pesha Plant-mother's voice.

Dooni jumped up when she heard Pesha. She spilled the

porridge. Roots rose to imbibe the rest. "What is it, what's happening?" Dooni cried.

"Roots," said Pesha, coming around the broad bushes of the twin plants. "Roots came up through the soil! Roots don't behave that way. Roots only go down!" She stared at the roots among the porridge. "What is this thing?" She unsheathed her knife and reached for a branch, which whipped away from her.

"Don't!" said Kethra.

"But—" Pesha said, reaching again. The plant rustled and arched. "Oh, very well. How am I to study it without a sample?"

"Find a way," said Kethra, "please." The plant-thoughts she was receiving scared her. The plants had already had a human sample, and analyzed it; the plants knew substances they could create that would upset a human system.

Dooni knelt beside the split porridge. "Kethra, I'm sorry."

"It's all right," said Kethra. She felt very strange, suddenly; her stomach still growled, but she could feel nutrients entering her through the needle-roots in her skin. "Oh," she said, "oh, no." The plants no longer needed to feed on her, so now the flow was reversed, as if the plants had decided she was a part of them that should be preserved and nourished. She remembered being one with the tap root and thinking about flowering and fruiting. These plants could learn. These plants had thoughts. These plants had their own plans, and somehow she knew them. "No, don't feed me," she said to the plants, "let me go. Just let me go."

"What?" said Dooni, who had gone to her handcart for more porridge.

Kethra breathed loudly and tried to move her fingers. She could feel that her hands were the cores of rootballs beneath the two plants. "You don't need me anymore," she whispered, and wriggled her fingers, tried to move her arms. The roots clamped tighter around her, sending in more needles to lock her into stillness. She felt a stirring in her gut and remembered how entwined she really was. "Oh," she said. No. There was no escape. She felt new rootlets snuggling against her in the soil, nudging at the ones that already held her. One crept up out of the earth to loop over her shoulder, growing fingers and settling on her like the hand of a friend.

She felt the utter despair she had had no time for the night before. She was buried in the ground and would never emerge again. Most of the colony's corpses were at least dead before they became plant food, but she was alive, and now the plants had discovered how to keep her that way whether she willed it or not. There were roots in her vitals; the only thing she could move was her head.

Dooni poured water down her throat. She coughed.

"Were you serious? You don't want anything else to eat?" Dooni asked when Kethra stopped coughing.

"No. I was talking to the plant. It's feeding me now."

Dooni stared into her face. Kethra looked back. "I had thoughts," Dooni whispered. She glanced behind her. Pesha Plant-mother was making notes, not paying attention. "I thought when we discovered whether the plant could live alone, whether it would sprout without you, we could cut you free; we can always make new plants, now that we have so much fruit. And I thought, if we could not cut you free, that a quick death might be a mercy. I hoped . . ."

"I did too," Kethra said. She had envisioned being eaten alive, and thought at some point the plant would interrupt some vital system and kill her, quickly or slowly, but somehow. "But I don't think it's going to happen."

After another glance at Pesha, Dooni reached into her sash and got out the pruning knife she always carried. "Sister," she whispered, laying the blade against Kethra's throat.

"No," Kethra whispered. "Not yet. I'm not ready yet. Thank you."

Dooni resheathed her knife. "Look." She held up a jerked strip of lizard meat. "Would you like some of this?"

"Yes."

Dooni pulled bite-sized shreds off the strip and fed them to Kethra. Kethra ate to quiet the hunger in her stomach. She began to remember: when she ate, she made waste the plant could eat. Perhaps her life would be orgy of eating; she had never had enough to eat before. She closed her eyes a moment, and suddenly she was loose again, no longer confined to a caged body, but in among all the roots and stems and leaves. The plants were in ferment, preparing to bloom.

And below the soil, the roots stretched for ages. Prompted by her dreams the night before, the plants had sent roots toward the mines below. Kethra reached out along them, channels of water and nutrients, only the tips and edges where the roothairs could sprout really aware of their quest, blind but sensitive to changes in the soil and to the pull of gravity. Suddenly the roots stubbed on little pebbles. They sent out the hairs, which would slip through smaller spaces, pioneer pathways; the roots followed. Beyond the shoal of pebbles, more soil, rich in ancient decayed life-stuff, and then, a little further, the roots broke through into open air, perceived as an area of aimlessness, no food or water or direction beckoning. *The mines*, Kethra thought. She sent herself out to the tips of the roots there, feeling the air as if it touched raw skin. Vibration tingled through the roots.

The air carried signals the roots didn't understand, but when Kethra tuned herself to them she realized the shifts and tingles were sounds. Excited, she focused on the variation of vibration, and the roots responded, changing their surfaces, growing things that were not like roots. With all her heart Kethra poured need and want into her presence at the edge of the roots, and the roots responded.

At first she found muddy mutters, but she listened, and words emerged. "—think the reef might continue over here," a voice was saying when at last she could sort it out from the other signals.

"You've got sand in your brain. Mishwa cleaned out this deposit fifty years ago."

"I've been studying the three-dee, and it looked to me like there might be another deposit *just here*," said the first voice, its vibrations growing stronger. "And look, here's a little flare gravel. I wish that damn core sampler still worked. I'd like to take a core from right through here, see if I'm right—hey, what's this?"

The roots sensed heat, moisture in breath. Something stroked along one of the sensitive areas the roots had made for her, and Kethra felt as if she had been burned.

"Roots," said the voice. "Roots? How can that be? The three-dee puts this tunnel under a fallow greenhouse. . .have you ever seen roots in a tunnel this depth, Kimli?"

"Get away! Didn't you hear the whispers at breakfast this morning? Some new crazy-plant that eats people—"

"Turn on your brights."

A moment passed. Her rootskin sensed a tiny change in temperature. Kimli said, "We should tell the supervisor. Raz, you stay here and watch them. Don't get too close. We don't know what they do. I'll go find Linnis."

Raz, Kethra thought. She twined roots around several of the little hard stones she had gone past on her way to the mine. She pushed the stones through the soil and out into the air. They dropped from the mine wall. She sensed Raz stooping to pick them up. He gasped. "Shimmerstones. How—what—?" He touched one of the root tips and she curled it around his finger. "What?" he said. He laughed and thrust his hand into the thick of the roots.

She was touching him. Before, only their murmurs and their breaths had mingled, and their minds, a little. She wanted to pull him into the wall, to own him, to have a companion with her under the earth. But he would surely smother. It would take much more preparation.

What was she thinking? How could she ask someone else to give up everything he knew and be buried alive?

A simple prick or two with a needle root, and she could pump something into him that would make him feel sleepy. Once he settled down to rest she could envelope him, make him a part of her.

That was crazy.

She pressed root fingers against his hand, then pulled them back into the soil, pushing three more shimmerstones out through the wall.

"Come back," he said, knocking on the wall.

Kethra sensed the arrival of two new people, heard Tarami's voice say, "Don't touch it!"

"What?" said Raz.

"Where has it gone? Were there really roots?"

"Yes. Look, Councilor! They gave us stones. What sort of plant is this?"

"Something called a fast plant, from a trader seed. It ate a girl last night. We are tending it to see if it will benefit us. Don't touch it!"

"Ate a girl? *Ate* a girl?"

"Mm. Kethra di Lukasai."

"What!" Raz came to the wall and put his hands flat to the earth, their heat and the exchange of air and moisture on the skin surface close, so close to her outer edges. "Kethra, come back!"

She thrust roots out and looped them around his fingers, tying them to the wall. He gasped.

"I told you not to touch it," said Tarami in a grouchy voice. "Now we'll probably have to forfeit you, too; the girl was sacrifice enough. Gods!"

"Forfeit me?" Raz said. He wiggled his fingers. "Kethra, let go," he said, and she released him. "Thank you. You won't hurt me, will you?"

"Come away from there," said Tarami. "What are you playing at? Do you understand lizard language because you have eaten a lizard? Does the bean plant have a voice because you have eaten its fruits? What makes you think a plant understands you? You're a trained laborer. We need your skills. Don't take any more foolish chances."

Raz leaned against the wall. "Kethra, we never had a chance to move past whispers," he said, "but I loved your voice and longed to kiss you." He put his lips to the wall. She sent a root tip between his lips, then had to retract it, for when it sensed the moisture in his mouth, it started sending out root hairs. She used other tips to touch his face; sensing in all of them, she built a composite image in her mind: long nose curved like the beaks of birds who hunted meat from the sky, in ancient vidpix; high cheekbones, deep-set eyes, heavy brows, and a high forehead.

"Leave that wall alone!" said Tarami.

"But—"

"Come up to the greenhouse! If you want to give yourself up to this foolishness, at least do it in a convenient place."

"Kethra!" Dooni was yelling in her ear.

"Quiet," said Kethra. "Gods' bones, I'm not deaf!"

"You are," said Dooni. "I thought maybe you had died. I've been speaking to you this past half hour."

"I was somewhere else," Kethra said.

"What?" Pesha knelt beside her. "Explain, please."

"No," said Kethra.

"Explain, or no more water."

"Sister!" said Dooni, outraged. "No threats. My sister has done enough for the community already. Leave her alone. I'll get you whatever you need, Kethra."

"Thanks. Here he comes."

Tarami, cloaked, led Raz, who was clad only in a loose tunic (arms, legs, thought Kethra; not so very different from a woman's) into the greenhouse with Sala, Wanira, and Holdin trailing after.

Raz stumbled forward and looked down at her. "Kethra? Is this you?" he said, falling to his knees before her. "Is this what you look like?"

"This is my face. Oh, Raz. I thought our meeting would be different."

He lay before her, gripped her root-capped head in his hands, and kissed her mouth. Heat rushed through her. She heard her plantselves rustling. She closed her eyes and embraced him, loving the firm lean length of him, imagining it lying against her.

A while later she opened her eyes. He leaned away from her a little and looked at her, his light brown eyes smiling. His face was different from the one she had constructed by touch, its peaks and valleys less severe than she had thought. "The councilor said the plant ate you," he said. "But—" and then he looked at himself. Strong roots anchored him to the ground. "Oh," he said. "Kethra?"

"Gods," she muttered.

Tarami stood above them. He emptied two waterskins over Raz's back and watched the roots swell and strengthen and lock down on Raz. "Still just as fast," he said with detached interest.

"Stop that!" said Sala.

"He volunteered to be a sacrifice."

"I did?" Raz said. He struggled. "Kethra, let go, all right?"

"I—"

"No, let's wait and experiment," said Tarami. He watered Raz again. "What would happen if we planted one of the seeds in the middle of his back?"

"Enough!" said Wanira. She knelt beside Raz and tugged at the roots. They were now as thick as her forearm. Kethra concentrated; by feeling her way into the roots Wanira touched, she was able to loosen them. For the moment, she left them on the surface.

Raz slid free. He sat back on his heels. "If I *am* going to join you, I want to do it upright," he said.

"Don't," said Kethra. "Please don't. Be safe."

"But—"

"Please, Raz. I don't want you." A root lifted and curled around his ankle.

He looked at it and smiled.

"Go away," she said. She had lost touch with the roots, but she knew they were stirring now, awake and active. "You don't want this. I will never escape, and if you stay, you won't either. It's up inside me." She took a deep breath, blew it out. "It's in my gut, and it's in my dreams. It's in my brain. Go away."

Another root lifted and clamped down on his other ankle. The roots were making noise under the earth now, and little piles of earth rose around her and Raz and the plants.

"You understand?" Kethra said. "You'd be stuck here. At their mercy." She pointed with her chin toward where the councilors and Pesha and Dooni stood. "Pesha already threatened to withhold water. Get up, Raz, go away while you still can."

"At *their* mercy?" Raz said. He laughed. He leaned back and pulled off his shoes, tossing them toward the greenhouse door. Then he gripped the roots that gripped him.

She felt strange. All the needle roots in her arms were pulling out of her, and the roots that had locked her into position were loosening. Something pushed at her palms. Her arms, which had been bent with hands in front of her for a day at least, moved out to her sides. It was not her muscles doing the work.

A pit opened in the ground before her between the plants. It was a well walled with roots. One reached up and caught Raz's wrist, pulling him forward, as the roots around his ankles relaxed. He made a fist and resisted the pull a moment. The room held deep silence. He breathed loudly. Then he laughed, came forward on his knees, slipped into the pit feet first, and ended up beside Kethra. "Much better," he said, and kissed her again, his arm around her shoulders. Roots whipped up and locked his arm where it was, as the others underground fastened on to him, gripping and exploring him. Still others pulled the dirt back into the hole.

"Wait," said Dooni. She came forward and poured fertilizer from a cloth sack Holdin had brought the day before. She pulled loose earth from the little piles everywhere and helped the roots pack it in around him, mixing fertilizer with it. Roots stroked her calves as she worked. She shuddered and ignored them.

Wanira brought over more water. She showered it over both of them. Raz looked up. Then his eyes widened, and he looked down. "Hey," he said, his tone outraged. He jerked. He shuddered. "Oh, well," he said, and closed his eyes. Kethra watched him writhe. She could feel her way into the roots again; she was in them as they crept around him, working in beneath his clothes, needling under his skin and tasting the different things he had in his blood, weaving him right into a web, entering him where they could.

Kethra's arms were still loose among the working roots, and she brought one forward, pushing between rough roots and smooth roots until she touched Raz's skin. He looked at her, astonished, and she smiled, because she had not known whether he would be able to tell the difference between her fingers and the plant's touch. Then she felt the familiar needles reentering her arms, the familiar clamping down that restrained movement, but she did not mind so much, aware of her hand flat against his side; aware still of his arm against her shoulders, a brief expanse of skin to skin where the roots did not penetrate. Roots grasped them, locked her hand on him as though they were one flesh.

"Are you directing them?" he asked.

"No," she said. She felt his ankles. She sent a little root beneath his foot and tickled the sole. "Maybe one or two." she said as he chuckled.

Then he sucked in breath between his teeth, a flat painful sound.

"What?" she said, then knew a root tugged at a toe which bent the wrong way. She pulled it loose. "Did you break it?"

"Two weeks ago. Thanks."

"What are you talking about?" asked Wanira, sitting cross-legged beside them.

Raz looked at her: Kethra watched his gaze move from Wanira's head to her bottom, and then he was sharing a glance with Kethra, one eyebrow lifted.

"No," she said, but she grinned, thinking of sending a root up to goose Wanira.

"Just wait," he said.

She stared at him and lost her smile. She thought of how he had talked those days at the whisper wall. One day, he had said, he would set law with the councilors, and talk tough to the traders until Spire got what it needed. So that was why— She closed her eyes. She let herself be all plant, everywhere.

The taproot had swollen since that morning, and had been joined by several others. Its root hairs had pulled minerals from the soil to armor it. She knew they would never lack for water; Pesha's threat was empty. The network of roots spread down to the mines, just because she had dreamed of Raz. She felt other roots creeping out toward the greenhouses presently in use, but most went toward the Spire's living quarters. She had a net of roots below the kitchen floors, and a thicker net under the store rooms where the fertilizer bags were stacked, and under the waste-processing works. Several roots had snuck up under the compost heap and were already pilfering from it. A scattered few lurked under the sleeping caves, both the men's side and the women's. And beyond the next wall, in another fallow greenhouse, roots had surfaced and started shoots, upper air plants with leaves spread for sunlight. These leaves were adapting to the desert, thickening their skin, trying different shapes. They were transforming sunlight and producing much food. The plant-self would survive.

Kethra stared at Raz and wondered how much of this he had understood. Had he realized he could grasp power by joining the plant? Did he love her at all? She remembered his laugh when he said, "At *their* mercy?" How had he known?

His eyes were sad. He bit his lip.

Wanira tapped him on the head and he looked up at her. "What are you talking about?" she asked.

"My toe. Please don't hit me again."

"Your toe?" she said.

Raz glanced at Kethra. "Cast me out if you want. I do love you."

"What did you plan to do with this?" Kethra asked.

"I don't know." He shook his head as if trying to shake off a fly. He turned. A root was creeping up his neck. "Oh," he said, "Oh, no."

"This is the important one," said Kethra. "Hold still."

"Don't. You don't trust me." He shook his head violently, evading the root.

"It won't matter," said Kethra.

"What? Why not?"

She dropped a root over his head and clamped it tight. "Hold still," she said.

"What if I'm stronger?"

"The plant is the strongest. It decides."

"All right." He closed his eyes. The root crept up his neck and needled in through the base of his skull. He grimaced, then relaxed. His face blanked.

"Are you directing the roots?" Wanira asked.

"Me?" said Kethra.

"Raz seems to think you are. Kethra, can you control the plant?"

"Not exactly. Sometimes it cooperates with me."

"By thought?" asked Wanira, her brow puzzled.

"It reached roots down to the mine and romanced Raz," Tarami said. "He called it Kethra and it obeyed him. That's why we came up here in the first place."

Kethra felt the roots tensing and relaxing against her skin. She looked at Raz, who was staring at her. A root lifted and tapped her chin. He was there, inside it. He tipped his head back and looked at the leaves above him. They rustled. Then the twin plants burst into bloom, buds folding back to reveal blue five-petaled stars. The scent was wild and strong, spicy on the warm still air. Dooni went to the plants; they thrust their flowers at her as if they recognized her. This time she pollinated back and forth between the two plants.

"It is very odd," Pesha Plant-mother said. "You said first flower was white, Dooni?"

"Yes," said Dooni, "and there were six petals to each flower, and the flowers were smaller." A cluster of flowers brushed her nose and she batted it away. "Stop that," she said, wiping pollen off her nose. "Wait your turn."

"How can we use this?" Holdin asked. "I still don't understand. Trade the fruit?"

"If a trader brought this seed, as Kethra said, surely traders know the properties of these plants. That they have never offered them to us means they have a value we are not supposed to have access to," said Sala. "The medic is analyzing the flesh of one of the first fruits. He says it is nourishing and not dangerous. Two have volunteered to live off the fruit for a couple of days and see how their health is." She watched the flowers. "If it grants us a crop a day without exhausting our resources, if we plant more of these plants and they prove reliable producers, we have our expansion begun."

"We can help with mining," Raz said. "Kethra pushed shimmerstones out of the wall for us with the roots down below."

"What?" said Sala. She grinned.

Tarami said, "We must plant some seeds without using people for food and see what happens. Perhaps this is not the way this plant normally behaves."

"No," said Kethra. She had an image of the plant's wants and desires. Growth, maintenance, propagation. Without a human mind in the mix, diverting the plant's attention, expressing her own needs . . . There were far more efficient ways to grow and spread. The plants knew the ways of plants in competition for survival. In all the places she had roots, it would be so easy to poison basic supplies, or just drug them, creating human-sized organic matter to feast on. She could kill the crops just coming ripe with a thought. She looked into Raz's eyes and wondered what he was thinking, if he knew.

"Why not?" Tarami demanded.

"Wait. Please, wait, Councilor," she said. When Kethra had spread her roots everywhere, so they could touch whatever was planted, she knew she could get the new plants to join her, the way the second one had when it sprouted. And if she cared for the life of the colony, the plants might too.

"Who are you to advise me, head on the floor?" asked Tarami.

A root touched her lips. She looked at Raz and knew he was right. They dared not tell what they could do. Water misters could spray poison, and there were still a few working lasers and flamethrowers in the colony armory. At her thought, the rootworks sent fingers out in that direction.

"I see no harm in waiting a while. We have plenty to explore here," said Sala.

"Kethra, when you think at the roots, they do what you want?" Wanira asked.

Kethra looked at Raz, who looked back.

Sala, carrying a shovel, squatted beside Wanira. "A good question, Councilor," she said. "Kethra, when you told Raz to hold still, a root gripped his head. Are these roots like your hands? What can you make them do?"

Kethra shook her head as much as she could.

Sala sighed. She closed her eyes a moment. Her lips moved and no sound came out. Then she opened her eyes and said, "Kethra, I name myself Salaketh. Forgive me." She raised the shovel two-handed above her head, then swung it at Kethra's head, putting muscle into it.

Roots shot up and grasped her wrists, crushing them until she screamed in pain. The shovel fell from her hands. Her face went white.

"Stop it," said Kethra. "Stop it! Let go."

The roots released Salaketh. She collapsed, groaning. She curled up, holding her arms against her chest. A thick dark root snaked out of the ground and curled over her, holding her down, and two others captured her ankles. She lay quiet a moment. Then she rolled her head to look at Raz and Kethra, her face still pale and shocked. "Well, that answers the question of whether you can protect yourself," she said. A pale root crept up the side of her head and entered her mouth.

"Don't," said Kethra. "She has to figure things like that out. She's a councilor."

"I know," said Raz. "It's water and dispa."

The root lifted from Salaketh's mouth. She swallowed. She shook herself, and the roots released her. She held her broken wrists above her and looked at them dispassionately.

"We can make dispa?" Kethra asked. The painkiller came from a plant very hard to cultivate, it needed so much care. A chill draft could kill it. Dispa was always in short supply.

"I think we can make anything we've ever tasted. We just have to learn how to think," said Raz.

"But dispa! How did you make dispa?"

"I thought its taste. I snuck some when I broke my toe, so it's taste was right in my mouth."

"Who's watering whom?" Salaketh asked them, rocking herself to sit up without using her hands. A broad brown root emerged from the ground behind her and pushed her upright. She shuddered. "No," she said, "I don't think we had better trade any of this fruit. Kethra?"

"Sala?"

"Anything you want. Mention it and it's yours. You too, Raz."

"Salaketh?"

"Raz?"

"What we want. We want to live. All of us, I mean every bit of us. That's all."

Salaketh scooted closer to them and sat, cradling her hands. "That's what we all want," she said. "That's what we're fighting for. Raz, you saw the overview sooner than anyone else. You embraced this thing. Why aren't you a councilor?"

"It wasn't time," he said. He glanced up at the leaves and flowers, then at Kethra. "Leaves, roots, no flowers or seeds yet. I needed to lay my groundwork, and I wanted to bond with Kethra. But now . . ."

Kethra, sensing and remembering what Raz had done in the root that had given dispa to Sala, glanced at him. *We just have to learn how to think.* She remembered the taste of steamed coney meat, and she thought about it to the plants, then thought, *No, not yet. Later. Here's what an apple tastes like.*

"Now," said Salaketh. She shivered.

"Salaketh, are you Chief Councilor?" Raz asked. No one who was not a decider knew who headed the group; speech to one was considered speaking to all.

Salaketh looked at Wanira, Holdin, Tarami. "I am," she said.

"Thank the gods," said Raz. "I thought it was Tarami."

"Ah," said Salaketh.

"We need someone who will listen to us."

"I will," she said.

"You won't destroy us?" he asked.

"No," she said, and then, "how could we?"

Kethra and Raz looked at each other. "It would be difficult," Raz said.

"We are part of the colony," said Kethra. "We don't want to lose that. Let us work with you."

"Yes," said Salaketh. She smiled. Then her smile eroded into a mask of pain. She stared down at her crushed wrists. "Should have tried it one-handed."

A slender root crept up her arm. When it reached her shoulder, she turned to it and accepted it between her lips. A little later it lifted away from her; she wiped her mouth on her shoulder. "What was what?" she asked.

"Strong-makers," said Kethra.

"Dispa. A little silidi?" Raz said. Kethra nodded.

"Thanks. Where do you get your water? Are you in the pool?"

Kethra and Raz exchanged glances. They kept silence.

"Ah," said Salaketh. "Never mind. I think I'll go to the physician now. Help me up?"

Roots grasped her upper arms and lifted her to her feet. "Thanks," she said again. "I will consult with you later." She left.

Tarami spat on the ground and followed her, but Holdin came and sat beside Wanira. "What just happened?" he said. "I didn't follow."

Wanira sighed. "Kethra and Raz are Chief Councilor," she said.

"Oh," said Holdin. "That's what I thought. I wasn't sure." He leaned forward. "Can you make wine?" he asked.

Raz looked at him, eyes alight. "What kind?"

"The best kind, whatever that is. We could expand our trade base." Something fell on his head. He looked up.

The fruit had ripened on the bushes. It was large and greenish gold. One fell and landed in Holdin's lap. He picked it up. "What are we supposed to do with this, anyway?"

"Eat it," said Raz.

"Look, I admire you, but I don't want to become you. Actually, I think you're crazy."

"Eat it," said Raz. "We don't want you to become us, either."

Holdin shrugged, lowered his veil, and bit into the fruit. "Oh," he said, and ate faster. He reached up and another fruit fell into his hand. When he had eaten a third, leaving only nine black seeds, he said, "Gods, it's the best thing I've ever tasted." he put his hand up to the plant, then lowered it before taking a fourth fruit. "And I've had enough." He held out the seeds. "What—"

"Over there," Kethra said, pointing with a leaf to a place a little distance away where she had a nest of roots.

Holdin lifted earth and set the seeds in a hole, covered and watered them, then frowned at Kethra. "You said not to plant."

"It's all right there."

Fruit began to fall. Holdin picked up another. "So this isn't dangerous?" he said, opening a pocket at his waist.

"Sure it is," said Raz.

"What?" He clasped his hands over his stomach as if expecting instant indigestion and stared at Kethra and Raz.

"They're addictive," said Raz. "Just wanted to try it. See how you feel in a couple hours, and tell us about it."

"Oh, yeah?" Holdin jumped up, got one of the empty fertilizer sacks and filled it with fruit. "I'll be comfortable for a little while, anyway."

"We're not going to kill you," said Kethra. "We don't kill anybody. We'll change it into something else later. Don't worry."

"I'll try not to." He left.

Wanira picked up one of the fallen fruits and smelled it.

"Gods," she said, but a root snagged her wrist before she could bite into the fruit. "Why not?"

"Because we're new," said Kethra. "Maybe we're not doing this right. Please, Mother, don't take a chance."

Wanira set the fruit on the ground. "Dooni?" she said. "Where are you?"

"Shh," said Raz.

"She's asleep. She has been up a day, a night, a day, taking care of us."

"And Pesha? She was here." Wanira stood up.

"I put her to sleep," said Kethra.

"Kethra," said Wanira, edging around the plants to where Dooni lay in an earth cradle with leaves spread to shelter her, and where Pesha Plant-mother sprawled, a knife near her lax hand. "Why?"

Kethra said, "She threatened me, and she was trying to sample me, though I told her not to. She should be all right; I only gave her a basic sleeper."

Wanira came back into sight. "I guess I'm on watch, then." Sighing, she sat down. "Just yesterday morning," she said, "I was telling you to be careful with seeds."

Kethra smiled, wondering if the Dorm-mother had felt this strange, sad, intense and tender caring for everything in her reach, this fear that so many things could go wrong. She felt the rootlets reaching from the seeds Holdin had planted, and sent her own roots to mesh with them. Bright green arrowhead leaves unfurled in a small thicket, catching sun. Raz's heart beat slow and sure; she could feel it where his skin touched hers and through rootneedles innumerable that bathed in and tasted that pulse. In distant dark places she felt the steps of the people of Spire above her root network.

She knew that now she would always have the sky. "I'm glad I didn't listen," she said.

BIOGRAPHIES

JOHN BETANCOURT is the author of a dozen books, including the acclaimed *Rememory, Johnny Zed,* and *The Blind Archer,* as well as a large number of short stories and nonfiction. He had two collaborative novels published in 1995: the YA fantasy *Born of Elven Blood* (with Kevin J. Anderson) and the *Star Trek: Deep Space Nine* novel *Devil in the Sky* (with Greg Cox). In 1993, he and his wife Kim were World Fantasy Award finalists for their independent publishing venture The Wildside Press. He also served as editor on the anthologies *The Ultimate Witch, The Ultimate Zombie, The Ultimate Dragon, New Masters of Horror,* and *The Best of Weird Tales.* Currently he lives in New Jersey, where he collects cats and computers with equal success.

CHRISTOPHER H. BING is a conceptual editorial and political illustrator for several national and international newspapers, among them *The Wall Street Journal, The New York Times, The Washington Post, The Japan Times, The Boston Globe,* and many others. He provided the illustrations for *The Essential Dracula* and *The Essential Frankenstein,* the annotated editions of those classic novels. He is presently working on the artwork for two children's books.

CAROL CARR was born in New York and now lives in the Oakland Hills Fire Zone. This is her second collaboration, which she says brings her oeuvrette to six stories, the most recent of which, "Tooth Fairy," appeared in *Omni* magazine in 1984. She was married to anthologist and writer Terry Carr, who said, "Her natural medium is the postcard. She sells everything she writes but she never writes."

ARTHUR C. CLARKE has published more than seventy books, including the groundbreaking *2001: A Space Odyssey* and its sequels, and made many appearances on radio and television, most notably with Walter Cronkite on CBS during the Apollo missions. His thirteen-part *Mysterious World* and *Strange Powers* TV programs have been seen worldwide. He is a Council Member of the Society of Authors, a Vice-President of the H.G. Wells Society, and a member of many other scientific and literary organizations. His honors include several doctorates in science and literature, a Franklin Institute Gold Medal, the Marconi Fellowship, the Charles A. Lindbergh Award, the UNESCO-Kalinga Prize, and an Academy Award nomination for the screenplay to *2001*. He has lived in Sri Lanka for the past thirty years, and in 1979, President Jayewardene appointed him Chancellor of the University of Moratuwa, which is the location of the government-established Arthur Clarke Centre for Modern Technologies.

LYNN D. CROSSON was born, raised, and currently resides on Long Island. This is her second published tale, the first having appeared in *The Ultimate Witch*. She divides her time between a full-time corporate job and several freelance careers. In addition to writing, she is also an accomplished portrait photographer and a practitioner of shiatsu and herbal medicine. She and her mother own and operate a mail-order business centered around her own line of aromatherapeutic herbal bath products. Lynn hopes her next major accomplishment will be extending a day to 48 hours.

Since the World and British Fantasy Awards-nominated *Narrow Houses* (1992) and its successors, *Touch Wood* and *Blue Hotel*, **PETER CROWTHER** has edited or co-edited a further half-dozen anthologies (including the recent *Heaven Sent* and *Tombs*), continued to produce reviews and interviews for a variety of publications on both sides of the Atlantic, and sold some fifty of his own short stories. He has recently adapted his story "Prime Time" for British television and sold *Escardy Gap* (with James Lovegrove) to Tor Books. A solo novel, more anthologies, and a sequel to *Escardy Gap* are all currently underway. Crowther lives in Harrogate, England, with his wife and two sons.

DON D'AMMASSA is the author of the novel *Blood Beast*, and has sold several dozen short stories to science fiction and horror anthologies, including *Hottest Blood*, *The Ultimate Zombie*, and *Deathport*, and to the magazines *Analog*, *Pulphouse*, and *Tomorrow*. For the past ten years he has been the book reviewer for *Science Fiction Chronicle*. He lives in Rhode Island surrounded by 60,000 books and 3,000 videotapes.

When he was young and impressionable, KEITH R. A. DeCANDIDO'S parents gave him Ursula K. Le Guin, Robert A. Heinlein, J. R. R. Tolkien, and P. G. Wodehouse to read. He was doomed. He has been a writer and editor in the science fiction, fantasy, and comics fields since 1989. His nonfiction has appeared in *Creem*, *Publishers Weekly*, *Horror*, *Library Journal*, *The Comics Journal*, and *Wilson Library Bulletin*; his short fiction has been published in the anthologies *The Ultimate Spider-Man*, *The Ultimate Silver Surfer*, and *Two-Fisted Writer Tales*, and he edits the series of novels and short-story anthologies based on Marvel Comics' super heroes co-published by Byron Preiss Multimedia Company, Inc., and Putnam Berkley.

Born in 1957, RON DEE grew up in Tulsa, Oklahoma, sneaking constant snacks of horror films and science fiction novels as he grew up. After a near-fatal car wreck shortly before high school graduation, he turned his obsessive nature to writing. His novels include *Boundaries*, *Brain Fever*, *Blood Lust*, *Dusk*, *Descent*, *Blood*, *Succumb*, *Blind Hunger*, *Shade*, and *Horrorshow* (the last three under the pseudonym David Darke). His short fiction has been included in *The Ultimate Dracula*, *Hottest Blood*, *Deathport*, and in TAL Publications' "Vampire Trilogy" chapbooks under the title *Sex and Blood*.

NICHOLAS A. DICHARIO was nominated for the John W. Campbell Award for Best New Writer of the Year (1992) and has also been nominated for the Hugo and World Fantasy Awards. His short fiction has appeared in *The Magazine of Fantasy and Science Fiction*, Robert Silverberg's *Universe* series, and several other original anthologies.

MEL GILDEN is the author of many children's books, including *My Brother Blubb* and its sequels, the "Fifth Grade Monster" series, and

The Pumpkins of Time. Books for adults include *Surfing Samurai Robots* and its two sequels. He has authored the *Star Trek* novels *Boogeymen* and *The Starship Trap*, as well as the YA *Star Trek: Deep Space Nine* novel *The Pet* (with Ted Pedersen). He's also perpetrated novelizations of stories from *Beverly Hills, 90210* and the live-action film *Rudyard Kipling's The Jungle Book.* Mel is a radio personality and has written and developed cartoons for television. He lives in Los Angeles, California, where the debris meets the sea, and still hopes to be in an astronaut when he grows up.

ED GORMAN has written several crime novels and many short stories. The *San Diego Union* recently called him, "One of the most distinctive voices in American crime fiction" and *The Bloomsbury Review* said, "Gorman is *the* poet of dark suspense." In addition, he has written three science fiction novels under a pseudonym.

KAREN HABER is the author of several science fiction novels including *The Mutant Season* (with her husband Robert Silverberg), *The Mutant Prime, Mutant Star,* and *Mutant Legacy.* Her short fiction has appeared in *Asimov's Science Fiction, The Magazine of Fantasy and Science Fiction, Full Spectrum, The Ultimate Frankenstein, After the King, Women of Darkness,* and other anthologies. Her nonfiction has been featured in *American Artist, Southwest Art,* and other art-related publications. She and her husband edited *Universe 1, 2,* and *3,* anthologies of original science fiction stories. Her latest novel, *The Woman Without a Shadow,* was published in March 1995, the first of a three-book series; the second, *Codename: War Minstrels,* will be published in November 1995.

NINA KIRIKI HOFFMAN is the sixth of seven children, and grew up in Southern California. One of her day jobs involves channeling other writers, most of them still living. Another involves selling their work to the general public. Her recent publications include *The Thread that Binds the Bones* (which won the Bram Stoker Award for First Novel), *Unmasking* (nominated for a World Fantasy Award), *Haunted Humans* (nominated for a Nebula Award), *Child of an Ancient City* (with Tad

Williams), and the recently released *The Silent Strength of Stones*. Her short fiction has appeared in *The Magazine of Fantasy & Science Fiction*, *The Ultimate Zombie*, and *The Ultimate Witch*, among other places. Presently she resides in Eugene, Oregon with four cats, a big TV, and a mannequin.

LIZ HOLLIDAY lives in west London with her cat Cassandra. In 1989 she attended the Clarion SF Writers' Workshop which was heaven and hell in one go. Since then her fiction has appeared in various British anthologies. Her story "El Lobo Dorado Is Dead, Is Dead" was nominated for the 1994 Eastercon Award; "And She Laughed" was shortlisted for the Crime Writers' Association Macallan Award for Short Fiction in 1994. She has written two novelizations for the *Cracker* TV series: *One Day a Lemming Will Fly*, (1994) and *The Big Crunch* (1995). Her nonfiction has appeared in many magazines including *Interzone*, *Science Fiction Chronicle*, and *Fear*. She is also the book reviewer and fiction editor for *Valkyrie*, the British role-playing magazine.

Born on April 1st, ANNE MCCAFFREY has tried to live up to her auspicious natal day. Her first novel, *Restoree*, was written as a protest against the absurd and unrealistic portrayals of women in the science fiction novels of the 1950s. It is, however, in the handling of broader themes and the worlds of her imagination, particularly the two series (*The Ship Who Sang* and the various "Dragonriders of Pern" novels) that her talents as a storyteller are best displayed. McCaffrey lives in a house of her own design, Dragonhold-Underhill (because she had to dig out a hill on her farm to build it) in Wicklow County, Ireland.

BYRON PREISS is the editor of the books *The Planets*, *The Universe*, *The Microverse*, and *The Dinosaurs: A New Look at a Lost Era*, which was featured in *Life* magazine. He has collaborated with Arthur C. Clarke, Isaac Asimov, and Ray Bradbury, and edited the Grammy Award-winning *The Words of Gandhi*. His monograph on *the Art of Leo & Diane Dillon* was a Hugo Award nominee. He is the producer of several CD-ROM titles, including the Invision Award-winning *Isaac Asimov's The Ultimate Robot*. He holds a B.A. from the University of

Pennsylvania and an M.A. from Stanford University. He currently resides in New York City.

MIKE RESNICK is the author of more than thirty science fiction novels, including *Santiago, Ivory, Soothsayer,* and *A Miracle of Rare Design.* He is also the author of more than 100 short stories and the editor of 21 anthologies. He has won two Hugo Awards, and has been nominated for nine Hugos, six Nebulas, five Sieun-shos (the Japanese Hugo), a Clarke (The British Hugo), and has won a number of lesser awards. His daughter Laura won the 1993 John W. Campbell Award for Best New Writer.

ROBERT SILVERBERG was born in New York City and educated at Columbia. His first book, *Revolt on Alpha C,* was published in 1955, and he has since penned over a hundred books and numerous short stories, among them *Nightwings, Lord Valentine's Castle, Tom O'Bedlam, Nightfall* (with Isaac Asimov), and more. He has won four Hugo Awards and five Nebula awards, as well as most of the other significant science fiction honors. He was President of the Science Fiction Writers of America from 1967–1968. He edited the *New Dimensions* series of anthologies from 1971–1980, the first volume of *The Science Fiction Hall of Fame* series, and *Robert Silverberg's Worlds of Wonder.* With his wife, Karen Haber, he edited *Universe,* a series of original science fiction anthologies. His newest book is *Hot Sky at Midnight.*

S. P. SOMTOW was born in Bangkok, Thailand, and grew up in Europe. He was educated at Eton College and at Cambridge. His first career was as a composer and performer; he turned to fiction writing in 1977. He won the John W. Campbell Award for Best New Writer in 1981, and two of his short stories have been nominated for the Hugo Award. His work has included science fiction (*The Darkling Wind,* a *Locus* best-seller), fantasy (the award-winning *The Wizard's Apprentice*), horror (*Vampire Junction,* called "the most important horror novel of 1984"), and children's literature (*The Fallen Country*). He is also a screenwriter, playwright, and film director. *The Laughing Dead,* the horror film he wrote and directed, was released in the U.S. this year.

LAWRENCE WATT-EVANS was born and raised in Massachusetts, fourth of six children, in a house full of books. He taught himself to read at age five in order to read a comic book story called "Last of the Tree People," and began writing his own stories a couple of years later. Eventually a fantasy novel, *The Lure of the Basilisk*, actually sold. Several more novels and dozens of stories have now made it into print, as well as articles, poems, comic book scripts, etc., covering a wide range of fantasy, science fiction, and horror. His short story "Why I Left Harry's All-Night Hamburgers" won the Hugo in 1988; his most successful novels to date have been the Ethshar fantasy series, beginning with *The Misenchanted Sword*. He's married, has two children, and has settled in the Maryland suburbs of Washington, D.C.